BEACHSIDE
Christmas

MW00657751

ALSO BY KAREN CLARKE

Being Brooke Simmons
My Future Husband
Put a Spell on You
The Beachside Sweet Shop
The Beachside Flower Stall

KAREN CLARKE

The BEACHSIDE Christmas

Bookouture

Published by Bookouture
An imprint of StoryFire Ltd.
23 Sussex Road, Ickenham, UB10 8PN
United Kingdom
www.bookouture.com

Copyright © Karen Clarke, 2017

Karen Clarke has asserted her right to be identified
as the author of this work.

All rights reserved. No part of this publication may be reproduced, stored in any retrieval system, or transmitted, in any form or by any means, electronic, mechanical, photocopying, recording or otherwise, without the prior written permission of the publishers.

ISBN: 978-1-78681-272-8
eBook ISBN: 978-1-78681-271-1

This book is a work of fiction. Names, characters, businesses, organizations, places and events other than those clearly in the public domain, are either the product of the author's imagination or are used fictitiously. Any resemblance to actual persons, living or dead, events or locales is entirely coincidental.

In loving memory of my grandparents, Charlie and Ethel Machin,
who always came to 'our house' on Christmas Day.

Chapter 1

'No one's died here if that's what you're worried about.'

I turned, surprised that the estate agent had misinterpreted my silence.

'I'm not worried,' I said, whipping out a smile. I looked a bit stern when I was being serious, according to Max.

Don't think about Max.

'Someone famous lived here a while back.' Alfie Blake ran a nervous finger between his neck and shirt collar. 'Isabel Sinclair?'

'Never heard of her.' I felt a bit sorry for Alfie. He looked too young to be selling property, as if he was on work experience. 'Is she an actress?'

'No, but she went on *Morning, Sunshine!* trying to get our local sweet shop closed down,' he said. 'It didn't work, and suddenly they'd moved out.'

'Well, I'm glad they did.'

My eyes switched back to the view through the latticed window. Despite the gunmetal sky, befitting early November, there was a triangle of sea just visible and I imagined jogging along the beach, the wind tossing my hair, blasting away the stress of the past six months. I hated jogging, but it was bound to be more relaxing by the sea.

'The garden doesn't look great at this time of year, but there's a decent-sized shed, and there aren't too many shrubs, and I know the apple tree looks a bit crap at the moment, pardon my French, and there's a shed. Did I mention that?'

'You did.'

Alfie joined me at the window, clutching his clipboard like a Bible. 'Have you been to Shipley before, Miss Ambrose?'

'Lily,' I said, automatically. 'I came here on holiday a few times with my family, years ago.' My lips curled in a smile as a succession of happy snapshots flooded my mind: eating sandy sandwiches on the beach; my brother chasing me into the sea, then mounting a panicky rescue when I floated out too far; Dad's startlingly hairy legs in his 'holiday' shorts, hurtling after our beach-ball; Mum, red-shouldered in her summer dress, trying to read a romance through her sunglasses.

'I always wanted to come back,' I said, though, in truth, I'd been perfectly happy in London, before my life blew up.

'It's a bit quiet.' Alfie's youthful brow puckered. 'I mean, it's nice for older people—'

'Hey, I'm barely thirty,' I protested, though that was probably ancient to him.

'Oh no, I didn't mean… I just meant… I mean…' Alfie's cheeks looked as if someone had taken a blowtorch to them. It was easy to imagine what he must have looked like as a toddler, with his wholesome face and swell of chestnut curls. 'What I meant was—'

'It's OK,' I said, putting him out of his misery. 'I'm planning to write a novel, so quiet is perfect for me.' I liked the way it sounded. *I'm a novelist* sounded more exciting than *primary school teacher*. Not that Alfie was impressed – or even listening.

'I bet it's noisy in London, what with all that traffic, the shops, and people.' He made it sound as if London was one long street, filled with ear-splitting car-horns and deafening music. 'There won't be any of that here,' he went on, wistfully. 'Most you'll hear is seagulls. They're bloody noisy, pardon my French.'

'I can handle that,' I said, glancing around the living room, which was painted the colour of mayonnaise (or Vanilla Dream, as Alfie informed me, faithfully checking his clipboard). The cottage was palatial compared to places I'd lived in before: a room in a student house, a poky studio flat, then my childhood home in East Finchley, where I'd been living for nearly three years, since Dad died.

'Your money goes a lot further out here,' Alfie said brightly, switching back into sales mode. Not that he needed to. I'd as good as bought the cottage already. I'd found it online a couple of weeks earlier, hunched over my laptop in the middle of the night, desperate to be somewhere else. I'd typed in *Shipley*, figuring it was as good a place as any to flee to, and some frantic scrolling had brought me to Seaview Cottage. The owners were so keen for a sale, they were even throwing in a few classy pieces of furniture they hadn't got room for in their new place, and after a tour through the gallery of photos, I'd booked a viewing.

'I couldn't afford anything like this in London,' I said, the words provoking a painful lurch as I recalled the daydreams I used to have of Max and me buying our own place, once his divorce was finalised.

'You're buying it on your own?' Alfie's eyes grew round, as if I was an heiress, or lottery winner.

'I've been at home for a while, saving for a deposit,' I said, which wasn't strictly true. I doubt I'd have moved back to Finchley if Dad hadn't died, and I'd already had a respectable nest egg, thanks to Granny Ambrose, who'd been squirrelling away money for me and my brother for decades. Chris had spent his on a hipster café in Shoreditch, while I'd put mine aside for a rainy day.

The rainy day had turned into monsoon season, and I'd never been more grateful to my grandmother for providing me with the means to escape.

'That famous woman I just told you about, she had it decorated proper like, so there's not much to do unless you fancy painting over it all.' Alfie's lovely Dorset vowels washed over me, and I began to feel oddly at home.

'The fireplace is an original feature, but hasn't been used for a long time,' he said, nodding at the copper façade, which was partly hidden behind an old-fashioned fireguard. 'It's decorative, like, but there's plenty of logs in the shed, so you might want to think about opening it up.'

Tucking his clipboard under his arm, he led me into the modest but stylish kitchen, and flourished an arm at the artfully rustic cabinets. 'Fridge-freezer's like another bedroom, see?' He opened and shut the shiny red door, then turned on the tap at the butler-style sink, leaping back when a whoosh of water splashed his skinny tie. 'Shit!' he muttered. 'Sorry,' he added, taking the tissue I was holding out and dabbing at his front. 'This is only my first week on the job…'

'Don't worry, you're doing fine,' I said, understanding all too well the horror of messing up at work. I shuddered at the memory of Max's wife, storming wild-eyed into my classroom a couple of months ago, in the middle of story time.

'Look at you!' she'd cried, as if she'd been expecting Beyoncé and encountered a Teletubby. 'You're… *homely!* And he doesn't even *like* blondes, *or* blue eyes!'

Actually, Max had professed to love both; claimed my hair was the colour of sun-ripened wheat, and my eyes the blue of the evening sky in summer (he'd fancied himself as a poet). I couldn't tell her that of course; especially not in front of thirty five-year-olds desperate to get back to *The Very Hungry Caterpillar.*

'It's caused quite a stir, Lily,' the head teacher had said, pulling me into her office the following day, her usually kind eyes frosted with disapproval. 'I'm afraid there've been complaints from some of the mothers about your affair.'

'They were separated and, anyway, we're not together any more,' I'd protested weakly. I'd just begun to get over our break-up – though it was hard seeing Max drop off and pick up his daughter every day – when he'd texted me to say that, in a fit of guilt, he'd confessed to his wife that he'd been 'seeing' their daughter's teacher while they'd been apart. The shame of that confrontation with his wife, which I'd stood through, sweaty and shaking, had meant I couldn't stay in my job, even without the head's veiled hints that I was no longer welcome at the school. The humiliation of being gossiped about, and eyed suspiciously by the parents, was more than I could bear.

'Do you want to look upstairs again?' Alfie balled the tissue into the jacket pocket of his baggy grey suit. 'I can show you how the shower works, if you like.'

I had a vision of us emerging, sodden. 'I'm good, thanks.'

'The garden?'

'Looks great, from what I've seen.' It was a raw day, even for early November, and I didn't fancy wandering around in a force ten gale.

'OK, so...' Alfie's eyes roved around, as if seeking something spectacular he could point out: a sliding ceiling, perhaps, or a panic room.

'How soon can I move in?' I said, smoothing a hand over the limestone worktop. I could see me baking in here.

His face brightened. 'You said you're not in a chain?'

'That's right, and you told me the couple who were also interested have pulled out so… I'd like to offer the full asking price.'

Alfie's grin was huge. 'Let's do this!' He tried to high-five me but I missed my cue, so he scratched his head instead. 'I'll phone the office,' he said.

He moved into the hallway, his mobile pressed to his ear, and I closed my eyes and imagined myself living on Maple Hill, where the houses on either side of the steeply pitched road were all different shapes and sizes. Seaview Cottage was one of the smallest, but that suited me just fine.

I'd already earmarked the back bedroom as a study, where I was going to write my book, and, once I'd settled in, Erin could come and stay, even if it was just to check her best friend hadn't made a terrible mistake, and Chris and his fiancée could visit—

A car door slammed, and I jumped. I crossed to the window and saw a man wearing a bandana, earrings and a trench coat, leaning into the boot of a black Explorer parked on the drive next door. He heaved out a cardboard box overflowing with fairy lights, and what looked like a deflated reindeer, and clutched it to his chest as if it were stolen jewellery.

'What are the neighbours like?' I asked Alfie when he came back in, watching as the man crept – he was definitely creeping – up his garden path, pausing to glance over his shoulder as if expecting a police car to arrive.

'Neighbours?' Alfie followed the line of my gaze. 'Ah, that's Barry Lambert,' he said. 'He's head of The Christmas Lights Society.'

'The what now?'

Alfie adjusted the tiny knot of his tie. 'It's a sort of committee,' he said. 'They raise money during the year for the lights in the town, and book someone to turn on the tree lights in the square, and there's a competition every year for best house display on Maple Hill. Blake's Properties – my dad – usually makes a donation.' He opened his mouth, as if to say more, then snapped it shut again.

'What aren't you telling me?'

'Nothing!' He snatched up his clipboard and held it like a shield. 'It gets a bit competitive, that's all.'

'I think it sounds lovely,' I said. Christmas was my favourite time of year and if I couldn't spend it with Max, then being in Shipley might be the next best thing. 'I should join the society, if it's not too late. It'll be a good way to meet my new neighbours.'

Alfie's round eyes widened. 'I think they've had all their meetings, and I doubt you'll be moved in before Christmas, anyway.'

'Why not?' Now I'd seen the cottage, I wanted to move in right away.

'Well, there's… stuff to do.' Alfie clearly needed training in what selling a house involved.

'How long, Alfie?'

He puffed out his cheeks. 'Could be six weeks, could be longer, it depends on lots of things.'

Six weeks? 'What sort of things?'

'Stuff?' His Adam's apple bobbed over the collar of his shirt. 'Paperwork, mostly.'

I couldn't bear to wait any longer than I had to. The wheels were in motion, and I wanted to start my new life in the place where I'd had such happy times as a child. It felt like I was destined to live in Shipley.

'Can you make it four?' I did a little twirl in my shiny new kitchen. 'I've already started packing.'

Chapter 2

Four weeks later...

'I think I've made a mistake.' I stared through the rain-speckled window at the soggy garden. There was no sea or sand visible today, just a hovering mist, and a bedraggled seagull on the gatepost.

'Oh, Lily, of course you do. You're just feeling funny because I'm going back home today.' Mum came over and wrapped her arms around my waist. In the distorted reflection she could have easily passed for my funkier sister, with her spiky white hair, and her favourite rectangular glasses with the leopard-print frames. It was only when you looked closely that the 'V' between her eyebrows and fine lines around her eyes were noticeable.

She'd lost weight after Dad died, which had brought out her cheekbones, and she'd kept it off with a diet of faddy eating and a frantic lifestyle.

'Can't you at least stay until the weekend?' I said, breathing in her familiar scent of fresh apples, and vanilla body lotion.

'I can't leave Annie for long, she gets flustered on her own,' Mum said, giving me a little squeeze. 'And I've got my play tomorrow night.'

As well as running a craft shop with her oldest friend, Annie Larkin, Mum was a leading member of Acting Out, an am-dram group that specialised in Agatha Christie mysteries and occasional adaptations of classic novels. The other players had been her saviours after Dad died, and I couldn't begrudge her (much) for wanting to get back to them.

'It's so quiet,' I said, cocking my head. Nothing but the patter of rain on the living- room window, and Mum's soft breath in my ear. I hadn't even heard a car door slam since arriving the day before.

'Isn't that a good thing?' Mum steered me back to the plush, oatmeal-coloured sofa that had belonged to the previous owner, and sat me down. 'I thought you wanted peace and quiet so you could write your novel.' She slightly emphasised 'novel', as if unsure of its meaning, still not fully on board with me giving up teaching.

'I do,' I said, lifting my mug off the coffee table, hot chocolate steaming my face. 'It's just so unfamiliar.'

Things had happened quickly in the end, as my four-week challenge was met with gusto, and I'd become swept up in organising the move. Once we'd arrived, I'd thrown myself into organising the rooms, with Mum's help, installing the few items of furniture I'd had stored in her garage, and rearranging the rest. Around midnight we'd sunk, exhausted, into my hastily made-up bed, and slept for eight hours.

It wasn't until this morning, over a breakfast of poached eggs (me) and black coffee, (Mum) that reality began to sink in. Soon, I'd be alone in a strange town, miles from everything I knew.

'It's a big step,' Mum acknowledged, sitting beside me, 'but once you've got to know your neighbours, and reacquainted yourself with the area—'

'We haven't been here for years, Mum, it's like a completely new place,' I said, invalidating my original argument for choosing Shipley in the first place.

'Seaside towns don't change that much.' She patted my knee. 'You'll be fine, sweetheart.'

I didn't know whether to be upset that she was trying to convince me, or relieved that she wasn't the sort of mother who wanted me tied to her apron strings forever.

'Won't you miss me?' I said, childishly.

'Oh, darling, of course I will, but you're not a million miles away, and we'll see each other at Christmas.' She bristled a little in the chunky-knit cardigan Annie had knitted for her birthday. 'I'm just happy to see you taking control after what that man did to you.'

Mum had been friendly towards Max, but after he broke my heart had branded him a 'shitbag', which had made me giggle, tearfully. She'd preferred 'Lovely Dan', who I'd dated since teacher-training, and I hadn't had the heart to tell her he'd given me an ultimatum when I told him I was moving back home after Dad died – him or my mother.

'I won't be able to come to your plays,' I said, though in truth it was quite a relief. As much as I supported Mum's acting endeavours, it was sometimes hard to watch her playing a murder victim, or pouting, sultry-eyed at her leading man, as she'd done in an adaptation of *Lady Chatterley's Lover*. 'There's probably nothing to do here in the evenings.'

'Where's that sunny girl of mine gone?' Mum looked around comically, as if the old me might be lurking on the oak bookcase that had belonged to the previous owners. 'We Ambroses are famed for our resilience, so don't you go letting the side down,' she said, wagging a playful finger.

I mustered a smile. She was right. Our family possessed an uncanny ability to bounce back from adversity, which had proved a blessing in the past, but since Max… *don't think about Max…* since leaving my job, my resilience had taken a battering, and, apart from the resurgence that had seen me uproot my life, was in danger of vanishing.

'Why don't we have a nice muffin before I go?' Mum suggested, as if I'd reverted to being seven years old. She shot into the kitchen and returned with the gingham-covered basket she'd found in the porch that morning, while putting out some rubbish. 'You can pop round and thank the woman who left them, and then you'll have made a new friend.'

'I guess so,' I said, taking the note she was holding out and scanning the untidy handwriting sprawled across the paper.

Welcome to Maple Hill, from Doris Day (Head of Neighbourhood Watch) Number 1 (blue door, brass knocker). The purple bits are blueberries, I didn't use nuts, just in case. If you aren't allergic I make a nice pecan tart, although I don't think people can be allergic to pecans. They're tree nuts, so not related to the peanut. Return the basket at your leisure. I'm in all day tomorrow.

'Doris Day?' I immediately thought of the old films that Mum and I used to watch on Saturday afternoons, when Dad took Chris to the football, and tears pricked my eyes.

'She's bound to be lovely with a name like that, and to have gone to all this trouble…' Mum peered into the basket and inhaled. 'They smell divine.' She often said actressy things like 'divine' since she'd joined Acting Out.

'I'm not hungry,' I said, then seeing worry unfold on her face, added, 'Go on then, maybe a couple of bites.'

She relaxed into a smile. 'We'll share one,' she said, which was a measure of her concern. She'd currently given up anything she couldn't throw in a juicer.

'They taste… odd.' I swallowed a mouthful, trying to pinpoint the flavour. 'Sort of… earthy.'

'They might be poisoned.' Mum grabbed it off me, her face contorting with horror. 'It could be laced with arsenic.'

'Mum!' A laugh bubbled up. 'This is real life, remember?'

All the same, I didn't eat any more, and once Mum had left in a flurry of hugs, goodbyes, reassurances, and promises to call, dashing to her little Golf in the sleety rain, holding her tapestry bag above her head, I slid the bolt across the door. After I'd checked that all the windows were tightly closed, I switched on the television for company.

Next, I took another tour of the cottage, acquainting myself with its twists and turns, soothed by the unaccustomed space, soft colours, and tasteful furniture – which I'd never have chosen, but which suited the little rooms.

The books and cushions I'd accumulated, and the fortifying photos of family I'd scattered around, made me feel a bit more anchored.

'I'm going to be fine,' I said out loud, determined not to imagine Max's head on the pillow in the bedroom, his athletic body in the shower, or his long legs stretched out on the sofa.

Shipley was going to be a Max-free zone. A *drama*-free zone.

A round of applause burst from the television and I gave a blood-curdling yelp.

This was ridiculous.

Maybe I wasn't suited to being alone with my thoughts.

'You're not used to it, that's all,' I said kindly, as if counselling one of my pupils. *Don't think about them.* Don't think of their shiny little faces, wondering where Miss Ambrose has gone, or my ex-colleagues, gossiping about me in the staff room.

My old life was over.

'DO something!' I ordered, my voice bouncing off the smooth, cream walls. Perhaps I could go for a bracing walk. I glanced through the window at a seagull being flung about on a gale-force wind. The rain was horizontal, and in the distance the sea was a frothing mass of crashing waves.

I should start my novel instead.

I rushed to the back bedroom, where I'd set up my laptop at the school-type desk I'd bought on eBay a few years ago, but had never found a space for. I plonked myself on the swivel chair Mum had given me, which used to be Dad's.

I spun around a few times.

The room was warm, thanks to the efficient central heating, but otherwise empty. I'd need a new bed if I was going to have people to stay. Mum had been happy to bunk in with me, but I could hardly share with my brother if he came to visit, and even though the sofa was big and squashy enough to sleep on, it would be nice to have a proper spare bed.

I logged on to the Wi-Fi, congratulating myself for setting it up before arriving, and started browsing websites. Before I knew it, I'd ordered a double divan, and some bedding and matching curtains.

I quickly checked my emails (nothing but Spam) and clicked onto Facebook. Max loathed social media, so thankfully wasn't on there, but reading updates from my old life made my throat ache. I was missing the build-up to the end of term before Christmas. We'd be living on a diet of Quality Street and mince pies in the staffroom, and someone usually brought in a bottle of Bailey's to share on the last day of term.

On impulse, I deactivated my account and scrolled through Twitter instead. Erin often posted pithy updates from the talent agency she worked for, but apart from a bland *congrats to Ellie Palladino on a job well done!* about a former soap star fronting a toothpaste advert, there was nothing recent. Or pithy.

I logged off, surprised to find that a couple of hours had shot by. I stood up and did some stretches to get my blood flowing, then sat back down and opened the document I'd imaginatively titled 'Novel'.

I stared at the blank page, wishing I'd written a paragraph or two already. The trouble was, I hadn't made up my mind what type of novel to write. I'd been hoping inspiration would strike once I began my new life.

Thrillers were popular, so it made sense to go down that route.

I looked out at the muted colours of the compact garden, where the light was fading and the naked apple tree was bent double, and tried to enter a murderous frame of mind.

A robin landed on a wavering branch, its feathers fluffed up for protection, and the sight of it reminded me it was Christmas in less than three weeks and I'd hardly bought any gifts before leaving London.

Perhaps I should do some more Christmas shopping now…

No.

'Stay focused,' I ordered myself, waggling my fingers above the keys.

Just type an opening line and the rest will flow.

I was sure I'd read that somewhere. Or maybe Max had said it, about his poetry writing.

I quickly typed: *It was dark and dreary, as Janet entered the garden…* Janet? I knew a Janet from school, and she was lovely, but hardly main character material.

It was dark and dreary as Maxine entered the garden… That was better. A strong, female name.

No, wait. Maxine? I was thinking about bloody Max.

... *as Camilla*... too royal. *Cerys*... tricky to pronounce? ...*as Jasminda, Belinda, Melinda, Toyota, Magenta, Placenta...*

Jessica!

I pressed delete and started again. *Rain lashed down as Jessica entered the garden...*

Why was she entering the garden?

...as Jessica entered the garden with a spade and began to dig...

More atmosphere.

...as Jessica drove her spade into the soil...

Drove didn't sound right... *dug*... didn't look right.

Jessica slashed the soil with her spade... Oh, for hell's sake, spades didn't *slash.*

I hated Jessica already.

And I didn't want to write a thriller.

I deleted it all and typed: *Jessica watched Marco enter the garden, his naked chest muscles rippling as he wielded his spade...*

Blood gushed to my face. Imagine Mum reading that! And why was I fixated on spades?

As I deleted the text, I became aware of an unnatural brightness filtering into the hallway, considering the sky was now black with no sign of a moon. I rose and went into the front bedroom, and my mouth fell open as I drank in a kaleidoscope of Christmas lights. In the house opposite, they twinkled in every window, around the garden, and even on the roof, while next to it was a perfect replica of a gingerbread house. There were candy canes and gingerbread men surrounding the perimeter of the garden, and icing-like snow trimmings attached to the edges of the house (how had they got that 'ginger' effect on the walls?) Moving closer, I noticed a house a couple of doors down decked out as a scene from *Frozen*, with vivid blue lighting, and an image of Elsa beamed onto the front wall.

'Wow,' I breathed. They really made an effort on Maple Hill, and I wondered if it was compulsory; whether I'd be shunned if I didn't participate.

Dragging my eyes from the festive lights, I slammed my laptop shut. What I needed was a cup of tea, and to plan my novel properly.

Down in the kitchen, I spotted the piece of paper Doris Day had written her note on, laid on top of some junk mail Mum had placed on the worktop. I picked it up and was about to throw it away, when I noticed Doris had written something on the back: *There's an emergency meeting of The Christmas Lights Society at No. 8 Maple Hill at 6 p.m. today (the 7th) if you fancy coming along. Refreshments provided.*

I glanced at the illuminated digits of the built-in oven: *17.55.* I checked my reflection in the glass door. My hair – recently chopped from shoulder- to jaw-length – had developed a kink, and my skin was chewing-gum pale, but I didn't have time to faff with straighteners and make-up.

I pulled my parka on over my sweater and jeans, stuffed my feet into my boots, and grabbed my keys.

My novel would have to wait. It was time to meet my neighbours.

Chapter 3

It was gone six o'clock by the time I realised that Number 8 was right next door. It shouldn't have been that difficult, as there were only ten houses on either side of the road, and one at the top of the hill, but I'd been too busy admiring the displays, distracted by inflatable Santas, prancing reindeers, and a galaxy of fairy lights to look for numbers.

I finally worked it out by a process of elimination.

'Well done, Sherlock,' I muttered, blinking at the dazzling assault on my eyeballs. My neighbour's was the gaudiest, most haphazardly decorated house in the street. It was as if he'd run amok in a Christmas decoration warehouse and bought every light, ornament and inflatable he could find and blindly flung them up. I remembered the owner, creeping up his garden path a month earlier, and thought I recognised the reindeer, now inflated and prancing in a bush.

I hesitated, knowing the meeting would have started, then marched past a row of illuminated angels and, after moving aside a winking Father Christmas on the step, and almost dislodging a flashing wreath on the door, gave a determined knock.

The woman who answered beamed a greeting as she stepped aside to let me in. She was fiftyish, and generously proportioned, with brass-coloured curls around a doughy face.

'They've already started, love, but go on through,' she said, as I entered a cluttered hallway, hung with coats and scarves.

As she pushed the front door closed, I was hit by a blast of heat from a radiator. On the other side of the wall, voices rose and fell, and I was reminded of a film I'd seen with Mum, about an elite society whose secret meetings had turned out to be orgy-filled nightmares.

Dismissing the image, I held out a frozen hand. 'Lily Ambrose.'

'Sheelagh Lambert.' Her grip was warm and vice-like. 'It's spelt the Irish way, which is a nuisance because I'm always having to spell it,' she said, with an extravagant eye-roll. 'At one point, I thought about changing it to the Aussie version.' She adopted a jaunty pose and boomed, 'G'day, Sheila!' before reverting to her Dorset lilt. 'But then I thought, why should I? I'm half Irish on my mother's side and proud of it. Two-thirds German, thanks to my great-grandfather, and a quarter Italian, courtesy of my dad's side, but slice me in half and I'm a West Country gal through and through.'

Brain reeling from the confusing introduction, and Sheelagh's terrible maths, I adopted what I hoped was an engaging smile. 'I've just moved in next door—'

'I know, love,' she said, tweaking her snowflake-patterned cardigan across her torpedo-like bosoms. 'We watched you from our bedroom window, me and Barry.' Her off-white teeth and raspberry-coloured lipstick made me think of a scone, bursting with jam and cream. 'We were thrilled to see a pair of young ladies moving in. We're very modern, Barry and me, and have nothing against same-sex marriage.' She lifted her chins. 'I kissed a lady myself many years ago, before I met my husband.'

'That's… good.' I swallowed an unexpected giggle, half tempted to play along. 'The other lady was actually my mother,' I said, deciding I'd better not. 'She was helping me move in.'

'Well, I'm sorry about that.' Sorry for assuming I had an older, female partner (Mum would be delighted to have been mistaken for a young lady), or sorry I wasn't gay? It didn't feel right to ask. 'Oh well, never mind,' she said, leaning past me and opening a door into a lamp-lit dining room, where several people were sitting round a table laden with food, talking over the top of one another.

As my eyes zigzagged around, trying to take it all in, they met the chilly stare of a coal-black cat on the windowsill, and I was prompted to ask its name.

'That's my darling boy, Marmite.' Sheelagh patted my arm with ring-crowded fingers. 'He's lovely, unless you get on the wrong side of him.' I wondered how you got on the wrong side of a cat. Steal its food? 'He can be a bit moody,' she added. 'Tends to divide opinion, hence his name. I love him, but Barry's lukewarm. He stands in front of the TV whenever he watches *Most Haunted*, and shredded his favourite pants. Marmite, that is, not Barry!' Her laugh was like a klaxon, and the heated conversation at the table stopped, as several pairs of eyes swivelled to greet us.

I'd never felt more like a stranger, my usual confidence – from years of dealing with pushy parents at school – trickling away in this over-heated room, where the leaf-patterned walls were hung with those photos of babies in flowerpots that used to be fashionable.

'Let me take your coat,' said Sheelagh, yanking it off, almost taking my arms with it. 'I'll go and fetch you some tea. Or maybe you prefer *coffee*?' She said it as though coffee was an illegal substance.

'Tea will be fine, thank you,' I said.

She nodded, apparently satisfied, then cleared her throat extravagantly. 'This is Lily, our new neighbour,' she announced grandly. 'Be gentle with her, folks!'

The cat shot past with a furious glare, as if I'd upset his plans, and I nervously approached the table to a chorus of, 'Hello, Lily', 'Welcome to the neighbourhood', and, 'Do you know what you're letting yourself in for?'

'Come and sit here,' said a woman who'd been discreetly buffing the edge of the table with a lacy handkerchief, which – along with her neat, greyish-blonde bob – was a clue to her age. Apart from James Bond, no one under sixty carried a hankie these days.

'Thanks,' I said, easing towards the dining chair she'd pulled out. The padded seat still held the imprint of someone's sizeable bottom. 'Wasn't somebody…?'

'Sheelagh won't mind. She'll fetch herself a stool from the kitchen,' said the woman, shifting slightly to give me a piercing look as I perched on the still-warm seat. 'I'm Doris Day.'

'Oh, you left the muffins,' I said, aware that everyone was listening, and that my London accent sounded more pronounced. 'Thank you so much.'

She rolled her eyes. 'I thought I'd put blueberries in them, but later realised I'd used some chopped-up beetroot by mistake.'

So that's what the weird taste had been. 'That's OK, don't worry.' I was practically gushing, in an effort to put her at ease. 'It was a lovely gesture.'

'I wasn't worried, because beetroot's very good for you, but I got distracted after putting a leg in the oven,' Doris said. 'My Eric loves his lamb, but a leg can be tough without the bone in, and I wasn't sure I'd got the temperature right. I had to consult Delia.' She chuckled. 'Good old Delia, what would we do without her?'

'Indeed,' was all I could manage.

'She means Delia Smith, the chef,' explained the woman on Doris's right, a cheerful smile crinkling her pale blue eyes, which looked tiny behind her glasses. She had frizzy brown hair, exploding from under a pink woolly hat with a pom-pom. 'I'm Jane, her next-door-neighbour,' she said, nudging Doris so hard she tilted towards me. 'I work on the flower stall in the square, if you get chance to have a look, and that's my husband, Dennis.'

She jabbed her finger at a broad-faced man sitting opposite, examining a chicken drumstick. 'If you want any shelves putting up, he's your man.' She gave him a love-struck smile. 'Hands off, though, he's mine.' She let rip an earthy cackle. 'Just joking,' she said, as if there was any doubt. Despite his friendly smile, Dennis was at least fifty-five, with a greying beard that was more dishevelled than hipster. 'My very own Christian Grey,' Jane continued, causing a pained expression to cross Doris's powdered face, and Dennis's ears to redden.

Unperturbed, Jane went on to introduce everyone at the table. I was good at remembering names – vital for a teacher – but it was hard to focus, what with the heat, and the weight of so many eyes on me.

'That's Mr Flannery, he owns the newsagent's in the square, and next to him is Marnie Appleton, and she runs the sweet shop along the parade.' I vaguely remembered visiting a sweet shop in Shipley on holiday, and sharing a bag of chocolate mice with my brother.

'Hi,' said Marnie, giving me a sympathetic smile, as if she understood how overwhelming it was to be thrust into a room of strangers. She was about my age, with a smooth curtain of brown hair I instantly envied. 'I'm only here because my grandmother, Celia, has a dog-training session today, and wanted me to represent her,' she said. 'I actually live in Wareham with my fiancé.' She pushed over a tray of pink and white coconut ice, just like my grandmother used to make. 'These are mine, if you'd like one.'

Impressed, I helped myself to a cube. 'It's delicious,' I said, as the flavour hit my taste buds, bringing back more happy memories.

'Marnie makes the sweets herself,' Doris said, dabbing the corners of her mouth. 'She had to really, after that woman's campaign.'

The air around the table grew chilly.

'Campaign?' I recalled Alfie mentioning the sweet shop being threatened with closure, and it being something to do with the previous owner of my cottage. *My cottage.* I hadn't got used to saying it, yet.

'Isabel bloody Sinclair.' Jane had adopted a doom-laden voice, and a disapproving murmur ran around the group. 'Thought she was a cut above us right from the start.'

'She's the lady who lived next door?' I made my voice extra warm, as if compensating for the awfulness of Isabel Sinclair.

'That's right.' The voice from the head of the table belonged to Barry Lambert, still wearing a bandana over his collar-length grey hair, like an ageing punk. He'd been silent since his wife left the room, but I sensed his impatience to get back to the important business of the day. 'She had a dog called *Pollywollydoodle.*' He said it with a lip curl, leaving no room for doubt about his opinion of the dog. 'It dug up our garden, the little... mutt.'

He cast me a baleful look through heavy-lidded eyes, as though it was all my fault.

'Well, I don't have a dog, and I'm definitely not planning to close down anyone's business,' I chirped, widening my smile until my cheeks hurt. 'And I can assure you I'm very normal and down-to-earth.' I inwardly cringed. People who were genuine didn't need to announce it. And was it normal to move somewhere new on a whim? Alone?

'Of course you are,' murmured Doris, surreptitiously scribbling something in a notebook. I caught a question mark next to my name, and the words *whereabouts in London?*

'East Finchley, born and bred,' I whispered.

Colour shot to her cheeks and she snapped her notebook shut. 'Just taking the minutes,' she said.

'So, what do you do, Lily?' asked Marnie, delicately.

I flashed her a grateful look. 'Well, I...' I took a breath, wishing I'd invented a cover story for why I was in Shipley that didn't sound like something from a soap. 'I *was* a primary school teacher...' I stopped, as a ripple of interest shot round the table.

'Isn't that strange, when we were talking earlier about Miss Anderson leaving school at the end of term?' said Sheelagh, returning with a mug of brick-coloured tea, which she placed in front of me, before moving to place her hands on Barry's shoulders.

'It must be a sign,' said Jane, with a delighted nod at the woman sitting next to Dennis.

'Jill Edwards,' she said, with a brisk but friendly nod. She looked to be in her forties, with solid features, and thick blonde hair cut just below her ears. 'I'm head teacher at Nightingale Primary School.' She'd been absently picking at a sausage roll, but now fixed me with a determined gleam. 'You should come for an interview, Miss Ambrose.' I smiled, recognising the unconscious teacher-habit of formally referring to adults. 'I expect you've got references?'

'Actually, I'm not teaching any more.' I was keen to put a stop to this line of conversation, unwilling to relate the story of my humiliating classroom confrontation with Max's wife, which had lodged itself so firmly in my mind it was as if a shutter slammed down whenever I thought about stepping in a classroom again. 'I'm writing a novel.'

'Ooh, how exciting!' squeaked Jane, and I dragged my gaze from Jill Edwards's thwarted frown. 'What sort of novel?'

'Well...' *Hellfire.* 'It's... I... I haven't quite decided yet.'

'My grandmother's always got her head in a thriller,' Marnie said, sweeping her fringe to one side. 'And my friend got me into historical fiction. She's mad about Victorian London.'

'Sounds great,' I said. *Historical.* I hadn't thought about that.

'You could do another *Fifty Shades*.' Jane leaned over, colour staining her cheeks. 'Something steamy, maybe set in Texas. I've always had a soft spot for Texans. And cowboys.'

Dennis's eyebrows quivered, as if it was the first he'd heard of it.

'You know what they say about men in big hats.' Jane gave a lascivious wink and shoved Doris again.

'I think you mean big hands,' Doris said.

She turned crimson when the newsagent, Mr Flannery, said with a smirk, 'You're a dark horse, Doris. I take it Roger was handy with his truncheon, back in the day?'

'Awful man,' Doris said in an undertone, which the newsagent clearly heard as his already thin lips tightened further.

'Ex-*cuse* me.' Barry's hand slapped the table, making everyone jump.

I picked up my mug and gulped some tea as Barry's meaty hands bunched into fists. 'Can we *please* get back to the agenda?'

'Everything was decided at the last meeting,' said Doris, flipping to a previous page in her notepad, and reading from it. 'All decisions approved by the council. The school choir, licences for the market stalls, PA system, stage and canopy organised, and the event's been advertised via local press, posters, newsletter, Facebook and Twitter—'

'Yes, yes, but we still haven't found anyone to switch on the Christmas tree lights and announce the winner of the best house display.' Barry looked about to explode with frustration.

'Isn't it a bit late for turning on the tree lights?' I ventured. 'I mean, the ones near where I used to live were switched on in November.'

'Therein lies a story,' said Doris, arching her slender eyebrows.

Barry gave a heavy exhalation, as if the thought of explaining was too much. 'It's a long-held tradition that the tree lights are switched on on the thirteenth of December,' he began, but was interrupted by Jane.

'For decades, a tree was donated every year by a long-standing Shipley resident called Harold Fletcher, who would turn on the lights himself on the last day of November at the Christmas Festival, as it was called then.' She spoke in the manner of someone reading an exciting story to a small child. 'But, one year, the lights mysteriously went out on the thirteenth of December at five o'clock on the dot. Poof!' She flicked her fingers to demonstrate. 'No reason that anyone could discover, and no one could get them to come back on.' She lowered her voice. 'Turned out Harold Fletcher died in his bed at the very moment the lights went out, and as a mark of respect they get switched on by a VIP at the exact same time, every year.'

'Amazing,' I said, as Jane sat back with the satisfaction of a tale well told. I suspected a dodgy power connection had been to blame – and guessed Doris did too, from the sceptical way she was tapping her pad with her pen – but there was no denying it made a good story.

'I was just admiring the displays outside,' I said, into the contemplative silence that had fallen. 'Are you all taking part?'

'Not all,' said Barry. 'Just me, him' – he gave Mr Flannery a glowering stare – 'the Jensens...'

'That's the *Frozen* house,' said Jane, her tone admiring. 'So clever.'

'...but they've got high-powered jobs in Poole, so probably won't be at the ceremony, *again*,' Barry continued, 'and them two.' He nodded to a harassed-looking couple, each cradling a baby.

'Ours is the gingerbread house,' said the woman, who looked like she hadn't slept for months, let alone had the energy to create a themed

Christmas display. 'Twins,' she added, seeing me looking. 'This is Jules.' She tipped the swaddled bundle so I could see a thatch of black hair.

'She's lovely,' I said, banishing an image of Max stroking my hair one evening, talking about how he'd like us to have children of our own one day.

'It's a boy,' she said, apologetically. 'Julius, after my grandfather.'

'Oh, sorry.' Heat rushed to my cheeks.

'And this is Robbie.' The harassed man, who also had dark circles under his eyes, tilted his twin forward, revealing a small curled fist.

'He's gorgeous,' I said.

'She's a girl.' He gave a tired smile. 'Roberta, after my grandmother.'

'Any*way*,' said Barry, stretching the word out. 'There'll be no point having a stage and a PA system if there's no one to switch on the flipping lights and announce who's won the best house display.'

'He's in a paddy, because he's hoping it'll be him,' said Mr Flannery, darkly. 'He's got no chance.'

'What's the prize?' I said quickly, as Barry turned furious eyes on him.

'A Christmas hamper, a fifty pound donation to a charity of the winner's choice by our sponsors, Blake's Estate Agents, and a weekend away at a Hudson Country House Hotel,' Mr Flannery reeled off.

'Nice,' I said.

'Bit of a palaver last year,' Doris said to me. 'Rumour has it Mr Flannery knew the judge and bribed him with a promise of free Mars bars for a year.'

'That's not true.' Mr Flannery's pale cheeks reddened. 'Reverend George is a man of the cloth and not open to bribery. And, anyway, he prefers KitKats.'

'Maybe you should have online voting instead,' I suggested. 'You could all send in a photo to the local paper, which they could upload onto their website. The public could pick their favourite and whoever's switching on the lights could announce the winner.'

The Trappist silence that fell was broken by a burp from one of the twins.

'Pardon me,' whispered his harassed mum.

'It's a good idea, but apparently it wouldn't be traditional,' said Jill Edwards, making quote marks, and I guessed she'd suggested it before. 'All this silliness is why I'm not participating this year.'

'Well, I'm not taking part in the competition either,' said Jane, 'but we still enjoy it, don't we, Dennis?' Her husband swallowed his mouthful of chicken drumstick and nodded.

'It's a shame Mr Hudson pulled out at the last minute,' she added. 'He's a fair man, as well as being very good-looking.'

'Who's Mr Hudson?' I whispered to Doris.

'The local hotel owner who donates the winning voucher,' she whispered back. 'He decided to go on a cruise, but forgot to let us know until about a week ago.'

'Donal Kerrigan would have done it, if he hadn't had other commitments,' Sheelagh volunteered. She was by the dresser, rearranging some ivy-patterned crockery, clearly not as invested in the topic as her husband was.

'Donal Kerrigan from *Morning, Sunshine!*?' I said.

'Oh, yes.' Marnie gave a sweet smile. 'He's got a soft spot for Shipley, but his daughter's getting married next week, in Ireland.'

'We don't need a celebrity,' said Barry. 'Just someone impartial.' He glared at Mr Flannery as if he'd like to bump him off. 'Someone who can't be bribed.'

'You're just a sore loser.'

'I won the year before,' Barry said, pushing out his chest.

'Only because I had a power cut,' growled Mr Flannery. 'There'll be no chance of that this year. I've got a back-up generator.'

'Here we go again,' said Jill, sitting back with a sigh. 'I can't believe I gave up an hour of my time for this.'

'Isn't it very expensive to run all these lights?' I chimed, hoping to distract them.

'LED,' Barry said, still glowering at Mr Flannery. 'You can run a thousand lights for the price of a hundred watt bulb.'

'Wow.'

A flurry of voices broke out.

'They still cost a lot to buy though.'

'All that flashing's enough to bring on a migraine.'

'I heard the Jensens paid someone to do their *Frozen* theme.'

'Let's face it, they can afford it with their high-powered jobs.'

'Annabel Williams, from Number 11, wanted to get a petition to cancel the competition, but no one would sign it.'

The voices grew louder, and as Sheelagh moved around the table, refilling everyone's mug from a giant teapot, an idea crept into my head.

'I have a friend who works for a talent agency in London,' I said, employing the voice I used to use when dealing with pushy-tiger mothers. 'I could see if we could get a proper celebrity to switch on the lights and judge the house displays.'

A hush fell over the room, as if I'd summoned a spirit.

'Why didn't you say so before?' Barry gave me an aggrieved stare. 'Go and give her a call, and tell her it's urgent.'

Chapter 4

Before I could respond to Barry's demand, a barrage of questions broke out.

'What sort of celebrity?'

'Will it be a proper one?'

'Can you ask for a comedian?'

Jane leaned across Doris and gripped my forearm. 'Could you actually get *him*?'

'Him?'

'Jamie Wotsit,' she said, a feverish light in her eyes. 'The one who played Christian Grey.'

Doris tutted. 'I'd prefer that nice man from *Midsomer Murders*,' she said, patting her hair. 'Barnaby Rudge.'

I compressed my lips.

'You mean John Barnaby,' said Jill Edwards, who'd been observing proceedings with an increasing air of irritation. 'Barnaby Rudge was a Charles Dickens character.'

'I know that,' Doris huffed. 'And I meant Tom Barnaby, if you must know.'

'Why does it have to be a man?' Mr Flannery sat forward, bony shoulders hunched. 'What about that actress from *Mamma Mia!*?'

Marnie shot him an incredulous look. 'I wouldn't have had you down as a musical lover.'

'I'm not,' he said. 'But I like that Meryl Streep.'

Meryl Streep? 'I'm afraid it's not—'

'Oh, I love her too,' said Sheelagh, nudging a stool between Doris and me and wriggling her bottom onto it. 'I loved her in *Pretty Woman*.'

There were several stifled snorts around the table, and one of the twins started to grizzle.

'Sorry,' said Harassed Mum, unbuttoning her shirt. 'He needs a feed.'

'I'm afraid it won't be an A-list actor,' I said, deciding to get it over with.

'Who, then?' demanded Barry, averting his gaze from the suckling twin. 'A *news* presenter?' He might as well have said toilet cleaner. 'Or someone from a *boy*band?'

'Ooh, our Calum's a huge fan of One Direction.' Jane's beaming smile returned. 'I like the one with the hair.'

'Didn't they break up?' queried Marnie, glancing at her watch.

'Only some of them.' Sheelagh shifted her buttocks. 'Or am I thinking of Take That?'

I was already starting to regret my impulsive suggestion. 'It's more…' I hesitated, sensing they wouldn't like what I was going to say. 'Reality stars.'

'*Reality*?' Barry pulled in his chins. 'You mean some loser who's been in the jungle, eating a kangaroo's arse?'

'Barry!' Sheelagh admonished, giving me an apologetic smile. 'I'm sure they're not all losers.'

'A lot of them have been in films and television dramas,' I pointed out, keen to calm ruffled feathers. 'I'm sure I could book one of those.'

'And how much will it cost to get one of these *reality* stars?' Barry was scanning a printout through narrowed eyes. 'Donal Kerrigan was going to do it for free.'

'We don't have the resources, and council cutbacks mean they can't pay either.' Sheelagh worried at a button on her cardigan.

'How much?' Barry repeated.

'Don't hassle her when she's just saved our skins,' said Mr Flannery, looking as if he'd like to punch Barry on the nose.

'I'm sure I can work something out,' I said, deciding that if there *was* a fee I'd pay it myself.

'That's very kind of you.' As Sheelagh gave my arm a motherly pat, I glanced down to see Marmite nestled on her roomy lap, his green gaze filled with contempt. I hadn't much experience of cats, but he didn't seem to like me.

'Give him a rub,' Sheelagh suggested, fondling his ears.

Worried he'd scratch me if I tried, I said, 'I'm good, thanks.' I scraped my chair back, banging my knees on the table as I stood up and squeezed out of the tiny space. 'I'll go and give my friend a ring now, and I'll let you know.'

'Sooner rather than later,' grumped Barry.

'Whenever you're ready,' Sheelagh qualified.

'Lovely to meet you, Lily.' Marnie gave a little wave as I backed into the hall and grabbed my coat.

'Don't forget to pop my basket back, dear, I'm in all day tomorrow,' Doris called, but the last word belonged to Jill Edwards.

'Let me know if you change your mind about an interview.'

'I don't think we've anyone available,' said Erin, five minutes later, as I drew the curtains in the cottage and switched on a couple of lamps. The air felt chilly after the hothouse atmosphere at the Lamberts', and

I crossed the living room and turned the heating up. 'Most of them are working, or going away for Christmas.'

'It'll only take a few hours to turn on some Christmas tree lights and judge a few houses,' I said. 'Half a day, tops.'

'These things are usually booked ages in advance.' On the other end of the phone, Erin sounded distracted, and I remembered that business wasn't too good since a colleague had opened her own agency, taking their best clients with her. 'And, with respect, Shipley's the arse end of nowhere.'

'Grimsby's not exactly Knightsbridge,' I pointed out, 'and didn't that talent-show winner turn on the lights up there, last year?' I couldn't fall at the first hurdle after promising my neighbours a celebrity. The thought of breaking it to Barry filled me with dread.

'Yes, but she was desperate for publicity after her record deal fell through.' Erin blew out a sigh. 'They're becoming fussy,' she said. 'They get paid shitloads more for a nightclub appearance.'

I pictured her at her messy desk at Stars For You, where she organised power lunches, negotiated auditions for her 'artists' and made sure they were where they were supposed to be. When I'd met her, Erin was staying not far from where I worked, helping to look after her niece while her sister recovered from an operation. She was late to pick up Tallulah one afternoon, explaining she'd had a meeting with a quiz host who'd tried to talk her into bed and, fascinated, I'd ended up grilling her about her job, while Tallulah sat on a beanbag, eating a packet of vegetable crisps.

With her thickly lashed blue eyes, and blonde Rapunzel waves, Erin had reminded me of an actress, but when I asked if she'd been in anything, she'd made a horrified face.

'You've got to be shitting me,' she'd said, her potty-mouth belied by her girly prettiness. 'I've seen how hard it is to get a break in show business. Believe me, I'm happier looking after the stars than being one.'

After making me laugh with a couple of anecdotes, she'd asked if we could meet for a coffee some time. 'I don't really know anyone around here and I might be staying a while.'

We'd clicked, despite our differences, and stayed friends after she returned to her life in Soho, where she rented a flat close to the agency. I liked the vicarious glamour of Erin's job, and she liked that my job put hers in perspective; 'dealing with *actual* children, rather than grown-up ones', as she'd summed it up.

'There must be someone who's got a kind heart, if you say it's for a good cause,' I said now, practically wheedling.

'Is it?'

'What?'

'A good cause.' Erin sounded wary. 'From what you've said, it's just an excuse for your neighbours to show off.'

'Well, I've only met them once, and I suppose the circumstances—'

'Don't people show their true selves during "circumstances"?' I knew where this was heading. I opened my mouth to head her off, but she was already saying, 'You-know-who certainly did.'

'We've been over that,' I said, plonking down on the sofa and easing my boots off. I pointed the remote at the television and turned the sound low. The weather forecaster was predicting a polar blast, due to bring snow to areas of the southwest. The bit where Shipley was, by the look of it.

'I still can't get over that you've moved to Dorset because of him.'

'He was just the catalyst,' I said. 'I fancied a change.'

'You left because you got shown up in front of your class, thanks to that idiot's wife.' A memory of the head teacher's disapproving face shot into my head. I shuddered, imagining the story she'd tell if someone called her for a reference. 'It's not likely to happen again, is it?'

'I needed to move out of Mum's anyway,' I said quickly.

'You had the house pretty much to yourself, with all her acting and shit.'

'Erin, you're supposed to support me.'

Her sigh was heavy. 'Sorry, Lils. I'm cross with him for making you believe you had a future together, then wimping out.'

My heart twisted. 'I told you, it was mainly because of his daughter. If he divorced her, she was going to apply for full custody of Harriet.'

'She wouldn't have gone through with it.'

'She would have, just to spite me,' I said, wishing, not for the first time, that I'd never clapped eyes on Max Bellfield (or Bellend, as Erin renamed him). If he hadn't dropped his daughter at my classroom on her first day at school, confessing he was a 'clueless' single dad, I doubt I'd have looked at him twice, but he was so gentle and patient with Harriet – even when she kicked Percy Shelton's shin and called him a douche – I'd been won over.

'Wasn't his daughter a handful?' Erin said.

'She was confused, that's all.'

'Hmmm. Lots of children are confused, but they don't try to burn their school down.'

'She didn't mean it,' I protested, though I still wasn't convinced that Harriet hadn't smuggled the matches in with the express purpose of starting a fire in the waste paper bin. She'd seen it done on an episode of *Chicago Fire*, she said afterwards, sticking her bottom lip out. 'She wanted to see a fire engine.'

'Why the fuck was a kid her age watching *Chicago Fire* in the first place?'

'Oh, Erin, we've talked about this, too,' I said, acknowledging a ripple of relief that I wouldn't have to deal with the issues raised by her parents' break-up now that Max was back with his wife. 'Can we get back to you offering me a nice celebrity, free of charge?'

'It won't be free of charge,' said Erin. 'It's not very sexy, but the local council normally foots the bill, at the taxpayer's expense. It can cost anything up to five grand.'

'*What?*' I wasn't digging that far into my savings. I was relying on them to get me through until I received an advance for my first novel. 'Not this year,' I said. 'Cutbacks. Plus, Donal Kerrigan was going to do it for free, but pulled out.'

'And you're getting involved because…?'

'I want to make friends.' It sounded pathetic, and I immediately wished I hadn't said it.

'Oh, Lily.' After a loaded pause, during which I heard someone in the background tell someone to 'fuck right off', followed by a slamming door, Erin said, 'There *is* someone who might be available.'

I straightened. 'Who?'

'Ollie Matheson,' she said, with a certain amount of caution. 'He's between jobs at the moment, and could do with some positive exposure.'

I didn't like the sound of that. 'Who's Ollie Matheson?'

Erin gave an exasperated laugh. 'Even you must have heard of him, Lily!'

'You know I don't watch soaps.'

'He's not in a soap, he was the breakout star of *Players*.'

The name rang a bell. One of my ex-colleagues used to rave about it. It was a reality show about wealthy playboys driving flashy cars and attending fancy nightclubs, their sole purpose seemingly to make females with names like Puffy and Twinkle fall for them.

'I don't watch reality shows either.'

'It's quite a good one actually, but Ollie was fired for hitting someone—'

'Isn't that par for the course on those shows?' I said. 'I'd have thought it would be good for ratings.'

'It was actually, but he doesn't want to go back. He's in love with the girl on the show, but there were rumours she'd slept with someone else… it's a long story,' she said, sounding unusually fed up. 'Basically, he needs another job, but other networks are reluctant to hire him, and Tattie Granger—'

'*Tattie*?'

'Yeah, I know,' she said drily. 'She's been bad-mouthing him in the press.'

'And you think he'll be up for a trip to Shipley to look at some Christmas lights?' I pressed my fingers to my temple. 'I can't imagine him jumping at the opportunity.'

'Well, maybe he doesn't have much choice.'

I tried to imagine the local reaction if Ollie Matheson was to turn up. Would anyone even know who he was? 'I suppose if he's the only option…'

'I'll give him a call, but I can't promise anything.'

'You'll try though?'

Erin relented. 'I'll do my very best, you pushy mare.'

'Thanks, Erin, you're the best,' I said. 'Let me know asap.'

'Yes, miss.'

Ending the call, I felt a flash of excitement. This was just what I needed.

Tomorrow I would visit the nearest town and buy some Christmas lights of my own. Not to compete – that would be impossible – but to get into the festive mood, and show that I was a part of the Maple Hill community.

When Mum called later, after she was home from her play, to check that I was OK, I said convincingly, 'Everything's fine, Mum. I think I'm going to fit in here.'

Chapter 5

'What do you mean, he won't do it?'

'He said it was beneath him and he's going to the Maldives for Christmas.'

'I don't believe it.' I stopped and a customer shoved past, arms loaded with boxes of brightly coloured baubles. I was in the Christmassy section at a super-sized garden centre, half an hour's drive from Shipley, and had been merrily humming 'Jingle Bells' as I browsed the aisles when Erin called. 'He actually said it was *beneath* him?'

''Fraid so.' She didn't sound too surprised, as if she'd guessed what Ollie Matheson's response would be.

'But I thought he needed some good publicity.'

'He does, but insists he'd rather lie low until the fuss has blown over, and re-emerge in the New Year.'

'To what?'

'Exactly.' I heard her tapping a pen on her desk, a habit she had when stressed. 'I told him his chances of joining another show are practically nil. And he's been dropped as the face of Snugz.'

My stomach tipped at the mention of the upmarket underwear brand, my mind zooming back to Max, stripped to his boxers, one foot thrust on my bed. Hips jutting forward, he'd raked back his hair with his fingers and asked huskily, 'Do I look like the Snugz guy?'

He'd been slightly peeved when I'd snorted with laughter, and said the Snugz guy probably removed his socks before trying to seduce a lady.

'He wasn't bothered about doing it for nothing, to be fair.'

'That doesn't really matter if he's not going to do it.'

'He's worried he might look like a "desperado".'

'He used that exact word?'

'Yep. Tosser.' I was getting the sense that Ollie Matheson wasn't Erin's favourite client. 'There might be a ventriloquist who could do it, next Thursday,' she said. 'He's appearing in panto in Bournemouth, so Shipley's en route.'

'Ventriloquist?' I moved out of the way of a toddler careering around with reindeer antlers on his head, while his flustered mother threatened to take away his iPad. 'I don't like ventriloquists, they're creepy.'

'It's the one with the rapping panda that swears a lot.'

'Oh, no.' I chucked a snow globe in my basket. 'I want Ollie Matheson.'

'You've changed your tune.'

'At least he's not a sweary, rapping ventriloquist,' I said, reluctant to admit that overnight I'd adjusted to the idea of Ollie Matheson. I'd tried googling him after talking to Erin, but the wild weather had played havoc with the broadband signal and I couldn't get online. Nevertheless, as I'd lain in bed listening to the howling wind, I'd played out various scenarios in my head – most involving my neighbours being overwhelmingly grateful that I'd allowed them to uphold their Shipley traditions. I'd drifted off to sleep, and dreamt that a faceless Ollie Matheson was begging me for a role in the film of my bestselling novel, *The Neighbours*, before waking with a start, disappointed I hadn't come up with a more imaginative title.

'Maybe I should speak to him,' I said, tipping some boxes of lantern-shaped lights into my basket. 'I could appeal to his better nature.'

'I'm not sure he has one,' Erin said grimly. 'I told him it was a favour for a friend, and he said *I* should do it.'

'What an idiot.' I was starting to despise Ollie Matheson.

'I know, I know, he's a moron.'

'What if it's for charity?' I said, as the thought popped into my head. 'He'd happily make a donation, he's pretty generous like that.'

'So you keep saying.'

'I don't know what else I *can* say.'

'Did you tell him he'll get good coverage in the local news, and—'

'Lily, I tried,' Erin interrupted, sounding torn. 'I'm really sorry.'

'But, Erin, I promised.' I was ashamed of my stroppy toddler whine. 'I don't want to let them down.'

'Let down people you don't even know?' Her voice softened. 'They're not going to hate you if you don't produce a celebrity,' she said, but remembering their excitement, and Barry's demand that I let him know as soon as possible (or else?), I wasn't so sure. 'There must be a local business owner, someone neutral, who could step in and do the honours.'

'I don't think there is, and anyway it wouldn't be as memorable.'

Disappointment nudged tears to my eyes. I imagined the reaction from my neighbours. I'd be a laughing stock. Worse, they'd hate me. It would be Isabel Sinclair all over again. They'd start referring to the 'curse of Seaview Cottage' and campaign to get me out.

'This isn't school we're talking about.' Erin spookily picked up my line of thought. 'Not producing a celebrity for neighbours you barely know is hardly the same as being confronted by your boyfriend's wife, in front of your whole class, at the place where you've worked for years.'

'Thanks for the reminder,' I said stiffly, twisting my mind away from the stinging memory. 'It's not that I'm desperate to be liked and approved of, I just want to fit in and be accepted.'

'That's the same thing, you prat.'

'Look, I know you think I was running away, but I really want to make a go of it here.' I squeezed a rubbery Santa so hard that one of his eyes pinged out, and I hastily stuffed him to the back of the shelf.

'Lily, I didn't mean—'

'I'm sorry for putting you on the spot,' I said. 'I should have checked with you before I made any promises.'

'Oh, Lily, you don't need to apologise. I just… I'm worried about you, that's all, over there on your own. It's such a bloody big change. I bet there isn't even a Costa Coffee there.'

'You pointing that out doesn't help.'

'You're right, I'm sorry.' Erin exhaled. 'Maybe I'm jealous that you've escaped and I'm stuck here, clinging to my job, wondering if I'm going to be single forever and end up being eaten by my Alsatian.'

'You don't have an Alsatian,' I said.

'Not yet.'

Relieved to be treading a more familiar path, I said, 'It's not like you don't have the opportunity to meet men. Maybe you should be less fussy.'

'I need to be *more* fussy after The Actor.'

'Understandable.'

A year earlier, Erin had broken her cardinal rule about not dating showbiz types and had fallen for the star of a hospital drama, only for him to dump her six months later to 'break America'. There had been a grim satisfaction in hearing that the only thing he'd broken was his leg, after slipping down some steps on his way to an audition.

'Maybe if you weren't babying your clients all hours of the day and night, you'd have time to meet someone normal.'

When she didn't respond, I realised I'd gone too far. 'Oh, Erin, I'm sorry.'

'Let's stop apologising to each other,' she said, briskly. 'I'll try Ollie one more time, see if I can work my magic.'

'No, don't.' I felt a surge of fury towards Ollie bloody Matheson. Because of him, Erin had had a dig about me moving to Shipley, and I'd been bitchy about her job. He'd made us apologise to each other, which had never happened before. 'Give me his number and I'll contact him myself.'

'You know I can't give out contact details.' Nevertheless, Erin sounded sorely tempted. 'I'll tell him he's off my books if he doesn't do it.'

'Will he care?' I quickly realised how that sounded. 'What I meant was—'

'I know what you meant,' she said, wryly. 'And, yes, I think he might.'

'Mention I'll go to the press otherwise, and brand him a mean-spirited, entitled…'

'Fuckwit?' Erin knew I didn't swear, from years of being around small children. 'I'll pass that on.'

'No,' I said, backtracking. 'I don't want to get anyone into trouble.'

I turned in time to see a pair of white-skinny-jean-clad mums speeding towards me with baby-buggies, and backed into a Christmas tree trussed with tinsel and baubles. It toppled over before I could grab it, spilling its decorations across the floor. 'Shoot!'

'What's going on?'

'Got to go,' I said, yanking the tree upright, but the damage was already done. It was squashed and misshapen, and only a bright-breasted wooden robin remained on a branch, staring glassily ahead.

An assistant approached with a chilly expression, as though I'd kicked the tree over on purpose. 'Leave it,' she ordered as I dropped to my hands and knees and scrabbled to rescue some baubles.

'I'm so sorry,' I said. 'Do you have a dustpan and brush?'

'I said, leave it.'

I rose and backed away, cheeks fizzing with heat, catching some sympathetic glances and a couple of sniggers.

'Good job I was going to buy one anyway!' I called out, heaving a boxed tree onto my shoulder and staggering to the checkout, throwing more items into my basket on the way.

As I stuffed the tree and several bags into my car, I cursed Ollie Matheson again. It was his fault I'd bought a tree too big for the cottage, and enough lights and baubles to decorate the whole of Shipley. 'The least he could do is turn up now,' I muttered, slamming the boot shut.

The sky was goose-grey, as if holding back snow, and my breath emerged in white puffs. On impulse, I drove to the beachfront and opened the car window a crack, breathing the ozone tang in the air, while I watched the waves flinging themselves at the empty beach. We'd often visited Dad's parents in France during the summer holidays, and one year we'd gone to Portugal, but it was our seaside trips to Shipley that remained the most vivid, when the sun had seemed to shine endlessly, and the sea and sky were just the right shade of blue.

The beach and parade had bustled with holidaymakers, and I remembered an ice-cream parlour where we'd eaten sundaes, my tongue lingering over a scoop of cold vanilla.

Today there were just a few dog-walkers, angled against the wind, but a café on the corner of the parade looked busy, and there were several people in the sweet shop. Resolving to pop in there soon, I drove back to Maple Hill and parked on the narrow driveway, hoping to avoid detection. I half expected Barry to pounce, even though I'd seen him drive off earlier, presumably to work, but there was a shiny Honda parked outside. I assumed it belonged to Sheelagh.

As I got out of the car, discreetly eyeing the endless rows of lights on the roof next door, which looked ghostly when they weren't lit up, I caught a glimpse of green eyes at one of the windows.

'Morning, dear.'

For a spine-prickling moment I thought Marmite had spoken, before realising that the voice was female and had come from somewhere behind me.

Slamming the car door, I turned to see Doris Day on her way up the hill, neatly wrapped in a navy belted coat, with her feet encased in black Ugg boots. 'Good morning,' I called after her.

'I'll see you later!' She waved a leather-gloved hand without turning.

'Later?'

'When you return my basket.'

'I can get it now, if you like.'

'Can't stop, dear, I'm having coffee with Celia.' Without breaking her stride, she motioned to a grey stone house at the top of the hill. 'About three p.m.?'

'I'll try, if I'm not too busy,' I called, but my words were snatched away by a gust of cold air, and she didn't appear to hear me.

Busy. The word had taken on a different shape over the past few months. Did wrestling unwanted Christmas items into the cottage count as busy? Making myself something for lunch? Going to the shops and doing housework? Being 'busy' used to be teaching, while home was where I slept and ate, but after leaving my job I'd found myself sleeping late, and spending hours at the library, or baking all afternoon to distract myself from how badly things had gone wrong.

But that was all in the past. A new start meant new routines, and I began by lugging the Christmas tree indoors and dumping it in the passage between the front door and the kitchen. It took up a lot of room, even in its box. I stacked my carrier bags on top, and went back outside to close the car boot, just as Sheelagh emerged from her house in a mustard coloured coat with black leggings, her brassy curls misshapen.

'How are you, love?'

'Fine, fine,' I said, rubbing my arms to indicate I was cold, hoping she'd get the message and let me go back inside. I couldn't face a probing about whether I'd booked a celebrity yet. 'Looks like it might snow!'

'Ooh, I hope so,' she said, and before she could speak again I dashed inside and closed the door.

From the kitchen window I watched her climb into her Honda and drive off, and was about to microwave some vegetable soup when my phone rang.

'I've spoken to him.' Erin's voice was taut. 'He said he'll do it.'

'That's great!' Relief swept over me as I imagined telling Barry, once he returned from work.

'On one condition.' I detected a note of caution. 'He wants to stay in Shipley for a few days beforehand and mingle with the locals.'

'*What?*'

'And…' Erin sucked in a breath. 'He wants his stay to be filmed for a one-off show.'

Chapter 6

I should have been elated, but I felt oddly nervous. Organising a visit for a Christmas festival was one thing – I'd hosted events for school in the past that had gone without a hitch – but being responsible for a celebrity for nearly a *week*?

It was the filming that bothered me. I had a sneaking suspicion the residents wouldn't like it, but Erin assured me there wouldn't be a crew, just a single cameraman, and the focus would be mostly on Ollie. No residents would appear on screen unless they'd given their permission, and she'd get clearance from the local authority for filming outdoors.

'I'm afraid it's that or the ventriloquist,' she said, when my silence stretched too far, 'and Ollie seemed really keen. He's convinced it'll be the fresh start he needs.'

I knew all about needing a fresh start, but didn't like that he'd only agreed on his own terms. 'You'd better tell him yes,' I said brightly, not wanting to sound ungrateful. 'What about payment?'

'He's self-funding the "project".' Erin put quote marks around the word with her voice. 'Like I said, money's not a problem.'

'Brilliant!' In danger of alerting her to my doubts, I asked her to email the details once they'd been sorted out.

'I'm on it,' she said, sounding chipper, as if she hadn't labelled Ollie Matheson a tosser less than two hours ago. 'I actually think this could benefit everyone.'

I doubted Ollie Matheson was thinking of anyone but himself, but reminded myself it would be good for Erin if her client got more work on the back of this 'one-off' show, and at least his appearance in Shipley meant I wouldn't be cast out by my neighbours. *Hopefully.*

Optimism bouncing back, I navigated my purchases in the hallway and headed up to the back bedroom, where I logged in to my email account. It was far too soon for Erin to have any details, but as the signal appeared to be working I googled *Ollie Matheson* and read a couple of articles about him being fired from *Players.* He'd declined to comment, but another cast member was quoted as saying 'good riddance' and that the show was better off without him. It didn't bode well. If the neighbours had heard of him, and knew he'd been fired, they probably wouldn't be welcoming him with open arms.

I scoured his Wikipedia page for more information. His family sounded impressive: his father had earned his money in the diamond-mining business, his mother was a barrister, his younger sister a respected concert pianist. He'd been Eton educated – no surprises there – had a degree in languages, played the trumpet, loved powerboat racing, and, apart from fronting the Snugz campaign, had designed a range of sunglasses, appeared in a low-budget vampire movie, and thrice been featured as one of *Tatler*'s 'eligible young bachelors'.

Great. He might as well be from Mars for all he had in common with me and my neighbours. And where was he supposed to stay?

I studied a head-and-shoulders shot of him on the Stars For You website, where he was smirking at the camera. He wasn't my type – not that I really had one. In my late teens and early twenties I'd been attracted to bad-boys with tattoos and attitude, who'd ultimately preferred their guitars or motorbikes to girls. 'Lovely Dan' had looked like Shaggy from *Scooby-Doo*, while Max was the brooding type: all floppy hair, intense eyes, and poetic gestures.

Ollie Matheson looked too… *polished*. He was clean-shaven, his even features set off by a tea-coloured tan, topped with a smooth thatch of honey-coloured hair. I could see him wielding a cricket bat, a sweater slung around his shoulders, or at the prow of a boat, gazing out to sea.

I considered watching an episode of *Players* online, but couldn't summon the enthusiasm. Everyone knew shows like that weren't real.

I closed the page and opened my novel document, determined not to get diverted. After re-reading what I'd written yesterday, I cringed and deleted it all. I couldn't carry off writing erotica, even if Jane had declared a rather unhealthy interest.

I remembered what Marnie had said about historical fiction set in Victorian London, and the words 'gothic mystery' bounced into my head, alongside an image of a moustache-twirling villain.

I flexed my fingers and typed: *Georgina rushed across the shadowy yard, her billowing cloak blending into the darkness, and entered the stable. Albert, the stallion, whinnied a greeting. 'Where do you think you're going?'* Oops. It sounded as though the horse could talk. *There was a movement, and Georgina smelt tobacco. 'Where do you think you're going?' It was Lord Gruffalo…'* Gruffalo? Imagining the fictional monster, I swallowed a bubble of mirth. Placing the Gruffalo in a Victorian mystery would certainly spice things up, but wasn't exactly credible – not to mention I'd be plagiarising a much-loved children's story.

Lord Gruffley, I retyped, *his eyes like marbles in the gloom, his nostrils flaring…'* Would she see his nostrils flaring in the darkness? Maybe Georgina should have a torch. No, not a torch, an oil lamp or… candle?

I plundered my brain, which was feeling increasingly flabby. I'd loved storing away fascinating snippets for my mini-students and often, in the evenings, I'd dream up interesting art projects, or ways to make spelling and number tests more fun, but now there was no need to do any of this, my brain had apparently seized up.

What if I never had an original or clever thought again?

Panicky, I leaned back in Dad's chair and looked out of the window to see it had started snowing. I remembered last year, when snow had carpeted the playground, and we'd rushed outside to build a snowman.

I got up and moved closer, pressing my forehead to the glass, wishing I had someone to share the moment with. *Not this again.* Was I incapable of enjoying things on my own?

Glancing at the square of garden, which looked like it had been sprinkled with icing sugar, I tried to imagine my heroine, Georgina – she would be a plucky seductress, I decided – in the stable with Lord Gruffly, but instead remembered I'd promised to return Doris's basket this afternoon.

I rushed downstairs, bundled my coat and boots back on, and wound a pumpkin-coloured scarf round my neck. Then I made my way down the hill with the basket, sticking my tongue out to catch snowflakes, like I'd loved to do as a child.

I was suddenly enveloped with a sense of well-being, half planning a walk on the beach afterwards, to think about my novel, so it came as a shock when Doris yanked open her door before I'd touched the knocker, and beckoned me inside.

'I'm glad you got my gist, earlier,' she said, fixing me with a meaningful look as I stepped into my second unfamiliar hallway in twenty-four hours.

'Gist?' I tried to glance round, but her gaze had gripped mine so hard I couldn't look away. I had a fleeting impression of extreme tidiness, and a scent of polish mingled with bleach that made my nostrils itch. 'I've brought your basket back, like you asked.'

'Thanks.' In one nimble movement, she took it from me and placed it on the bottom stair without breaking eye contact. 'Have you seen any unusual activity next door, since moving in?'

'Next door?' I wanted to unwind my scarf, shake out my hair, and have a normal 'getting-to-know-you-better' conversation; perhaps talk about the snow – which I was ridiculously excited about – but it was obvious from the glint in her eyes that Doris had an agenda.

'Barry and Sheelagh,' she said slowly, as though I was slow on the uptake. She lifted her chin, and I was reminded of Mum preparing for one of her acting roles. 'Goings on,' she added, arching her eyebrows.

'Goings on?' I was echoing her, in the hope things would make more sense. 'What do you mean, "goings on"?'

She looked from side to side, as if someone might be listening behind the open living-room door, affording me the opportunity to peer inside. I'd no sooner glimpsed an army of ornaments behind gleaming glass cabinet doors, and a photo of a baby with golden curls, than she said, 'I think he's having affairs.'

My head whipped round. '*What*?' She looked so serious, I let out a laugh, only for it to die when Doris's whole face stiffened. 'Sorry,' I said, dipping my hands in my coat pockets. She clearly had no intention of getting cosy over a cup of tea. 'Affairs? Don't you mean "affair"?'

'There's more than one woman, from what I can gather,' she said, pursing her lips. 'I've been trying to study his movements, but he's clever.' She smoothed her neat little bob. 'I'm amazed any woman would want him, let alone more than one. He's a grumpy bugger, and not good-looking like my Roger was, God rest his soul.'

I was starting to feel a bit sorry for Barry, who couldn't really help his looks – or lack of them. 'Just because he's a bit' – I chose my word carefully – '*blunt*, doesn't mean he's running around with other women.'

'If he was running around, we'd know,' Doris pointed out. 'He's being cunning, and I don't like a cunning man.' Her eyes slid to a framed photograph on the wall, and following her gaze I saw a well-muscled man with a thick shag of black hair, sporting a seventies-porn-star moustache. He was dressed in tennis whites, wielding a racket as if it was a truncheon, a ball gripped in his other hand. 'My Roger had to be cunning, it was the nature of his job, to catch criminals, but outside work he was a scholar and a gentleman.'

Looking at his indecently tight shorts and manic smile, I had a feeling Roger Day had been neither, but wasn't about to say so.

'Doris, it's none of our business what Barry's up to,' I said, tearing my eyes from Doris's former husband.

'If he's cheating on his wife, what does that say about him?' Doris looked quite het up. 'He doesn't deserve to be head of The Christmas Lights Society for a start. I didn't agree to him taking over after Leonard Appleton died. Barry's only lived on Maple Hill for three years, but he just appointed himself. *I* could have taken over. I'd have been very good in the role, and things wouldn't have got out of hand.'

I wasn't sure about that. In my experience, competitions brought out the best and the worst in people, regardless of who was in charge.

'You want to discredit him?' I said, trying not to sound critical. 'So you can take over?'

'Certainly not.' Doris looked affronted. 'I just don't trust him, that's all, and think I could do a better job.'

'*R... ight.*'

'Anyway, I'd like you to keep an eye out, look for evidence, that kind of thing,' Doris went on, as if nothing I'd said mattered. 'Being right next door means you're in pole position, because even with my binoculars—'

'Binoculars? Doris, is that even legal?'

'I'm head of Neighbourhood Watch, it's my job,' she said, matter-of-factly. 'I like bird-watching too, as it happens. I've seen every kind of tit you can imagine.'

I digested that for a second. 'So, basically, you're asking me to spy on my neighbour.'

'Not *spy*, no.' A crease appeared between her eyebrows. 'Just keep an eye on him, that's all.'

'That's spying—'

'He was in the army, you know.' That didn't surprise me, somehow. 'My friend Ellen Partridge got that information – don't ask, she never reveals her sources – but Barry's a builder now and has never mentioned his military background.' She widened her eyes. 'See what I mean? He's cagey.' Her eyes grew round. 'I wouldn't be surprised if he's killed people.'

'That's a bit much,' I said, my mind reeling at the unexpected swerve our exchange had taken. I'd expected a welcoming heart-to-heart, perhaps a slice of cake, not wild and unfounded accusations about my next-door neighbour.

'Have you found someone to switch on the lights?' Abruptly switching topic, Doris's gaze homed in on mine like a hypnotist's, but I managed not to tell her, having promised I'd let Barry know first.

'It's not confirmed yet, but I'll keep you posted,' I managed, reaching behind me to grasp the doorknob. 'I'd better go, I'm expecting a call any minute.'

I hurried away, trying not to slip on the snow that had settled. Certain I could still feel her eyes on my back (binoculars?) I looked round, but her door was closed. She was standing at the front window, waving a yellow duster.

'That was weird,' I said, letting myself into the cottage, wishing Mum was there so I could tell her about it. *Great.* Now I was missing my mum, like a six-year-old on a school trip.

I'd left my phone charging in the kitchen, and there was a message from Erin.

'Check your emails!!!!'

After shedding my coat and scarf, I opened up my inbox and read:

'Ollie will be with you day after tomorrow, arriving around 1 pm. The local guest house is closed for the winter for refurb, so because he wants to be among locals, get to know them etc, I said it would be OK if he stayed with you, hope that's OK.'

WHAT THE FLAMINGOS???? Ollie Matheson was coming to stay at MY HOUSE?

'I've sent a press release to News South-West about him switching on the lights etc on the 13th, so you just have to entertain him until then.'

HOLY SHIRTSLEEVES!

'*Be warned,'* she finished. *'He's hot, and you'll fancy him, but don't go there. X'*

There was no way he was staying with me. I immediately tried to phone Erin, but it went to voicemail. She'd probably guessed my response and was avoiding my calls.

'Dustballs!' I wished I could swear properly, but I was too far out of the habit. 'Figgy, pillocking dustballs.'

I thought a bit more, letting my breathing slow down. Maybe it made sense for him to stay here. It would only be for a few days, and I had the feeling that once he'd met the locals, and realised there wasn't a nightclub in Shipley, he wouldn't want to hang around.

And maybe it would win favour with my neighbours, having a celebrity living among them.

Providing he doesn't punch anyone.

Forcing down a surge of misgivings, I replied:

'Thanks!! Not remotely happy about accommodation arrangements, but I owe you (depending on the outcome). Love, L XX'

Then I phoned the bed company to check when my new bed was arriving. I couldn't imagine Ollie Matheson slumming it on the sofa, no matter how big and squashy it was.

Chapter 7

I spent a restless night, veering between excitement and trepidation. At 2 a.m., convinced the cottage was too ordinary to accommodate an upper-crust celebrity, I decided to look for a bigger property to rent nearby, preferably with a pool and gymnasium, and pass it off as my own. I got as far as fetching my laptop, shivering in my fleecy pyjamas, because the heating had gone off, when something Dad used to say floated into my head: *Let people take you as they find you. If they don't like it, it's their problem, not yours.*

It was hardly ground-breaking, but it brought me back to reality. If Ollie Matheson didn't like the cottage, he could go and stay somewhere else. Maybe Doris would put him up. The thought of him in her pristine house made me smile, and I finally drifted to sleep and dreamt I was on the roof, my hands and feet wrapped in tinsel, while Sheelagh danced on the pavement below in a flashing Santa hat.

I must have forgotten to set my alarm, and woke with a jolt when I heard a door slam outside and man's voice shout, 'See you later.'

Barry. I needed to let him know the news before he left for work, to give him time to let everyone know about Ollie's arrival, and do whatever else he needed to do.

I stumbled downstairs, flung my coat on over my pyjamas, and shot outside in my slippers, to see Marmite crouched on the path, eyeing something in the hedge.

'Shoo!' I cried, clapping my hands. 'Go away!' He blanked me, and I felt oddly embarrassed. 'Please yourself,' I muttered, stepping over him.

The snow had melted overnight, and the garden looked extra bright, like a child's drawing that had been coloured in. For a second I savoured the fact that I was standing *in my own garden*, with a shiny green hedge on one side and a low, wooden fence on the other; something I couldn't have imagined six months ago.

Shivering, I looked over to see Barry standing by his dusty Explorer on the driveway (the sort of car an ex-military man would drive?). He was wearing his long black trench coat and some army boots, his grey hair tied in a ponytail at the nape of his neck. I found myself seeing him through Doris's eyes, and gave myself a mental shake.

Barry was gazing at his over-decorated house with something approaching awe, as if it had metamorphosed into a magic carpet. 'I don't know why anyone else is bothering,' he said, and as there was no one about I assumed he was talking to me. 'I think I've got it in the bag this year.'

'It's not over 'til it's over,' I said, fastening my coat and stamping my feet. On the concrete path they felt like slabs of ice, even in furry slippers.

'Once I get the inflatable angel and the Three Wise Men in the garden, it'll be game over.' He was rubbing his hands and smacking his lips, as if watching a lap dancer slip money into her thong. (Possibly adulterous behaviour?) 'You got some?'

'Sorry?'

'Christmas lights.' His pale eyes flickered over me, probably assessing how likely I was to better his display, and for a split second I was tempted to pull out all the stops and create something that could be seen from outer space. Then I remembered the gingerbread house, and the *Frozen* theme, and knew I didn't stand a chance. 'Not much point, seeing as you'll be bringing the judge on board. You'll be exempt, see?'

The way he said 'judge', as if it was a competition worth thousands of pounds, or came with a contract that would catapult him into the realms of the rich and famous, was almost laughable.

'I can still put up some lights,' I said, stiffly. 'I'm not bothered about winning.'

'Everyone's bothered about winning.' Barry planted his feet wide and folded his arms across his barrel-like chest, and I could definitely see him, shaven-headed and tattooed, with a rifle slung over his shoulder. 'Why do you think the others are bothering, if they don't want to win?'

'I'm sure they like decorating their houses for the fun of it, especially if they have children,' I said, wishing my teeth weren't chattering. 'Christmas is for children, really, isn't it?' I didn't really believe that for a second, but I was making a point about him being a bit juvenile.

'Nothing childish about my display, not like some of the others,' he said, with a rather pained expression, and I suddenly realised I hadn't seen evidence of a family next door, and hoped I hadn't touched on a sensitive subject.

Before I could speak again, the door flew open and Sheelagh appeared in a fire-engine-red sweater, clutching several books.

''Morning!' she called, tugging at her black leggings. 'Bitter, isn't it?' Her orange lipstick clashed with her jumper, and her blusher was a bit 'pantomime dame', but her smile was warm. 'Shame the snow's gone, but apparently it's coming back.' She said it fondly, as though expecting a much-loved relative. 'I do love the snow.'

'Me too,' I said, relieved that Barry had moved back to his car, a sullen set to his jaw. 'I just wanted to let you know that I've booked someone. A celebrity. Like I promised.' I hadn't meant to say the last bit – it sounded too much like I was seeking their approval – but the effect on Barry was startling.

He swung round, smiling broadly, revealing a set of greyish, uneven teeth. 'Good girl!' he boomed. 'Who is it?'

Oh jeepers… 'Well, you might not have heard of him,' I warned. It was probably best not to get their hopes up too much. 'He's called Ollie Matheson, and he's from a show called—'

'*PLAYERS*!' Sheelagh's screech could have stopped traffic, and she dropped the books she'd been holding to clutch at her curls. 'Oh my days, I *love* that show!'

Barry's unkempt eyebrows bristled together. 'It's the first I've heard of it.'

'I record it and watch it before I go to school,' said Sheelagh, stooping to pick up her books. I couldn't help noticing one was titled *The Other Woman* while another asked *If Running Away isn't the Answer, What is?*

Maybe Doris was on to something. It looked like Sheelagh might be too.

'School?' I said, pretending I hadn't noticed the books.

'I'm a dinner lady at Nightingale Primary,' Sheelagh said, tucking them back under her squashy arm. 'They have lovely food there, proper school dinners.'

I smiled. 'It was packed lunches only at the school where I worked, and there was quite a variety, not all of it very healthy—'

'So, which one is it?' Sheelagh butted in, cheeks wobbling with excitement. 'Please tell me it's Francis DeVere.' She mimed swooning, and Barry made a sound like *humph*. 'Or Sebastian Dooley-McBride.' Her eyes popped open. 'He's such an old-fashioned gentleman, and he plays the flute like a dream. He's a horse whisperer too,' she went on, her face soft with affection, 'and a qualified surgeon. He's leaving the show at the end of the year, because he wants to go to a disaster zone and help the refugees.'

'That's... impressive.' Not what I'd have expected of a reality star.

'Unless he accepts an offer he had, to appear in a Hollywood movie with Ryan Gosling.'

'Wow.' I was quite keen to meet Sebastian Dooley-McBride myself, and almost dreading revealing the truth.

'Oh, no!' Sheelagh's features hardened. 'It's Quincy Cuttlingtonson, isn't it?' she said. 'I'm going to tell him exactly what I thought of him cheating at water polo, and getting his brother's fiancée into trouble.'

'What sort of trouble?'

'Let's just say it involved a baby.'

'He got his brother's fiancée pregnant?' *Players* sounded far more gripping than I'd imagined.

'No, no, nothing like that.' Sheelagh gave a mirthless laugh. 'He shopped her to the police for diamond-smuggling.'

'I don't get it.'

'She was carrying her brother's child,' Sheelagh said in a 'keep up' tone of voice.

'She was pregnant by her *brother*?'

Barry made a choking noise.

'What? Of course not.' Sheelagh boggled at me. 'She was carrying her nephew as she came through customs,' she clarified. 'The diamonds were hidden in his nappy.'

I digested this in silence. 'All the more reason to arrest her, I would have thought.' What was I *saying*? 'Anyway, it's none of those,' I said, teeth rattling with the cold. 'It's... it's Ollie Matheson.'

'Oh, I *love* him!' Sheelagh's face brightened. 'He got a raw deal, being kicked off the show, poor fellow. I'll tell him so, too. Ooh, I can't wait!' She turned to Barry, who looked a lot less thrilled than his wife, though I couldn't work out whether it was because he'd discovered her secret love of *Players*, or because he'd never heard of Ollie Matheson. 'So much for your theory that Lily was all talk,' she said to him, cheerfully. 'She clearly *hasn't* got better things to do.' She swept us a beam, seeing it as a compliment, while Barry neatly avoided my gaze altogether. 'Aren't you going to thank her?'

'Thanks,' he mumbled, scratching the back of his neck. 'And he'll be available on the thirteenth?'

'He will.' I debated telling them the rest, but Sheelagh, hugging her books to her bosom now, was growing agitated.

'Will we get to talk to him properly after he's switched on the lights and everything?' she queried. 'I mean, will that be allowed? Because I've a friend who lives in Poole, and she tried to get an autograph when those children's TV presenters The Giggle Sisters turned on the lights last year, but they were whisked away in a chauffeur-driven car. Brenda swore that one of them gave her the finger as they drove past.'

'You'll get to talk to him,' I promised, trying not to laugh. *Tell them Ollie's staying with you.* But, for some reason, I couldn't. I hadn't come to terms with it myself, and I had a feeling that Sheelagh might burst a blood vessel if I told her. And that Barry might go further, and erect an actual stable in his garage, depicting the birth of Jesus, if there was a chance it would influence the judge. *Oh fudge. Why had I moved to Shipley?*

'Well, that's just marvellous!' Sheelagh's face collapsed into a smile. 'I can't wait to tell everyone.'

'It'll be in the press,' I said. 'And his agent will be liaising with the local authority.'

Barry wrenched open the door of his car as though expecting to find a fugitive hiding inside, then turned to salute me with a hint of respect. I felt ridiculously gratified – as if my whole reason for existing depended on pleasing Barry Lambert: ex-military and probable love-rat.

'Thanks again, Lily,' said Sheelagh. 'You've already turned out to be a million times better than Isabel Sinclair.'

'Oh. Well, thank you.' I couldn't help basking in her approval. 'Happy to do my bit.'

'It's more than a bit,' she said, sincerely. 'It means a lot that you've helped.'

Flushed now, with embarrassed pleasure, I said, 'I'd better go and get dressed.'

'Don't forget to pop up and have a proper chat with Jill Edwards.' Sheelagh gave a persuasive smile that made her eyes disappear. 'I'm sure you'd be a great asset to that school.'

Not this again. 'I'm committed to getting my novel written,' I said, as I backed up the path. 'I'll see you soon.'

I'd left the door open and it was frigid inside the cottage. I kept my coat on while I made some toast and coffee, but I could only manage a couple of mouthfuls, because I kept thinking about Ollie Matheson turning up and invading my space.

I might have been feeling lonely the day before, but only because I hadn't had a chance to properly settle in. Could I cope with a total stranger being thrust into my life? Someone undoubtedly high maintenance. My instinct was a resounding 'no'. For a second, I considered calling Erin and telling her to cancel his visit, or at least find somewhere else for him to stay. But it had gone too far, and I'd just told Barry and Sheelagh he was coming.

With a groan of despair, I threw my toast in the bin and surveyed my surroundings. The cottage was clean and tidy, so I had nothing to worry about there, but there was something missing. I hadn't lived in it long enough to make it my own.

Perhaps if I put up the Christmas tree and decorations, it would make the place more homely, and I could bake some mince pies, which would create a welcoming aroma – once I'd bought the ingredients. In fact, I needed to do a big shop. There was barely anything in the cupboards.

I remembered something else. Hadn't Erin mentioned a cameraman, to film Ollie's visit? Where would he be staying?

I tried to call her, but there was no reply, so I fired off a text: *'What about the cameraman?'*

'*What about him?'* she texted back.

'Where's he staying?'

'Don't you have a sofa? LOL!!'

We always wrote LOL ironically, as we didn't approve of people who 'laughed out loud' in messages, but I couldn't raise a smile. She *was* joking, surely?

'*You are joking?'*

'*Nope. You'll need a chaperone around Ollie, as you're bound to fancy him, and the cameraman's a good guy, one of the best.'*

Swear words filled my head, but all that came out was '*Fart!*' So I had to house a sweaty cameraman, as well as Ollie Matheson? I hadn't signed up for this. I'd tried to do a favour for my neighbours, and it was snowballing out of control. And what did Erin mean, I was bound to fancy Ollie? Apart from anything, she knew I was off men, and I'd never be attracted to someone from a reality show. What was she *thinking*?

As I stormed into the hallway to unpack the Christmas tree, with a sense of things slipping from my grasp, I wondered whether Erin knew me at all.

Chapter 8

After a quick shower, I threw on some jeans and a sweatshirt and drove to the nearest supermarket, where I found myself tossing duck pâté, Earl Grey tea, macaroons, quail's eggs and smoked salmon into my trolley, and asking at the meat counter whether they had any grouse.

So much for letting Ollie Matheson take me as he found me.

'There's some kangaroo steaks in the freezer section,' the girl behind the counter said. 'It's a new range. There's alligator too.'

I'd never cooked a reptile before, and didn't fancy starting now. 'It's OK, I'll take a couple of partridges instead.' What if he only ate fish, or was a vegetarian?

Ambushed by a surge of panic, I dashed to the fish counter and bought a turbot and some mackerel, then picked out the most exotic vegetables I could find. I could always google how to cook a Jerusalem artichoke.

In the drinks' aisle, I started checking out vintage champagne, wondering whether Ollie would prefer cocktails and, if so, how I could learn to make them. Snapping back to my senses, I settled on a bottle of £5.99 red wine, put back the macaroons and Earl Grey tea and threw a packet of crumpets into the trolley, along with some bacon and a jar of coffee, and the ingredients to make mince pies.

Maybe Ollie Matheson will appreciate my homemade pastry.

With that thought, something inside me unclenched. Maybe I should embrace the situation, instead of getting worked up. OK, so it was completely random, and if I had to entertain a celebrity at home I'd have preferred a female, but nothing like this was likely to happen again, and it might even be fun. Hadn't I wanted a total change? Wasn't that why I'd moved to Shipley? I might even get some material for my novel.

Returning to the drinks' aisle to get some vintage champagne, I decided to scrap my gothic mystery and write something contemporary instead. A satire, perhaps, on the fickle world of reality television. Ollie would have plenty of anecdotes, and might even give me a quote for the cover, in return for my hospitality.

'That'll be ninety-eight pounds forty,' said the assistant, looking sideways at my shopping, which she'd thrust down the conveyor belt with unnecessary force. 'Looks like you've got royalty coming to stay.'

'Something like that.' I was ashamed to feel a treacherous thrill. Ollie Matheson was hardly royalty, even if he had attended the same school as princes William and Harry.

Perhaps he'd met them! He was a couple of years younger than Prince Harry, but must have been there at the same time. I'd had a little crush on Harry, which Max had been jealous of, criticising him whenever he appeared in the press, as if there was a possibility he might rock up at the school one day and sweep me off my feet.

Back at the cottage, I put away my shopping, put some washing in the machine, and spent the afternoon cleaning the already clean cottage to work off my nervous energy, before baking enough mince pies to feed the whole of Shipley. I also made a fruit cake soaked in brandy, and a couple of apple pies, snacking on dried fruit while I worked. I sang along to a medley of Christmas songs on an old radio

I'd brought from Mum's, and by the time I'd finished, the cottage was warmly fragrant with baking smells, and I was pleasantly tipsy on half a bottle of red wine. Outside the window, darkness had fallen, punctuated with brightness and colour from the Christmas displays. I looked out for a moment, enjoying the twinkling lanterns gilding the branches of the tree in the garden opposite, and the flashing 'Happy Christmas' sign on the gate.

My new home! I sighed happily as I liberally dusted the mince pies with icing sugar, and poured some more wine.

'Deck the halls with boughs of holly, tra-la-la-la-laaaaaaaa la-la-LA-LAAAA!' I warbled, grabbing my glass as I danced into the hallway, where I screamed with fright as a pair of gleaming orbs appeared at the top of the stairs.

'Marmite, you… *beast*,' I shrieked, clutching my chest as the cat sauntered down, sleek as a panther. 'What are you *doing* here?'

Figuring he'd crept in that morning while the door was open, I hurtled upstairs to check for damage. After a few hours cooped up, he'd probably wreaked havoc, or at least done his business somewhere. But apart from a still-warm indent in the middle of my duvet, there was no sign he'd done anything but sleep.

Back downstairs I attempted to shoo him out, but he was stretched along the back of the sofa, staring at the blank television screen as though waiting for his favourite programme to start.

Intimidated, I backed out, banging my heel on the corner of the boxed-up Christmas tree in the hall. I should probably put it up. It would save me a job in the morning, when I would be busy with the new bed arriving, and getting myself ready for Ollie's arrival. I hadn't shaved my legs for a while, and even Mum had commented that they'd taken on the appearance of a hairy, mythical monster.

Not that I cared about a reality star seeing my furry shins; it was personal pride that was all. I needed to wash my hair too, which I hadn't bothered brushing after my shower that morning, so it had dried in a tangle at the back.

I poured another glass of wine and took a long drink, before tearing open the Christmas-tree box with the help of some scissors and plenty of brute force.

The tree was in three separate pieces and far too tall to inhabit any of the rooms.

'Boggle,' I mumbled, dragging it all out, sweating in the heat from the kitchen and the radiators. I pulled off my top and threw it over the banister. Bending over the pieces of tree, I was aware of my waistband cutting into my stomach. The dried fruit I'd ingested, not to mention the wine, had made me bloated. I unfastened my jeans to release my muffin-top, and puffed out a breath of relief.

'Come on!' I cried, yanking the tree segments into the living room, leaving a trail of fake pine needles in my wake. Marmite looked round, as though finally registering my presence. 'Fat lot of help you are,' I scolded. 'Sitting there like a king.'

I scratched my head, staring at the parts of tree, sipping more wine. Then it hit me – I could put it together without the middle bit! '*Genius!*'

Marmite yawned and closed his eyes.

'I'll do it on my own then, shall I?'

By the time I'd wedged it together the tree looked bottom-heavy, like a lady in a crinoline dress, but no one would notice once it was laden with baubles and lights – and at least it fitted nicely in front of the window. I stuck my tongue out at Marmite, and returned to the bags in the hall. After retrieving the tree lights and decorations, I ripped open the boxes and emptied them on the floor.

'There's an awful lot of them,' I said, but it turned into a burp. 'Oops, pardon me.' I looked sheepishly at Marmite and giggled. His eyes were still shut. 'God, you're boring.' Sheelagh was probably wondering where he'd gone. 'You need to go home,' I said.

Didn't cats like playing with string? Perhaps I could lure him to the front door, and trick him into leaving.

I had some string tucked away in a kitchen drawer. Erin had laughed when she'd discovered the stash of 'emergency' equipment I'd brought back from my studio flat to Mum's, and kept in my bedroom.

'What emergency will ever require you to whip out a ball of string?'

'You'd be surprised,' I'd said, unable to think of anything in the moment.

After scrabbling my phone out of my back pocket, I texted Erin: *'aBOut to get my string out HA HA HA XCCX'*

I noticed I'd had a missed call, but didn't recognise the number. Probably one of those annoying home insurance calls I kept getting since ringing around for a good deal on the cottage.

I swayed towards the kitchen, widening my eyes as the floor tilted towards me. Mixing alcohol with dried fruit had clearly been a mistake. It must have fermented in my stomach and become more potent. I swallowed the final drop of wine, surprised to find the bottle was empty. I'd better eat a meal to soak it up.

I retrieved a cooked chicken leg from the fridge and plonked it on a plate, then turned to admire my mince pies. Mary Berry couldn't have done better. Impulsively, I picked one up and crammed it in my mouth, groaning with pleasure as the butter-soft pastry melted on my tongue. I took a selfie and sent it to Mum with the caption 'PIE-FACED!!!!!'

She'd be glad I was settling in and having fun.

Next to the tray of cooling apple pies was a mud face-mask I'd bought in the supermarket, and I picked it up, doing a little shimmy as Justin Bieber's new song came on the radio. I was startled by the sight of my naked, bouncing breasts reflected in the window, and fuzzily remembered I hadn't put a bra on after my shower that morning, before dashing to the supermarket.

'Booby boobs, booby boobs, boobies *all* the way,' I sang, to the tune of 'Jingle Bells'. 'Oh what fun it is to have, a pair of booby *booooobs.*' I jiggled them for effect, then tore open the sachet with my teeth and slathered the gooey mask all over my face. The last time I'd used anything like it had been on my sixteenth birthday, in the hope it would eliminate an outbreak of spots, but all it did was trigger a rash, and I'd spent my party hiding in the bathroom.

Obviously the ingredients were more sophisticated these days, but it still felt as though I'd smeared quick-setting concrete on my face.

'No pain, no gain,' I intoned through gritted teeth, arms outstretched like a Dalek, suddenly remembering why I'd come into the kitchen.

After washing my hands and drying them on my jeans, I found the ball of string, which I took to the living room, staring in shock at the baubles and lights scattered all over the floor. Hadn't I put them on the tree? I was *sure* I had. And why was the tree so fat on the bottom and leaning to one side?

'Blasted cat,' I muttered. 'Don't you know I've got visitors coming tomorrow?' I looked around, a prowling headache making my eyes scrunch up. 'Marmite?'

Hearing a crash behind me, I pelted back to the kitchen to see the cat on the worktop with the chicken leg clamped in his mouth.

'Drop it!' I ordered, feeling my face mask crack. 'That's my dinner, you little... varmint.' Unwinding the ball of string I dangled a length in front of him and jigged it about. 'Here, kitty, kitty.' I tried to make my voice enticing, but Marmite was having none of it.

He leapt to the floor and slipped past me, the chicken leg jutting from his jaws.

'Come here, you… son of a banana.'

As I dived to grab him, I became aware of a bright white light shining under the front door, as if a spaceship had landed in the garden.

'What the…?'

Marmite paused, as if spotting the light too, and I took the opportunity to grab him and scoop him up. 'Give me that.' I tried to wrench the chicken leg from between his teeth, as if I could possibly eat it now. He held on, writhing in my arms. Extending his claws he lashed out at my upper arm.

'*Ow*!' I howled, dimly aware that someone was rapping urgently on the door. '*What*?' I cried, tugging it wide, reeling from a rush of cold air. A beam of white light filled my vision, and I remembered a programme I'd seen about people convinced they'd been abducted and probed by aliens. 'What's going on?' I whimpered. Shielding my eyes with the forearm that wasn't wrapped around Marmite, I could just make out the shape of a man on the doorstep. His head wasn't typically alien-shaped, but that didn't mean I was safe. 'Who… who are you?'

'Wow!' said a male voice, with a hint of comedy poshness. 'Now *that's* what I call a greeting! Is it a Maori thing, with the bare breasts and face paint? Should we press our noses and foreheads together?'

Too late, I remembered I was half-naked, and tried to arrange the cat across my chest, but he chose that moment to make a bid for freedom, erupting from my grasp with a yowl.

'Switch that thing off, Craig,' the man said, in cut-glass vowels, and as the bright light abruptly vanished I had a vague impression of another man, holding the sort of camera normally used for filming.

Filming. Nooooooooooooo! It couldn't be. Unless I'd entered some sort of time warp, surely it was still the same day?

'You're early,' I whispered, my stomach rolling queasily, trying to fix my gaze on Ollie Matheson's features. My eyes wouldn't focus properly. It was dark without the hall light on, and his face was cast into shadow, despite the flashing lights from the surrounding houses.

'I wanted the element of surprise,' he said, cheerily. 'Plus, I fancied going incognito.' His head moved, as if looking behind him at the street, his voice unnaturally loud. 'Didn't want the selfie brigade out because they knew I was coming.'

I tried to blink my way to some sort of clarity, but it was no good.

'Lily Ambrose, I presume?' I sensed him looking more closely. 'Is it a make-up thing? Contouring I think it's called. I saw something about it on an episode of the Kardashians.'

Oh god, the face mask. 'It's got moisturising properties,' I said, squiffily. Behind Ollie Matheson, the other figure made a sound that could have been a yawn or a groan signifying either boredom or displeasure. 'Gotta go,' I said. With one arm fastened across my upper half, I stepped back and slammed the door.

The letter box rattled. 'Hey, are you OK?'

Stomach rising, I grabbed my top from the banister and dragged it over my head, then stumbled upstairs and made it to the bathroom in the nick of time.

Chapter 9

My eyes were broken. Also, my head was too heavy and my tongue felt fat. My whole body felt like it didn't belong to me. *Had I come down with the flu?*

As I tried to peel back my eyelids, a memory rushed in. I'd opened the door to a shadowy figure – *two* shadowy figures. There'd been a light, shining in my eyes. Maybe that's why they were broken.

Had I been attacked?

Where was I?

I really, really needed to open my eyes.

Heart thrashing, I ran my fingers over the duvet and felt the familiar imprint of embroidered butterflies on the cover.

Phew.

Prising open one gummy eye, I saw pale sunlight slanting through the window and across the rug on the floor.

Not kidnapped, then.

A rush of relief brought another memory, of me sloshing wine into a glass. *Of course. I'd had too much to drink.* It was so long since I'd had a hangover, I'd forgotten how awful they were.

My stomach gave a queasy roll, and I closed my eye again.

There was a smell in the room that I couldn't identify. Nice, but unfamiliar. Maybe it was another hangover symptom, affecting my battered senses.

'Never drinking again,' I moaned. Even my voice sounded wrong – as if I'd swallowed something fluffy. I blindly felt for my phone, impressed I'd placed it on my bedside table as usual before falling into bed. If only I'd closed the curtains. It was far too bright in the room, even with my eyes shut.

'Well, hello!'

My phone clattered to the floor.

There was a man in my bedroom. *There was a man in my bedroom.*

My mind hurtled through the possibilities.

I'd gone to the pub… and brought someone home?

No. I'd have remembered, and anyway it wasn't my style. Plus, I didn't know any pubs in Shipley.

The man on the doorstep. Perhaps I'd invited him in and…

No. I'd definitely have remembered that.

The floorboards creaked, and I managed to hold in a scream. Perhaps if I pretended to be asleep he would leave me alone.

'I know you're awake, your nose is twitching.'

My nose was twitching in response to his cologne wafting over me – the scent I'd detected on waking and now recognised as fresh linen with a hint of basil, and something exotic that made me think of palm trees. It was surprisingly soothing, and my panic subsided a little.

'Please wake up, Miss Ambrose.'

My eyes pinged open. That cut-glass voice definitely belonged to the man on the doorstep, but why was he in my bedroom if I hadn't invited him in?

Then it came rushing back. The man had been Ollie Matheson. He'd turned up early. He'd seen my boobs. He was in my bedroom. *He'd seen my boobs. And my muffin top. Had he put me to bed?*

A panicky sweep of my body confirmed I was fully dressed. In fact, I was wearing more clothes than I had been when I answered the door, and I remembered pulling my top over my head before rushing upstairs to be sick.

I struggled upright, clutching the duvet to my chin, wincing as the hammering in my head increased. 'Why…' I cleared my throat. 'Why are you in my bedroom, Mr Matheson?'

'Oh, please, do call me Ollie,' he said. 'I wanted to make sure you didn't die in the night. I couldn't have your death on my conscience.' His accent reminded me of the time Mum was cast as a toff in one of her plays, and spent several weeks in character, saying things like, 'Oh, *yah*, absolutely, how WAAANDERful!' to everyone's bemusement. Except Ollie's voice was lower pitched and unexpectedly sexy. 'You snore like a bear,' he added.

'I do not.' My eyes swivelled painfully in the direction of his voice. He was standing between the bed and the door, his hands braced on his hips, and although I'd intended to order him out, a gasp jammed in my throat.

Ollie Matheson was – I blinked and double-checked – *gorgeous*. Like a fairy-tale prince. He looked so different to his photo, his browny-blond stubble giving him an edgier look, and his golden hair was longer – thick and wavy, swept back from a broad, tanned forehead. He was taller than I'd expected, with a presence that hadn't translated in his picture. I felt almost cheated, even as a hot flush travelled through my body. He was supposed to be weedy, not look like he worked out for twelve hours a day, giving the impression he could handle himself in a fight. And those eyes! What was that shade even called? Brandy or cognac – something alcoholic – sprang to mind. Deep-set and intensely twinkly, framed by gold-tipped lashes, they radiated a flirty warmth that was matched by a wide-lipped smile. His mouth was almost indecently sensuous, and his teeth, although white, weren't blindingly so.

In short, he was very handsome.

At least the outfit was *exactly* what I'd expected: turned-up shirt collar, paisley cravat, navy blazer, and narrow-legged trousers in a shade my grandmother would have called maroon. He wasn't wearing socks – a pet hate of mine – with his tan brogues, and the laces were unfastened.

'You'll trip over those, if you're not careful,' I croaked, resorting to teacher-speak to counteract the way my traitorous body was reacting.

'What?' He glanced down in surprise, and it was as if a spell had been broken and I could finally tear my eyes away. 'I didn't want to dirty your carpet so I removed them, but when the heating went off my feet got cold, so I—'

'Wait!' My gaze wandered to the palm-print armchair in the corner of the room. My dressing gown was flung over the arm, and there was a cushion on the floor, next to one of my mugs. 'Have… have you been in here all night?'

'Most of it, yah.' He gave a frisky smile that set my insides twanging. 'Like I said, I wanted to keep an eye on you. I have a younger sister, you see, and would do the same for her. In fact, I have done.' He cocked a shoulder. 'She was a bit of a tearaway in her teens.'

The thought of a coffee-sipping stranger watching me sleep was deeply unnerving. Even one as good-looking as Ollie Matheson. 'You didn't have to do that,' I said, pushing my matted hair back. 'As far as I know, I didn't even ask you in, which means, technically, you're an intruder.'

'Hey, look, you don't need to worry,' he soothed, his eyes dancing over me as though I resembled a sex kitten, rather than someone horribly hung-over and smelly. 'I felt bad, that's all. You didn't lock your front door. Anyone could have come in.' *Like he had.* 'I couldn't leave you in that state.'

That state. I'd assumed that *I* would be the one making judgements, once we finally met, and was scalded with embarrassment that his first impression of me had been so unflattering. And what about during the night? I might have broken wind, or talked in my sleep. Thank god I hadn't been sick again.

'In case you're wondering, you crashed onto the bed once you'd finished in the bathroom, and I covered you up and made sure you were comfortable.' He smoothed the air with both hands. 'Not everything you've read about me is true. Here.' He slipped a smart-phone from his blazer pocket, tapped the screen a few times and thrust it under my nose. 'This is me with the fam.'

'Fam?' Nothing was making any sense.

'Family,' he said. He sat on the side of the bed, knees spread wide, the fabric of his trousers straining over his well-built thighs. 'Ma, Pa, Aunt Belinda, Uncle Toby, and that piece of grey fur is Prissy's Miniature Schnauzer, Bentley.' His chuckle was affectionate. 'He tends to do his business around the house, but gets away with it because he once saved Prissy's life. She got into trouble in the swimming pool, and Bentley dived right in and pulled her to safety.' He hitched a bit closer, his proximity making my head swim. Or perhaps it was the hangover, heightening my senses.

I goggled at his 'fam' who were all as good-looking and expensively clothed as Ollie, with perfect teeth and salon-styled hair, posing in what looked like the grounds of a stately home.

'That's your house?'

'One of them,' he said, shooting his fingers through his hair. 'They mostly live in the Kensington pad these days, except in the summer when they decamp to the chateau in France.' His head was so close to mine I could almost see my reflection in his hair. 'This is the family shack in Hertfordshire, where I was raised.' *Shack?* 'We were celebrating Uncle Toby winning a world conservation award.' A smile tilted the corner of his mouth. 'He's big on saving badgers.'

'That's… amazing,' I said, aware that I probably smelt of vomit. A sideways peek at the mirror propped against the wall shot back an image of my bed-ruffled, puffy-eyed appearance, the remnants of the mud-mask clinging to my face as if I'd slept in a swamp. Ollie Matheson looked like my ridiculously handsome carer.

'Your family seem lovely and I'm sure I'm not in any danger,' I said, adopting a no-nonsense tone that was undermined by a hiccup. 'Sorry.'

'Hey, I should be the one apologising, for scaring the life out of you and your pussy.'

I shot a look at his face, but he looked genuinely repentant. Was this the same man who'd declared that turning on Christmas lights was beneath him? That Erin had said was a tosser? He seemed… *nice.*

'He's not my cat,' I said, remembering how Marmite had lashed out and clawed my arm. *That's* why it was sore. 'He'd just stolen my dinner, actually. I hadn't eaten much, and I'd had rather a lot of wine, which is why…' I gestured at my face.

'You look ravishing,' he said, which was clearly a lie – unless he liked the madwoman look.

'I wasn't expecting you until lunchtime today.'

'Yah, I guess I should have called ahead,' he said. 'Craig actually told me to, but I wanted to fly under the radar—'

'Craig?'

'My cameraman, Craig Daniels.' The other shadowy figure from last night. So, where was *he*, I wondered? 'You see, the last time I did a public appearance was at a book-signing in Soho—'

'You've written a book?' I loosened my grip on the duvet. If Ollie Matheson was a writer, we at least had something in common.

'It was an autobiography, *Ollie Uncovered.* Sort of a play on words, because I was in my pants on the cover.' He gave a twinkly eye-roll. 'Crazy, I know, to write my life story at my age, especially when I haven't done anything magnificent or brave. But, the point is, at this book-signing someone took a swing at me for something I'd supposedly said on Twitter, and broke my jaw.'

'That's awful,' I said. Although, hadn't Ollie hit someone on *Players*? Still, two punches didn't make a right.

'She had quite a right hook,' he conceded, adjusting his cravat. 'Goes with the territory, unfortunately. That's the deal when you sign up for a reality show.'

It was too early to be having a heart-to-heart in my bedroom with a hot reality TV star, especially when I looked such a state, but I couldn't deny I was curious about how he'd got on to the show in the first place.

I wanted to ask, but my bladder was full to bursting, my skull was throbbing relentlessly, and my mouth was like the Sahara. 'I need a drink,' I said. 'Of water, I mean.'

'Oh, I left some. Here.' Ollie bent to pick a glass off the floor by the bed, his hair flopping forward. 'I found these in a drawer,' he added, flicking his hair back again as he handed me a packet of aspirin with a flirty smile.

'Thanks,' I mumbled. The idea of him going through my house was almost as unsettling as him watching me while I slept. Where were his boundaries? Maybe he didn't abide by the same rules as lesser mortals – ones who lived normal lives, away from the glare of cameras, in houses that weren't the size of castles, or chateaux in France. All the same, I relinquished my grip on the duvet and took the tablets and water.

'So, you wouldn't rather be in the Maldives?' I said when I'd finished, handing him the glass.

He gave a charmingly apologetic grin. 'I was in a bit of a strop when Erin called,' he said. 'Tattie, my so-called girlfriend, had just sold a story about me to the press, and I wasn't in the best of moods.' He looked suddenly crestfallen, and I guessed he must be in love with this 'Tattie', and wondered whether any of the females in his circle possessed an ordinary name. 'I suddenly figured a gig like this was a step in the right direction,' he added. He rose in an easy movement so my eyes were level with his crotch, planting his hands in his trouser pockets so the material tightened around what Erin would call his 'package'. 'A show about the real me, you know? To show… certain people that I'm a nice, normal guy, and persuade them I'm worth their time.'

So, he was here to win back his girlfriend. Still, as long as he did what he'd come to do, with minimum fuss and disruption, that was all that mattered.

'I need a shower,' I said, hoisting my eyes to his face.

'Oh, of course.' He gave me a devilish grin. 'Can I help? I'm very good with a loofah.'

'I think I can manage,' I said politely, as if he'd offered to do a spot of painting.

His twinkly gaze lingered until my cheeks felt hotter than Venus. 'In that case, I'll go and tell Craig you're awake and we'll have breakfast together, make a plan.'

I assumed the cameraman must have crashed out on the sofa. *Brilliant.* Two strange men in my house, and I'd slept soundly for nearly ten hours.

'Give me twenty minutes,' I said, and waited until he'd descended the stairs, letting my pulse rate settle, and trying not to think about the mess I'd left down there. I hadn't even washed up or put my baking away. My mince pies would be stale.

'Did that really just happen?' I looked in the mirror and groaned. Twenty minutes wasn't long enough. I needed a week, and several extensive beauty treatments – possibly a body lift – to turn me into the sort of female Ollie Matheson was used to hanging around with.

Chapter 10

After the quickest shower of my life, I called Erin and brought her up to speed.

'What the eff is wrong with him?' she exploded, when I'd finished babbling. 'He should have kept me in the loop. I'd organised a car for today.'

'That's your response?' I said. 'I think he drove up with his cameraman.'

She made a noise like a cow in distress. 'And what do you mean, he's better-looking than you thought? I *said* you'd fancy him.'

'I don't *fancy* him,' I said. 'I'm not a teenage girl.' I put my phone on speaker while I towelled my hair dry. 'I was just saying, he comes across better in real life.'

'Oh god, you've been Ollied.'

'I haven't been Ollied,' I said, lowering my voice, even though I could hear that he was downstairs. *What was he doing?* I bobbed in front of the mirror and winced. I looked pale, and my eyes were pink, but at least my skin felt softer, thanks to the mud-mask, and my hair smelt of fruits-of-the-forest shampoo. 'He seems nicer, too,' I added, retrieving my phone. 'I thought he'd be a total nightmare.'

'Oh, Lily.' I pictured Erin with her palm pressed to her forehead. 'You've only just met him,' she said. 'You've never even seen the show.' She sounded annoyed.

'First impressions count,' I fired back. I'd been feeling quite chipper, despite my hangover and the stubbornly clinging face mask – not to mention the peculiarity of the circumstances – and her words were like a reprimand. I hadn't done anything wrong. In fact, I was being extremely forgiving, considering I could have called the police and had Ollie Matheson arrested for breaking and entering. Well, entering without permission.

'I *warned* you.'

'Why do I need to be warned?'

'Because this is what he does, Lily.' I didn't like the way she kept saying my name. It was a tactic teachers employed when taking a child to task. *Harriet, you know that stamping on someone's foot isn't nice.* 'He'll get under your skin, then he'll move on. That's how the show works.'

'This isn't a show,' I said, with a disbelieving laugh. 'And he's not even on it any more.'

'He's been there long enough for that sort of behaviour to seem normal. And he wouldn't have signed up in the first place, if there wasn't something in his character that enjoyed acting up.'

'Well, apart from all that, I'm not his type,' I said. 'I'm not thin enough, or the right shade of blonde.'

'You know you're bloody gorgeous, but that's the point,' she said. 'I doubt he's met anyone like you, which means you'll be a challenge.'

'He's seen me at my absolute worst.' I flashed back to myself, hunched over the toilet bowl, and cringed. 'If that doesn't put him off, nothing will.'

'I still can't believe you were topless when you answered the door.' A trace of laughter came back to Erin's voice. 'And why did you send me that weird message about string?'

I told her about Marmite.

'I wish I'd been there,' she said, chuckling.

I paused in the act of wriggling my underwear on. 'I've just remembered, they were filming.'

'Don't worry. It'll get cut.'

'But they can still play it back and watch it. It could end up on YouTube.'

'They're not twelve years old, Lily. It's a job to them. And I'm sure they've seen plenty of hooters before.'

'Not my hooters,' I protested.

'The cameraman's probably deleted it already.'

'He's called Craig Daniels. Do you know him?'

'Not really,' she said. 'They're old friends. He left the show when Ollie did, which I imagine is why Ollie brought him.'

Going off on a tangent, I flipped through the clothes in my wardrobe. 'I've no idea what to wear.' I studied the array of dresses, skirts and cardigans I'd worn for teaching. There were some jeans and T-shirts, and baggy sweatshirts – my 'casual-wear' – and a couple of 'best' outfits, comprising a floral jumpsuit and a strappy low-cut dress, neither of which were suitable for eating breakfast with Ollie Matheson.

At the thought of breakfast, I felt suddenly ravenous.

'Why are you looking for something special to wear?' Erin's voice dripped suspicion. 'What's wrong with your usual clothes?'

'Nothing, I just… need some new ones.' I'd never mastered the art of on-trend dressing like Erin had. She could carry off cuffed skinny jeans with lace-up shoes, or mid-calf culottes, which would have looked tragic on me. 'It's fine, I've found something.' I settled on one of my nicer dresses; knee-length with long sleeves, and little blue flowers on a black background.

'It's for him, isn't it?'

'Erin, give me some credit.' I was starting to wish I hadn't called her. 'Even if I was looking, I'd never fall for someone based on their appearance.'

'You're vulnerable,' she persisted. 'I'd love you to meet someone new, but he's not the one.'

'What do you mean, I'm vulnerable?' I put the phone back on speaker while I shimmied into my dress. I needed some thick black tights to hide my hairy shins, and pulled a pair out of the chest of drawers and tugged them on. 'Erin?'

'Oh, nothing,' she said, rather huffily.

'It was clearly something.' I plucked out a cornflower-blue cardigan that matched the flowers on my dress. 'Erin?'

'Just that since your dad died—'

'Erin, don't.' I snatched up the phone again. 'This has nothing to do with Dad.' I couldn't believe she was still pursuing her ridiculous theory that Dad's death had been the reason I'd fallen for Max in the first place; something about my judgement being off, and me rushing into it because I wanted to feel happy again. 'And, anyway, Ollie's in love with someone else.'

To my relief, she let it drop. 'Tattie Granger?' She snorted. 'I doubt it, after how she's treated him.'

'Well, he seemed to think coming here and doing this one-off show might win her back.'

'He said that?'

'Well, not exactly—'

'You seem to have had a good chat, considering he's been there less than twenty-four hours, and you were asleep for most of it.'

Before I could work out her tone, Ollie's voice drifted up the stairs. 'Miss Ambrose, do you have any goose fat?'

Goose fat? 'Erin, I've got to go, he's calling me.'

'Lily, wait, I—'

'I'll call you later.' Pulling on my cardigan, I left the bedroom and jogged downstairs, reminding myself I had no need to feel bad or apologise to my guest for the mess. If Ollie had turned up when he was supposed to, the Christmas tree would have been properly decorated, and my baking wouldn't have been ruined.

'I'm in the kitchen,' he called.

Obviously. I wouldn't keep goose fat in the hall. Not that I had any. Goose fat didn't feature in my life, any more than partridges normally did. 'On my way,' I called back, wondering where the cameraman had got to.

I peered round the living-room door, expecting to see him snoring on the sofa, a blush rising as I imagined explaining my behaviour the night before… but the room was empty.

Too empty.

Where were the baubles and decorations I'd left scattered about? My eyes travelled round. They were on the tree, that's where. It was in the corner, and no longer looked like something I'd pulled out of a canal. In fact, it looked rather magnificent, even if the top was squashed against the ceiling, leaving no room for an angel.

My mind raced back. Had I done this in the night? A creative sleepwalking session? Impossible. Even sober, I'd never have managed such a coherent scheme of red, gold and green, or managed to evenly entwine the softly glowing lights around the branches. As my eyes surfed the rest of the room, I noticed my snow globe positioned next to my favourite family photo on the mantelpiece, and a garland decorated with holly leaves and red poinsettia flowers draped around the fireplace. The few Christmas cards I'd brought from home were hanging on the wall on a strip of ribbon, and there was a wooden candle bridge on the windowsill, with battery-powered bulbs for flames.

'Hey, you look scrumptious, that colour really suits you.' Ollie eased past me into the room, which immediately shrank in size, and gave me an appraising look that made my blood rise. 'What do you think?'

In the nick of time I realised he was referring to the room and not my choice of cardigan. 'Where did all this stuff come from?'

'Well, most of it was in bags so you must have bought it, and I found some drawing pins in a really handy drawer in your kitchen.' His eyes heated up. 'I did bring some mistletoe with me, but I left it in the car. You never know when you might need it.'

'I carry paracetamol for the same reason,' I said, trying not to look at his lips.

'Super,' he said with a slightly puzzled smile.

'The tree looks amazing.'

'Ah, yes, you'd missed out the middle section.' He lifted a brow, as if that had been the only thing wrong with the scene that must have greeted him.

'You did all this by yourself?' I stared, unable to get over how pretty and perfect the room looked.

'Yah, is that OK?' His brow contracted. 'It's just that I got a bit bored around dawn, plus it was pretty damn cold up there and I couldn't find any spare blankets, so I thought I'd nip down and I saw all the stuff you'd left out...' He brandished an arm. 'Prissy and I used to decorate the tree in the drawing room when we were tiddlers.' He sounded nostalgic. 'It's like riding a bike, I suppose. Haven't done anything like it for yonks, but it all came flooding back. Rather relaxing, actually.'

'Well… thank you,' I said, trying to imagine him as a child with his sister, in their stately home, fixing gold-plated trinkets to a gigantic tree. 'I'm sorry it's not real, I sort of *had* to buy it.'

I imagined Erin asking why I was apologising. *I'd do the same with any guest,* I argued in my head. *Everyone knows a real tree is better than a fake one.*

'Oh, I love a fake tree.' Ollie tilted his head to admire his efforts. 'I'm actually allergic to the scent of pine, so a real one would have been a no-no.'

'Oh, yes, of course.' My voice was dangerously close to effusive. 'Me too!' *What?* 'Well, it's not an allergy as such, more that I'm allergic to hoovering up pine needles.' *What was I talking about?* 'So, goose fat?'

'Ah, yes.' Ollie perched his nicely moulded bottom on the arm of the sofa and folded his arms across his chest. Our faces were almost level, and I couldn't help noticing tiny dark flecks around his irises. 'I found some rashers in the fridge, and thought it would be totally retro to have bacon sarnies.'

'Right.' Looking at him felt dangerous – like staring into the sun – so I ripped my gaze away and fixed it through the window, where the sky had forgotten it was winter and had turned a vivid blue. 'I don't cook bacon in goose fat, I tend to grill it.'

Ollie let out a guffaw. 'Oh, the way you said that, with your eyebrows scrunched, it was like you were talking in code.' He adopted a stern expression and flicked his eyes from side to side. '*Listen very carefully, I shall say this only once.*' His French accent was impeccable. 'I used to love *'Allo, 'Allo*.'

My breath caught for the second time that morning.

'What is it?'

'My dad loved that show, too,' I said.

His expression changed, as he picked up on the past tense. 'I'm so sorry,' he said. 'I didn't mean to upset you.'

'You didn't.' Plastering on an answering smile, I clapped my hands as though assembling a class. 'Now, where's this cameraman of yours?' I scoured the room, pretending to look under the coffee table. 'Unless he's very tiny, I can't see him anywhere.'

'He's very tiny indeed,' Ollie said, catching on. 'Practically Lego-sized.' Swinging round to look at the window, he lightly touched my arm. 'Look, I think he's behind the curtain.'

I snorted inelegantly, feeling my nerve-endings tingle where his fingers had rested. 'Seriously, where is he?'

'You read a lot,' Ollie said, crossing to the bookshelf and pulling out my favourite Bill Bryson and flipping through it. 'I must send you a copy of my autobiography, though there's quite a lot in there about my, ah, sex life.' He arched an eyebrow. 'I've been told it's pretty hot stuff.'

I squashed an image of him, naked on my bed. 'Your cameraman?' I said.

'Oh, he hasn't read it. Not his cup of tea. Prefers to read a camera manual.'

'I meant, where is he?'

'Ah, yes.' Ollie slid the book back on the shelf, and picked several satsumas from a bowl I'd placed on the coffee table. 'He insisted on sleeping in the car,' he said, juggling with the fruit.

'What?' My head snapped up. 'He must have been freezing out there.'

'It's a very nice car.' Ollie expertly peeled one of the satsumas and popped half in his mouth, then gently pressed a segment to my lips so I had no choice but to eat it. 'He's slept in it before, in worse conditions.'

So, I'd been alone with Ollie. Was that better or worse than there being *two* strange men in my house? I swallowed. 'But why not just sleep on the sofa?'

'Because he's funny like that.' Ollie made a 'what can you do?' face. 'After you slammed the door in our faces, he said we should find a hotel to stay in, but I told him that was silly because there wouldn't be anywhere suitable, and even if there were, we wouldn't get a room at short notice.'

So, he'd stayed for convenience, not out of concern for me?

'And I was worried about you,' he added quickly, running warm eyes over my face.

Hmmm. 'You might have got in somewhere, at this time of year. Out of season, I mean.' *Why was I discussing hotel bookings?* 'You should go and get him,' I said, reluctantly. Having barely adjusted to Ollie's presence, the idea of someone new turning up wasn't very appealing. Especially when I felt delicate. 'I'll put some bacon on.'

'Actually, I popped out while you were in the shower, and he wasn't there,' Ollie said. He put down the remaining satsumas and stretched, arching his spine so his shirt rode up, revealing a strip of taut stomach. 'I expect he's gone for a run.'

'A run?' I said, staring. Thankfully, he tucked his shirt back in.

'On the beach, probably; he was oddly keen on taking a trip to the seaside. Plus, he loves running. Lord knows why. I tried to get him to join my gym, but he's not into pumping iron.' He flexed a bicep, twinkling his eyes at me, and while I wasn't normally impressed by gym-honed muscles, it had clearly paid off for Ollie. 'Do you want to give it a squeeze?'

'I'm fine, thank you.' I laced my hands primly in front of me.

Ollie suddenly released a yawn. 'I might scrub up after breakfast, if you don't mind?' he said. 'I feel a bit grimy and probably smell dreadful.'

'You smell nice.' The words popped out unbidden and his mouth curved into a smile. 'I mean, yes, of course you can. You can do it now if you like, while I make breakfast. There's plenty of hot water.'

'Super, if you're sure you don't mind.' He was proving to be as polite as he was good-looking. 'I'll fetch my bag from the car and get changed.'

As I reversed from the room, I sucked in my stomach, wishing I hadn't when it let out a noisy gurgle. He touched my elbow on his way past, and I jolted against the door frame.

'Sorry,' I said, feeling foolish. I drew myself up to my full five feet four, which only brought my gaze level with his shoulders. Wide, strong shoulders.

'You've a hole in your tights.'

'Oh.' Looking down, I saw that one of my toenails was poking through, the pink varnish chipped and worn. 'Sorry,' I said again. I felt somehow exposed, which was ridiculous when he'd already seen me naked from the waist up.

'Please don't keep apologising,' he said, so close I could feel his warm breath on my cheek. He seemed fixated by my attempt to wiggle my toe back inside my tights, and we both jerked when the doorbell chimed a series of tinkling notes through the cottage.

'Jumping Jesus!' Ollie clutched his chest. 'That scared the sh… life out of me.'

'I was wondering what the doorbell sounded like.' Giving up on my holey tights, I slipped my feet into my sheepskin slippers at the bottom of the stairs. 'It's probably your cameraman.'

'*Our* cameraman,' Ollie said, right behind me. 'I want some slippers like that.'

Flustered, I couldn't quite understand what was happening when I opened the door.

'It looks like your mother was right to be worried.' It was Doris Day, in a red woollen coat and a matching knitted scarf tucked around her neck. Her mouth was set, and her eyes stretched as she glanced over my shoulder at Ollie. 'Not one man in the house, but two, and you've been here less than a week.'

'Wha…?'

'She was going to call the police, you know. Your mother.'

'I don't understand.'

A man was letting himself through the gate, carrying a holdall and a rucksack, and he threw a small smile at Doris as he drew level. 'I said you'd explain everything,' he said to me. He had bright eyes and a faint scruff of beard, the same sandy shade as his tangled hair.

'What's my mum got to do with anything?' I said, switching my gaze back to Doris and cuddling my cardigan around me. Despite the brightness of the day it was arctic, with a thick coating of frost on the ground.

'She called me last night.' Doris's red-gloved fingers clutched the handle of her scarlet handbag, and I was reminded of Little Red Riding Hood without the hood. 'She was very worried about you.'

I pulled my chin back. 'My mum called *you*?' I frowned. 'How? *Why*?'

'Oh, yah, I forgot to say your phone rang a couple of times last night,' Ollie said. 'I popped it by your bed.' So that's how it had got there. 'Craig, my man, come in,' he went on, to the man hovering with the bags. 'Thought you'd got swept out to sea.'

'There was a café on the seafront, so I stopped and had a coffee,' the man – Craig – said, stamping his black trainers on the doorstep.

'I was just coming to get my bag.' Ollie pulled the door wider, like the man of the house, seeming oblivious to Doris's outraged bewilderment.

'I'm sorry about this,' Craig said to me, a salt-scented tang of the sea coming off him. His voice was pitched deeper than Ollie's, and he had a polite London accent. 'I'm Craig Daniels, by the way.'

'I know,' I said, aware of Doris attempting to assess the situation with her eyes, trying to stem a blush as I remembered my doorstep encounter with Ollie and Craig the night before. 'Lily Ambrose.'

He nodded. He was shorter and leaner than Ollie, with a slightly crooked nose, but his eyes were a clear, greyish-green beneath strong brows, and he had a steady gaze. His layered running gear seemed inadequate for the cold. 'I'll' – he nodded towards the hall – 'see you in there?'

'Right.'

'Thanks.' He slipped through the door, and there was the sound of some friendly back-slapping behind me.

'Why don't we all go inside?' Ollie suggested, and I turned to see him blowing on his hands. 'It's brass monkeys out there.'

'No, thank you very much.' Unmoved by his winning smile, Doris glared at him.

'As you wish.' He widened his eyes at me as he retreated. 'I'll go and clean up.'

When he'd gone, Doris sharpened her gaze. 'Your mother received a rather alarming picture of you yesterday evening, with hardly any clothes on and white powder around your nose.'

'What?' Then I remembered. 'It was *icing sugar*,' I said, feeling slightly hysterical. 'I'd been baking. I was eating a homemade mince pie.'

Doris drew back. 'In the nude, dear?' She looked behind her, as if checking no one was listening. 'Are you one of those naturists?'

'Of course not, I was just… hot.'

She pulled a bag of sweets from her coat pocket and held it out. 'Pineapple cube?'

'No. Thanks,' I said. 'How did my mum know your number?'

'She remembered my name from the note I left with your muffins, and looked me up.' Doris sounded approving of Mum's detective skills. 'She mentioned you'd had a break-up with a married man a while ago and a nasty encounter with his wife, and might be having regrets about moving away—'

'He was *separated*,' I said, surprised that Mum had been so open. 'And I'm absolutely fine, it was months ago.'

'Well, I told her I'd keep an eye on things.' Doris popped a sweet into her mouth. 'Anyway, I thought I'd call in, and I saw a man getting out of that car.' She turned to point at a black saloon, like a witness for the prosecution. 'When I asked what his business was, he said they were FBI and you were under arrest, but it appears he was *joking*.'

'I'm sure he was just being friendly,' I said, trying not to be annoyed by her interfering. The point of living somewhere like Shipley was that everyone knew everyone's business, and that's what I'd chosen – for better or worse. 'Thank you for your concern.'

'So, who are they?' Doris craned a neck for a glimpse inside. 'Is one of them your lover?'

'Of course not,' I spluttered, and she looked momentarily crushed. 'Did Sheelagh call to tell you I've found a celebrity to switch on the tree lights?'

Her gaze shifted back to me. 'The chap from reality television?' Her mouth turned down at the corners. 'Not my cup of tea, but Sheelagh could barely contain herself.'

'Well, that was him.' I figured it would come out soon enough, or else Doris would work it out, once she'd stopped concocting dubious set-ups in her overactive mind.

'Him?' She sounded stunned. 'The chap in the funny shorts? I thought he was supposed to be handsome, according to Sheelagh.'

'No, the other one,' I said, feeling a bit sorry for Craig. Imagine living in the shadow of Ollie Matheson.

'Oh, him.' Doris sniffed and patted her hair. 'Looked a bit full of himself, if you ask me.'

'He's nice actually. The other one's his… friend.'

'But it's not happening until the thirteenth,' she stated. 'Why are they in your house?'

'They, er, want to get a feel for the place first, and as I was the one who invited Ollie I'm… welcoming him to Shipley.' I decided the whole truth could wait. If she knew Ollie Matheson was my house guest, she might take it upon herself to pass the news around, and then everyone would be turning up at my door. 'I'd better get back.'

'Of course.' Doris tweaked her collar. 'I've got to get on anyway, I've got a Zumba class at ten.' She swivelled at the gate, just as I was closing the door. 'Oh, and your mother said to expect her around four o'clock.'

Chapter 11

With Doris's words bouncing around my head, I pulled my phone from my cardigan pocket and shot into the kitchen. I didn't need Mum turning up, her head full of Doris-fuelled nonsense. And I couldn't believe she'd told Doris about me and Max.

As I pressed in her number, I glanced up and my mouth fell open.

The kitchen had been transformed. The limestone worktops shone, the washing up was tidily stacked in the drainer, and my pies and cake had been covered neatly with foil.

Unless a cleaning lady had snuck in while I wasn't looking, Ollie must have done it after decorating the living room. As well as being charming, and extremely good-looking, he was house-trained, too. He was hardly living up to his stereotype – apart from the flirting.

As I waited for Mum to pick up, I switched on the grill and manhandled some bacon out of the fridge, determined to give him a proper welcome breakfast. I was going to prove I was more than a wine-swigging loser with a penchant for topless baking, who wore holey tights and apparently snored in her sleep.

'Lily, thank god! What's going on over there?' Mum's voice exploded into my ear as I placed strips of the bacon under the grill and my temples throbbed in protest. 'I was worried sick when I got that photo after my play, and you didn't reply to my call—'

'How was your play?' I interrupted, in an effort to deflect her.

'Oh, it was fine, though Stuart forgot his lines and said the "c" word instead of "count", which threw things off a bit.'

Stuart was a single ex-fireman who'd taken up acting after early retirement, and I'd started to wonder lately if their relationship was more than professional.

'If Doris hadn't promised to look in on you this morning, I'd have phoned the police,' she said, getting right back on track.

'Mum, it's OK, I'm perfectly fine.' I half laughed to show I meant it, looking around for the eggs. *Damn.* There were only quail's eggs and they were tiny. Still, it would be nice to make a posh English breakfast for my guest. *Guests,* I reminded myself, wondering where Craig had got to.

I could hear the shower running, and assumed it was Ollie, and for the briefest second imagined joining him, and helping to soap his quads – although I would have to shave my legs first. A fiery heat rose to my face, which had nothing to do with cooking, and I realised Mum had stopped talking and was waiting for an explanation.

'Look, I'd been baking,' I said, telling her what I'd told Doris, trying to make light of it by adding the bit about the face mask. 'My skin feels quite nice this morning,' I said, smoothing a hand over my cheek.

'Didn't you use one on your sixteenth birthday, and it brought you out in a rash?'

'I was hoping you'd forgotten about that,' I said, glad she was finally distracted.

'We had to coax you out of the bathroom to attend your own party.' She laughed, fondly. 'Your dad said to tell your friends you'd got sunburnt—'

'But it was the wettest February on record,' I finished off, smiling – though it hadn't been funny at the time. 'Then Chris thought it would be hilarious to announce that I'd got my period.'

'Your brother always had a silly sense of humour.'

'No wonder Perry Edwards didn't hang around to give me a birthday kiss.'

'I think that was the idea,' Mum said. 'Chris was being protective of you, because he knew what Perry was like.'

'How's my brother's hipster café doing?'

'It's very popular, as you well know, and not at all hipster,' she reproved. 'He's using barrels as chairs now, and he's applied for a licence to do cocktail nights.'

Totally hipster, then. Chris had always been good at spotting a trend, and had made a big success of Ambrose and Bell – though Mum hadn't approved of him adding his fiancée's surname, despite her helping him run it.

'Anyway,' Mum went on, 'stop changing the subject. Did Doris tell you I'll be there this afternoon?'

'Yes, that's why I'm ringing.' I turned on the grill to cook the bacon, took out an artisan loaf I'd bought from the supermarket's instore bakery, and returned to the fridge for butter. It was rock-hard, so I popped the packet in the microwave and switched it on. 'You don't need to rush over,' I said. 'I'm settling in brilliantly, and you'll never guess what's—'

'Miss Ambrose, do you have another towel I could use, this one's a little small and I didn't think to bring one with me.'

I whipped round to see Ollie's head and one tanned shoulder thrusting round the door. He was vigorously rubbing his hair with a hand towel, which meant... 'You're naked.'

'Sorry?' He stopped rubbing.

'You, er… you're… I mean…' I blinked to clear a mental image of what he might be hiding. 'I mean… um… I left the big towel in my bedroom,' I said, eyes darting everywhere but at him.

'You only have one?' He sounded vaguely scandalised.

'I shoved a couple in the washing machine, and haven't got round to putting them in the dryer.' *Sexy.*

'Right.'

Why hadn't I thought to buy more towels while I was out, instead of quail's eggs? 'I'll, er, you can go and get the one in my bedroom, but I might… I mean, it might be damp.'

'No probs.' He gave his hair a final ruffle, then raked it back with his hand. 'I am wearing underwear,' he said, and gave me an intimate smile as though sharing a secret.

He winked and withdrew, and I finally remembered how to breathe again, drawing in a lungful of air like a drowning woman.

I stared at the gap where he'd been, then lurched into the hall in time to catch a glimpse of jersey-clad buttock and muscular thigh. As I gawped, the front door opened and Craig materialised. I hadn't even realised he'd gone back outside.

'What's happening?' he said, lugging in his camera and another holdall.

'Ollie couldn't find a towel,' I said, stupidly.

Craig shut the door on a blast of cold air and gave me a steady look, no doubt registering my dilated pupils and heightened colour, and jumping to all sorts of conclusions. 'I meant, something's burning,' he said, and I became aware of smoke billowing from the kitchen, and an acrid smell in the air.

'Oh, mother-of-pearl, the bacon!'

I scooted back, but Craig beat me to it. Wrapping a dishtowel round his hand, he pulled out the grill pan, which was leaping with flames, and flung it into the sink, before leaning over and pushing the window open.

'Haven't you got a smoke alarm?' he said, and succumbed to a coughing fit.

'Obviously not.' As I lifted my hand to cover my nose and mouth, I realised I was still holding my phone, and that Mum had hung up. Through a haze of smoke, I read the text she'd left. *'A naked man in your house??? I'm on my way. XXX'*

'Oh crabsticks.'

'Don't worry,' Craig said, straightening up and wiping the back of his hand across his forehead. 'No harm done.'

'I don't know about that.' I stared at the message, as if it might change its meaning. 'My mum's on her way.'

'I'm guessing from your tone that's a bad thing?' Craig tore off a length of kitchen roll, scooped the charred mess from the sink, and looked around for the bin.

'Over there,' I said, pointing.

He deposited the mess and wiped his hands on his running shorts, which were layered over black leggings – not a good look on a man.

'She's worried about me having a strange man in the house.'

'Isn't that's a good thing?' He bent his leg and tugged his trainer off. 'I should think most mothers would be worried.'

'I'm thirty years old,' I said, stung by the implied criticism. 'I could have a houseful of men, if I wanted.'

He opened his mouth and seemed to be searching for a suitable response. Clearly not finding one, he removed his other trainer and said, 'I'll put these outside, shall I?'

'Please,' I said, shortly. I unlocked the back door, feeling hot and bothered. There'd be no stopping Mum, now she'd made up her mind to visit, and all the bacon had burnt. What was I going to cook for breakfast?

'I can make some scrambled eggs if you like.' As Craig bent to place his trainers outside the door, I let the air cool my face and clear the lingering smoke from the kitchen. 'It doesn't seem right you waiting on us, especially after the way we showed up last night.' It sounded like he hadn't approved – or maybe he was recalling the state I'd been in when I answered the door. 'You will be paid for your trouble,' he added.

'I don't want paying, and it's hardly running around,' I said, tetchy with embarrassment, even though I'd never been in the habit of cooking men breakfast; even Max, who'd preferred a coffee and a cigarette. He'd struggled to quit smoking, despite being desperate to give up for his daughter's sake. 'I've only got quail's eggs,' I admitted.

Craig turned, his eyebrows inching up. 'I don't think I've ever eaten them,' he said mildly. 'It'll be a new experience.'

'Please yourself.' My headache had returned, and I didn't have the strength to argue. 'The eggs are over there, and the pan's in the cupboard.' I opened the fridge. 'I bought some oyster mushrooms, if you fancy a go.' I slapped the carton on the worktop.

Craig glanced at me, but didn't comment, before crossing to the cooker and turning it back on. 'You must have a lot of questions.'

'Not really,' I said, in a mean little voice, wishing Ollie would come down and lighten the mood. I reached for the loaf and a knife, feeling like a visitor in my own kitchen, despite agreeing to let Craig cook the eggs two minutes ago. 'I'll slice the bread.'

He scratched the back of his head, leaving a tuft of hair sticking up. 'Your butter's melted,' he observed. 'How long did you leave it in there?'

'About five minutes.' I looked at the microwave and, seeing a greasy pool leaking from under the door, thought of several swear words. 'I'll get a cloth.'

While I attempted to mop up the mess, Craig silently began cracking quail's eggs into a bowl, and the sight of his long fingers, handling the tiny shells, melted my irritation.

'They're fiddly, aren't they?'

He looked at me sideways. 'Just a bit.'

I tossed some of the remaining butter into a pan, then spread the rest on thinly cut slices of the artisan loaf, which was small and rather hard.

When Ollie came in, smelling of expensive shower gel, his hair freshly blow-dried, Craig was scrambling the eggs with the mushrooms, while I took out some cutlery, pleased it was the solid silver set my grandmother had given me when I moved in to my studio flat.

'Wow, what a treat,' Ollie enthused, rubbing his hands together.

'Thanks for cleaning up in here, you didn't have to,' I said. He'd changed into loose black jeans and a grey hooded top that deepened his tan. The overall effect was a lot more appealing than his public-schoolboy/nightclub-owner look.

'Hey, it was my pleasure,' he said, grinning. 'Ages since I put my hands in bubbles. I covered the pies and your yummy-looking cake, so they didn't go stale. Used to help Nanny in the kitchen with that sort of thing, as a boy.' I guessed he was referring to an actual nanny and not his grandmother. At least she'd taught him a thing or two. Max could barely tell one end of a tea towel from the other. Washing up didn't fit with his self-image as an aspiring poet and passionate lover.

'Thought I'd dress down a bit and go for a more urban vibe,' Ollie said, catching me checking out his clothes. 'What do you think?'

He rested one bare foot against the wall, squashing a hand in his pocket as he gazed moodily into the distance, like someone in an advert.

'Suits you,' I said, briefly catching Craig's eye. 'Much better, actually.'

'You think?' Ollie's face relaxed. 'I don't look like I'm trying too hard?'

Was he asking for fashion advice? 'I don't think so,' I said, although now I thought about it, wasn't he supposed to be on a higher plane than the rest of us, with a sprinkling of stardust thrown in? Otherwise, someone from the council might as well switch on the Christmas tree lights. 'I like it.'

'You look like you're auditioning to be someone's love interest in *Coronation Street*,' Craig said. 'Stop fishing for compliments.'

Ollie gave another of his guffaws. 'He's bloody hilarious this bloke,' he said, aiming a playful punch at Craig's upper arm. 'He keeps my feet on the ground.'

Shaking his head, Craig dished up two portions of food.

'Aren't you having any?' I said, seeing the pan was empty.

'I had something to eat at the café while I was out.'

'You could have invited us, mate.' Ollie looked around, as if seeking waiter-service in a restaurant.

'Come and sit down,' I said, gesturing to the little pale wooden table I'd squeezed into the corner with four mismatching chairs. 'Or we can sit in the living room, if you like.'

'Oh, no, here's fine. This place is so cute.' Ollie stretched his arms wide, demonstrating he could practically touch the walls, before straddling a chair the wrong way round, hands dangling over the back. 'It reminds me of the Wendy house that Pa had built for Prissy's sixth birthday,' he said. 'Remember, Craggers? She'd invite us in to pretend dinner parties.'

Craig handed Ollie a plate and a fork. 'Of course,' he said, quietly.

'His pa was our chief gardener,' Ollie said to me, shovelling some egg into his mouth. 'Wonderful cook, just like his ma.' He jabbed the fork in Craig's direction, and I felt a prickle of interest. I'd assumed they must know each other from Eton, but it somehow made sense that they were from totally different backgrounds.

'It's only eggs,' Craig said, modestly.

'They're quail's,' I added, as if it mattered, sitting self-consciously at the table with my plate.

'Is he a farmer?' Ollie looked quizzical. 'I'm all for people buying local produce.'

I laughed a bit too loudly. 'That's a good one.'

Ollie's brow puckered. 'I don't follow.'

As Craig massaged the point between his eyebrows, it dawned on me perhaps Ollie hadn't been joking, and thought I was actually referring to a Farmer Quail. 'Oh, I… er, I was talking about the bird the eggs came from.'

'Ah!' He let out a laugh. 'Of course you were. I didn't make the connection for a second.'

'It's a ground-nesting bird,' I said, as if he was five.

'Every day's a school day, big man.' Craig's tone was dry. 'Next, you'll be telling him those mushrooms came from oysters.'

He gave me the tiniest of smiles, but it felt as if he was making fun of Ollie so I looked away and picked up a slice of the bread from a few that I'd fanned out on a plate. As I'd suspected, it was like chewing cardboard, and I wished I'd bought a squashy white loaf instead.

'So, we need to sort out an itinerary,' Ollie declared, once he'd cleared his plate and eaten four slices of the bread with apparent enjoyment. I was impressed that, despite his background, he seemed perfectly at home and wasn't remotely judgemental – apart from his comment about the size of the kitchen (what must he have made of the tiny shower cubicle?). 'Did Erin give you any deets?'

'Deets?' I pushed aside my half-eaten food, my appetite having diminished under Craig's watchful eye. Eating when someone else wasn't just felt wrong.

'Details,' Ollie said, handing Craig his empty plate. 'A plan of action.'

'You know she's my friend?' I said. It was odd, hearing him say her name. 'Erin, I mean. And no, no deets.'

'Yah, of course I do, she asked me to come here as a favour.'

'It's a favour for you, too,' I felt moved to point out, as Craig rinsed Ollie's plate at the sink.

'She's a great girl, isn't she?' Ollie said, perhaps not hearing me.

'She is.' I smiled. 'The best.'

'She's so great at her job. She got me the gig with Snugz.' My head grew hot as I pictured him in his pants. 'Shame the bastards dumped me, excuse my language.'

'I'm sorry,' I said. 'About them dumping you.'

He shrugged. 'I can sort of see why they had to, but they didn't know all the facts.'

'Oh?' I waited for him to say more, and when he didn't, added, 'Had you been on the show a long time?'

'Hey, let's not talk about that.' He jumped up, smiling widely. 'I'm trying to get away from that whole scene. This is my fresh start.'

'I know all about that,' I said, talking in a similarly jaunty way, as if it was catching. 'This was my fresh start.' I gestured around me, and noticed Craig had quietly made some tea and there were three steaming mugs on the counter.

'Oh?' He looked interested.

'Let's not talk about that either,' I said.

His half-smile disappeared. 'Right.'

'Do you know Prince Harry?' I said to Ollie, the words leaping out before I could snatch them back. 'He must have been at Eton at the same time as you.'

He gave me a broad smile and tapped the side of his nose. 'Now, I definitely can't talk about *that*,' he said. 'Except to say, he's a jolly nice chap.'

'That's… great.' What had I expected? That he'd offer to set us up on a blind date? Hardly likely, especially as the prince was now dating an American actress. I was relieved when Craig picked up one of the mugs and said, 'Let's go and sit in the other room.'

'Good idea,' I said, gratefully.

'God, he's bossy.' Ollie's grin was admiring as he picked up his tea. 'You can see why I need this guy, can't you?'

It was clear they got on well, despite their obvious differences, with Craig taking on an older-brother role – I guessed – from years of familiarity.

Ollie crept comically after him, as though trying to avoid triggering a landmine, and threw me a pretend–scared look that made me smile.

'I'll be with you in a minute,' I said. 'Make yourselves at home.'

I added two sugars to my tea, taking the opportunity to catch my breath.

Was this really happening?

I looked out of the window and watched a couple of seagulls wheeling past. The sky was white again, as if holding back more snow, and I thought how much had happened in a very short time. I didn't know whether to be excited or scared.

How was I going to fit in working on my novel? I'd have to make some time, or I'd never get past chapter one.

Peeling back a corner of foil, I reached for a mince pie and ate it quickly.

The doorbell chimed and I started, slopping tea over the clean worktop.

Mum couldn't be here already!

'I'll get it!' called Ollie, and before I could tell him not to, he'd already opened the door. I entered the hallway to see him scribbling on a piece of paper for a swarthy man in a brown delivery uniform, gloved hands gripping a clipboard.

'I don't know how word got round,' Ollie said, seeming not at all put out despite his clandestine arrival, and protestations about avoiding attention. 'It's been an absolute age since I've actually signed my autograph. People usually want selfies.'

'I don't think he wanted your autograph,' I said, smiling at the confused-looking man as I spotted the Sweet Dreams van behind him on the road. 'He was asking you to sign for a bed.'

Chapter 12

Craig helped the driver wrestle the bed frame and mattress upstairs, while Ollie issued directions from the foot of the stairs – 'mind the bend, you don't want to bring the paint off the walls, old chap' – seemingly unembarrassed by his autograph faux pas.

As I went to close the door, Sheelagh came up the path, resplendent in a tight black jumper adorned with glittery red hearts, tucked into a voluminous skirt. She'd artfully arranged a couple of curls on her forehead, mascaraed her eyelashes into spider-legs, and painted her mouth blood-red.

As soon as she clapped eyes on Ollie, her pudgy hands shot to her cheeks. 'I knew it was you!' she cried. 'I was taking Marmite to the vet's for his monthly health check and saw you looking out of that bedroom window.' She jabbed a finger upwards. 'I recognised you right away, from a scene in *Players,* when you were caught in Gabriella Forsythe's suite at that fancy hotel, after your cousin's wedding, and hid behind the curtains so her husband didn't find you.' She drew breath, and Ollie gave a broad grin as he thrust his newly washed hair back, clearly not minding at all that he'd been 'discovered'. 'You weren't wearing much then either, as I recall.' Sheelagh's twinkle rivalled Ollie's, and I realised she must have spotted him fetching the towel from my bedroom.

'Your eyesight is superb, ma'am.' Ollie gave a little bow and, with a girlish giggle, Sheelagh said, 'Oh, please, call me... Loretta.' *What?* 'It's my middle name.' A vivid pink stain crept up her face as her gaze fluttered towards me and away again, as though I'd turned invisible.

'Charmed to meet you, Loretta.' Swooping forward, Ollie lifted one of her hands and pressed his lips to the back of it, and from the look of wonder and gratitude on Sheelagh's face, it was obvious that meeting her idol was exceeding her expectations.

'I knew you'd be a gentleman,' she simpered, when he released her fingers. 'And if you don't mind me saying, you're much handsomer in real life.' She smoothed both hands over her jumper and hips, as if drawing attention to her waist. A waist that hadn't been there the last time I'd looked. Sheelagh hadn't just raided her make-up bag and wardrobe since returning from the vet's, it looked like she'd squeezed herself into a corset. No wonder her face was slowly changing colour. Or maybe it was the Ollie effect, which I was starting to see was considerable. He'd switched up the charm, as if the presence of an adoring audience – even one as humble as Sheelagh Lambert – was feeding into an inherent need to be admired.

It was disconcerting, but before I could analyse it further, there was a muffled curse from upstairs and Craig hopped into view, clutching one socked foot.

'Sorry about that,' boomed the delivery man. 'I thought you'd moved out of the way when I let my end go.'

'It's fine,' Craig muttered through gritted teeth, leaning over the banister. His eyes were closed, and his lips moved soundlessly. He was either swearing or counting to ten, and I felt a stab of guilt for not helping with the bed.

Finally unhooking her gaze from Ollie, Sheelagh watched as the delivery man came downstairs, his fleshy cheeks even redder than hers. He shot out to the van to fetch the bedding and curtains I'd ordered. 'That's the lot,' he said, thrusting the packages at me, and fled.

'You should have said, love, I've plenty of spare blankets going.' Sheelagh placed one shiny, square-heeled shoe on the doormat. 'Is he staying with you, then?' Her eyes darted from me to Ollie, with poorly concealed excitement. 'Oh my!' she said, when I failed to produce an adequate answer, fanning herself with her hand. 'Just wait until I tell everyone the latest. That there's an actual star living in the house next door!'

Both feet planted on the doormat now, she looked at me properly. 'You've done yourself proud, my dear.' Her eyes shone. 'To bring someone like Ollie Matheson into our neighbourhood…' She shook her head, as though words had momentarily failed her. 'It means an awful lot.'

'Hey, it's my absolute pleasure,' said Ollie, drawing her adoring gaze back. He placed a strong arm around her, and as Sheelagh looked down in awe at his broad, tanned hand on her shoulder, her lip wobbled as if – in that moment – everything she'd ever wanted had finally come to pass.

I was almost envious of the purity of her emotions. Had I ever felt as passionately about anyone? My feelings for Max seemed puny in comparison. I almost felt sorry for Barry Lambert, suspecting he'd never evoked such a strong display of emotion.

'You got a raw deal, being sacked from the show,' she said, turning in the curve of Ollie's arm, as though she'd remembered vowing to say this very thing, should she get the opportunity. 'It was obvious to me that it wasn't the whole story,' she continued, her voice juddering with gravity. 'I'm certain it was all a big game to Tattie Granger, you could see it in her eyes. She engineered the whole thing, you mark my words.'

Ollie's features shifted slightly, though he didn't take his eyes off Sheelagh. 'It's a perfect opportunity for me to try new things, my sweet Loretta.' He was using a late-night radio voice that had Sheelagh swooning towards him, her expression pained, as if it was almost too much, and I knew she'd be replaying this moment for weeks to come – if not for eternity.

'Do you want a hand putting the bedding on?' From the top of the stairs, Craig's flat voice was like a gust of cold air. I shivered, suddenly noticing the temperature had dropped with the door standing open for so long.

'I can do it myself,' I said, wondering whether he was jealous of the effect Ollie was having, even if the recipient was a woman the wrong side of fifty, with questionable dress sense. I had no idea whether Craig was in a relationship, but there was something contained about him that suggested he was used to being single.

'I can't wait for you to see our Christmas lights,' Sheelagh was saying to Ollie, clearly not ready to get back to her mundane life. 'I know you'll make the right decision when it comes to judging the best house.'

'I can't wait, either,' said Ollie. 'I had a look last night, and I have to say I was terribly impressed.' For a horrible moment, I thought Sheelagh was going to raise one leg and wrap it around his.

Maybe the same thought had crossed his mind, as he eased her gently away. 'I'm looking forward to meeting all the residents of' – he shot me a questioning look – 'what's the street called?'

'Maple Hill,' I said, adding rashly, 'I'd be happy to host a meeting for the society here, tomorrow afternoon. Say, four o'clock?'

'Sounds wonderful.' Sheelagh was still gazing at Ollie, as if he was a priceless piece of art.

'I'll do afternoon tea,' I said, wanting to impress her. 'Make sure you let the other members know.'

'I will,' she said, though I doubted she'd even heard me properly.

Craig was limping downstairs. 'We'll need you all to sign waivers because of the filming—'

'Filming?' Sheelagh's head shot round. 'We're going to be on the telly? Like Ollie in *Players*?'

'He's not in *Players* any more, and I thought you knew about the filming.' Craig gave me a questioning look. 'Didn't you tell that woman about it, earlier?'

I gave him a frosty stare. 'No, I didn't,' I said. 'I was waiting until I knew more about what was happening.'

His jaw tightened. 'Sorry.'

Sheelagh was half out of the door now. 'I can't believe I know something that Doris doesn't.'

I couldn't believe Doris hadn't already called Sheelagh to tell her that Ollie was in my house. She was already halfway down the path.

''Bye!' I called. 'Don't forget! Afternoon tea here, at four tomorrow.'

She raised her hand, slipped and almost fell, and I held my breath as she mustered her dignity and carried on through the gate, fiddling with her jumper as if her corset had worked loose.

'Well, she was quite a character,' Ollie said, when I entered the living room, feeling oddly shy as I pressed myself against the radiator to warm up. He'd flung himself on the sofa, legs stretched out, one arm along the back, while Craig hovered by the window, staring out. 'How wonderful if they're all like that. I don't come across folk as' – he screwed up his eyes, as if searching for the right word – 'as *quirky* as that, very often.'

Now that Sheelagh – or *Loretta,* as I would never think of her – had gone, he'd dialled down the charm, and his posture was more relaxed. Not that I thought he'd been acting – I was certain lavishing his attention on every female he met was in his nature – but he couldn't maintain that level of intensity without something slipping, eventually. Like people in high-demand jobs, who burnt out at thirty-five. I'd seen it happen to a teaching colleague, and a friend of my brother's who'd been a social worker. Not that I was comparing what Ollie did with someone in social services – that would be ridiculous. But being Ollie Matheson was clearly tougher than it looked.

'They are pretty quirky,' I agreed, thinking of the neighbours I'd met at the Lamberts'. 'But they might not all be as welcoming as Shee… Loretta.'

'Oh?' Ollie sat forward, elbows on his knees, eyes frisking me like an airport scanner. 'Pray tell.'

Blood whooshed to my face. 'Just that some of them… well, they probably won't have heard of you, no offence, and a few might be a bit resentful that you're not… more famous.'

Craig released a barely audible sigh and looked at me over his shoulder.

What? I said with my eyes.

He shook his head and turned back to the window, as if something fascinating was happening in the street.

'More famous?' Ollie's brow creased. 'Like, Tom Cruise famous?'

'Well… maybe,' I said, carefully. 'An actor, definitely, or a singer.'

The brightness briefly left Ollie's eyes, and I felt terrible for bringing it up.

Across the room Craig's shoulders tensed, as if he was dreading what might come next, but Ollie simply smiled and said, 'Well, I'm a terrible singer, but acting's actually my passion, and it's kind of where I'm hoping to go with my career.'

'Really?' I said, as if one of my pupils (*former* pupils) had announced he wanted to be an astronaut when he grew up. Then I remembered Ollie's Wikipedia page. 'Weren't you in a vampire movie?'

'You *have* done your homework.' His gaze was so openly admiring that I felt as if I'd announced my intention to train for the next Olympics. 'Yes, I was, though it was more of a foray into the acting biz really. The film wasn't critically acclaimed.'

Craig coughed into his fist, which I interpreted as meaning it had bombed, and I wondered why he wasn't being more supportive. If Ollie was making a move into acting, surely that meant there'd be a role for his favourite cameraman. 'I'll look it up online,' I said. 'I'm sure you were very good.'

'It was a small part.' He flapped a dismissive hand. 'I barely wet my fangs.'

'Shall we get on?' Craig unzipped his Nike running top, and took a notepad from his rucksack, which he'd brought in from the hall. 'I thought we could keep things discreet,' he said, flipping open a page and running his eyes over it.

'Only guy I know who won't use a tablet for storing info,' Ollie said, winking at me. 'Complete luddite.' I smiled, but didn't admit I preferred pen and paper too, and wondered briefly whether the words might flow more easily if I tried writing my novel by hand.

'I'll film a short segment in here, or outside the house if you'd prefer, Lily.' Craig glanced up, and I nodded, somehow surprised at the ease with which he said my name.

'In here's fine,' I said, though I hadn't really thought through the filming aspect, and still wasn't sure I was comfortable being part of

Ollie's one-off show. I didn't voice my doubts, though, unwilling to cast a pall over his career-revival plan.

Craig looked back at his notepad, pushing a hand through his hair, revealing a subtly darker shade beneath and a faint scattering of freckles across his forehead. 'Once we've worked out a schedule, I'll follow proceedings with my camera and we'll just let things unfold.' He paused, tapping the pad with his pen. 'That's about it, really.' He lifted his head, eyes fixing briefly on mine. 'We'll try not to get in your way too much, and if at any point you're not comfortable feel free to say so, we—'

'Woah!' Ollie raised a hand, like a traffic controller. 'Steady on, old chap. You're scaring poor Lily witless.' He patted the cushion, indicating I join him on the sofa. 'Of course she won't be uncomfortable. I simply won't let that happen,' he said, as I obediently shifted from the radiator and sat beside him, smoothing the hem of my dress over my knees and trying to curl my toe back into my tights.

'You're used to having a camera on you, Lily's not,' Craig said, bending to put his notepad away so it was impossible to see his face. 'I'm just saying, once things are underway she might not like it, and I don't want her to feel like she can't tell us to stop.'

Ollie made a yapping-mouth motion with his hand, and I gave a guilty smile. Craig probably had health and safety in mind, but it was nice of him to be concerned. 'I'm fully insured,' he went on, 'so if there should be any damage to any properties, we're covered for repairs. Not that I'm suggesting that would happen.'

Ollie pretended to stifle a yawn and Craig glanced up, just as I was biting my lip to stop myself laughing.

He quickly looked away. 'Any questions?' he said, reaching for the mug he'd put on the windowsill, and turning his back.

'Are you planning to sleep outside every night?' I said.

'We won't be here very long. I can manage a few nights in the car.' He gulped some tea, and my gaze settled on his feet in their plain black socks. 'I've got a thermal sleeping bag, and my outdoor clothes are insulated,' he said, as if compelled to defend his reply.

Ollie sat up straight. 'It's true,' he said, swivelling to face me with endearing eagerness. 'It's from when he spent a week on Everest, a few years ago, before his pa had his accident.' Admiration crept into his voice. 'We'd wrapped *Players* for the season, so Craggers took off with this idea of shooting a talking-heads type show, interviewing people on their way up the mountain about why they were doing it, bearing in mind they're risking their lives and a lot of them don't make it back.'

'That sounds amazing.' I eyed Craig with fresh interest, but he didn't look round. 'That's definitely a programme I'd watch.'

'Yah, well, like I say, his pa needed him and it didn't get finished, so—'

'I don't think Lily wants to hear the story of my life,' Craig cut in, though I couldn't deny a stirring of curiosity. 'Let's get back to the topic in hand, shall we?'

Ollie winced at me and mouthed, 'Sorry.'

'It's OK,' I mouthed back, hoping Craig wasn't lip-reading our reflections in the window.

'So.' Ollie slapped his hands down on his knees and assumed a serious expression. 'I was thinking of a little narrative we could use.'

That got Craig's attention. 'I thought you wanted to be yourself,' he said, turning to face us. 'No more "structured reality", right?'

Ollie stood up and crossed to the fireplace. 'You should open this up,' he said, smoothing a hand over the mantelpiece. 'There's nothing like a real fire during the winter. We had them in every room when I was growing up, even the bathroom.'

'If you can do it, that would be great,' I said, trying to imagine bathing in front of a roaring fire. 'Apparently, there are loads of logs in the shed. The previous owner wasn't here long enough to use them.'

'It would be my pleasure.' Ollie beat his fists on his chest. 'Man makes fire. Me Tarzan.'

I couldn't help laughing, even as I worried about the technicalities of restoring the fireplace to its natural state, while Craig muttered something that might have been, 'For Christ's sake.'

'What's that, bro?' Ollie dived over and hooked an arm around Craig's neck, ruffling his hair with his other hand. 'Speak up, old chap.'

Craig tolerated the assault with surprising ease, cuffing his arm as Ollie let him go. 'So, what's this narrative you had in mind?'

'Ah, yes.' Ollie's expression switched from playful to lustful, and he hauled me off the sofa and attempted to twirl me round. It didn't quite work, as I wasn't expecting it, and I ended up stumbling against him, then reeling away. 'I was thinking it might be nice if I got myself an "ordinary" girlfriend while I'm here.' He let go of me to scratch quote marks in the air with his fingers.

My heart bumped. 'I'm sure there'll be no shortage of offers,' I said, straightening my cardigan, aware Craig had tipped his head back, as though seeking strength from the light fitting. 'My neighbour was definitely smitten.'

Ollie threw back his head and laughed, seeming not to notice that no one joined in.

Wrapping his arms around himself, he looked at my scalding face, his eyes boring into mine. 'I'm offering you the post, Lily Ambrose. As long as you promise me something.'

'Oh god,' Craig muttered.

'What?' My voice was faint.

'That you stop wearing holey tights.'

Chapter 13

'Lily, do *not* pretend to be his girlfriend,' Erin blasted. 'I can't believe he even thought it, let alone suggested it.'

'I didn't say yes, for crumble's sake, what do you take me for?' I shivered as I paced around the shed in an attempt to warm up. 'He was probably joking.'

After Ollie's girlfriend-pitch, which I'd tried to laugh off – not very convincingly –Craig had jumped in to propose I fetch some logs so he could get the fire going.

Ollie had graciously agreed and, too dumbfounded to argue, I'd grabbed my keys and phone from the kitchen, and headed down the garden on a wave of adrenaline.

'He's such a shit.'

'Erin! I don't think he meant any offence,' I said. 'He got a bit carried away, that's all. I'm sure it'll be forgotten about by the time I go back indoors.'

I banished an image of me crushed to Ollie's broad chest, wondering whether the air in Shipley was affecting my brain cells.

'Lily, you don't get it.' Erin sounded despairing. 'This is part of his routine, to pull you in. It's how he finds validation, even if it's subconscious and he doesn't realise he's doing it. Don't think for a minute he's *actually* going to fall in love with you.'

'Thanks for thinking I *want* him to fall in love with me,' I huffed. 'And for assuming that he wouldn't. It's a good job I don't have self-esteem issues.' There was a momentary pause. 'I don't have self-esteem issues, Erin.'

'Of course you don't.' Her voice turned soothing, as if I was one of her rabidly insecure clients. 'That's not the point, though,' she added. 'He's a persuasive bastard, which you'd know if you'd ever watched the show.'

'Don't make it sound as if I haven't got a mind of my own.' I was getting heated now. 'I've been a teacher for several years, and an adult for even longer. I'm capable of assessing a situation and deciding on the best course of action.'

As Erin remained silent, no doubt resisting the temptation to fling my impulse-based move to Shipley in my face, I slumped down on a bag of kindling and glanced around.

Although the padlock had been a bit rusty, requiring some frantic key-jiggling, the inside of the shed was almost as immaculate as the cottage, with only one visible cobweb draped across the window. Apart from a lawnmower, and a shiny spade leaning against one wall, it contained only stacks of logs and bags of kindling. A fire waiting to happen, Dad would have said. The air smelt pleasantly of seasoned wood and I breathed it in, trying to soften the knot of tension in my stomach.

'I'm starting to think this might not have been the best move for him,' Erin said at last. 'Or you.'

Now it was my turn to be exasperated. 'It's too late to back out,' I said. 'He's here, and it's happening, and he seems perfectly happy about it.' I remembered something he'd said. 'Did you know he wants to be an actor?'

The noise she made was like an old-fashioned foghorn. 'I thought he'd got all that out of his system,' she said. 'He tried it once and was bloody terrible.'

'The vampire movie?'

'Honestly, you should look it up,' she said. 'It mostly flew under the radar, which is where it should stay.'

'Didn't you get him the part?'

'No, I did not.' She sounded horrified. 'He did it when *Players* was on a break, without telling the agency. A friend of his father's was directing, and agreed to give him a part. Big mistake.'

'It clearly hasn't put him off.'

'Clearly,' she said. 'He said he'd be better next time, but hasn't mentioned it for a while.'

'And you don't think there'll be a next time?'

'I doubt it,' she said. 'Unless he signs up for acting lessons for about twenty years.'

'So, what kind of future *does* he have?'

She sighed. 'If this one-off show goes OK, then maybe a crawl back to the reality circuit. I've been working on the idea of a series, maybe something themed. *Ollie Goes to…* could be the title, and he'd visit different countries and go white-water rafting, or play the slots in Vegas, and soak up the culture.'

'But do the public want to see some privileged posh boy doing things he could easily afford to do anyway?' I felt a twinge of disloyalty at referring to Ollie as a 'posh boy' when I actually really liked him. 'I would have thought that… if this thing they're doing here's a success… it would be more interesting for him to take on something out of his comfort zone. Working at a food bank, or visiting the homeless, that sort of thing.'

Erin was quiet for a moment. 'Can you honestly see Ollie Matheson mixing with the poverty-stricken at a food bank? Surrounded by cans of baked beans?'

'Who knows?' I said. 'It would be different.'

'He'd just make a donation,' she said, rather wearily. 'He gives a lot to charities, I'll give him that, but he won't want to do the dirty work.'

'Maybe I could persuade him?'

'By sleeping with him?' Her voice rose. 'Don't sleep with him, Lily. You don't want to be one of those girls.'

'Erin, what are you talking about?'

'Another notch on his bedpost.'

'Erin, for goodness—'

'I think I should come over.'

'What? No!' I stood up. 'Honestly, it's as if you and Mum think I'm completely helpless.'

'What's your mum got to do with it?'

'She's on her way, already.' I told Erin about Ollie coming into the kitchen to ask for a towel, while Mum was on the phone.

'Shit a brick,' she said. 'Don't tell me he was parading around in his undies.'

'He… concealed himself.' I blinked away a momentary flashback. 'He wasn't showing off, or anything.'

'Oh, Lily.'

'Will you *stop* saying my name like that!'

'I should call him,' she said.

'What, and warn him not to sleep with me? That doesn't show much faith in your *client*,' I said. 'Or me, for that matter.'

'Fine,' she said, after a long pause. 'Sorry. I didn't sleep much myself last night.'

'Oh?' I perked up. 'Did you have a date?'

'A date?' she said, in an old-lady voice. 'People don't date any more, Lily. They sext and swipe, and send photos of their ugly genitals.' She sighed. 'No, I wasn't on a date, I went for a curry with some friends and got the runs.'

'I wish I hadn't asked.'

Back inside, Craig was kneeling in front of the open fireplace, and had arranged some scrunched-up newspaper in the grate. 'I had one in my bag,' he said, looking round to see me gaping.

'How did…?'

'Oh, it was easy.' He gestured at the sheet of copper lying on the rug. 'It was a false front, that's all. The grate hasn't been used for a while, but the chimney looks clean.'

How could he tell? 'Thanks,' I said, wishing I'd thought to check the fireplace myself. Feeling silly, I dropped some logs in the basket by the hearth, and passed over a bag of kindling. 'I've some matches in the kitchen drawer, I'll go and get them.'

'No need.' Craig reached for his rucksack. 'I always carry some, just in case.'

In case of what? 'Something I picked up on a survival course.' He swiped at a smudge of soot on his nose. 'If you can start a fire you can keep warm, have a light source, boil water, and keep predators away.'

'Brilliant,' I said. 'That must come in handy.' I was immediately ashamed of my sarcastic tone, but a faint smile tugged at his mouth.

'Let's just say, I've never needed to start a fire… yet.'

'Good to know.' I scanned the room, aware of how quiet it was, in spite of Craig rustling about. 'Where's Ollie?'

Craig arranged some kindling, placed a log on top, then struck a match and held it steady until the whole thing caught alight. 'I told him to have a sleep.' He pushed back onto his heels, watching the flames leap to life. 'I hope that's OK.'

'But I haven't sorted out his room,' I said, realising I hadn't had a chance to check out the new bed either. 'The duvet and bedding…'

'We sorted it out, while you were doing whatever you were doing in the shed.'

What did he mean by that? OK, so I'd been gone a while, but only because I'd wanted to talk to Erin. What had Craig said to Ollie while I wasn't there? He was looking up at me, as if he could read my thoughts, a faint flush of colour on his cheeks.

'He probably won't pursue the fake girlfriend angle,' he said, and I felt a flash of annoyance. Maybe I'd *wanted* to be Ollie's fake girlfriend. I hadn't had much luck being a real one, and perhaps a pretend relationship would have been fun.

'He didn't seem tired to me,' I said, peevishly, 'and even if he had been, surely he could have asked me himself if he wanted to have a lie down?'

Craig placed his hands on his thighs. They were broad hands, with faint dark hairs on the back. 'Shall I go and wake him up?'

'What? No, of course not.' I shrugged my coat off. The fire was blazing away now, the heat scorching my cheeks. 'I think I'll just go and check on him.'

Craig's eyes widened slightly, but he didn't comment. We looked at each other for a moment, the only sound the crackling of wood in the grate. 'I'll be back in a moment,' I said, when the silence stretched and grew awkward.

His voice stopped me at the door. 'He's a good person, Lily. He's just… used to a different way of living, and getting his own way, and that awful show didn't bring out the best in him.'

I swung round, clutching my coat. 'I happen to like Ollie, and don't need you to speak up on his behalf.' Craig got to his feet and rotated his shoulders, as if to alleviate some tension. 'Why did you even agree to work on the show if it was so awful?'

He stopped in the act of massaging his upper arm. 'Agree to work on the show?'

'You were glad enough to accept Ollie's offer of a job, and yet—'

'Just a minute.' His frown deepened. 'I got Ollie a place on the show, after I started working for the TV company that were making it. He'd been looking for a challenge and I thought, because of his background, it would be a good fit for him, but…' his voice trailed off. Dipping his head, he rubbed the back of his neck. 'I sometimes regret it,' he finished.

I tried to think back, and realised that in my hung-over state I'd assumed that Ollie must have brought Craig onto the show, instead of the other way round. 'Sorry,' I mumbled. 'My mistake.'

He didn't seem to have heard, his gaze lowered, as if there was something meaningful carved in the floorboards.

Keen to change the subject, I said, 'You can put the kettle on if you like, and help yourself to a mince pie or two.'

Before he could reply, I slipped into the hall and hung up my coat, removed my boots and crept upstairs, careful to miss out the second step from the top where I'd noticed it creaked. My mind heaved with snippets of all the conversations I'd had since waking up, and I was overcome with an urge to crawl back under my duvet and have a sleep myself. Perhaps, when I woke, I'd realise it had all been a dream, and the only things I had to think about were my novel and what to cook for dinner.

My novel.

If Ollie was taking a nap, there wasn't much point going back downstairs just yet. I didn't fancy trying to socialise with Craig, and Mum wouldn't be here for at least an hour – more if traffic was bad. I could take my laptop into my bedroom, and focus on some writing.

The door to the spare room was ajar, and I pushed it open to see Ollie sprawled on his front in the new bed, the duvet rucked up to reveal he still had his jeans on, though he'd shed his top, which was hanging over the back of the computer chair. One tanned arm was flung up, hiding most of his face, but from the rise and fall of his shoulders it was obvious he was deeply asleep.

Ollie Matheson was asleep in my spare room. It was so bizarre, it felt unreal. If I hadn't left my phone in my coat pocket, I might have been tempted to take a photo and post it on Twitter. Imagining it, I bit back a giggle. No one would believe it was him. I crept closer, intending to pick up my laptop, and froze when a floorboard squeaked, the sound deafening in the silence. I couldn't bear the thought of him opening his eyes to see me looming over him, like Kathy Bates in *Misery.*

I backed out and stood for a moment, holding my breath, but he didn't even stir.

Perhaps I should go back downstairs. It wasn't polite to ignore a guest, and Craig had got the fire going, as well as putting one out this morning, *and* he'd cooked quail's eggs without complaining.

I entered the living room, with a smile in place, ready to make small talk and find out more about him – after all, a writer should be interested in people – and stopped dead when I saw him stretched out on the sofa, asleep.

One arm dangled towards the floor, and his face looked softer, his lashes dark against his skin. His foot twitched, as though he was dreaming about running, and I carefully picked a throw off the armchair and shook it over him.

The room felt cosy with the Christmas tree lights casting a warm glow, and the fire blazing – Craig had sensibly put the fireguard across – but I didn't feel comfortable parking myself in the armchair.

I felt like a visitor in my own home.

My gaze fell on Craig's open rucksack, where his notepad was poking out, and I remembered my earlier idea to write my novel by hand. Perhaps I could go to the café on the seafront, which Craig had mentioned, and spend an hour there before Mum turned up. It might be the last chance I had for a while.

The only problem was, I didn't have a notepad. *Why* hadn't I got a notepad? What kind of writer was I? Would Craig mind if I borrowed some sheets from his? I'd replace the pad, obviously.

Moving stealthily, I crossed the floor, keeping one eye on Craig. Clearly, his night in the car hadn't been that restful after all.

As I eased the notepad out, it struck me that I could just as easily buy one. Perhaps from the newsagent's, if it wasn't too far away. About to put it back, I noticed the first page was folded over and covered with scribbled words and I couldn't resist a peek.

Behind Closed Doors I read, in sloping handwriting that practically ran off the page. *Idea: talk to the people behind the Christmas lights. Ask what Christmas means to them. Human interest – could be humorous/personal stories/link with shots of the displays outside – do they reflect their inner life, or disguise some inner pain? Outside vs inside? Challenge the competitive element – do they really care about winning? Why??*

Behind me, Craig gave a snort. I dropped the pad and held my breath, waiting for him to ask what I was doing.

His breathing deepened and, hot with relief, I stuffed the pad back in his bag.

Picking up a discarded sheet of newspaper, I carefully tore off a corner, located Craig's pen on the floor, and wrote *Gone for some fresh air, back soon. Lily.* I placed the note on the floor, where Craig would be sure to see it if he woke up, then slipped out of the room like a ghost.

Chapter 14

I parked my car and rushed across the square to the newsagent's, where, under Mr Flannery's watchful eye, I found a basic reporter-style notepad.

'Sheelagh told me about this Oliver bloke,' he said, when I reached the counter.

I smiled politely, relieved she hadn't yet spread the news about seeing him at Seaview Cottage. 'His name's Ollie, not Oliver.'

'Never heard of him before.' He took my money, probably disgruntled that I hadn't secured Meryl Streep – or anyone else from the cast of *Mamma Mia!*

'Don't you read your newspapers or magazines?' I cast an eye over the front covers. 'I'm sure he's been featured on their gossip pages.'

Mr Flannery laid his bony hands on the counter. 'I don't go in for gossip,' he said, which I didn't believe for a second. Everyone I'd met so far seemed keen to know what everyone else was up to. 'I don't understand this reality lark. Why would people want to watch ordinary people do silly things?'

There's nothing ordinary about Ollie, I wanted to say, but mindful it might sound fangirlish I refrained. 'There'll be an update very soon,' I promised.

'I hope so,' he said darkly. 'Those tree lights aren't going to switch on by themselves.'

I managed not to say that anyone could flick a switch if it came to it, and left him grumbling at another customer, who'd dared to ask if he had any paperclips. 'We're not a bloody stationery shop. Try WH Smith's, up Main Street.'

Outside, I paused to admire the silver mesh balls on the fir tree planted in the square, which was wrapped in LED lights just waiting to burst into life. A chalkboard bravely proclaimed a 'Special Guest' would be doing the honours at 5 p.m. on 13th December, and that Santa would be handing out presents to children who'd been 'good'.

I smiled, remembering my last Christmas at Kingswood Primary, and the children's expressions when Santa – one of the dads dressed up – had popped in to tell them a story. They'd looked so joyful – until little Todd Lafferty, whose parents were 'free-thinkers' said, 'Everybody knows that Father Christmas isn't real,' and the rest had burst into tears.

Across the cobbled square was the flower stall Jane had mentioned, its green-and-cream canopy strung with fairy lights, beneath which a rosy-faced woman, surrounded by buckets of flowers, was chatting to a customer. I didn't recognise the woman, but there was a wheelbarrow nearby with *Ruby's Blooms* painted on the side, so I guessed she must be Ruby.

Spotting Cooper's Café on the corner of the parade – surely the café Craig had visited – I hurried over, keen to get out of the cold. The interior was warm and steamy, the air filled with chatter and laughter and the clink of spoons, against a background of Christmas music. After ordering a hot chocolate and a toasted teacake, I removed my coat, then sat at a table by the window. I ate slowly, enjoying the sensation of buttery dough and raisins on my tongue.

Outside, the sky was powder-white, and the wind had whipped the sea into foamy peaks. The tide was out, and the beach and pier were deserted. I dismissed the brief but ridiculous idea of going for a run on the sand. I kept a pair of trainers in my car, just in case, but the thought of going to get them wasn't appealing. Anyway, I didn't have much time. Leaning back, I wrapped my hands around my mug, and watched a couple of seagulls soaring high, before dive-bombing the choppy water.

If I hadn't had guests to get back to, I might have taken a drive to Corfe Castle, recalling the last time I was there, when my brother Chris had decided to play hide-and-seek, wedging himself inside a stairwell so we couldn't find him. Mum had grown hysterical, running around, pleading for help. I'd cried and wet myself, and Dad had finger-whistled as though Chris was a sheepdog, before bellowing his name. When the security guard found him, Chris confessed he'd stayed hidden for so long because we were 'embarrassing'.

Smiling, I sipped my drink, enjoying the anonymous buzz of conversation around me, and Bing Crosby crooning 'White Christmas', and when the window grew too steamy to look through, I pulled my new notepad and a pen from my bag, and placed them on the table.

I thought again about what Craig had written, wondering why neither he nor Ollie had mentioned wanting to interview the neighbours 'behind closed doors'. Perhaps they hadn't got round to it; or Craig was planning a spin-off show of his own. How could I ask without outing myself as a snoop?

I pushed up the sleeves of my cardigan and doodled a couple of hearts in the margin of the notepad, and a whiskery cat that might or might not have been Marmite, then idly checked the time. Would Ollie and Craig be awake now, annoyed I'd gone out? Should I have left them alone in my cottage? Not that I had anything worth stealing, even if Ollie hadn't been the heir to a fortune, and Craig's camera worth more than anything I owned. I had nothing hidden away that I wouldn't want them to find, and if either were tempted to rummage through my underwear, they'd be disappointed by my sensible bras and pants. And, considering how helpful they'd been since arriving, the cottage seemed more theirs than mine, anyway.

Impulsively, I accessed the Internet on my phone and tapped *The Vampire and Me* into a search engine. Once it had loaded, I fast-forwarded the clip until Ollie appeared – and wished I hadn't. Erin had been right. Ollie was a terrible actor; wooden and stilted, sporting a disastrous moustache and a terrible Irish brogue. None of his natural charm came across, as he and his winsome girlfriend strolled through a night-time city, stalked by a vampire with a Colgate-white complexion and staring eyes.

I shut down the clip as Ollie – or Paddy, as he was unimaginatively named – turned to the vampire and shouted, 'I know what your game is, sir,' his accent dipping towards Liverpool.

Evicting the image of his panic-stricken eyes, I forced my attention back to my notepad and, after a moment's contemplation, wrote: *The sight of Carlos in his tight-fitting pants made Jessica's heart race.* I scribbled it out. I wanted to write something a child could pick up, without fear of them seeing a word or sentence their parents would be embarrassed to explain.

Jessica turned to the cameraman, a short, bad-tempered man with a scruffy beard. 'I don't think I'm cut out for the show,' she wept, throwing herself on his mercy. 'It's so shallow and unimportant.'

'Remember, you're under contract,' he growled, his eyebrows wriggling like caterpillars across his forehead. Jessica rolled her eyes at him... I had an image of her eyes whizzing like marbles across the floor, and changed it to: *Jessica tossed her raven hair back...* Ugh. Too soapy.

Maybe I should write about what I knew. Wasn't that what writing tutors advised? But I didn't want to write about teaching. My career was forever tainted by the memory of Max's wife barging into my classroom and shouting at me in front of the children. After she'd flounced out, one child had asked if the 'nasty witch' was coming back to put a spell on her, while another demanded to know what a 'slut' was.

With a shiver of revulsion, I blinked away the memory and turned to a fresh page. Perhaps a stream of consciousness would get things flowing. I tapped my pen for a minute then, catching the irritated glare of a woman at the next table, started to write: *Once upon a time—*

'Hi, Miss Ambrose.'

I looked up to see Alfie Blake hovering by the table in the same baggy suit he'd worn when he showed me around the cottage. 'You settled in alright, then?'

'Oh! Yes, it's lovely, thank you.' His gaze skittered over the page in front of me and, thankful my writing was too untidy to read, I snapped my notepad shut. 'I just popped out for a breath of fresh air,' I felt obliged to explain. 'But Shipley's lovely, I really like it here.'

'Oh?' He sounded so doubtful, I couldn't help smiling.

'It's honestly not that bad,' I said. 'Look at that.' I gestured towards the view, but the window was still foggy, and all that was visible was a giant penis someone had drawn in the steam, which I hadn't noticed before. 'I mean, it's a very pretty place.'

'S'alright in the summer, I s'pose.' His tone was grudgingly polite, and looking more closely I noticed he'd lost the air of enthusiasm he'd had when he took up my challenge to push the house sale through. His shoulders sloped forward, as though weighted down with worry, and his curly hair looked limp.

'How's work?'

He rubbed the side of his nose. ''S'okay.'

'Are you on your lunch break?'

Before he could reply there was a kerfuffle, and I looked round to see a pair of youths at the counter, grabbing some cake from beneath a glass dome while the assistant's back was turned.

'Oi!' A customer had clocked what was happening and was rising from his chair, as the beefy boy squashed a wedge of carrot cake into his skinny friend's spiky hair.

'You're such a twat, Biff.' The boy scraped off the cheesy frosting and smeared it over Biff's face.

'DAZ, you absolute pillock.'

'Language,' said a woman I recognised as the Harassed Mum from The Christmas Lights Society meeting, with the twins in a double buggy. 'There are impressionable ears over here, and you're setting a terrible example.'

The skinny youth had the grace to mumble an apology, but Biff turned on her with a swagger and stuck two fingers up – the effect somewhat spoiled by lumps of cream cheese clinging to his acne.

The door to the kitchen swung open and a man I assumed was the manager emerged. 'Get yourself back to college before I call the cops,' he ordered, his face like thunder. 'And you're both barred. Again.'

'Fuck's sake, Dad.' Biff deflated like a popped balloon as he reached for a serviette and scrubbed at his face. 'You can't bar me. Mum won't let you and, anyway, we live upstairs.' Grabbing his friend by the strap of his rucksack, he tugged him towards the door, pausing when he caught sight of Alfie. 'Ooh, look, Daz, it's Mr "convenient for local amenities",' he said, in a clipped, high-pitched voice.

'I have to say that, it's part of my job.' Alfie's cheeks glowed red. 'And I didn't know you'd only showed up at that flat to take the piss.'

'As if I could afford to buy it, you knob. I 'aven't even got a job.' He caught Daz's eye and winked. '"Easy to maintain, and a great use of space, with plenty of original features",' he continued, in the same falsetto, but although Daz smiled, his eyes didn't join in.

'Leave 'im alone, Biff.' He tugged his rucksack free and brushed some of the crumbs out of his hair. 'Least he's got a job.'

Biff wrinkled his nose, as if he'd smelt something bad. 'I'd rather clean toilets wiv my tongue, or be a snot collector than an estate agent,' he said.

'Collecting snot's not a job, you tool.' Daz's attempt at bravado fell on deaf ears, as Biff continued to inform Alfie about what he'd rather do than sell houses – including wiping horses' bottoms, and unblocking sewers with his bare hands – before switching his squinty gaze to me.

'This your girlfriend, Alfie? Bit old, in't she?'

'That's enough,' I said sharply. 'Alfie's earning a good living, doing something respectable, which is something to be proud of. I suggest you grow up fast, or the only thing you'll be good for is unblocking sewers with your hands, and then you'll be laughing on the other side of your face.' It was the sort of thing my grandmother would have said, but had the effect of wiping the smirk off Biff's face.

'Sorry, miss,' he said, glancing at Daz who looked mortified. 'No offence, like.'

'Plenty taken,' I said. 'Now, get lost.'

'You sounded just like my old form tutor, Mrs Latchford, then,' said Alfie when they'd gone, deliberately leaving the door open so some of the heat rushed out. 'Biff backs down when someone stands up to him, and she always used to.'

I decided not to reveal that I was, in fact, a teacher (*ex*-teacher). I didn't like that I sounded like one outside the classroom, but I supposed it was a habit that was hard to break, and at least it had its uses. 'You were at the same school?' I said.

'Yeah, they were a couple of years below me, but Biff always took the pi— the mickey 'cos of my dad being an estate agent, see, and 'cos I'm working with him now they think it's hilarious and a bit sad.'

'Do you think it's sad?'

'Not really,' said Alfie, shifting from foot to foot. 'I mean, I used to want to be a footballer, but I was cr— rubbish, and I get good commission, plus Dad's teaching me a lot.'

'Well, you should be proud then,' I said.

'Yeah, but not many kids want to be estate agents, do they?' My heart melted when I spotted his leather man-bag. He'd been holding it behind his back, presumably to avoid more taunting from Biff and Daz. 'At school, when they ask what you want to be, you're supposed to say scientist, or doctor, or something cool.'

'You're earning an honest living,' I persisted, despite having balked at the admin fees I'd paid Blake's Properties, grumbling to Mum that it was a pity you couldn't buy a house direct from the owner, without being fleeced by a middle man. 'It's a shame so many children want to be famous, instead of becoming plumbers or electricians. Or estate agents.' An idea unfurled. 'You should give a talk at the local primary school,' I said, packing away my notepad and sliding my coat back on. 'Every month, a parent or relative came to the school where I used to work—'

'I knew you sounded like a teacher!'

'—and talked about their job, to inspire the children,' I continued, deciding to pretend I hadn't noticed my slip-up. 'I think it would be a lovely thing to do.'

He chewed his bottom lip, appearing to give it some thought, and I was pleased to see that his skin had resumed its normal, robust shade of pink. 'How do I go about that, then?'

'I'm popping over to see Jill Edwards at Nightingale Primary sometime this week,' I said, to my surprise. 'I'll have a word with her, if you like.'

Chapter 15

As I drove the short distance to the cottage I couldn't help smiling at Alfie's parting words.

'Thanks a lot, Miss, that's ever so nice of you,' he'd said, the apples of his cheeks bunching up in a smile. Before I could respond 'no promises', he'd gone, clutching his takeaway coffee, his man-bag over his shoulder.

I'd had no intention of going to see Jill Edwards, but Sheelagh's suggestion from the day before must have implanted itself in my head. Still, if Alfie could make being an estate agent sound cool to a bunch of eight- or nine-year-olds, it would be worth it. Not everyone could end up working in television, I reflected, still fuming over Biff's derisory comments to Alfie, wishing I'd thought of a more cutting put-down than what had amounted to a schoolmistressy ticking off.

As I drove up the hill, Doris – out in her front garden, despite the cold – gestured for me to pull over. I stopped and wound down my window as 'Careless Whisper' finished playing on my *Christmas Number Ones* CD and 'Mr Blobby' blared out. 'Sorry,' I said, switching it off as Doris approached, still in her red coat and scarf, a cloth in one hand and a can of polish in the other.

'I like a bit of "Mistletoe and Wine" myself,' she said, peering into the car, taking in the box of chocolate liqueurs, which I'd bought on my upmarket shopping spree, on the passenger seat. 'You can't beat *Cliff at Christmas*, though my Roger preferred that awful Slade song.' She tutted fondly. 'Gave himself a sore throat every year at the policeman's ball, singing along to that,' she chuckled.

'I much prefer traditional songs,' I admitted. 'I used to love going carol-singing with the children…' I trailed off, aware that I was talking about school again.

'Where you used to work?' Doris's gaze gripped mine.

'That's right.' Keen not to get drawn in, I changed the subject. 'Isn't it a bit chilly to be cleaning your windows?' Although the wind had dropped, the air was crisp with the threat of snow.

'I'm not cleaning my windows.' Doris glanced at the polish in her hand, as though surprised to see it. 'I was cleaning the lights on my bush,' she said, nodding to her front garden. 'They get a bit grubby if you don't attend to them.'

Hiding a childish smirk, I said, 'What did you want me for?'

'Oh, yes.' Her glance darted up the road, and she craned her neck. 'I think you have a visitor,' she said. 'She arrived about half an hour ago in a black Golf, registration delta tango two four, bravo Charlie echo.'

'Wow.' So, she'd stopped me to tell me my mum had arrived, and in doing so had delayed my arrival even further. 'I'd better go then,' I said, gunning the engine.

'She looks lovely in blue,' Doris called, as I wound the window up, and I wondered why she even needed me to spy on Barry Lambert. Perhaps she actually worked for MI6.

Pulling the car up behind Mum's, I sat for a moment and took a couple of long breaths. Being out of the house had reinforced the strangeness of my situation, and the thought of facing Mum, as well as Ollie and Craig, felt like an uphill task.

A curtain twitched next door, and I guessed it was Sheelagh, hoping for a glimpse of her hero, but Marmite appeared and gave me an assertive stare.

'Why do you have to be so creepy?' I muttered, grabbing the box of chocolates as I got out of the car. Unless I worked out how to cook a partridge, we'd be eating the chocolates for dinner.

As I entered the hall, I was hit by a wall of warmth, and several things struck me at once.

1. The cottage was starting to feel like home, and I liked the way it enveloped me as I came in.
2. Mum was laughing her actressy laugh; the one she deployed when she really, really wanted to impress someone, or was rehearsing for a part more over-the-top than usual. As she was currently in the middle of a run, it had to be the former, which meant she'd been Ollied.
3. There was a mouth-watering smell wafting out of the kitchen, which probably meant we wouldn't be eating chocolate liqueurs for dinner.

I'd been about to call out, but instead removed my coat and boots and slid my feet into my slippers, rather liking that no one knew I was there. I could slip upstairs and have a little nap. Or at least visit the bathroom to freshen up.

I ran lightly upstairs, and checked the spare room. The bed was a rumpled mess, and there were clothes spilling out of Ollie's holdall, but my mouth opened when I realised he'd hung the curtains. Despite being impressed that he'd tackled such a mundane task, I regretted my impulse buy. In reality, the pink floral pattern looked more like chickenpox.

I locked myself in the bathroom, listening to the rumble of Ollie's voice downstairs, followed by more of Mum's ringing laughter, and smiled at my reflection as I washed my hands at the basin. For a few months after Dad died, I couldn't have imagined her ever laughing again, and I marvelled – not for the first time – at the resilience of the human spirit. *The Ambrose spirit*. Dad always said that if he went first he'd want Mum to be happy, and even to marry again, but that was when he'd been fit and healthy, unaware of the heart condition that would cut short his life at fifty-eight.

As often happened, if I thought about Dad no longer being around to see his children get married, or become a grandfather, or grow old disgracefully with Mum like he'd planned, I felt as if someone was squeezing my heart, and I had to grip the edge of the basin until my breathing settled.

I decided I'd better change my tights before going back downstairs, conscious that Ollie seemed bothered by the hole. I thought again of Craig warning him off the fake-girlfriend idea, and wondered whether I was relieved or disappointed. It was months since I'd been anyone's girlfriend.

As if I'd conjured him up, I heard Mum say Max's name as I stepped out onto the landing.

'He told her he was getting divorced, but changed his mind, and later he confessed to his wife he'd been seeing Lily, and she went and confronted her at school and said some *awful* things, in front of everyone.' I froze, one hand on the banister rail. 'Would you believe, he dumped Lily by *text*?'

Ollie said something I didn't quite hear, though I thought I caught the word 'cad'.

'And he did it in the form of a *poem*.' Closing my eyes, I willed Mum not to repeat it. '"My tender sacrifice", he called it.' I groaned. '"Love leaves a memory no one can steal, but I must return to my old life, to heal."'

Mum's tortured delivery elicited a stunned, '*Please* tell me you're kidding, Fiona,' from Ollie. *Fiona?* It hadn't taken them long to get cosy.

'"Think of me kindly, for I really do care, but let yourself find a new love to share."' I hadn't realised Mum had memorised Max's poem, and I wished with all my heart I hadn't shown it to her. '"I will always keep you in my heart, but beg you, sweet Lily, to make a fresh start."'

'Chr-i-i-i-st,' said Ollie, sounding genuinely aghast – as if ending a relationship with poetry was worse than punching a rival, like he had. 'Not just terrible poetry, and I'm talking absolute kindergarten level, but he made out like he was doing her a massive favour.'

'I know.' Mum lowered her voice. 'I wanted to throttle him.'

'I didn't realise you were back.'

I jolted. Craig was at the foot of the stairs, looking up at me.

'A few minutes ago,' I said, jogging down to join him. *Had he overheard Mum and Ollie's conversation?* 'I just needed… I just wanted to, er, change my tights.'

His gaze dropped to my feet, where it was evident I was wearing the same pair.

'I didn't have any spare,' I improvised, tugging my cardigan sleeves over my hands. 'Did you get my note?'

He nodded. 'I'm sorry I fell asleep like that,' he said, raising his eyes. 'I hadn't realised I was so tired.'

'It's fine.' The light outside had faded, and I was glad he couldn't see me clearly in the dimness of the hall. 'I needed some fresh air, anyway.'

'I thought I'd start dinner, I hope you don't mind.' He jerked his thumb in the direction of the kitchen, clearly as awkward as I was. 'Your mother's here.'

'Yes, I saw the car.' I tucked my hair behind my ears, for something to do. 'I intended to be back before she arrived.'

'Ollie's keeping her company.'

A peal of laughter erupted from the living room. 'Evidently.'

I noticed he'd changed out of his running gear into a dark green sweater and black jeans, and that his hair was freshly washed and combed back off his face. He'd neatened his beard too, and looked altogether more groomed.

'I took a shower,' he said, and I realised I was staring. 'You weren't here to ask, so…'

'No, no, it's fine.' *Could this be any more stilted?* 'Was there enough hot water?'

He nodded. 'Plenty. But it was just a quick one, in case you wanted to take a bath later on.'

'Good. I mean, not good. But… thanks.' *This was torture.* 'What are you cooking?'

'Roast partridge and apricot stuffing, with celeriac mash.' *Wow.* 'It shouldn't be too much longer.'

'I didn't know I had any celeriac,' I said.

'You've got quite a selection of unusual vegetables.'

I felt the beginnings of a blush creep up my throat. 'Well, it sounds delicious,' I said. 'You didn't have to do all that.'

He scratched the top of his head. 'There wasn't any point in filming without you here, and I like cooking. It's relaxing.'

'I prefer baking.'

His teeth flashed in a smile. 'I ate a couple of mince pies. They were good.'

'Thank you.'

A powerful, metallic note erupted from the living room.

'Ollie brought his trumpet in,' said Craig.

'O-*kay*.' I wasn't keen on the sound. I preferred the saxophone, or guitar.

'You should go through and say hi to your mum. Put her mind at rest.'

Annoyed at being told what to do in my own home, I retorted, 'I was just about to, when you came out and started talking to me.'

His eyebrows lifted. 'Don't let me keep you.'

'Don't worry, I won't.' I silently berated myself as he walked back to the kitchen without another word. He was cooking dinner for us, and I was being rude. He could easily make me look bad once he started filming, I reminded myself, and resolved to be nicer.

When I entered the living room, Ollie was playing 'When the Saints Go Marching In', while Mum watched from the sofa, her face lit with admiration. Her peacock-blue coat was flung across the armchair, and she was wearing a long-sleeved top in a matching shade with black jeans and low-heeled boots, and a flamingo-pink scarf bunched into a silver clasp.

'Oh, Lily, you're back!' She looked at me over her glasses and flashed a smile of relief as I sat beside her. 'Isn't he clever?' she stage-whispered, returning her gaze to Ollie, who was giving it his all by the Christmas tree, knees braced, head thrown back as he blew into his trumpet. His cheeks were puffed out, and his fingers pumped the valves, while one bare foot tapped along to the beat.

'*Oh when the saints. Go marching in. Oh when the saints go marching iiiiiin. I wanna beeeeeeee, in that number,*' Mum sang lustily, earrings swinging as her head bobbed to and fro. 'Join in,' she said, nudging me with her shoulder, but I was too busy trying not to giggle at the absurdity of it all. There was a cameraman cooking dinner in my kitchen, and a celebrity in my living room, playing a trumpet for my mother. Why wasn't Craig filming this? At least the public would see that Ollie had a talent – even if it was playing an instrument associated with the Salvation Army.

He finished with a triumphant flourish, and took a bow.

Mum applauded wildly. 'He's marvellous,' she gushed, out of the side of her mouth. 'You should have told me who your naked man was.'

'He wasn't naked, and I didn't exactly get a chance,' I replied, out of the side of mine. 'And if you'd have known, you'd have come anyway.'

'True,' she acknowledged, while Ollie replaced his trumpet lovingly in its case. 'I nearly died when Craig answered the door and said you weren't here, but then Ollie introduced himself and explained what was happening, and couldn't have been more delightful.' She threw him a smile, which he returned full force, adding a wink for my benefit. 'I thought he got a raw deal being kicked off that show.'

'I didn't know you watched *Players*.'

'Oh, yes. It's fascinating. He's *so* much better-looking in real life.'

'Why are you two talking like gangsters?' said Ollie, plopping in the armchair on top of Mum's coat.

'Just saying hi to my mum,' I said, leaning over to kiss her cheek. It *was* nice to see her, even if she couldn't take her eyes off Ollie. 'Thanks for making her welcome.'

'The pleasure was all mine,' he said, sincerely.

Seeing him afresh brought home how out of place he looked in my house, despite his dressed-down appearance. He should be sipping cocktails by a tinkling fountain, or flying a jet to a swanky awards ceremony, not making small talk in an ordinary living room in Shipley.

'He's made it look wonderful in here,' Mum gushed. 'Quite the transformation.'

'He's good with a tree, I'll give him that,' I said, while Ollie assumed a faux-modest expression, and pretended to twirl a handlebar moustache. 'What are those?' I'd spotted a couple of parcels under the lower branches, wrapped in shiny red paper and tied with extravagant gold bows.

'Oh, they're for you from Annie,' Mum said. 'She insisted I bring them. Just some of her lovely woollies, I'm afraid.'

'You can never have too many,' I lied. Annie Larkin, Mum's best friend, had knitted me so many 'lovely woollies' over the years, I'd been gradually re-gifting them.

'And your crackers,' Ollie said, with a smirk.

'I'm sorry?'

Mum tittered. 'I brought some of our handmade crackers, too.' She pointed to a neat little bundle beside the parcels, tied with curly ribbon. 'In case I forget at Christmas.'

So she hadn't been worried enough not to think ahead before she came rushing over.

'Did you remember to put paper hats in them this year?'

She gave Ollie an exasperated look. 'Honestly, I forgot once and she won't let me live it down.'

He chuckled obligingly, then turned to me. 'So, where did you go?' he said, leaning back and crossing his ankles, his smile as warm as the fire still burning in the grate. 'When I came downstairs, Craig was on his back on the sofa, and you were nowhere to be seen. I thought you'd shot him and done a runner.'

Mum's laugh went on for ages. 'Oh, Ollie, you're funny,' she said. 'Lily doesn't have a vicious bone in her body.' She angled herself towards him, her face mischievous. 'When she was seven, she found a dead mouse on the playing field at school and brought it home in her school bag.'

'*Mum*,' I protested.

Ollie seemed charmed. 'Did it recover?'

Mum shrieked. 'Hilarious!'

'Very funny,' I muttered. 'I didn't realise it was dead, I thought it was—'

'In a coma?' Ollie was feeding off Mum's delight, and it struck me again how he thrived on female attention – any female. 'You know, I asked her to be my girlfriend this morning.' His eyes wandered lazily back to mine. 'She hasn't said yes, yet.'

Mum sobered up, looking from Ollie to me, as if trying to work out whether he was being serious. 'That seems a bit soon,' she said, uncertainly.

'It's for the show I was telling you about, but I actually really do like her,' he said, one hand caressing the arm of the chair. 'She's a great girl.'

'I know she is, but…' Mum's eyes flicked away from my face, and I guessed she was feeling bad that she'd told him about my last, disastrous relationship. 'I'm sure you could make a good show without that element.'

'I can speak for myself, you know.' I stood up and threw another log on the fire, trying not to think about what it would be like to be Ollie's girlfriend in real life. I imagined there would be a lot of competition. Not to mention leg-shaving.

'Of course you can,' said Mum. 'I was just saying.'

'Listen, I'm sorry if I was out of order. It was just a thought, and my trusty cameraman friend has already ticked me off.' He smiled. 'Let's leave it there for now, shall we?'

'Good idea,' said Mum, clearly keen to get on his good side again, and I felt a little pang that he wasn't going to pursue it. *Did that mean I* did *fancy him?* 'So, what's the plan for this show of yours?' she added.

'Why don't we discuss it over dinner?' said Craig, sticking his head round the door. 'It's ready, if you'd like to come through.'

'Marvellous!' Ollie leapt up and stretched. 'And then we can discuss me directing one of your plays,' he said to Mum.

Chapter 16

'What did Ollie mean about directing you?' I grilled Mum after dinner, which Craig had produced with seemingly little effort, waving away our compliments and claiming that partridges were no more difficult to cook than tiny chickens.

Ollie had kept up a string of anecdotes designed to make us laugh, but Craig hadn't spoken much, despite Mum doing her best to draw him out. Plans for the show hadn't been discussed at all.

Now, Craig and Ollie were doing the washing up, while Mum and I relaxed on the sofa with mugs of tea.

'Before you came back, I was telling Ollie that our director's walked out,' Mum said, 'and he's offered to help. Apparently, he directed a couple of episodes of *Players* and was rather good at it.'

I was beginning to wonder whether there was anything Ollie *wasn't* good at – apart from acting. 'Why would he want to direct a bunch of amateurs?'

Mum looked offended. 'Why wouldn't he?' she said. 'I expect he likes a challenge.'

'I'm surprised he doesn't want to be on stage instead.'

'Ooh, I can see him being a big hit, with those looks.' Mum went a bit swoony.

'Maybe his looks, but that's about all.' I told her about *The Vampire and Me*, keeping my voice low so Ollie couldn't overhear. 'Perhaps he'll be better suited behind the scenes.' *If he meant to keep his word.* I couldn't imagine him rocking up in East Finchley to direct the Acting Out bunch, who regularly fell out over who did what, according to Mum, as they all vied to be top dog.

She put down her mug. 'Lily, I'm sorry I thought you'd got drunk and been taken advantage of by a stranger,' she said. 'I should have known better.'

'You should, but it's OK.' I didn't add that I suspected she'd wanted an excuse to come over. I was glad that she had.

She glanced in the direction of the kitchen, where Ollie was singing the *Ghostbusters* theme in a bizarre baritone. 'I actually think you're in good hands with those two.'

'Craig's a bit quiet, don't you think?' He'd barely contributed to the conversation over dinner, although he'd been quietly attentive. At one point, while Ollie was helping himself to a slab of fruit cake, which I'd been planning to smother with icing and keep for Christmas, I'd been ready to quiz him about the 'ideas' I'd read. But then Mum had asked what I wanted for Christmas, and when I said, 'Someone to massage my feet for an hour every night,' Ollie's grossed-out face had made us laugh.

This had led to us naming our worst-ever gifts: an empty DVD case for me, from my brother (though, to be fair, I'd given him a pine cone the year before); a motorised rolling pin for Mum from her mother-in-law; and for Ollie 'a scuba-diving kit, because I already had two.' Craig had smiled along when Ollie added, 'For Craggers it was probably the Ferrari I bought him a couple of years back, because he made me take it back,' but hadn't commented.

'I thought he was quiet, but he's a nice man.' Mum said it so firmly I looked at her in surprise. She had good instincts about people, and was rarely wrong, despite her misjudging 'Lovely Dan', but I couldn't help thinking she was giving Craig more credit than he deserved. She'd always rated men who could cook, perhaps because Dad had been handy in the kitchen, his roast potatoes second to none. 'I think Ollie needs someone like Craig around, to balance him out a bit.' My surprise grew. I'd assumed she was completely captivated by Ollie. 'Just don't fall in love with him,' she said, looking at me over her glasses.

'Craig?' I gave a snort. 'Not much chance of that.'

'No, silly. I mean Ollie.' She patted my arm. 'I can see he'd be very hard to resist, but a man like him…' She pursed her lips. 'He's a heartbreaker, and you've had enough of those.'

'I'm not planning to fall in love with anybody, and anyway, he's in love with someone else,' I said, repeating what I'd told Erin.

Mum shook her head again. 'He might be, but he's obviously very persuasive and not immune to a pretty face.'

'Well, I'm glad you think I'm pretty, but I won't be falling in love with anyone. If anything, I'm only having casual flings from now on.'

'That doesn't sound very sensible, either.'

There was a sound at the door, but when I looked round there was only a sliver of light cutting through from the hallway.

'I'm a big girl, Mum.' I stifled a yawn as tiredness descended. 'I can look after myself.'

She looked as if she was going to say more, then glanced at her watch. 'It's almost eight. I think I'll make a move.'

'Sure you won't stay the night?'

She wrinkled her nose. 'Better not. I've got to open the shop in the morning,' she said, standing up and stretching. 'Annie's going Christmas shopping with her daughter.'

'I can't believe you came all this way because of a silly selfie.'

'I think any mother would have done the same.' She pulled me up into a hug. 'And I'm really glad I did.' She drew back, eyes dancing. 'Now I can tell my friends I've met Ollie Matheson.'

'Will they know who he is?'

'Oh, they all watch *Players*.'

Did everyone watch *Players* apart from me, Barry Lambert, and Mr Flannery?

Ollie did his best to persuade Mum to stay, offering the new guest bed, joking that he could 'bunk up' on the sofa with Craig.

'I'll be sleeping in my car,' Craig said, leaning against the kitchen door frame, his jumper sleeves pushed up to reveal hairy forearms.

'You'll do no such thing.' Mum glanced at me for support. 'Will he, Lily?'

'No,' I said obediently.

'Lily could cuddle up with me.' Ollie gave me a merry look and my heart nearly sprang out of my chest.

Mum lightly slapped his arm. 'Enough of that,' she scolded.

''Bye, Mum,' I said, steering her to the front door, where I enfolded her in a hug. 'Let me know when you're home.'

Once she'd left, Ollie suggested we go to the pub and 'start mingling', but my eyelids were starting to droop and I knew I'd be terrible company.

'I'm tired,' I said, unable to stop a yawn escaping.

Ollie did a boyish little pout. 'Where *is* the nearest pub?' His eyebrows rose. 'Me and Craggers can go for a pint and chat to some locals.'

'There's one called The Anchor, but I don't know what it's like.' It seemed incredible, when so much had happened, that I'd only been in Shipley a few days and still hadn't had chance to have a good look around.

'Let's turn in and start afresh tomorrow,' Craig said, coming over and clapping Ollie on the back. He looked as tired as I felt, despite his earlier nap. 'We could all do with some sleep.'

'But I've already had some.' Ollie leapt from foot to foot, like a boxer warming up. 'I'm feeling pumped.' Lowering his chin, he raised his fists and punched the air around him, his hair flopping up and down. 'I haven't been to the gym today. I've tons of energy to work off.'

'You could go for a run,' I suggested. 'Or do some push-ups?'

'Hey, that's a great idea.' Without warning, he did a combat roll over the sofa and started doing one-armed press-ups on the rug.

'You've started something now,' Craig muttered, as Ollie swapped arms and started counting out loud. 'He could be at this for hours.'

We exchanged looks.

'I need to sleep,' I confessed. 'Today's been a bit much.'

'Go on up.' Craig jerked his head at the stairs. 'I'll keep him entertained.'

'Don't sleep in your car,' I said, impulsively. 'I haven't got a spare duvet, but you could use your sleeping bag on the sofa.'

'...nine, ten, eleven,' Ollie puffed, barely breaking a sweat, the tendons in his neck standing out alarmingly.

'I might do that,' said Craig. 'I could grab some more logs and keep the fire going.'

'What is it about men and fires?' I said. I'd meant to be jokey, but it came out as a criticism.

'Maybe it appeals to our inner caveman.' Craig's smile deepened the fine creases around his eyes. 'Luckily, we're good at putting them out as well.'

Touché.

'Make sure you put the fireguard across,' I said primly.

'Yes, miss.'

I wished people would stop saying that.

'...twenty-five, twenty-six, twenty-seven.' Ollie was using both hands now, to lever himself up and down, and for a split second I imagined lying beneath him and heat washed over my face.

'I'll... er... I'll just...' I bit my lip.

'Go,' Craig said, and I had a horrible feeling he'd read my mind. 'We'll be fine.'

I didn't need telling a third time. I hurried upstairs to the sound of Ollie counting, and heard Craig say, 'If you can make it to a hundred, I'll let you beat me at arm wrestling,' before closing the living-room door.

Trying not to think of Ollie stripped to the waist, his biceps flexing, I undressed and brushed my teeth, then dived under my duvet with my phone. In the darkness, I strained my ears for voices downstairs, but they were faint and intermittent. After a while, the television came on and sitcom laughter flared, then someone went into the kitchen and I heard the crackle of foil. *Ollie's at the mince pies again.* I'd have to bake a fresh batch.

I thought about Mum telling Ollie how Max's wife had been horrible to me at school, but for once the memory didn't bring the burn of mortification. Instead, I remembered Ollie's response to Max's poem and gave a stifled giggle. His poetry *had* been kindergarten level. In fact, my class of five-year-olds could have done better.

While I waited for Mum to text, to say she'd arrived home safely, I tried to fix a first paragraph for my novel in my mind, but only got as far as *Nellie the elephant packed her trunk and said goodbye to the circus…* before sleep dragged me under.

Chapter 17

It was blissfully quiet when I woke, and I lay for a moment, absorbing the peace, feeling a lick of excitement about the day ahead.

Checking the time on my phone, I noticed Mum had texted around eleven to say she was back home, and Erin had Whatsapped *How's it going?* and a salvo of angry faces when I didn't respond.

Tempted to reply that Ollie and I were snuggled in bed, I typed instead, *'Mum reassured, so should you be.'* I attached a photo of me grinning and doing a thumbs-up.

'Well, that was scary,' she replied. *'I see you're still in bed.'*

'On my own.'

'Obviously.'

'Why obviously?'

'OK, I'm going to work now. Love you.'

'Love you more.'

'Ha ha. Keep me posted.'

'Will do. X'

On my way to the bathroom I pressed my ear to the door of the spare room. I hadn't heard Ollie come to bed, but detected some rhythmic snoring. So much for him not being tired. He was like a child, determined to stay awake in case he missed something, but out like a light the minute his head hit the pillow.

Unsettled at considering him childlike (*with those muscles?*), I headed for the shower, and after deciding not to fuss with my appearance – it looked a bit desperate and I couldn't compete with Tottie or Puffy, or whatever the women he usually mixed with were called – and settled for jeans and a sweatshirt before tiptoeing downstairs, expecting Craig to be sleeping on the sofa.

The room was empty, the curtains drawn back to let in the pale morning light. A fire still glowed in the grate, but the sofa was bare apart from a sleeping bag folded up at one end. At least he hadn't spent the night in his car.

He wasn't in the kitchen either, but there was an empty mug by the sink, and a smell of toast lingered in the air. I opened the back door, shivering a little as cold air prickled my skin. His trainers weren't there, so perhaps he'd gone for a run.

I felt oddly put out, as if his absence signalled his desire to be somewhere else, and was more convinced than ever that the plans I'd read on his notepad were nothing to do with Ollie. Perhaps he was sussing out the neighbourhood – filming without us knowing…

The floorboards creaked upstairs, and my pulse quickened. Closing the door, I busied myself making porridge, flicking the radio on to cover the toilet-flushing and showering sounds upstairs. I accidentally sloshed too much milk into the pan and compensated by tipping more oats in, until it was a bubbling mass.

Did Ollie like porridge? I should have bought some organic granola, or ingredients for a protein-based smoothie. And a smoothie maker.

I scoured the cupboards, shifting my favourite chocolate Rice Krispies to the back, and jumped violently when Ollie yodelled, 'Honey, I'm home!' behind me.

His hands landed on my waist and spun me round, and I barely had time to catch my breath, and register that his stubble had gone, before his head came close to mine and he murmured, 'Look at you.'

'S… sorry?'

'You're gorgeous,' he said, lifting his hands to cradle my face, drinking me in with his eyes. 'I've always loved the natural look.'

'Natural?' My voice had gone husky with shock.

'Make-up free, no hair dye, no extensions.' His gaze swept over my head, and I was conscious of having left my hair to dry naturally, and that it had probably lost its shape. 'Proper curves.' Dropping his hands back to my waist he gave it a gentle squeeze, and suddenly his mouth was on mine.

In the split second it took me to react, I imagined my lips parting and my hands snaking around his back and pulling him closer. I knew he'd be a good kisser, like Max had been – even though Max had sometimes kept his eyes open to check my reaction – but something didn't feel right.

As I pushed him away, I saw Craig, holding his camera aloft, his face crowded with disappointment, or distaste – possibly both – I couldn't tell in the heat of the moment, and as I sprang back, my elbow jogged the handle of the pan on the hob. It flipped over, tipping its gloopy contents over the floor, and some of the scalding mixture landed on my foot.

'*OW*!'

As Ollie dived for a cloth, I bent to peel off my sock, glad to be free of whatever that look on Craig's face had been. Had he assumed that I'd only pushed Ollie away because I didn't want to be caught on camera?

'There's so much,' Ollie said, snapping back to normal with enviable ease. 'Are you OK?'

'Not really.' My heart was still thundering, my nerve-endings jangling as I hopped over to the table and sat down, darting a quick glance at Craig.

'You should run it under cold water,' he said in a neutral tone, but it was obvious from the way he was gripping the camera that there was plenty going on in his head. 'Your foot,' he added. 'It'll take away the sting.'

'Thanks, I… I will in a minute.'

'You should do it now.'

'Fine.' I still didn't move, wishing Ollie would say something instead of spreading the porridge around with the inadequate dishcloth. His T-shirt was rucked up at the back as if I'd yanked it, and with a rush of nausea I realised how close I'd come to returning his kiss – to becoming one of 'those girls'.

You've been Ollied.

I batted Erin's words away, as Ollie turned to Craig.

'Did you get that?' he said, nodding to the camera dangling by Craig's side.

Craig caught my eye and looked away. 'Of course I did. We agreed I'd start filming this morning.'

What? Had Ollie staged the almost-kiss, knowing Craig would come in with his camera at any moment? 'When did you decide that?' I said.

'Last night, after you'd turned in.' Ollie flashed his easy smile.

'The filming, not the kissing,' Craig said abruptly.

'It wasn't really a kiss,' I challenged. 'I mean, I didn't respond, I was...' *thinking about it*? 'Please don't use that, will you?'

'Not if you'd rather I didn't,' said Craig, stiffly.

'Are you sure, Lily?' It was obvious from the crease that appeared between Ollie's eyebrows, he was disappointed. 'It's just that I thought we'd agreed to go for a natural feel for the show. You know, me doing stuff in an ordinary setting, for a' – more finger quotes – 'glimpse of the *real* Ollie Matheson.'

'Kissing your hostess wasn't part of that agreement,' Craig said, as if I wasn't there.

'But it's the sort of thing I do.' Ollie straightened and gave me a roguish smile. 'Rather well, don't you think?'

'On *Players*, yes. Not in real life.' Craig laid his camera on the worktop and unzipped his jacket. He had his running gear on again, minus his trainers.

'The sort of thing you *do*?' I couldn't believe what I was hearing. 'It was for the camera, then, all that rubbish about liking natural girls, with *curves*?'

'Oh crumbs, Lily. No.' Ollie tossed the dirty cloth into the sink and came over to kneel in front of me. He looked different without his stubble – too clean-cut. More like he had in his studio shot. 'That kiss was one hundred per cent genuine.' His eyes were so… twinkly. And he sounded sincere. 'At that moment in time.'

Right. 'I don't like being used.'

'Lily, my lovely, I wasn't using you, I was expressing my deepest admiration.'

'Aren't you supposed to be in love?' Craig's face darkened. He was no doubt thinking about Tattie, and wondering – as I had – why Ollie was kissing me if he was hoping to win Tattie back. Unless it was to make her jealous.

'She'll understand it's for the show,' Ollie said, but he didn't sound convinced, a wave of doubt sweeping over his features. 'Oh crap. Have I messed up?'

'I'll delete it,' Craig said, catching my eye, and I wondered if he was recalling the other bit of footage he'd have to delete.

My cheeks began to throb in time with my burnt foot.

'I'm deeply sorry if I've offended you, Lily.' Ollie seemed genuinely bewildered, and I was reminded again of a child being told his behaviour was inappropriate, and not quite getting why.

'I'd better go and soak my foot,' I said, as if Craig hadn't already suggested it. I was aware I must look a total mess in my baggy top and jeans, with my hair all over the place. 'Would you mind moving out of the way?'

'Sure.' Ollie's eyes dipped down, and he seemed to notice my bare toes for the first time. 'Remember to put a sock back on, won't you?'

Chapter 18

'He's got a thing about feet,' Craig said, an hour later. 'He's never liked them.'

'Women's feet, or feet in general?' I bundled a scarf around my neck, relieved that Craig had made no further reference to the scene in the kitchen.

We were about to take in the sights of Shipley, and Ollie was upstairs changing into something 'more suitable', though his outfit had seemed fine to me.

'Feet in general,' said Craig. 'Apart from his own.'

'Obviously.'

Our eyes grazed, then Craig picked up his camera. 'I've been looking forward to using this, I haven't had it long,' he said unexpectedly. He was fussing with the shiny casing and lens, pressing buttons and checking the SD cards were inserted, though he must have known they were. I noticed that his wrists were thick and strong. 'Surprisingly lightweight for such a comprehensive piece of kit,' he added.

'It looks more professional than ones I've used,' I said, matching his professional tone. 'I used to film assemblies for parents at the school where I worked, but the results were a bit dodgy if the light wasn't great.'

'Technology's moved on a lot.' Craig raised the camera to shoulder-height and I noticed the way his bicep flexed under his sleeve. He trained the lens on me. 'It's got a built-in light meter, and the audio's really good.' He gave it a look I imagined a girlfriend might be jealous of. 'I think a subject's more likely to open up if there's not too much equipment in their face.'

It was the perfect opportunity to ask about his plans to interview the neighbours, but he'd started speaking again.

'You're a teacher?'

'Used to be,' I said. 'I'm writing a novel now.'

Expecting him to ask what it was about, I prepared to explain that I was toying with a number of ideas, but he was giving me a curious look.

'A good teacher can make a real difference,' he said, thoughtfully, scraping his thumbnail across his chin. 'I still remember Mr Bradley, in year seven, telling the class that if we found a job we loved, we'd never work a day in our lives.'

'Sounds a bit grown up for year seven.'

'I don't think I properly understood it then, but his words stuck with me. He loved his job and it really came across.'

'I teach... *taught* five-year-olds,' I said, smiling as a memory of Erin's niece, Tallulah, popped into my head, asking, *In the olden days, was everything black and white*? 'They're so receptive at that age.'

'Where was the school?'

'Near East Finchley, where I grew up.' It struck me that Ollie hadn't yet asked me anything about myself – though he knew far more about my break-up with Max than I'd have liked, thanks to Mum discussing my private life with all and sundry. 'It wasn't one of those tough inner-city schools, I'm afraid.'

'Why do you say that?'

I paused in the act of pulling one of my boots on. I'd run my foot under the cold setting on the shower head, but it still felt sore. 'Oh, I don't know,' I said, wishing I hadn't started this line of conversation. 'Someone once told me I'd taken the easy option when it came to teaching.' It had been another trainee teacher, and her words had stung. 'She said doing art with five-year-olds was a cop-out and that it wasn't as valuable as shaping the minds of teenagers, or helping to turn round a failing school, or teaching children with special needs.'

'And you agree?' Craig's voice held no judgement and for the first time in ages, I found myself really considering a topic I'd turned over more than a few times during my teaching career.

'No,' I said, finally. 'I have this really strong memory of my first day at school, of crying and wanting to go home, but my teacher had this little hand puppet of a rabbit called Bugsy, and she made it talk in a funny voice until I laughed. After that I loved going to school.'

'Maybe that's when you decided to become a teacher.'

'I think it probably was,' I said, the memory of Miss Larchwood's blue woollen cardigan and generous smile as fresh as if I'd seen her only yesterday. 'Apart from a blip when I was ten, when I wanted to drive an ice-cream van, I never wanted to do anything else. I even used to play schools at home with my brother, until he got fed up with his little sister bossing him around.' I smiled, remembering. 'Oh, and my dad was a teacher,' I said. 'That probably had something to do with it.'

'He must have been proud of you.'

'He was.' My voice wavered, remembering the steady heartbeat of his love. 'He taught maths, though. My worst subject.'

'Mine too,' said Craig. 'I preferred English and science.'

'You're not filming me, are you?' I noticed he was still pointing the camera in my direction, but before he could answer, Ollie bounded downstairs.

'Are we ready to hit the road, guys?' he said, lightly touching my shoulder. I jumped as though I'd been scalded, and when I saw what he was wearing, my mouth fell open.

'I thought you were dressing down?' I managed, taking in the spray-on trousers. He looked like a jester – fitted white shirt with the collar flicked up, long black leather coat and, most puzzling of all, a trilby hat on his head.

'Yah, when I'm indoors, sure,' he said, slipping on a pair of sunglasses that covered half his face. 'Designed these myself,' he said, giving them a wiggle. 'These shoes don't scream "dinner at The Ivy", do they?' He stuck out a tasselled, moccasin loafer.

'Well, no, but… I don't think you need the shades.' *Or the crotch-grabbing trousers. And definitely not the hat.*

'I think they add a little *je ne sais quoi*.' He struck a rock-star pose, pretend-strumming a guitar, and I had to admit he still looked incredibly handsome. Something to do with his height and the width of his shoulders.

'I think a more subtle look might work better.'

'But how will I get mobbed if I don't stand out?'

Was he joking? He did an Elvis hip wiggle with his knees turned in, and sang a couple of lines of 'Since My Baby Left Me'.

I cast Craig a helpless look.

'It's a bit nineties indie boyband,' Craig said, hitching up his camera. 'Maybe lose the hat?'

Ollie whipped off his shades, apparently unoffended. 'Hang on a tick, I'll get changed.'

He sped upstairs, and Craig sighed and ruffled his hair. He wandered back to the kitchen and dug some headphones out of his rucksack, hooking them around his neck. As he didn't seem inclined to speak, I finished putting my boots on. By the time I'd located my keys on the radiator cover in the hall, Ollie had reappeared.

'Tah-dah!'

He'd replaced the leather coat with a lilac jacket, added a dove-grey tie, and changed the trousers for the loose black jeans he'd worn the day before.

'It's a bit insurance salesman slash cowboy,' said Craig, probably in reference to the cowboy boots Ollie was wearing. His holdall clearly held a lot more than its size suggested.

'It's better,' I said, though I doubted the jacket was a match for the cold weather, and it didn't really go with anything. 'Are you ready?'

'Sure.' Ollie twitched his cuff and glanced at a super-sized watch that looked like it might be a Rolex, and I noticed he'd slipped a gold signet ring onto his pinky finger.

It was if he couldn't help reverting to Ollie Matheson, reality star, but I sensed that saying so might only inflame the situation.

As we stepped outside, I had a sudden sense of being on holiday, despite the bitter cold, and felt a fizz of anticipation.

'We could have a wander along the seafront,' I suggested, locking the door while Craig dug his feet into his trainers. 'There's a lovely sweet shop along the parade. You could pop in and buy some humbugs and chat to the owner. She seems really friendly.'

'Good plan,' said Craig, a smile warming his eyes as he zipped his jacket back up.

'Wouldn't it be better to look around the town first?' said Ollie. I gaped when I saw that he'd picked up Marmite and was stroking him under the chin. 'I can take a look at this famous Christmas tree and maybe practise my speech for the switching-on ceremony.'

'Oh, you won't need to do a speech,' I said. 'Just, "I declare these lights switched on", or something.' I held out my hand to touch Marmite's ears, but he flattened them out of the way.

'Isn't he magnificent?' Ollie raised him in the air and they eyeballed each other with apparent affection.

'He's OK,' I muttered, annoyed at being snubbed (again) by the cat. My heart plunged when I noticed Barry striding up the road with a paper tucked under his arm. I had a feeling he wouldn't be as enamoured of my visitor as his wife had been.

He paused by the gate and gave Ollie an obsequious smile that didn't suit him. 'You're him off the telly, then.'

'At your service.' Ollie put Marmite down and the cat wound through his legs, purring like a traction engine.

Barry's head whipped back. 'He likes you,' he said. 'That's odd.'

'Not really.' Ollie gave him a dazzling smile. 'I have a natural affinity with animals.' It sounded so silly – as if he was auditioning for *Doctor Dolittle* – that I began to worry I'd misjudged Ollie after all and he really was a tosser.

Barry recovered and said, in a restrained sort of way that suggested he was angry, 'I couldn't get my car out of the road, thanks to you. Had to walk to the shop.'

'It's not that far,' I piped up, sensing Barry was spoiling for an argument.

'That's not the point.' He squared his considerable shoulders under his trench coat. He had a plaid cap on and grey strands of hair hung limply as though stitched to the edges. 'It's up to me if I want to drive there, without a van load of females blocking my way.'

Craig and I looked at each other.

'Females?' I said, as though the word was new.

'For him.' Barry jabbed his paper at Ollie, whose smile wavered slightly. Next to Barry, who seemed entirely made of muscle, he looked less imposing. Perhaps it was the cowboy boots.

'What's he talking about?' I said.

'Word must have got out that I'm here. I've quite a big fan-base you know.' Ollie spoke casually, bending to swipe his hand over Marmite's back. 'I'll make sure they're not a nuisance, sir.'

'Humph.' Barry looked slightly mollified at being referred to as 'sir', but gave me a dirty look, as if it was all my fault he'd had to walk to the newsagent's. 'Make sure they don't start roaming about up here,' he said, moving on to his own gate. 'We don't want bombarding.'

I turned to see Sheelagh at the open door of their house, fully made up, a black-and-white-striped tunic top flaring out from her bosoms.

'We'll see you later!' she called with a wave. Ollie straightened and blew her a kiss that made her giggle and blush.

'What do you think of my lights then?' As if suddenly remembering the purpose of Ollie's visit, Barry turned and gave him a combative glare – hardly conducive to gaining favour if he wanted to win the competition.

'Oh, yes, well, they're marvellous.' Ollie rubbed his hands together as he scanned the house, eyes widening slightly as they took in the inflatable reindeers on the roof. 'I haven't had a proper chance to make up my mind yet, so no decisions have been made,' he added, tactfully.

'I think you'll find this lot hard to beat.' Barry attempted what was probably meant to be an appeasing grin, but it actually made him look slightly manic. Ollie took a step backwards and trod on Marmite's tail.

The cat didn't even flinch.

Craig was by the car, his camera raised, but I had a feeling Ollie wouldn't want the exchange with Barry to be filmed. More footage that would need deleting. He'd have nothing for the show at this rate.

A few neighbours had come out, swaddled in winter coats, presumably to see what was going on and to get a look at the celebrity they'd heard about via the Sheelagh/Doris grapevine. They didn't look particularly excited to see Ollie – in fact, they were giving off distinctly hostile vibes.

'Come to see how the other half lives?' someone called.

'We don't need you to tell us we're special,' said a skinny woman. Half her face was buried in a woollen scarf, so the words came out muffled. 'You hit somebody on that show, and we don't approve of violence.'

Someone else who watched *Players* – and who clearly didn't take Sheelagh's and Mum's view that Ollie had had a 'raw deal'.

'Two sides to every story, folks!' Ollie threw out his trademark smile. Then, sensing their antipathy, he dived through the gate and into the back of the car.

Fixing a smile to my face, I ducked into the passenger seat. I was embarrassed to be the focus of so many staring eyes, none of them particularly friendly. Even Sheelagh had gone back inside, as if she felt she was betraying her neighbours by being besotted with Ollie.

'Don't they know who I am?' Ollie said, rather plaintively, as Craig got in and passed me the camera to hold.

'Did you really just say that?' He glanced at Ollie in the rear-view mirror, as he revved the engine, and Ollie subsided, a rather moody set to his clean-shaven jaw.

I tried to catch his eye, but he was looking out of the window with a brooding expression. It was as if our almost-kiss had never happened and he hadn't declared me gorgeous. If it wasn't for my foot still throbbing from my porridge injury, I might have dreamt the whole thing.

The van load of females had gone when we reached the bottom of the hill, and there was no sign of it as we drove towards the harbour, past a row of brightly coloured beach huts, and the parade of shops where Marnie's sweet shop nestled. Perhaps Barry had got it wrong and they'd been tourists who'd got lost, and nothing to do with Ollie at all.

Craig pulled the car into a parking space and switched off the engine. 'Shall we do a few shots around here first, of the view?' He peered through the windscreen. 'The castle looks good up there, and the way the light's coming off the sea adds a lot of atmosphere.' He was animated, his hand making a sweeping gesture at the horizon. 'The sky's amazing.'

He was right. The sea was calm with a glassy appearance, and the castle looked as if it had been sketched in charcoal against the milky sky. The poster-paint-bright fishing boats, bobbing in the harbour, provided an eye-catching contrast.

'I can't believe I've never been here before,' Craig murmured, his knuckles brushing against mine as he reached for his camera nestled in my lap. 'It's nicer than some places I've been abroad.'

'It really is,' I said, watching a family on the pier with an excitable dog straining on its leash. The parents were chatting while their two young children danced around them, their faces pink with cold and bright with laughter.

It could have been me and Chris with Mum and Dad, only it would have been summer, and we'd have had melting ice creams in our hands, and there wouldn't have been a dog.

'I don't really like the seaside.' Ollie's voice broke in and I turned to see him glancing at his watch again. 'The salt plays havoc with my hair.'

He raked a hand through his mane, dancing his eyebrows up and down, and I couldn't work out whether or not he was joking. 'I think I'd rather walk through the town, if that's OK with you folks,' he said. 'I'm assuming there *is* a high street.'

Craig looked at me, mouth curving into a resigned sort of smile. 'It won't be like Oxford Street,' he said, 'but, yeah, I'm guessing there is one.'

'It's called Main Street.' I remembered the sign I'd seen the other day. 'Come on then.' I opened the car door, keen to restore Ollie's good humour after his less-than-warm reception at Maple Hill. 'Let's go and mingle.'

Ollie leaned over me to rummage in the glove compartment. 'Should I bring my mistletoe?'

'No,' Craig and I said together.

Chapter 19

It seemed the whole of Shipley had descended on Main Street, which was an eclectic jumble of shops, old and new, all prettily decorated for Christmas and buzzing with shoppers. Bob's Bakery had a queue of customers snaking out of the door. I recognised a figure coming out, clutching a 'special of the day' – a gingerbread Santa. It was Biff, from the café the day before, with a woolly hat pulled low over his brow. He glanced around to check he hadn't been spotted, before hurrying away, nibbling at Santa's hat.

'I didn't think places like this actually existed,' Ollie said, doing a slow spin with his hands outstretched, his head tilted theatrically to the sky. He looked as if he was about to twirl around a lamp post, like Gene Kelly in *Singin' in the Rain*, but instead of whipping an umbrella up, he checked his watch again.

'Why do you keep looking at the time?' I said, aware that we were attracting some curious stares. We must make an odd trio, with Ollie in his lilac jacket, gazing around as though he'd arrived in Oz, me limping along beside him in my parka, and Craig bringing up the rear, his camera perched on his shoulder like a parrot.

'I'm just checking my watch is still there,' he said, dodging to let a man with a shopping trolley manoeuvre past, while scanning the area as though looking for someone he knew. Apart from his obviously expensive attire, he had a refined air that set him apart from most of the passers-by, and as he paused to look at a grinning snowman sprayed on the chemist's window, I noticed a middle-aged woman discreetly take a photo on her phone and show it to her companion. They kept glancing over their shoulders as they moved on, clearly trying to work out who he was but, for once, Ollie seemed oblivious.

'Shame it's not snowing for real,' he said, dipping his eyes to his watch again. 'I should organise a snow machine for when I switch on the lights. It would add a festive vibe. I could get somebody to helicopter one over.'

I felt a snap of irritation, probably due to my throbbing foot, and because I was cold, even in my scarf, with the hood of my parka pulled up over my hair. 'How would that be authentic?' I said. 'People watch the weather forecast. They'd know it wasn't real snow.'

He drew his head back. 'You're right,' he said, eyes twinkling as he linked his arm through mine and gave it a little squeeze. 'I just think snow in December is so…' He snapped the fingers on his other hand, as though trying to summon the right word.

'Unlikely?' I said. 'Winter doesn't officially begin until the twenty-first so, statistically, it's more likely to snow in January or February. It's why we hardly ever have a white Christmas.'

'Hey, have you thought of becoming a teacher?' he said. 'You'd be really good at it. You have a' – he rubbed the air in front of my face – '*vibe*, about you. In a good way.'

He wasn't joking. The 'classroom' part of Mum's revelation about Max's wife confronting me at school clearly hadn't registered. 'I'll give it some thought,' I said, pulling my arm away.

'Not that you aren't brilliant at what you do,' he said quickly, as if picking something up from my expression.

'And what is that?'

Confusion crossed his face. 'You're um… oh, heavens.' His nose was red with cold but it didn't diminish his good looks, whereas I probably resembled someone with a heavy cold. 'I don't think I actually asked, did I?' He made a 'what am I like?' face. 'We haven't really had time though, to do all that "getting to know you stuff", have we?' He cupped his hands and blew on them, his breath puffing out in a mist. 'Mind you,' his tone dipped confidingly, 'I think there are many ways to get to know someone. A kiss, for instance, can tell one a heck of a lot about a person, don't you agree?' His smile was disarmingly warm, but his eyes had shifted, and when I turned I saw he was looking at the clock above the post office.

'Not really,' I said, lurching forwards as a pair of teenage girls pushed past. 'Only whether they're any good at kissing.'

Why was I talking about kissing? We hadn't even kissed; not really. I turned to check that Craig wasn't filming our exchange, and saw an elderly man with a purplish complexion trying to attract his attention. 'Do you want to know what I think of Brexit?' he said.

Craig lifted one side of his headphones. 'Not really,' he said, turning the camera on the man. 'Tell me what you like most about living in Shipley, and what Christmas means to you.'

His straggly eyebrows shot up. 'Well, I've lived here all my life,' he said, swiping some strands of white hair across his bald patch. 'I s'pose I've got roots here, 'cos my parents and grandparents lived here, and my children and my children's children grew up here, and probably their children will, too.'

'But what do you like about it?' Craig persisted, as though it wasn't freezing cold and we weren't all wishing we were somewhere warmer – like the bakery. In fact, the aroma of fresh baking was making my mouth water, and reminded me I needed to buy fresh bread for this afternoon. I had a feeling sandwiches were a pre-requisite of afternoon tea in Shipley. Egg and cress, probably. I'd need to buy eggs as well. Proper ones.

'Well, I like the pace of life,' the man began, 'and the beach has been voted one of the best in the country. And I like that I know everyone who lives on my street and that we all look out for each other.'

'All good reasons,' said Craig, offering a smile of encouragement that crinkled his eyes and made him seem approachable. If he was cold it wasn't obvious, despite his fingerless gloves. Perhaps his running gear really was insulated.

'We like the quiz nights at our local pub,' said a dumpy woman at the man's side, threading her arm through his. Her hair had been dyed the colour of prunes and matched her coat and gloves. 'We were married in the church where my mother got married and where I was christened and our great-granddaughter's getting christened there next week and, for us, Christmas means family.'

'Falling out with family,' her husband said with a chesty laugh. 'Only joking,' he added, hastily.

'OH MY GOD, IT'S OLLIE MATHESON FROM *PLAYERS*!' The excited, high-pitched shout ripped through the air and everyone turned to stare. The source was a twenty-something female with a sheet of raven hair, wearing a black fur-trim Puffa jacket and towering heels. She grabbed her friend's arm and they hurried over, undeterred by the uneven pavement. 'I thought it was you!' Her expertly made-up face was ablaze with devotion, her lashes so long and thick I was surprised she could open her eyes. 'We adored you in *Players*,' she said. *Adored*? That wasn't a very Shipley thing to say. 'The show's *so* not the same without you.'

Ollie attempted a modest expression as she pouted her glistening pink lips. The French-manicured nails of one hand pressed against her high, round breasts, which looked ready to escape the tight top beneath her jacket. 'We love him, don't we, Jemima?' She shared a look with her companion, who had a stylish brown fedora squashed on her ash-blonde hair, and was wearing a poncho-style coat with ripped jeans and chunky boots beneath.

'So much.' She rested a slender hand on Ollie's sleeve and gave an orgasmic shudder. 'I mean, I actually *dream* about you.' She gave a girlish giggle, showing off shiny white veneers. 'You don't even want to know what we did in my dream.'

'Oh, I think I can guess,' Ollie smouldered back, before looking round at the curious faces and tipping his head back to laugh. 'It's hard work but someone's got to do it,' he said to no one in particular, placing an arm around each girl so Raven-hair could take a selfie on her diamanté-encrusted iPhone. She pulled a sprig of mistletoe out of her pocket and held it above their heads, and Ollie obliged by placing a kiss at the corner of her mouth.

'So much for him not wanting to be recognised,' Craig muttered, as the girls posed and pouted, pushing themselves against Ollie like cats on heat.

'You getting this?' Ollie turned to grin at Craig, but Craig had lowered the camera and moved aside to continue talking to the elderly couple.

By now, a crowd had gathered, and several women had recognised Ollie and were jostling for photos and autographs, while I stamped my feet and tried not to look fed up. Ollie was lapping it up, pushing his hair back and mock-protesting, then happily planting kisses on proffered cheeks, and even crouching to smile at a wise-looking toddler in a pushchair.

More shrieks erupted and a whole group of identikit females elbowed their way to Ollie and started fawning over him, snapping pictures and asking him to sign various body parts. It was a cleavage-fest of low-cut tops, despite the polar temperature, and Ollie seemed only too happy to oblige, cracking jokes about his signature being worth a fortune one day, so 'You'd better not wash it off!'

I looked around for Craig, but couldn't see him. He'd probably gone to get a coffee, if he had any sense, and for a second I wished he'd asked me to go with him.

On the point of making my way to the bakery, I spotted a youngish, thin-faced man with a goatee, pushing his way through the crowd, and a feeling of panic rose. Ollie's level of fame and wealth hardly warranted a bodyguard, but there were several people who'd probably like to hurt him, especially after his conduct on *Players*.

Scoping the street for Craig, I finally spotted him outside a charity shop, filming a man dressed as Santa holding a collection box. He'd clearly lost interest in Ollie and was striking out on his own.

Furious now, I shoved my way to where Ollie was holding fort and tugged his sleeve. 'It's time to go,' I said firmly.

He looked at me in surprise. His expression was glazed, as though he'd taken something, and I realised he was high on attention. 'This is Lily, my lovely new… friend,' he said to the weasel-faced man, drawing me close and resting his cheek on my hood. 'Isn't she adorable?'

'What are you doing?' I hissed.

'Just telling this nice reporter from the…' he looked at the man. 'Who are you, again?'

'Chris Weatherby, *The Shipley Examiner*,' the man said, holding up the camera slung round his neck and snapping a series of pictures. 'So, you'll be turning on the Christmas tree lights on Friday?'

'Absolutely,' said Ollie. I tried to duck away, but his arm was like a vice. 'Make sure you put it on your website so we have a good turnout.'

'And will you be appearing in *Players* again in the future?'

'I doubt it,' said Ollie, to a chorus of disappointed boos from the crowd. He guffawed, clearly delighted. 'Watch this space,' he said, with an enigmatic twitch of his eyebrows.

'Whereabouts are you staying?' the reporter asked.

Don't tell him.

'With this lovely lady.' Another squeeze. I felt trapped and badly wanted to kick him.

'Can we please go, I'm freezing?' I ground out.

Ollie blinked, as though he'd just woken up. 'Of course, lovely Lily.' Before I could look away he grazed my lips with his and the camera snapped again.

'So, what was that all about?' Craig said in the car, breaking the awkward silence that had descended on the short walk back. Ollie had decided he didn't want a 'chat with the baker', while I bought some bread, or to 'have a little go at shaping some loaves in the kitchen', while Craig filmed him. After a cursory look at the Christmas tree in the square, and a charming tug of his forelock to the smiling flower-stall holder, he claimed he wasn't keen on 'freezing his balls off' on the beach, or wandering around Corfe Castle. Even when I pointed out that there would be people there, dying to meet him.

'It was about me connecting with the public,' he said to Craig. 'And I'm not keen on ruined castles,' he added to me. 'If it was tea with the Duke and Duchess at Alnwick Castle in Northumberland that would be a different matter. They shot bits of Harry Potter there, you know. Well, not *shot* him, but you know what I mean.' He laughed, and Craig gave a despairing groan.

'I thought this visit was all about you behaving like an ordinary person.'

'I am, old boy.' His voice took on a soothing note, as if keen to get Craig back on side. 'I'd normally be at the villa in St Barts by now, but I'm here, aren't I? Making an effort.'

'I thought you were going to the Maldives?' I said.

He gave a one-shouldered shrug. 'Same thing.'

As Craig released a long-suffering breath, something occurred to me. 'Those girls who spotted you, they didn't sound local,' I said, swivelling round to face Ollie, who was sprawled in the back seat, his knees wide apart. His whole demeanour was different now that he'd had his fix of being recognised and adored. 'You didn't have them bussed in, by any chance?'

Craig gave a low whistle. 'Please tell me you didn't.'

Ollie made a face that said… *you've got me.*

'Ollie, for Christ's sake.' Craig's hands tightened on the steering wheel as he swung the car up Maple Hill. 'Who did you call?'

'Ghostbusters!' When no one laughed, Ollie stuck his bottom lip out. 'I might have persuaded Flossie Bembridge to round up a few of her mates and send them here on a day trip and pretend to "spot" me,' he said, in the manner of a boy confessing his naughty behaviour in the hope of getting off lightly. 'She thought it was a hoot,' he went on, when neither of us responded, and I wondered whether, like me, Craig was starting to wish that he and Ollie hadn't come to Shipley.

I watched Ollie hoist his foot on his knee and polish his boot with the sleeve of his jacket, and longed to rewind to a couple of days ago when his name hadn't entered my consciousness.

'Who's Flossie Bembridge?' I managed. *And do any of the women you know have names that don't end in a vowel?*

'One of my exes,' he said blithely, as if there were hundreds. 'We're on good terms,' he added, as though that was the issue. 'She owed me a favour and thought it would be a laugh.'

'*We're* not laughing,' Craig said, parking behind my car. 'We're pissed off.'

'Oh, you two.' Ollie leaned forward, smiling. 'You're adorable.'

So, now it was Craig and me against Ollie. So much for me being his 'gorgeous new girlfriend'. Not that I wanted to be. I was furious with myself now for even thinking about responding to his kiss.

I slammed out of the car and stormed inside, ignoring a cheery wave from Sheelagh, who was watching from her window, and vaguely aware that Barry was up a ladder, no doubt adding another layer of lights to his already overcrowded house front.

'Let me make a brew,' Ollie said, following me into the kitchen, watching with apparent interest as I threw off my coat and scarf and kicked my boots across the floor, wincing as my foot protested. 'Why don't you go and put your feet up?'

'Because I've got The Christmas Lights Society coming round and I want to bake some more mince pies as you've eaten most of the ones I made.'

'Only because they were delicious.' With infuriating calm, he filled the kettle with water and flicked it on. 'I'll make a pot of tea.'

'I don't have a pot,' I said, churlishly. 'I suppose you're used to drinking tea out of a tiny china cup.'

He wagged a playful finger. 'I only take coffee in a tiny china cup. I prefer my tea from a flask.'

I didn't want to smile, but felt my mouth twitch. 'I don't have a flask either.'

'In that case, I'll have to make do with one of your mugs.'

I gave in. 'The teabags are in that cupboard.' I looked round. 'Where's Craig?' I said, realising he hadn't followed us in.

'Oh, he said he was going to do some external filming, get a few shots of the beach, that sort of thing.'

'The sort of thing we were supposed to be doing just now?'

Ollie pulled a mournful face. 'I'm not really outdoorsy, unless I'm on a horse,' he said, releasing yet another mince pie from under its foil covering. 'Not during winter anyway.' He put the pie in his mouth, and made muffled noises of pleasure. 'Not in this country, at least,' he said when he'd swallowed. 'I ski in Verbier, but that's different.'

'Cold is cold, wherever you are.' I was easily able to picture him on a ski slope, or urging a stallion over a jump at the Badminton Horse Trials.

'It's different in nice surroundings, doing nice things.'

'So, what we were doing out there... that wasn't nice?'

He jerked his shoulders. 'It was work, I suppose.'

I stared. Was *I* part of his job? A new cast member in Ollie Matheson's ongoing reality show?

'I really would like to get on,' I said, as he poured water into our mugs from a great height while flourishing his other arm, like a magician. It was dawning on me that most things Ollie did were for effect. I wondered how he coped alone in a room without an audience.

'I thought we could have a quick getting-to-know-each-other session.' He passed my mug across the worktop, eyes turned up to full twinkle. 'We could ask each other questions while you work.'

He assumed a serious expression, as though about to be interviewed on *Newsnight* about Syrian refugees, but before I could reply there was a burst of trumpets from his jacket pocket.

'Hold that thought.' He pulled out his phone, face tightening when he saw who was calling. 'It's Tattie,' he said, already backing into the hall. 'Sorry to be rude, Lily, but I'd better take it.'

'Go ahead.'

'What do you want, Tats?' he said, as he took the stairs two at a time.

I strained my ears but only heard the bedroom door closing, followed by the creak of floorboards and the lancing tone of his voice. They were obviously having an argument.

Sighing, I turned my attention to the mince pies, and wished Mum was here to talk to. Or Erin. Or anybody from my old life. I thought of Max, but couldn't locate any pangs of longing. I switched on the radio instead, and listened to Mariah Carey singing about what she wanted for Christmas, while I started making pastry.

As usual, baking took on a soothing rhythm. I soon had a stack of fresh mince pies and then rustled up a batch of scones.

As I cleared up, and checked I had enough plates and cups to go round, I wondered whether Ollie was still on the phone. I turned off the radio as Noddy Holder stretched his vocals to breaking point yelling, 'It's Christmaaaaaaaaaaaaas', which suddenly made me think of Doris.

I cocked my head. *Nothing.* Maybe Ollie was deep in contemplation after his conversation. Hard to imagine, but possible.

I glanced through the window, wondering what Craig was up to. The car was there, so he couldn't have gone far. Then again, the beach was only a short walk away, and he clearly wasn't bothered about the cold. Maybe he was taking exterior shots of the houses on Maple Hill, where the daylight was fading and house lights were beginning to glitter.

I dried my hands and checked my phone. Mum had texted: *'Hope all's well, good luck with your gusts! Xx'*

Guessing she meant 'guests' I replied: *'All under control, good luck with your plap! Xx'*

'I think you meant play', she responded. *'Call yourself a teacher!! Xx'*

Smiling, I made some more tea and took out my notepad, a new idea for my novel popping into my head.

Leaning on the worktop, I wrote: *Jennifer's cupcakes were enormous…*

Cupcakes sounded like a euphemism.

Jessica's cupcakes were the envy of all her friends.

It still sounded like a euphemism.

You should open your own café,' her friend Craig kept saying. He was the biggest fan of her baking and never stopped trying to encourage her to…

Craig? I scribbled it out and wrote *Carl.*

'If you find a job you love, you'll never work a day in your life,' he was fond of saying. But Jessica already had a job she loved. She was a police officer and currently in the middle of a grisly murder investigation.

I read it through, then tore out the page, balled it up and aimed it at the bin. It missed, but I couldn't be bothered to pick it up.

The cottage was far too quiet.

I tore upstairs and knocked on Ollie's door. No answer.

Taking a breath, I turned the handle and peered inside, spotting his cowboy boots lined up beside his brogues and moccasins at the end of the bed.

I'd half expected to find him upset – or perhaps watching clips of *Players* on You Tube – but his phone was lying on the duvet beside him and he was flat on his back, fast asleep, snoring noisily.

'Wow,' I whispered. So that's how Ollie Matheson coped with being on his own.

He slept through it.

Chapter 20

'What a lovely spread.' Doris cast an approving eye over the table I'd brought into the living room and piled with plates of sandwiches, mince pies and scones. I'd also put out a bottle of lychee-and-guava juice, which I'd bought on my pre-Ollie shopping spree. I'd thought about putting out champagne, but had worried that my neighbours would think I had a drink problem – or was showing off. 'And the Christmas tree looks so pretty.'

'Thank you,' I said, admiring it with her. I'd set the multi-coloured lights to twinkle on and off and the colours reflected along the wall, disguising the fact that I hadn't had a chance to hang any pictures yet. Or buy any.

'And you've got the fire going.'

I looked at the grate, where flames were dancing behind the fireguard. 'I thought it made a nice touch.'

'I noticed smoke coming out of the chimney yesterday and I thought to myself, Felicity Meadows would be delighted. She loved a nice fire. She was the original owner of Seaview Cottage,' Doris explained. 'Said she'd only ever leave this place in a coffin.'

'Well, I hoped she lived a full life.'

'Oh, she's still alive,' said Doris. 'She got sick of seeing the sea and moved to the countryside.'

'Right.'

'Is that your family?' Doris headed for the photo on the mantelpiece. 'You look like your father,' she said, studying his smiling, suntanned face. 'Around the eyes.'

'Thanks,' I said, touched. It was nice to hear, though I knew I looked more like Mum, and that Chris was the one who'd inherited Dad's dark hair and eyes. 'He passed away a few years ago.'

'I know.' She turned. 'Your mum told me.' *What?* 'He'll always be with you, like a handprint on your heart, just like my Roger is with me.'

'That's… lovely,' I said, meaning it.

'So, where are your men?'

'Men?'

She peered around the room. 'Your… *guests.*'

'One's out, and one's upstairs,' I said, wondering where Craig had got to. He knew the meeting was due to start.

'I wasn't sure whether we were meant to contribute, so I brought a few things.' Doris handed over a heavy, canvas bag. 'Nothing much,' she added, as I peeped inside at a heap of Tupperware containers. 'Just a few sausage rolls and some of my birdseed muffins, a chocolate cake and my version of Viennese whirls – I use lemon curd. Oh, and I popped a few dog biscuits in.'

'Dog biscuits?'

'Celia Appleton said she might pop by and she'll probably bring Chester, her dog. He's getting on a bit and doesn't like being left on his own.'

'That's fine.' I was a bit scared of dogs, having been bitten as a child, but decided not to say so. Just like I hadn't pointed out that Doris was fifteen minutes early. 'This is very kind of you.'

'No trouble,' she said, though it was obvious she'd gone to a great deal of effort. 'And I popped in some paper plates and plastic cups.'

'Wow,' I said. 'That's very kind, thank you.'

As I made room for everything on the table, Doris said, 'Any sightings next door?'

I looked round to see her angling her head, eyes swivelling in the direction of the Lamberts'. 'Sightings?'

'My friend, Ellen Partridge, says she saw Barry in the underwear department in John Lewis in Poole and he was picking out lacy bras with his other woman,' she said.

'I haven't noticed anything.' I thought for a second. 'Maybe he was with his sister, choosing a Christmas present for Sheelagh.'

'He hasn't got a sister, just an older brother called Nigel,' she said. 'Now, shall I put the food on plates while you go and get changed?' She looked askance at my flour-covered jeans and sweatshirt. She'd hung up her coat and was straightening her lavender twin-set over her grey woollen skirt. 'Unless you already have?'

I felt torn, guessing she'd love an opportunity to snoop around, but knowing I looked a mess. In the end, vanity won. 'That would be great,' I said. 'I won't be long.'

'Take your time, dear.'

Upstairs, I barged into the spare room to find Ollie still sound asleep, one hand cupping his privates. I couldn't believe he'd slept through the doorbell chiming.

'Ollie!' I leaned over and shook his shoulder.

'Sweetie.' Reaching out, he pulled me down on top of him. 'You smell like a tart,' he mumbled into my hair.

'*What?*'

'Mmmm, mince tarts,' he whispered, nuzzling my ear. 'I was dreaming about them.'

I wriggled out of his grasp. 'Ollie, you have to get up.'

He turned over, sliding his thumb into his mouth.

'OLLIE!'

He shot upright, as if I'd fired a gun. 'Lily, what is it?'

'It's time for the Christmas lights meeting,' I said, noting that his hair looked immaculate. 'Doris Day turned up early.'

'Doris Day?' He looked thrown.

'You met her, briefly.'

'Where have I heard that name?'

I suppressed a sigh. 'Your grandmother might have watched some of her films.'

'Your neighbour's an actress?'

Doris was singing the chorus of 'Mistletoe and Wine' in a high voice and I knew it would be stuck in my head for the rest of the day. 'Could you try and charm her, while I get changed?'

'Oh god, yah. Absolutely.' He leapt off the bed, smoothing his hands down his cheeks as if rubbing away the last vestiges of sleep – or checking for non-existent wrinkles.

'You look fine,' I observed. His shirt wasn't even creased.

He tweaked his sleeves and collar. 'Ollie Matheson saves the day,' he said, striking a Superman pose. 'The *Doris* Day.'

'Ha, ha,' I said.

'Shall I fetch my mistletoe from the car?'

'Definitely not,' I said. 'It's probably dead by now.'

He grinned, and ruffled my hair as he passed.

As I hurriedly changed into a plum-coloured dress and teamed it with a fluffy cream cardigan, I heard Doris bark, 'Put that sausage roll down, young man. It's bad manners to start before everyone's here.'

I smiled as I pulled a brush through my hair and swiped some nude lipstick on. I had a feeling Doris wouldn't be as easy to win over as most of the females Ollie met. I doubted she'd be asking for his autograph or requesting a selfie with him.

I pulled on some tights, after checking for holes, and ran downstairs as the doorbell sounded again.

It was Sheelagh this time, in a sequin-embellished V-necked dress beneath an emerald-green coat. 'Jill Edwards is still at school and can't make it,' she said, as she came in. 'But I told her you're going to look in before the end of the week and she's looking forward to seeing you.'

About to protest that I hadn't made any such arrangement, I remembered my promise to Alfie the day before and stammered out my thanks.

'The Jensens can't make it either, on account of their high-powered jobs.' Her smile vanished as Doris's voice drifted out.

'You can put your trumpet away, dear,' she was saying to Ollie. 'Nobody likes a show-off.'

'I might have known she'd be early.' Sheelagh removed her coat and thrust it at me, along with a bottle of white wine. 'I'd better go and rescue that poor young man.' She hurried through, her feet puffing over her pointy black velvet pumps.

'Nice to see you too,' I murmured, hanging her coat over Doris's on the banister post. Before I could catch my breath, Craig slipped through the front door, bringing with him a blast of icy air.

'Sorry,' he said, swinging his camera to the floor. 'I forgot the time.' His eyes were bright in his flushed face and his hair was untidy. 'There's a lot of potential around here to make a decent programme,' he said, clearly fired up as he removed his jacket and placed it on top of Sheelagh's coat.

'Interviewing the neighbours, by any chance?' I sounded like the fun-police and probably looked like them, too, holding the bottle of wine as though I'd confiscated it. 'Behind Closed Doors?' I added, widening my eyes in a meaningful way, not sure why I was cross with him when he hadn't done anything wrong.

He looked at me for a moment, as though weighing up how to respond. 'I'm not getting much good stuff with Ollie,' he said at last, smoothing a hand over his tousled hair. 'Every time the camera's on, he starts performing—'

A set of knuckles rapped on the door.

'I'd better go through,' he said, breaking eye contact as he bent to retrieve his camera. 'I'll try and blend into the background,' he added, as I opened the door to let in the Harassed Couple – minus their twins – and Jane and Dennis.

'Ooh, it's changed a lot since Felicity Meadows and her brood lived here,' said Jane, divesting herself of a thickly quilted purple coat and piling it on top of Craig's jacket. 'She was like the old woman who lived in a shoe, wasn't she, Dennis?' She turned to her husband, who'd dressed in a suit and bow tie, as if attending a film premiere, and had tamed his greying beard into something almost stylish.

'She certainly had a lot of children,' he agreed, adjusting the knot of his tie. 'This thing's strangling me.'

'Doesn't he look gorgeous?' Jane whispered, squeezing his bottom as she followed him into the living room.

'You OK with dogs?'

I spun round to see an older woman in the doorway, leaning on a wooden walking stick, an ancient, but friendly looking Labrador at her side. Trying not to goggle at her patchwork leather coat and flat cap, I waved them in.

'You're both welcome,' I lied, shrinking back from the dog. 'I don't think we've met.'

'Celia Appleton, Marnie's gran. She said you'd saved the day by ordering some celebrity to switch on the Christmas tree lights.'

'Something like that.' It came out more apologetically than I'd intended.

She nodded brusquely, seeming to take in me, the house, and the situation with a sweep of her shrewd, blue eyes. 'I'll go through, shall I?'

'Please do.'

As she flung her coat on top of the others, revealing several layers of clothing all in the same shade of pale grey – like mist – Chester plonked his bottom down and lifted a front paw. 'He's saying hello,' she said. 'He's got beautiful manners.'

Not wanting to seem rude, I obediently shook the dog's clammy paw, trying not to meet his eyes in case I inadvertently annoyed him.

The doorbell chimed again, and Chester gave a woof that made my heart jolt.

'Come here, boy,' said Celia, and he returned to her side, tail wagging as they went to join the others in the living room.

Mr Flannery was outside, a sour look on his face. 'I've had to leave my nephew in charge of the shop but he can't be trusted,' he said by way of a greeting, stamping his feet on the mat as he unfastened his black anorak. Unless it had started snowing again, he had a scattering of dandruff on his shoulders.

'I'm sure he'll be fine,' I said, thinking, *You didn't have to come, you miserable toad.* I checked that Barry wasn't lurking outside before I closed the door. 'Would you like a drink, Mr Flannery?'

'Call me Clint,' he said, tetchily. 'I'll have a mug of Ovaltine, please.'

Ovaltine? 'I'm afraid the nineteen seventies wanted their Ovaltine back.' It was a lame attempt to get him to crack a smile.

He narrowed his eyes. 'I hope there's some orange juice then.'

'Lychee and guava?'

'Never heard of them.' Still in his anorak, he loped into the living room, where the noise level had risen to mildly deafening. Following him through, I saw Sheelagh was monopolising Ollie, who seemed relieved to be playing to an appreciative audience again.

'Doris Day is terrifying,' he whispered, as I edged past him to where my phone was plugged into a speaker on the windowsill. I'd been downloading some Christmas music when Doris had turned up. 'She reminds of me of Nanny,' he added, his mock-fear tinged with deep admiration. I dreaded to think how he'd have turned out if his nanny had been like Sheelagh.

'Ooh, we should have a little dance,' Sheelagh squealed, as Shakin' Stevens sang 'Merry Christmas Everyone', swaying her hips and clicking her fingers. Her face was suffused with colour and I feared for her blood pressure – especially if she was wearing her corset again.

'Is Barry running late?' I asked her, checking the time. As head of the society, I'd have expected him to arrive with Sheelagh.

A funny look flickered over her face. 'He got held up,' she said, thrusting a hand through her curls. Her face contorted. 'Ow! My ring's stuck.'

Ollie sprang to the rescue, making her giggle as he released her fingers one by one. 'What are you like, Loretta?' He planted a kiss on the back of her hand.

'Ooh, you are lovely,' she simpered. 'Your mother must be very proud of you.'

'Not really,' he said, and Sheelagh let out a gasp. 'I mean, yah, she loves me loads, *obviously*, but she wanted me to be a lawyer or doctor, or full-time musician like my sister.' He made a horrified face. 'I much prefer doing things for fun,' he said. 'But Ma's never watched an episode of *Players*, on principle.'

'You poor lamb,' Sheelagh cried, as my own sympathies stirred. 'We're very proud of our daughter, Bryony, although she was never the brightest crayon in the box. She runs a meat-packing company in Nebraska now.' Even Ollie seemed stumped by this nugget of information. 'She doesn't have time to get home very often. It's been three years now.'

'Skype?' suggested Ollie.

'She doesn't do social media.' Her voice held a trace of sadness I suspected ran deep. I'd assumed she and Barry didn't have children, and it struck me I'd been judging a lot of things on appearance.

'Well, it's her loss, Loretta.'

Jane seemed equally taken with Ollie, hanging on his every word as she positioned her birdlike body at his side. She looked almost stylish in pair of black, wide-legged trousers and a loose, sand-coloured top. It was just a shame her trousers were a tad too short, and that she was wearing violent pink socks with crocs. 'Have you thought about going into acting, now you're off the show?' she asked him, her frizzy hair vibrating, and I turned away as he started telling her about his little foray into the acting world.

Craig was over by the tree, his camera on the floor, chatting to Dennis, who didn't seem to mind that his wife was now asking to touch Ollie's hair, to see if it was as soft as it looked. They both had paper plates piled high with food, and Craig looked relaxed, his expression open and enthusiastic. Glancing over, he caught my eye and raised a sausage roll as if in a toast.

About to smile back, I jumped as Barry's voice boomed out, 'I see you've started without me then?' He strode into the room, wearing his coat, his stomach straining under a tartan waistcoat. 'Afternoon, Miss Ambrose.'

'Please call me Lily,' I said. He stopped directly under the overhead light, and I caught a faint scent of perfume hanging about him.

'Sorry I'm late, I got held up at the building site.'

Hmmm. That didn't exactly fit with the scent of perfume. Unless he'd squirted on some of Sheelagh's to disguise the smell of brick dust. Had Doris's instincts been right? I glanced over at where she was happily doling out food and drinks, like a seasoned waitress. Was Barry having an affair? It would explain that look I'd seen on Sheelagh's face – as if she suspected something was up – and the real reason why Barry was late.

Perhaps he'd been with a lover.

It seemed so unlikely, but who knew what went on in people's marriages? I was hardly an expert.

Before I could ponder any further, Barry had gone over to shake Ollie's hand, and although he'd switched on an almost friendly smile, I had the feeling he'd rather get Ollie in a headlock. 'So, you know what's happening tomorrow?' he said, getting straight to the point.

Ollie inclined his head, freeing his fingers from Barry's grip and shaking them out. 'I do indeed.'

'After the switch-on and presentation, we usually decamp to The Anchor for a celebratory drink. Providing I win,' he said, casting a black look at Mr Flannery, who picked up my snow globe and gave it a violent shake, as if wishing it was Barry.

'Sounds grand,' said Ollie, keenly. 'I rather fancy sampling the local ale.'

The Harassed Couple exchanged a look that suggested they couldn't wait to get home and send up his accent.

'Seen all the displays yet?' said Barry.

Celia threw him a black look. 'Don't bother looking at my house,' she said. 'I'm not taking part.'

'Well, they're all… spectacular.' Ollie clearly wasn't at ease with a man like Barry, who oozed testosterone, and not in the manner of someone who enjoyed a workout. More like a man who'd slam you against a wall and get you to spill your secrets. 'You've done a splendid job.'

Barry's nod suggested his light display was indeed splendid. 'Covered the whole house,' he said. 'You can hardly see a brick for fairy lights.' He looked around and chuckled, his belly wobbling. 'These lot are amateurs, but they do their best.'

Had he seen the gingerbread and *Frozen* houses? I sensed he was attempting to be matey, but Ollie tilted his head so he was literally looking down on Barry.

'Ah, but have you ever heard the saying, "Less is more"?' he said. 'Not a concept you're familiar with, I take it?'

'Less is more?' Barry looked around for support. 'Are you kidding me? More is more, when it comes to Christmas lights.'

'I just think there's a tendency for them to look a bit… well, tacky.' Ollie narrowed his gaze. 'My mother has a saying, "There's beauty in simplicity." I think there's a lot to be said for that.' *Shut up, Ollie.* 'Clearly the message hasn't reached…' he turned querying eyes in my direction. 'Where am I, again?'

'Maple Hill,' I said, trying to warn him to be quiet with my tone.

'That's the one.' He resettled his gaze on Barry, who'd gone ominously still. 'I think if you removed some of the more common elements – the flashing Father Christmas, for instance, and those dreadful angels – it would all come together in a much classier fashion.' He cast his gaze around the room, seemingly oblivious to the fact that everyone had frozen in unnatural poses, like children playing statues. Even the music had stopped in the middle of 'Frosty the Snowman'. 'I'm not that keen on themes, either,' he continued. 'They're a bit too "try-hard".

The Harassed Couple joined hands, as if what they'd heard required some support. 'So, basically, you're saying you hate them all?' they said at the same time.

'No, but I rather like that lovely Lily' – he flung out an arm in my direction – 'hasn't bothered with a single light outside, which makes the effect of the candle display over there' – he swung his arm to the windowsill, where the little golden bulbs glowed against the glass – 'all the more effective.'

I wanted to say something about it not being planned, but Ollie had moved on.

'I'll tell you what you could all do to impress me even more.' He paused for dramatic effect. 'How about you all reveal a secret talent, and Craig over there can film it? I'm sure Loretta can carry a tune.' He jiggled his eyebrows at her. 'She's certainly got the lungs for it.'

'Pervert,' muttered Mr Flannery.

'Who the hell's Loretta?' said Celia, jamming a handful of Viennese whirls into her skirt pocket.

'Why are you using my wife's middle name?'

'Oh, is it?' Ollie looked at Barry, in obvious confusion. 'I didn't realise.'

Barry bristled. 'I'll show you my secret talent in a minute, you hoity-toity twat.'

Sheelagh laid a restraining hand on Barry's arm. 'You're here to judge the lights,' she said to Ollie. 'We're not performing monkeys.' She looked deeply wounded at having to scold her hero, and Ollie finally seemed to register that he'd misjudged the situation.

'It was just a bit of fun, you know that, don't you?' He directed his words at the Harassed Couple, perhaps hoping that because they were closer in age, they'd agree.

'No,' they said in tandem.

I glanced at Craig, half expecting him to have switched on his camera now that 'reality' had snuck in, but he was merely observing while pushing crisps into his mouth.

'The public like our displays,' Dennis offered. 'They come especially to see them and then donate money to local charities.'

Jane nodded, adjusting her glasses as though to get a clearer look at Ollie. 'My flowers in the summer, our Christmas lights in December,' she said.

'"Less is more" doesn't apply to Christmas.' Celia's tone suggested it was a fact she'd read, rather than her opinion.

Chester sank down on the rug and sighed.

'None of the houses will win if that's your criteria,' Mr Flannery pointed out. 'Everyone's gone to town, as it were.'

'OK, I get it,' said Ollie, rallying. 'I'm very sorry if I've caused any offence.' He placed his hands on the sides of his head and said in a monotone, 'Less isn't more. More is more. Keep an open mind.'

'Is he taking the piss?' said Mr Flannery, putting down the plastic cup of lychee-and-guava juice he'd been holding.

'Sounds like it to me.' Barry's chest swelled and even Celia looked like she wanted to thwack Ollie with her stick.

I cleared my throat. 'I'm sure Mr Matheson didn't mean to upset anyone and that he'll judge your displays with a fair and open mind.'

Barry rounded on me. 'Not a very good choice of judge, if you ask me.'

'Leave her alone,' said Sheelagh, but the look she flung me was wounded.

'Shame you couldn't find someone who lived on this planet.' Mr Flannery seemed pleased when everyone agreed, and knowing I was the cause of this rare event brought me close to tears.

'Don't talk to her like that.' Ollie came over and placed a protective arm around my shoulders. 'You should be thanking Lily. I'd planned to go abroad for the season.'

'Not helpful,' I muttered.

'Like that, is it?' Jane's smile was knowing, and slightly excited. 'We can't expect you to be impartial if you're... *involved*.'

'We're not *involved*.' I shrugged Ollie's arm off. 'Mr Matheson's here to do a job, and he's going to do it to the best of his ability.' I nudged him with my elbow and he nodded.

'Yah, absolutely.'

'Or, his friend could do the judging.' I swung round to see Doris pointing at Craig. 'He seems like a very nice man.'

There were murmurs of agreement.

How did they know that Craig was a very nice man?

'Not up himself like the posh one,' the Harassed Wife muttered.

'Charming,' said Ollie, his mouth turning down. 'What a bunch of ungrateful—'

'Shush,' I hissed. 'You've done enough damage already.'

Craig was shaking his head. 'Thanks, but that's not why I'm here.' He placed his empty plate on the arm of a chair. 'Ollie will do a good job, I promise.'

No one looked convinced.

'Frosty the Snowman' burst back into life, but the mood had gone flat.

With a heavy feeling in my chest I waved the bottle I was still holding. 'Would anyone like some wine?'

They all shook their heads without looking at me.

I tried to think what I would do if I was in the classroom, but I didn't fancy my chances of getting them to sing a song or listen to a story. 'Help yourselves to sandwiches,' I said. 'There's plenty more.'

'I think we'll make a move.' The Harassed Husband glanced at his watch. 'The twins are due back from their gran's any time,' he said, as though they were catching the bus.

'Thanks for the food,' his wife said, not meeting my eye as they hurried past, trailing a scent of baby milk and nappies.

They didn't even glance at Ollie, who'd slumped on the sofa with a look of bewilderment, as if nothing like this had ever happened to him before – which it probably hadn't.

'I'm staying with my sister tonight and need to pack a bag,' said Sheelagh, throwing Ollie a sad look, while Barry stomped by without a word. 'Sorry, Lily.'

One by one they all trooped out with vague, muttered goodbyes. Snapping into teacher mode, I positioned myself in the hall and made sure everyone picked the right coat off the pile.

'Hope to see you all for the switching-on ceremony,' I said brightly to each of them as they left. 'And I promise your lights will be judged fairly.'

Chester nudged my hip as if in sympathy, before trotting out after Celia, and it was all I could do not to cry. Dogs might have sharp teeth, but at least they weren't judgemental – and they didn't give a stuff about Christmas lights.

Doris was the last to leave, her canvas bag tucked in the crook of her elbow. 'It'll be fine, you'll see,' she said, patting my arm. 'You can return my containers any time.' Halfway down the frost-coated path to the gate, she turned. 'Oh, and I had a nice chat with your mother earlier. She's invited me over after Christmas, to see one of her plays.'

Chapter 21

'Well, that didn't go as planned.'

'It could have been worse,' said Craig. 'At least no one took a swing at him, like they did at his book-signing.'

He was helping me clear up in the kitchen, while Ollie – clearly unsettled by everyone's hasty departure – was watching *A Muppet Christmas Carol* on the television, saying he'd always liked Miss Piggy's interpretation of Emily Cratchit.

'Were you there?' I said. 'At the book-signing.'

Craig shook his head. 'He was pretty upset though. He called and asked me to take him to hospital.'

'I suppose it's a shock to find out someone dislikes you enough to want to hurt you.'

His gaze searched my face. 'Speaking from experience?'

I thought of Max's wife and gave the washing-up-liquid bottle an extra-vicious squeeze. 'Maybe,' I said.

'I can't imagine anyone wanting to hurt you.'

I looked at him, surprised. He was poised, bin-bag in one hand and one of Doris's sausage rolls in the other. 'You don't really know me,' I pointed out, heat spreading over my face.

He shrugged. 'What can I say? I'm good at reading people.'

I thought again about Ollie having his jaw dislocated. 'Have you ever been attacked?'

Craig ate the sausage roll in one quick bite and swallowed. 'No, but I'm not in the public eye like Ollie.'

'It's horrible, being judged,' I said. 'It's the injustice of it, when you haven't done anything wrong.' I thought of the parting shot Max's wife had hurled before she stormed out of the classroom. '*If it wasn't for you, he'd have come back sooner.*' As if I'd single-handedly wrecked their marriage – a marriage which I'd thought was over. I'd tormented myself afterwards that I shouldn't have got involved until Max was divorced. Before I met him, I'd been a poster girl for sensible decision-making.

'Ollie does get it wrong sometimes,' Craig was saying. 'He's not always diplomatic. He tends to say the first thing that comes into his head.'

'I quite like that about him.' I flushed again, remembering that Craig had caught us almost-kissing. It felt like ages ago.

'You and I might, but not everyone will.'

'No, I suppose not.'

'Anyway, as long as you like yourself, who cares what others think?' He tied up the bin-bag and put it by the back door.

I was about to reply with a quip about him sounding like a therapist, when Ollie came into the kitchen.

'Let's go out on the town,' he said, good humour seemingly restored. 'The Mop Hill bunch might not have warmed up to me yet—'

'Maple Hill,' Craig and I said together.

'That's what I said.' He widened his eyes, innocently. 'They might not like me yet, but I'm sure I can win over the locals in the pub.'

'How about we have a wander up and down *Maple* Hill and you make a final decision about which display you like best?' I suggested. 'You have to pick one, even if you hate them.'

'I don't hate them, that's not what I meant,' he said. 'And anyway, it'll only take me a couple of minutes to choose.' He held out his hands to me. 'We could go dancing. I'll show you my moves, if you show me yours.'

He broke into a Charleston with jazz hands and twisty feet, but although I laughed, and was relieved that he seemed back on form, I felt my energy draining as though a plug had been pulled. 'There's nowhere to go dancing in Shipley, as far as I know.'

'Just as well with those moves,' Craig said drily.

'So Shipley's a cultural wasteland,' Ollie said, panting lightly. 'Maybe further afield?' He looked at Craig, though I wasn't sure he knew the area any better than I did.

'Mate, I'm knackered.' Craig sagged against the worktop to demonstrate. 'Can't we carry on eating in front of the TV? *Elf* might be on.'

'That's my favourite Christmas film,' I said, pleased.

Craig grinned at me. 'It's a classic.'

'Watching telly's a bore,' said Ollie, faking a yawn. 'Anyway, I've seen *Elf* a hundred times.'

Craig shook his head. 'What about an early night?'

'Ooh, I didn't know you felt like that.' Lunging forward, Ollie pulled him into a bear-hug and half danced, half dragged him round the kitchen, planting noisy kisses on top of his hair. I was reminded of Chris and me, play-fighting when we were young, and felt a pang for those carefree times.

'Gerroff,' Craig said, pummelling Ollie's sides. He broke free, aiming a friendly kick at Ollie's midriff, and I could suddenly see what Mum had meant about Ollie needing someone like Craig to balance him out.

Ollie grabbed one of Doris's Tupperware containers and stuffed a couple of biscuits into his mouth. He chewed for a moment, then spat into his hand. 'Jesus, what are they?' he said, while Craig and I erupted into laughter.

'They're dog biscuits,' I spluttered. 'Doris brought them for the Labrador.'

Still laughing – a surprisingly warm and hearty sound – Craig twisted his head away as Ollie tried to push some into his mouth. 'You should try one of her birdseed muffins,' he said. 'Apparently, it's cheaper to buy millet from the pet store than those fancy, overpriced sunflower seeds that you get at the supermarket.' He did a passable impression of Doris's Dorset twang, and I wondered when she'd told him that.

'No, thanks.' Ollie wiped the back of his hand across his mouth and shuddered. 'Well, I definitely need a drink after that and I don't mean your sorry excuse for wine.' He nodded at the unopened bottle Sheelagh had brought.

'Ooh, I've got some good stuff,' I said, pleased I'd bought the vintage champagne after all, my apathy lifting at the thought of us settling in front of the telly with the Christmas lights twinkling in the corner. It would be like going back in time, to when I'd shared a house with two trainee teachers and a drummer, only I wouldn't be trying to keep the peace, or the only one who thought to lock up the house before going to bed.

Perhaps I could go and fetch some logs and get the fire burning again.

But Ollie was shaking his head before I could cross to the cupboard and get some glasses out.

'No offence, lovely Lily, but I fancy a change of scenery.'

My insides sagged. It was clear he'd set his mind on going out and wasn't going to be swayed. 'Craig can bring his camera, get a bit of local colour,' he added, as if that might swing things in his favour – as though Craig could only be happy filming Ollie.

Craig nodded with a faint air of resignation. 'Sure,' he said. 'But no filming. Let's just have a drink.'

'Oh.' For a moment Ollie looked perplexed and I thought he was going to argue, but then he said, 'OK, well I'll go and get my glad rags on.' He backed out of the kitchen, swinging his hips and winding his arms above his head, giving me a fierce look from under lowered eyebrows.

I couldn't help laughing again. 'I'd better see if there's somewhere nearby, if he wants to go dancing,' I said when he'd gone upstairs. I reached for my phone and did a search. 'It's blues night at the Shipley Conservative Club or there's a DJ playing at Jonny's Bar, but the place has got terrible reviews. "Music too loud and grumpy bar staff. There was a number two on the floor in the ladies."' I winced. '"A bouncer slapped my mum." Wow. I can't imagine Ollie in there, can you?' I said. 'We might have to drive to Poole.'

Craig looked at me sideways. 'I thought you were tired.'

'I am,' I said, 'but—'

'But nothing.' He wrapped some cling film over a plate of leftover sandwiches and slid it into the fridge. 'If you're tired, you don't have to come.'

'But he's my guest.'

'That doesn't mean you have to run around after him.'

'I'm not, I just...'

'Want to please him?'

'You make me sound like a nineteen-fifties housewife.'

'It's not good for him to get what he wants all the time.'

'Now you're making him sound like a spoilt little boy.'

'He is, in some ways.'

'Why are *you* going, then?'

'Because…' Craig's shoulders dropped. 'Force of habit, I suppose.' He fiddled with his watchstrap. 'We go back a long way and I… I feel responsible for him.'

'Because of the show?'

'I guess, and because his family have been good to me.'

'Well, maybe it doesn't do him any good, you always being there for him,' I said, stung by Craig's assessment of me as a sappy people-pleaser. 'Maybe he needs to stand on his own two feet, find out what he really wants, without you always being there to pick him up and dust him down.' I'd got my teacher-head on and couldn't seem to stop. 'Perhaps if you hadn't agreed to film this one-off show he'd have brought someone else – someone who wouldn't pander to him so much.'

'Like you were doing this morning?'

Just when I'd been beginning to like Craig (a bit) he went and ruined it. 'I wasn't pandering, it was a moment of—'

'Insanity?'

I glared. 'I told you, I didn't respond,' I said, a quaver in my voice. 'Maybe you're just seeing what you want to see.'

'I didn't want to see that,' he shot back. 'I've seen it all before anyway.'

'Bully for you.' I swiped some crumbs off the worktop. 'I'm sorry to be a disappointment.'

He briefly closed his eyes. 'Look, all I was trying to say is, you don't owe him anything.'

'I know *that*. I have free will. I'm not an imbecile.'

He gave a humourless laugh, as if he doubted it. 'I hope you're not actually hoping to become his girlfriend, because I can promise you that won't happen.'

'Psychic, are you?'

'No. I just know him very well.'

'Sounds like you're secretly in love with him.' It was the most childish thing I'd ever said, and I could hardly blame him for not responding. 'Anyway, maybe you don't know him as well as you think you do.'

'You've known him for five minutes.'

'An outsider can be more objective.'

'Was kissing him objective?'

'So now we're back to that.' I shook my head. 'If I didn't know better, I'd say you were jealous.' Maddeningly, he didn't comment. 'Have you ever been in love, Craig?'

'Oh, so now you're in love with Ollie?'

'No, of course not, I—'

'Good, because he's in love with Tattie,' he said wearily, as if he'd tired of the subject. 'He'll be trying to make her jealous.'

'How, when she's goodness knows where, doing whatever she's doing?' I said, aware that wasn't the argument I should be having, and that he hadn't answered my question about being in love. 'Unless he told her about it... but even so, nothing actually happened between us—'

'He spoke to her?' Craig's brow wrinkled.

'She called him while you were out.'

'Shit,' he muttered, rubbing a hand round his jaw. 'How did he seem, afterwards?'

'I don't know, he didn't mention it,' I said. 'He fell asleep.'

Before I could say anything else, Ollie reappeared, hair brushed back and shiny, wearing the skinny trousers and leather coat he'd discarded earlier. 'Ready?' He scanned my appearance. 'You're coming like that?'

I looked at Craig out of the corner of my eye. His expression was benign, as if we'd been discussing the weather. 'I'm not coming,' I said. Even if I'd wanted to, there was no way I could go after everything

Craig had said. 'I think I'll work on my novel for a bit and then turn in.' *Turn in*? It was something my gran would have said.

'Oh, Lilliput.' Ollie pouted his bottom lip, but I had the sense he wasn't too distressed. No doubt he was anticipating all the ladies he could charm. 'I was relying on you to show us the Devon nightlife.'

'Dorset,' Craig and I said together. He caught my eye and I looked away.

'Same thing,' said Ollie. He slapped Craig's shoulder, seeming oblivious to any tension in the air. 'Put your decent trousers on and lead the way, my man.'

'They're in the car.' With a barely detectable sigh, Craig rooted in his pocket for his keys. 'Shall I bring some logs in?' he said to me.

'No, thanks.' My voice was stiff. 'I can manage.'

'Do you have a spare key?'

'I'll leave the door on the latch. Just remember to drop it when you come in.'

'We'll be as quiet as mice,' said Ollie, compounding the feeling that I'd morphed into my grandmother by dropping a kiss on my cheek and squeezing my shoulder. 'Ciao, lovely Lily.'

Once they'd gone, I slumped against the sink and released a sigh.

The air seemed to settle as I ate a couple of leftover sandwiches and one of Doris's sausage rolls. They were delicious.

Determined not to dwell on my conversation with Craig, I opened the wine and poured myself a glass, then drew the curtains in the living room and set the tree lights to static. All that flashing was giving me a headache. *The Muppets* had finished and *Home Alone* was starting as I slipped outside to fetch some logs from the shed.

The night was cold and still and a full moon had risen high in the sky. Along the street, Christmas lights flashed and twinkled and a few sightseers wandered past, exclaiming at the displays. In the distance, I could hear the pure voices of some carol-singers throwing their hearts into 'We Three Kings of Orient Are', and felt both Christmassy and sad. It had been Dad's favourite carol. Whenever he'd had a few drinks on Christmas Day he would launch into song, and my grandparents would join in, while Chris and I squirmed with embarrassment and Mum went gooey-eyed.

As I came out of the shed, laden with logs, I noticed a female figure in the upstairs window of the Lamberts', silhouetted by a soft, pink light in the room behind her. It didn't look like Sheelagh, unless her hair had grown in the last few hours. It was long, tumbling around her shoulders, and as she reached up to close the curtains I saw she was wearing a silky, purple camisole.

Barry's lover! He must have invited her over while Sheelagh was at her sister's.

I watched the shadow move away, swishing her hair back, and told myself it was none of my business. Or Doris's, for that matter.

I felt sorry for Sheelagh, though. Hopefully, she wouldn't come home early and catch them in the act. The thought of Barry in bed with a woman – any woman – wasn't exactly pleasant, and I hurried inside and busied myself getting the fire going.

Once it was blazing, I ran upstairs and brought down the bag containing the few Christmas gifts I'd bought before leaving London, along with some sparkly wrapping paper, sticky tape and scissors. It would be nice to pop some presents under the tree, even if there weren't many. There was a book about cocktail making for Chris (I'd guessed it was only a matter of time before he was serving them at his café); a scarf for Mum, patterned with shuttlecocks – she and Dad used to play badminton; and a pair of silver sea-horse earrings for Erin, because I knew she'd like them.

Previously, I'd have bought something for the Secret Santa lucky dip at school, competing with my colleagues to see who could buy the silliest gift for less than ten pounds. Last year, I'd received a pair of wind-up racing grannies, which had gone down a storm, but I'd left them in my desk drawer when I resigned.

Turning my mind away from the past, as I wrapped the presents, I wondered whether it would look bad if there wasn't a gift for Ollie and Craig beneath the tree. I ended up shoving the parcels back in the bag when I'd finished, and then into my wardrobe.

I brought my laptop downstairs and plumped myself on the sofa with my wine, wondering where Ollie and Craig had ended up. Trying not to think of them surrounded by giggling, wide-eyed girls, I opened my 'novel' document and swiftly typed: *Jessica entered the nightclub and felt her body throb to the music. No one would know there was a body in the trunk of her car.*

I sipped some more wine, feeling my shoulders relax. I thought about calling Mum, to ask why she kept ringing Doris, but remembered she'd be onstage.

'Break a leg', I texted her. *'Not literally xx'*

I jumped when my phone rang in my hand.

'Hi, Erin.'

'You bloody snogged him!'

'What?' I sat up, my laptop sliding to the floor. 'How did you know? And I didn't!'

'Look online,' she said. 'You're famous.'

Chapter 22

I *wasn't* famous. But there was a photo of Ollie and me on *The Shipley Examiner*'s website; the one where he'd dropped his lips to mine.

The headline read PLAYER COMES OUT TO PLAY and I skimmed the words underneath:

> Former *Players*'s bad boy, Ollie Matheson, is in Shipley to turn on the Christmas tree lights on 13th December, and to judge the Maple Hill lights display. Ollie – who was booted off *Players* last season – arrived early to immerse himself in local life with local resident, Lindsay Anderson... [*I was glad Chris Weatherby had got my name wrong, but shouldn't he have checked his facts?*] ... who invited Matheson to stay at her home and is showing him the sights. One sight he's clearly enjoying is Lindsay herself, who seems to have won his heart. [*More fake news.*] So, folks, be at the square or be square [*!*] this Friday for festive fun and frolics, and to meet *Players*'s most infamous player.

I studied the image again. 'Is my backside really that wide?'

'That's all you've got to say?' Erin's voice rose. 'You're *kissing* him!'

'He was kissing *me*, actually, and the photo's misleading,' I said. 'It was just a friendly peck.'

My upturned face was barely visible, but in my parka and 'boyfriend' jeans (they were going in the bin) I looked to be a decade older than

Ollie and punching above my weight. My hair stuck out at one side and his eyes were fixed elsewhere, as if checking the reaction of onlookers.

'Why were you looking on their website?' I said, going hot as I recalled the other almost-kiss that Erin knew nothing about.

'I was checking to see if his visit had been reported.' Her voice sounded disjointed, as if she was pacing around. 'It would be bad for his ego if no one turned up to watch him switch on the lights.'

'Turning the lights on is a yearly event,' I pointed out. 'Celebrity or no celebrity, people will be there.'

'I thought his visit was supposed to be low-key,' Erin persisted. 'What's he doing kissing you in front of a crowd?'

Ollie's stay had hardly been low-key so far. I wondered whether to mention the visit he'd organised from fans, and that he'd insulted my neighbours, and that Tattie had called him, but Erin would probably give him a roasting, and then he'd be annoyed that I'd told her. He might even decide to leave and, while I suspected my neighbours wouldn't exactly be heartbroken, I was still hoping to turn things around.

'It was a spur of the moment thing, after a few people recognised him in the high street,' I said. 'And then that reporter turned up.'

'Handy,' said Erin. 'There was supposed to be a paragraph about his visit, and a mention on the local news, not the equivalent of a spread in *heat* magazine.'

'Someone must have tipped off the paper.' *Ollie, probably.*

'They're implying you're his new girlfriend.' Erin was working herself up again. 'I thought you said you weren't going along with that bullshit.'

'I'm not.' I rubbed my hairline, feeling another headache brewing, my gaze dropping to the Comments section.

What a slut, letting him stay at her house.

Wonder what else he's turning on??

Waste of tax-payers money, him switching the lights on.

I was tempted to reply that Ollie was doing it for nothing – apart from exposure – but knew engaging with trolls was a bad idea.

I'd turn on the lights for nothing and give her one.

Ollie Matheson's a posh twat.

Bet he's got a tiny willy.

She's obviously a gold-digger. Ollie, you can have me!!

Shaken, I slammed my laptop shut.

'Lily!'

I realised Erin had asked me something. 'I said, why the fuck did you let him kiss you?'

'He took me by surprise.'

'He had his arm around you, for god's sake.'

'It's just a stupid picture.' I was starting to feel hounded. 'No one will care in a week. Isn't that what you say when one of your stars gets caught in a compromising situation?'

'Don't use my words against me.' Erin sounded equally rattled. 'You'd better put him on.'

'Sorry?'

'I'd like to speak to him.'

'He's not here.'

'What?'

'He wanted to go dancing.' Put baldly, it sounded ridiculous. 'I don't know where.'

'And you let him go?' she snapped.

'I could hardly stop him,' I snapped back. 'Craig's gone, too.'

'Footage of him smooching doe-eyed fans in a dingy nightclub is hardly going to endear him to the public. *Jesus*!'

'Not all nightclubs outside London are dingy.'

'How do you know, have you been to any?'

'Have you?'

She hesitated. 'No.'

'Well, then. And Craig hasn't taken his camera.'

'Oh.' Her annoyance seemed to subside. 'Look, I just… I thought he was supposed to be lying low, living like an ordinary person.' She emphasised *ordinary*. 'Why didn't you talk him out of going?'

'For heck's sake, Erin, make your mind up. First, I shouldn't get too close, now I'm supposed to be controlling his every move.' I felt on the verge of tears. 'You're starting to sound like you care a bit too much.'

She sucked in a breath, as if I'd hit a nerve. 'I want his career to get back on track, but not at your expense,' she said, uncertainly. Erin never sounded uncertain. Even when The Actor had left her, she was unequivocal in her summing up that he was a bastard who didn't deserve her.

'That's not what you were going to say.' I waited. 'What's going on?' I felt the weight of her silence. 'Erin?'

In a rush she said, 'I kissed him too, OK? A couple of times, ages ago, before he started seeing Tattie Granger. It was stupid and I regret it, but I can handle myself and I'm not sure you… I'm worried you'll start thinking you might have a future with him.'

My mouth was hanging open. '*You* kissed Ollie Matheson?'

'I know,' she wailed. 'I still can't believe it.'

'Why didn't you tell me?'

'Why do you think? I was embarrassed,' she said. 'When he first called the agency, looking for representation, I had no idea that when I met him he'd be so…'

'Good-looking?'

'Exactly!'

'Oh my god, Erin!' I swallowed some wine, trying to get my head round it. 'You were Ollied, too!'

She groaned. 'Don't remind me.'

'And all this time, you never said a word.'

'I've been trying to forget it.'

'Did he want to take things further?'

'Of course he did,' she said. 'But only because it's what he expects. Luckily, I came to my senses.'

'Not your type?'

'Do you need to ask? I could never be one of "those girls".'

'How did he take it?'

'He kept asking if I was sure I wouldn't change my mind, in that gentlemanly way he has. He tried to win me over for a bit, then he started seeing Tattie and lost interest. It's not like he's short of options.' She sounded a bit gloomy, probably at being reminded that she'd been briefly taken in by him. Maybe she wasn't as immune to showbiz types as she made out.

I was quiet for a moment, letting her words settle in. 'Was kissing Ollie a reaction to… you know?' I meant The Actor leaving.

'Oh god, no.' It was said with such conviction, I believed her. 'I fancied the pants off him, pure and simple. Like I told you he's…'

'Very persuasive.'

'Exactly.'

'Not that ours was a proper kiss.'

'I'm glad to hear it,' she said. 'Maybe he hypnotises women, like those vampires in *True Blood*.'

The funny side hit and we were suddenly helpless with laughter.

'You called him a tosser,' I said, between unladylike snorts.

'He is.' Her runaway giggle made me laugh even more. 'A handsome, trumpet-playing tosser with amazing hair and abs.'

'He does have amazing hair,' I whimpered. 'How does he get it so shiny?'

'I think it's gold-plated,' she yelped.

'Or he washes it in Windowlene.'

'Or uses a special serum made of unicorn milk.'

I felt a bit bad for laughing behind his back. 'Poor Ollie,' I said, wiping my eyes, recalling my first impression of him as a fairy-tale prince. 'He probably thinks a kiss is enough to make any woman fall for him.'

'Probably because they do. At least in the television world.'

'Maybe that's why he'd like an "ordinary" girlfriend.'

'But not you,' said Erin, sobering up.

'Or you.'

'Never.' It came out a bit strangled, probably from laughing, but I sensed she felt a bit guilty too.

'It's hard not to like him, though,' I said, pouring myself some more wine.

'I know.'

She broke the little silence that fell by asking, 'How come you're home alone?'

I didn't want to tell her about my conversation with Craig. 'I fancied getting on with my novel,' I said.

'How's that going?' Like Mum, Erin had initially expressed doubt about my new venture, before declaring that teaching's loss would be the reading public's gain.

'Slowly,' I admitted. 'I haven't settled on a genre yet.'

'Well, you've plenty of material there. And you've heard enough stories from me to fire your imagination.'

'True.'

'In fact, I'm having dinner with a potential new client tonight. She's an ex-mob wife, so she'll have a few tales to tell.'

'Better stay on her good side,' I said.

Once she'd rung off, after extracting a promise that I'd keep her updated with Ollie's movements, I picked up my laptop and looked at what I'd written, but my thoughts leapt and crackled like the flames in the grate and kept circling back to Ollie.

It wasn't that I'd nurtured any illusions about him falling for me. This wasn't *Maid in Manhattan* – I was no J-Lo – but I couldn't help wondering what it was about Tattie Granger that had captured his heart. Maybe he just wanted what he couldn't have, now that Tattie had dumped him. I had the feeling that women didn't finish with Ollie Matheson very often.

A yawn escaped. The heat from the fire was making me drowsy and I couldn't concentrate on writing.

After checking the fire was safe, I finished my wine, switched off the tree lights, and made my way upstairs, where I paused outside the spare room. Spotting the contents of Ollie's holdall all over the floor, I tiptoed over to tidy up. There wasn't much apart from his designer clothes, a few pairs of Snugz, and a monogrammed wash bag of classy grooming products – just a chewing-gum wrapper, and a receipt for a meal for two at Chiltern Firehouse that had cost £296. *How much had they eaten?*

Hoping Ollie wouldn't think I'd been snooping, I went to draw the curtains, pausing as a movement next door caught my eye. A woman came into the garden, banging a cat bowl with a fork, presumably to entice Marmite in for his supper. In the pool of light from the open door was the woman I'd seen through Barry's window, her vivid red hair falling forward and a towelling robe hugging her considerable rump.

How could she be so blasé? Anyone could spot her – if they happened to be having a nosy out of their bedroom window – but maybe that was the idea. Perhaps she was hoping Sheelagh would find out she'd been there, and order Barry to leave, and then she could have him to herself.

As if my thoughts had beamed down to her, she shuffled backwards into the house with her head down – an odd movement, reminiscent of a Japanese geisha.

So, she *did* care about being spotted.

As the garden was plunged into darkness, I spotted Marmite posed on the fence post, silhouetted by the moon, like a witch's cat in a storybook. If only he'd bring some good luck, instead of emitting unfriendly vibes whenever he looked my way.

Finally, I got into bed and after fretting for a while about Craig and Ollie, I slipped into a deep sleep and dreamt they were doing the Argentine tango, while Doris pelted them with muffins.

Chapter 23

I woke suddenly, another dream fresh in my mind, involving loud voices, a shout, and the sound of a bolt sliding back. It must have been Ollie and Craig coming home, their return filtering into my subconscious.

I felt instantly alert, as though I'd been rebooted overnight, and glanced at my phone.

It was just after eight and the cottage was silent, a faint strip of light visible through a gap in the curtains.

I threw off the duvet and slipped out of bed, pushing my feet into my slippers. The door to the spare room was shut and I tiptoed to the bathroom like a cartoon burglar, even though Ollie seemed capable of sleeping through a police raid.

I decided not to have a shower until everyone was awake and, as I crept downstairs, I told myself I was being considerate of my guests, rather than pandering to Ollie, as Craig would have me believe.

It was dark in the living room, but I could just make out the shape of him on the sofa, one arm flung out, which seemed to be his default sleeping position. Embarrassed to be looking when he was at his most vulnerable, I moved into the kitchen and quietly closed the door. I switched on the kettle, wincing when it started to boil. I hadn't realised bubbling water could sound so deafening.

After making some tea, I took the plate of leftover sandwiches from the fridge and ate a couple, chewing quickly, in case Ollie came down and caught me.

I shook my head at myself. What did it matter if he caught me eating cheese sandwiches for breakfast, or a mince pie for that matter? It was nearly Christmas, after all. I could always start eating kale in the New Year.

I ate two mince pies, then one of Doris's Viennese whirls – the lemon curd element was surprisingly successful – and when I'd finished, I opened the back door for some fresh air, and did a few stretches to offset my carbohydrate intake. The air was bracing and the sky still held a trace of night, the moon just visible above the roof next door.

There was the rattling of a door opening and Barry's voice called, 'Marmite! Come and get your breakfast, before Mummy comes home.'

Mummy? It wasn't something I'd have imagined him saying. His voice sounded softer – almost *loving*. He was obviously feeling affectionate after a night of passion with his mistress. I felt another surge of pity for Sheelagh.

Unless she knows about it.

Maybe they had an open marriage and she wasn't visiting her sister at all, but off with her lover, too.

Shivering now, and not keen on Barry catching me in my Dalmatian-patterned pyjamas, I shut the door. As I turned I spotted Craig's camera and headphones on the worktop. After checking it was silent in the next room, I padded over and lifted the camera like a weight. Craig had been right; it wasn't heavy, despite its sturdy build and sizeable lens. I raised it to my shoulder, like I'd seen him do, and swung it around, pausing on the fridge.

'So, what do you make of your new contents?' I asked, in my best newsreader voice.

It didn't respond.

After checking the buttons on the side, I figured out 'rewind' and 'play' and decided to check that Craig had deleted the footage of me answering the door half-nude, and of Ollie and me almost-kissing. He might have forgotten. Or decided to leave it in and use it as part of the show. After all, he'd made notes about interviewing the neighbours, which he hadn't seen fit to share, so who knew what else he was planning?

The camera felt weightier now I'd been wielding it, so I took it across to the table and sat down. After a bit of fiddling the viewfinder sprang to life, images moving at triple speed like a clip from *The Benny Hill Show*, which my grandfather had loved.

I jabbed some more buttons until the images slowed and I recognised the elderly couple from yesterday, their lips moving soundlessly. Pressing pause, I got up and grabbed Craig's headphones, jamming them to one ear, while I wound the footage forward.

Doris appeared and I pressed pause, the frame freezing on a close-up of her holding the photo of a golden-haired baby, which I'd glimpsed in her lounge. Craig must have 'interviewed' her yesterday, while I'd assumed he was out running.

Heart racing, I pressed play.

'…my granddaughter, Erica,' Doris was saying, her chin proudly lifted. 'I only wish my Roger had been alive to meet her. He'd have loved being a granddad, almost as much as he loved being an officer of the law and looking after his garden, though he was always a bit regimental with the flowers, planting them in straight lines as though they were on parade.' Her eyes were hazy with memories. 'I must say, since he's gone, my borders have had a new lease of life, though that doesn't mean for one second that I'm glad he's dead...' I stopped it, even though I was riveted, and fast-forwarded the footage until Doris was replaced by her neighbour, Jane, her hair a frizzy explosion around a checked scarf.

'...our marriage was on the rocks until that holiday.' Her eyes sparkled through her glasses, which slowly slipped to the end of her nose. 'Now that our boy, Calum, is moving in with his girlfriend, we're thinking of turning his room into a red room, only I'm not keen on red, so it'll be pink and we're not really into pain, so it'll be more fluffy handcuffs and scarves than riding crops and ropes.' With horrified fascination, I realised she was referring to *Fifty Shades*. 'Dennis said it was like breaking in a horse, rather than pleasing his wife...' I quickly rewound, marvelling that she could talk so freely about her sex life.

Craig clearly had a way of drawing people out – like the elderly couple the day before – by asking a pointed question then remaining silent while they talked, probably revealing more than they'd intended.

I could see how it would make a compelling TV series, provided the participants didn't mind their innermost thoughts being laid bare. *Ordinary Lives* was a better title than *Behind Closed Doors* and I wondered whether to suggest it.

Glancing up to check Craig hadn't crept in, I rewound to the beginning of the recording. There were no bare boobs and no Ollie and me in a compromising pose, and even as I puffed out a breath of relief, I realised I'd known deep down that Craig wouldn't have lied.

I wound through the footage again as something else niggled at me. Ollie wasn't featured at all. Not in a single frame. Craig hadn't been joking when he'd said he wasn't getting anything worth filming. But then, during the rare moments that Ollie behaved naturally, the camera hadn't been rolling. Like that first morning in my bedroom,

Ollie sitting in a chair in the dark, watching a stranger sleep. OK, it wasn't exactly normal, but his manner and attitude after I'd woken had seemed more real than any of his behaviour since.

Scrolling back, I spotted my own face and pressed pause, freezing the frame mid-word, so my mouth was oddly twisted as if I'd swallowed a wasp.

Cringing, I pressed play. I normally hated the sound of my recorded voice, which was higher and more girly than it was in my head, but for once I sounded like me… but better.

Maybe it was the camera's superior quality. Or perhaps it was what I was saying.

I even used to play schools at home with my brother, until he got fed up with his little sister bossing him around.

I wasn't wearing make-up, but my skin looked clear and my shorter, choppier hair framed my face quite nicely. *Oh, and my dad was a teacher. That probably had something to do with it.*

I was looking straight at the lens, my face so full of emotion suddenly that tears swam to my eyes.

I quickly rewound. *A good teacher can make a real difference,* Craig was saying, his voice low-pitched and steady. *I still remember Mr Bradley, in year seven, telling the class that if we found a career we loved, we'd never work a day in our lives.*

The camera was fixed on my face, just as his gaze had been, and my expression gave me a jolt. It was as if he'd delivered a complex riddle and I was about to reveal the answer.

The sound of curtains being pulled back made me twitch with fright.

I turned off the camera and hastily replaced it, stumbling against the counter. My foot had gone numb from sitting on it and I hobbled back to the table and sat down to massage my toes.

Craig came in, rubbing his eyes, his hair standing up at the back.

''Morning!' It came out too loudly and he staggered backwards, bashing his shoulder on the door frame.

'Lily! Christ!' He did a double take. 'I didn't see you there.'

'Sorry,' I said.

'I thought you'd be asleep.'

'Why?'

He drew his head back. 'Er, because it was so quiet?'

'Oh, right.' I gave a nervous laugh, guilt coursing through me. *What if he'd caught me looking through his film?* 'Would you like some tea?' I said. 'I was just about to make some.'

He glanced around, one hand on his hip, the other flattening his hair. He was wearing his running gear again and I wondered whether he slept in it. 'Looks like you've had breakfast already.'

'Yes, I was... hungry.' I noticed the trail of crumbs I'd left and the uncovered plate of sandwiches on the table. 'How was your night out?'

At the same time, he said, 'Listen, I'm sorry about last night.'

'What?'

He looked at me, surprisingly clear-eyed. 'You didn't hear?'

'Hear what?'

His teeth grazed the skin beneath his lower lip, and I fleetingly wondered whether his beard felt as soft as it looked. I'd never been keen on beards, but his was close-cut and suited him. 'Ollie got a bit... boisterous,' he said, as if wishing he hadn't mentioned it. 'The club we found wasn't really...' He scrunched up his face. 'It wasn't exactly Raffles, if you get my drift.'

I did. Raffles, a private members' club on London's King's Road, had welcomed royalty and rock stars for years. I doubted there was anywhere equivalent in Shipley. 'Wasn't that the point?'

Craig crossed the kitchen in bare feet and switched on the kettle. Despite my offer to make tea, I couldn't seem to move. 'You might have thought so, from the brief for the show,' he said, taking two mugs from the cupboard. 'But, sadly, no.'

'Ah.' I drew my feet up and wrapped my arms around my knees. 'So, what happened?'

'Too much drinking's what happened,' said Craig. 'He decided to take his umbrella in, for a start—'

'Umbrella?'

'His statement umbrella.' He shot me a look. 'You really haven't seen the show?'

'Ollie has a statement umbrella?' Somehow, I wasn't surprised. 'I bet that went down well.'

'About as well as you'd expect, considering there was a football crowd in.' I winced. 'They thought it was quite funny actually, but then a bunch of students came over and one of them puked on his shoe.'

'Ugh.'

'The barmaid mopped up the mess and recognised Ollie, and started telling him how he was everything she hated in a bloke.'

'Oh cripes.'

'He tried to lighten things up by saying he was a feminist and that set the students off.' I could imagine the scene. 'There was a heated debate that ended with one of them taking a swing at Ollie with his satchel.'

'Oh dear.'

'Ollie opened his umbrella and started wielding it like a shield, or a sword, and the manager came out and threatened to call the police.'

'Yikes.'

Craig brought over two steaming mugs and sat opposite me. We were silent for a moment while he ate half a sandwich.

'These are good,' he said, reaching for the other half.

'Cheese and pickle.'

He nodded. 'Can't beat the simple flavours.'

'So, what happened next?'

'We left and found a pub and I let Ollie drink too much—'

'Let him?'

He shrugged. 'I normally keep tabs on his drinking, because when he's had too much he starts re-enacting scenes from his favourite films and things can get a bit messy.'

'Uh-oh.' I felt like I was at the cinema myself, watching a film unfolding in my head.

'His favourite's *Titanic* and he tried doing the bit where Jack and Rose are on the bow of the boat and he spreads out Rose's arms so it looks like she's flying?'

I nodded, holding my breath.

'Well, he started manhandling this woman at the bar and she threw her drink over him.'

'*Noooo*!'

Craig gave a solemn nod. 'When he explained, she just looked at him as though he was crazy and told him to sling his hook.'

'It could have been worse,' I said. 'He could have tried to re-enact the nude drawing part and asked her to take off her clothes.'

Craig almost choked on his tea. 'I think she'd have given him a right hook,' he spluttered.

I liked hearing him laugh, and the way it transformed his expression. He wasn't Ollie-handsome, but his face had interesting angles and his mouth was nice – soft and wide – which I hadn't noticed before. 'Going out wasn't his best idea,' I said, taking a sip of tea. 'It's probably all over Twitter.'

'I daren't even look.' Craig rubbed his eyebrow. 'When we got back, he started doing his Robert De Niro impression from *Taxi Driver*, staggering around shouting, "You talkin' to me?" in this aggressive voice. Someone across the road leaned out of her window and told him to go back to where he'd come from and he said, 'What, my mother's womb?'

It was such an accurate impression of Ollie, a giggle popped out. 'I heard voices, but I thought I was dreaming,' I said.

'At least we didn't disturb you, coming in.'

'Did you have to put him to bed?'

'He crashed on the sofa. I slept in the armchair, mostly.'

'But…' I glanced upwards. 'He's in bed now, right?'

Craig looked at me over his mug. 'He's gone to visit your mother.'

'*What*?' I stood up.

'I thought you knew,' he said. 'Didn't she invite him to direct a play she's in?'

'Yes, but…' I remembered the sound of a bolt sliding back. It must have been Ollie leaving as I woke up. 'I didn't think she meant *today*.'

'Apparently, there's a matinee this afternoon.'

'When did he decide this?'

'He woke up around seven, right as rain – he never gets hangovers – and said he was going into London.'

I crossed to the window, feeling jittery. 'Is he safe to drive?'

'He's taking a train.' I saw the car was still parked outside. 'He got a cab to the station.'

I spun round. 'Why didn't he tell me he was going?'

Craig's forehead contracted. 'He probably would have, if you'd been up.'

'But…'

'It's nothing personal. He tends to act on the spur of the moment, in case you hadn't noticed.' Craig's voice was dry.

'But he's supposed to be *here*.' I pointed at the floor, as though he should be lying at my slippered feet.

'He will be, later.'

My thoughts felt scrambled. It might have been nice to go with him to see Mum, but Ollie was meant to be staying in Shipley. 'What about filming and sightseeing?' I glared at Craig as though it was all his fault. 'We could have gone to Lulworth Cove and had a picnic, or some fish and chips. I know it's cold, but you'd have got some lovely shots, and Ollie could have visited some of the neighbours he upset, to apologise.'

'He's already said he was sorry if he offended anyone.'

'Not like he meant it, though.'

'How do you know he didn't mean it?' Craig was frowning. 'If he says he's sorry, he generally is. He can't help it if people are still offended.'

'But isn't the whole point that he's trying to turn his image around, to offset all the bad press? If…' I was about to say, *If you'd been filming, the public could have judged for themselves*, but then he'd know I knew he hadn't been filming Ollie.

Craig drained his tea and stood up. 'As long as he does what you booked him for, which is turn on the tree lights and judge the displays, isn't that all that matters?'

'But, the show…'

'The show won't happen.' Craig's voice was calm. 'If he wanted it to, he wouldn't be behaving the same way he always does when there's a camera on him.'

'Why are you even here, then?'

'I was hoping he'd figure out what it is he really wants to do with his future and that it wouldn't involve a return to reality television.'

I glared at him. 'So, you knew all along there wouldn't be a show?'

'Not entirely.' Craig sounded a bit fed up now. 'I think his intentions were good, and getting away from his usual crowd seemed like a great idea, but as soon as he suggested turning up early to surprise you, I suspected it wouldn't work. He's just not used to this kind of normality.'

I made a snorting sound. 'I thought you were his *friend*.'

'I am,' he said, crossing his arms. 'That's why… Look, I'm trying to let him figure things out without his family or anyone else interfering. Don't worry, I'll make sure he's here to turn on those bloody Christmas tree lights tomorrow.'

'I'm not worried.' I was breathing too fast. 'How come he didn't ask you to go with him to London?'

'He did,' said Craig, taking his mug to the sink. 'I said no.'

'Why?'

'Because I thought about what you said, when I accused you of pandering to him.' He glanced at me over his shoulder. 'I suppose I realised that's what I do, too.'

I stared at him. 'How do you know he won't go and find his friends, or that he isn't planning to meet Tattie?' Her name felt wrong in my mouth, like a bitter olive. 'You know that she called him.'

'Maybe he will,' he said, rinsing his fingers under the tap and drying them on a sheet of kitchen roll. 'I'm sure she's got plenty to say, if she hasn't already said it.'

I couldn't work out his tone or what he meant.

'But I don't think he will,' he said. 'If there's one thing Ollie is, it's honest. If he said he's seeing your mum, that's what he'll be doing.'

'And if he doesn't come back?'

'If he doesn't, I'll go and fetch him, OK?'

I deflated. 'Fine.'

'Sure you can live without him for a few hours?'

I picked up the dishtowel and threw it at him.

He caught it and pretended to mop his brow. 'Well, that was intense,' he said. 'Why don't we go for a run, as we've got a few hours off?'

'What?'

'Do you want to come for a run with me?' He spoke with exaggerated patience, as though I was slow on the uptake. 'It's great for releasing stress.'

As he said it, I felt the ache of tension in my muscles and knew I wouldn't be able to settle to writing or anything else, for wondering what Ollie was doing, and whether he'd be back. We didn't have a contract, but I'd promised Shipley that Ollie Matheson would be turning on the tree lights, and a portion of them might be angry if he didn't.

'He'll be back,' said Craig, as if he'd read my mind. 'Are you coming?'

'I suppose so.' Aware of his eyes on my pyjamas, I said, 'Don't worry, I'll get changed first.'

'You should probably leave those,' he said, nodding at my chest.

My boobs? I looked down and heat rushed to my head.

I still had his headphones slung round my neck.

Chapter 24

I'd hoped the beach might be empty, but we immediately ran into a dark-haired couple walking a muscular dog, and I recognised the woman as one of the neighbours who'd told Ollie 'his sort' weren't welcome.

'Our Brian was awake the rest of the night after your *visitor* woke him up.' Her voice was ripe with disapproval.

I glanced at her husband, who was trying to control the dog as it strained on its lead. 'I'm sorry,' I said to him, jogging on the spot.

'I'm talking about *Brian*.' The woman pointed at the hound, her expression darkening. 'He's a rescue dog and Celia Appleton told us to keep him calm, but how can we do that when there's rioting on the streets?'

'Hardly rioting,' I panted. I stopped jogging, grateful for a reprieve, even if the woman looked murderous. My lungs already felt on fire and we'd only run from the car, parked by the harbour. 'But it won't happen again,' I said, watching Craig back up when he realised I wasn't beside him.

'I should hope not.' The woman was shorter and skinnier than me, but had a ferocious air not dissimilar to the dog's. 'And we don't want someone like him passing judgement,' she continued. 'What does he know about Christmas lights?'

'What do any of us know?' I kept my voice buoyant, while wishing a wave would sweep in and knock her off her feet. 'He'll be fair, don't you worry.'

'Not after I told him off last night, he won't.' She jutted her jaw at me, while her husband, throwing me a rueful smile, allowed himself to be dragged away by Brian. 'You should never have invited him to stay with you, it's… unethical.'

'Unethical?'

'He's meant to be impartial, but how can he be now he's met us? He's bound to have formed opinions.'

She had a valid point. 'Emotions won't come into it,' I assured her, with more conviction than I felt. 'He'll make a decision based solely on which display he thinks is the best.'

'But isn't it subjective?' She dug her hands in the pockets of her navy fleece. 'I mean, one person's *best* is another's *worst.*'

Flaming Nora. 'Surely the same could be said of any judge.'

'Exactly!' Her face lit up with triumph. 'That's always been my point.'

'What has?' I willed Craig to intervene but he was a little way off, doing lunges, though I had the sense he was listening.

'We shouldn't be judged at all,' she said, shaking a strand of black hair from her eyes. 'The lights are there for everyone to enjoy. It shouldn't be a competition, or if it is, *everyone* should win.'

I'd heard similar comments about school sports days, which is why all the children were now given a star and told they were winners, even when they came last.

But these people aren't children.

'It's just a bit of fun,' I said, copying Craig by rotating my shoulders. I should have warmed up before setting off, but I'd been so distracted at being caught with his headphones, which I'd blushingly said I'd been 'trying on' because I needed a new set, that when he'd asked if I was an experienced runner, I'd said yes. 'Being competitive has all sorts of benefits.'

'Such as?' She looked at me sceptically, seemingly unbothered that her husband was being yanked along the shoreline by a bounding Brian.

'Well, it can encourage innovation and creativity, and make people more goal-orientated, and it teaches us that losing is part of life.' OK, so it was a speech more geared to schoolchildren, but it still felt salient.

'It leads to arguments, falling out, feeling pressured, and some people thinking they're better than everyone else.'

One nil to grumpy neighbour. 'The first rule of competition: in order to win, you have to want it more!' It was a quote from *Desperate Housewives* and intended to make her smile – if she was capable of such a feat.

Her skinny eyebrows knotted together. 'You're encouraging that kind of behaviour? Triumphing over others?'

Oh jeepers. 'No, not at all,' I said, doing some star jumps to work off some nervous energy. I should have worn a sports bra, but didn't possess one. 'Don't you think you're taking it a bit too seriously?'

'Lambert and Flannery are the ones who take it seriously.' She made them sound like a comedy double-act. 'It used to be fun, when everyone had a chance of winning.'

'You don't have to take part,' I risked pointing out.

'Of course we don't take part.'

I paused, mid-lunge. 'You don't?'

She rolled her eyes, as if I was the stupidest person she'd ever met. 'Don't you listen? I just told you, I don't believe in competing.'

As I struggled for an effective response, Craig finally came over. 'Hello, Annabel,' he said, in a friendly fashion.

'Oh, hi!' Her face melted into a smile that took years off her and revealed a pair of dimples. 'I didn't realise it was you.' She looked at me as though I'd tricked her. 'I'm sorry about having a go at you last night,' she said to him, sounding like a different person. 'But Ollie whatsisname was making *such* a racket, and like I was telling you the other day, I don't believe that celebrities should be allowed to get away with doing whatever they want.' *Was she actually batting her lashes*? 'I wouldn't really have called the police, I just wanted to scare him.'

'Glad to hear it,' he said, in a warm voice. 'We'll soon be out of your hair but in the meantime, I hope you'll bear with us.'

She dimpled at him again. 'I think we can manage that.' She gave a low, provocative laugh. 'Seeing as you asked so nicely.'

Craig dipped his head, modestly. 'You'll be there tomorrow, to see Ollie switch on the tree lights?'

'Be at the square or be square.' She giggled – *giggled*! – and gave him a double thumbs-up. 'You can count us in.'

I sensed her staring after us as we jogged away, before a piercing whistle brought Brian bounding up the beach, the red-faced husband still clinging to its leash.

'Well, aren't you the dark horse?' It came out breathy, due to the jogging, and sounded as though I was flirting.

Craig's feet were pounding the beach in a steady rhythm, whereas mine felt encased in concrete. My trainers were full of sand. 'She's OK,' he said, mildly.

'Maybe with you.'

'I can't help having the knack.' He flashed a grin to show he was joking – even though clearly it was true. He fixed his eyes back on the pier, where we'd agreed to run to, before circling back along the parade to the car. 'Everyone has a story.'

'What's yours?' I said. It seemed easier to ask out there, surrounded by the elements, though I was having trouble hearing above the roar of my heartbeat.

'You probably know some of it, if you've talked to Ollie,' he said.

'Not much.'

I thought he wasn't going to answer and took the opportunity to try to steady my breathing. Then he said, 'My father worked as a gardener for the Mathesons for most of his adult life and my mother died when I was sixteen.'

I threw him a look. 'I'm so sorry.'

'It's fine. I mean, it's not fine, but I'd had a good childhood up until then, and the Mathesons were very good to us. And I had Ollie, who always treated me like a brother.'

'Are you an only child?'

He nodded. 'You?'

'Older brother and we had a happy childhood, too.'

'When did you lose your dad?'

I stumbled and almost fell. Craig shot out a hand, but I recovered and kept on going. 'Nearly three years ago,' I said. 'I miss his voice.' *His warm, comforting hug of a voice.* He'd loved to talk on the phone. After I'd moved out, I'd call home every Sunday evening and we'd put the world to rights. My friends had teased me about it, but I'd looked forward to those conversations. 'We came here on holiday a few times.'

I remembered how, once, Dad carried me along this stretch of beach on his shoulders, because I didn't want to get sand in my new sneakers, and, when I went to splash in the sea, he put them in a bag to protect them.

'I still miss my mother,' Craig said, elbows slicing the air. 'It gets easier, but never really goes away.'

'I suppose it's not love if it doesn't hurt.' Chris once said that, in a rare moment of brotherly insight. It hadn't helped much, at the time.

'Exactly,' said Craig.

I waited for the usual punch of grief, and when it came a sob escaped but I didn't stop running. I kept going, even though my chest was burning and I knew my cheeks were beetroot. I picked up speed until I was in synch with Craig and, as the pier grew closer, the salty wind tossed my hair and dried the tears on my cheeks.

When we arrived I felt like I'd burst through a barrier. 'WOO-HOO!' I cried, waving my arms in the air. Then I doubled over, hands on my knees, and swallowed some sick.

'Not bad.' Craig was barely out of breath as he smiled down at me. His hair was windswept too, but he radiated health and well-being, whereas I felt like my organs had shifted.

'I'll race you to the end,' he challenged. 'Last one there puts the kettle on when we get back.'

I launched after him but a stitch took hold and I hobbled most of the way, clutching my sides.

'You're not an experienced runner, are you?' he said, when I finally reached him. He was leaning against the rail at the end of the pier, eyes bright with amusement.

I rested my chin on the cold metal beside him and let my arms dangle over. 'How can you tell?'

'You were clutching your boobs at one point and your feet were sort of turned in.'

'Sand in my shoes.' I waited for my supercharged heartbeat to slow down.

'You might want to get some proper running shoes.' His arm nudged mine. 'And maybe warm up, next time.'

I straightened, elated to realise that I wanted to go running again. *I liked running*! 'I will,' I said, stretching my arms out and doing a couple of side bends. 'See, I'm cooling down as well.'

'It's cold enough already.' He tipped his eyes and scanned the cloud-laden sky. 'Maybe more snow's on the way.'

'I'm really hot,' I said and grew even warmer when his eyes widened slightly. He bit his lip as though holding back a response, and I realised I was grinning.

We walked back to the car, arms occasionally brushing, and he told me how his dad had been paralysed from the waist down in a car accident, four years earlier. 'Drunk driver,' he said, mouth tightening around the words.

'Is that why you went back to *Players* instead of finishing your Everest show?'

He shot me a look. 'I needed a regular income to help pay for his care, plus I needed to be around.'

'Couldn't Ollie help out?' It was a stupid question, and I regretted it instantly, but Craig didn't seem offended.

'He's offered, more than once, and so have his family, but it's my responsibility,' he said. 'And we're managing just fine.'

I felt a flare of admiration and back in the car was emboldened to ask, 'What would you do if you weren't a cameraman on a reality show?'

He looked through the windscreen as he fastened his seat belt, as if seeing the future unfold in the car park. 'I'd move to a small seaside town, meet a beautiful girl and settle down. Then I'd pitch a brilliant idea to television companies and let them fight it out.'

Heat rushed to my cheeks. 'Don't you have a beautiful girlfriend at home, wherever that is?'

'I've been living with my father, not far from the Mathesons' place in Hertfordshire.'

'The shack?' I said, remembering what Ollie had called it.

Craig gave a small smile as he started the car and turned the heating up. 'Let's just say our place is a lot less grand, but it's home.'

'You have someone to care for your father?'

He nodded. 'When necessary. I had the house adapted and our neighbour, Linda, is more than happy to pop in and keep him company. I think they might have got married if he hadn't had his accident, but he wouldn't hear of it afterwards. Said he didn't want to be a burden.'

I was silent for a moment as his words sank in. Dad had gone quickly, with no suffering. Wasn't that better than lingering in pain?

'He gets plenty of enjoyment out of life, believe me,' Craig said, reading me like a book. 'And to answer the rest of your question, there's no girlfriend.' My face zinged with warmth. 'Let's just say my lifestyle hasn't lent itself to having a serious relationship.'

'You must have met a lot of women on *Players*.'

His jaw clenched. 'Not really my type, and none I'd want a serious relationship with.'

'Is the show you mentioned pitching, *Ordinary Lives*?'

He slid me a look. 'Do you mean, *Behind Closed Doors*?'

Whoops. 'I saw your notes,' I confessed, a flush enveloping my whole body.

'I know.' He gave a slow smile. 'You didn't put my notepad away properly.'

'I'm sorry. I'm not used to spying.'

'It's OK.' Craig's smile broadened. 'But I like my title better.'

'Well, keep mine in mind, in case the producers want to change it.'

He held my gaze, and my heart danced against my ribcage. 'The night you arrived,' I said, pushing the words out with difficulty. 'When I answered the door, did… did you see… anything?'

He nodded gravely. 'A very surprised, and possibly tipsy, woman in a face mask, clutching a cat with a chicken part in its mouth.'

I tried to read his expression, which didn't waver. 'And… and that's all?'

His face softened. 'No,' he admitted. 'I could have throttled Ollie for catching you out like that, but I promise I didn't look… for too long.'

I gave an embarrassed laugh and covered my face. 'Oh god.'

His fingers gently circled my wrist and drew my hand away. 'I wasn't filming, anyway,' he said. 'There was never any footage to delete.'

When we arrived back at the cottage I noticed Barry's Explorer had gone, but Sheelagh's car was parked on the drive.

Craig was looking, too. 'I might try them again this afternoon,' he said.

'The Lamberts?' I was glad we weren't pretending he was only here to film Ollie, though I wasn't sure how Ollie would feel when he found out. 'I'm surprised you haven't tried them already.'

'I have,' he said, as we got out of the car. 'But he wasn't keen. I think Sheelagh might talk to me if he's not there.'

'There's something funny going on,' I said, once we were inside, and I told him about seeing the woman at the Lamberts' house the night before.

Craig looked thoughtful. 'Maybe Sheelagh will open up.'

'Is that ethical?' I sounded like Annabel now. 'I mean, probing people's feelings for entertainment?'

'A show like this could help other people going through something similar. It's not just entertainment.' He faced me squarely, his gaze earnest. 'But I would never let anything go out if it didn't feel right, or I thought it might hurt someone.'

'That's OK, then,' I said. 'I'll call you Saint Craig, shall I?'

He swatted my arm. 'Go and put the kettle on.'

'I was hoping you'd forgotten,' I said, glancing at my watch. 'Besides, there's somewhere I have to be.'

Chapter 25

I parked outside Nightingale Primary School, and called Mum.

'Is Ollie there?'

'Oh, Lily, he is!' She sounded overexcited. 'I couldn't believe it when he showed up at the shop this morning.'

'He came to the shop?'

'I told him about it the other evening, and he remembered what it was called.'

'I suppose Crafty Bitches is a memorable name.'

'Annie nearly fainted when I introduced them,' she rushed on. 'She used to prefer Sebastian Dooley-McBride, because he plays the flute and so does she. But Annie says he got too big for his boots, when he got that Hollywood offer, so she switched her allegiance to Ollie.'

'Let me guess; she thought he got a raw deal being kicked off the show?'

'We all did!' Mum sounded surprised that I might think otherwise. 'It was obvious that Tattie Granger was playing him off against someone else. Somebody not on the show, according to Annie. She records it and watches it on Catch-Up TV as well. She said Tattie looked right at the camera with a knowing smile when Ollie was dragged away.'

'Oh, well, that's settled it,' I said. 'He definitely got a raw deal.'

Mum tutted. 'Anyway, he's going to be f*aaab*ulous at directing, I can just tell. He got the gist right away and everyone's *so* excited he's here they're falling over themselves to please him.'

'Even Stuart?' I said.

'Oh, yes.' Mum's voice softened. 'Bless him, he'd like to move into directing… Ollie promised to give him some tips about how to communicate a vision for the show and managed to win him over.'

In the background, Ollie called, 'Let's run that scene again with more feeling, yah?' and I felt an exasperated pang that he hadn't established the same rapport with my neighbours.

'Are you and Stuart seeing each other?' I hadn't meant to say it, and from Mum's sharp intake of breath it was the last thing she'd expected me to ask.

'We've been out for dinner a couple of times and he… he makes me smile,' she said, after a lengthy pause. 'But he'll never replace your father, Lily. Nobody can.'

Hearing the layer of anxiety in her voice prompted me to say, 'It's OK, Mum, you're entitled to have a boyfriend.' I didn't mean it. The thought of her laughing with a man who wasn't my dad; of someone like Stuart being in our house, sitting at the table where Dad helped me with my homework, and built Lego spaceships with Chris, made me want to howl. But I knew it might happen one day and I had to prepare myself.

'I think you'd like him,' she said tentatively, and I made myself murmur something appropriate. From the little I'd seen of them at the theatre, Stuart seemed respectful of Mum, but I hadn't been looking at him as potential boyfriend material.

'Would you like a word with Ollie?' she said, clearly keen to switch topics. 'I thought his cameraman might have come. Isn't he supposed to be filming?'

'It's fine, Mum,' I said. 'As long as you send Ollie back to switch on the lights tomorrow.'

'I will,' she said. 'Though I suspect Annie's planning to drug him and take him home with her.'

'Now, that would make an interesting show.'

'Are you ready, Fiona?' It was Ollie again, and I tried to picture him in director mode, but could only imagine him jousting with an umbrella after what Craig had told me about his performance at the nightclub.

'Sounds like I'm wanted,' Mum said, with the playful giggle that Ollie seemed to inspire in older women. 'I'd better run.'

After she'd hung up, I went straight online and tapped in *Ollie Matheson, punch-up*. It felt a bit disloyal, somehow, but I wanted to see it for myself. See whether he'd really had a 'raw deal', or if his fans were deluded.

While the clip loaded, I checked my face in the car mirror. It looked like it used to when I was teaching: hair held back off my cheeks with a couple of clips, and a light layer of make-up to stop me looking shiny. Beneath my knee-length coat I'd teamed a black skirt and fitted blue sweater with heeled boots, and had immediately felt more purposeful.

'You're dressed to impress,' Craig had observed from the kitchen table, as I'd collected my handbag. He'd been fiddling with his camera and picking at leftover food.

I'd gone a bit hot. 'Too much?'

'Yes, if you're going swimming.'

'Hilarious. I'm visiting the local primary school, actually.'

Something had flashed through his eyes and was gone before I could pin it down. 'You're applying for a job?'

'No,' I said, crossly. 'I promised someone I'd ask the head teacher for… something.'

His eyes had narrowed, but he merely nodded and said, 'Good luck,' before turning back to his camera. I could have sworn he was stroking its shiny casing as I left.

The *Players* clip loaded and I lifted my phone and peered at the screen. The setting, predictably, was a bar, studded with velvet armchairs. Gleaming chandeliers hung above the heads of expensively clad toffs with shiny hair, all holding champagne flutes.

Ollie – who looked somehow smaller onscreen – was jabbing the air in front of a man with particularly glossy black waves, and a sneer on his hawkish face.

'I know you made a move on her, Cuttlingtonson, you bastard.' Even swearing, Ollie sounded posh. 'You might have got away with cheating at water polo, but you won't get away with this.' The sneering man must be Quincy, the one Sheelagh had professed to be angry with, and it was easy to see why. My fingers itched to slap his supercilious face.

Quincy gave a big, bold laugh, and swept a hand through his hair. 'You need to get out of my grill, dude. I wouldn't touch your trollop with someone else's bargepole.'

The woman at his side – presumably Tattie Granger – gave a dramatic gasp. 'Thanks a lot, Quince,' she snapped. She tossed her poker-straight, honey-blonde hair and turned Bambi-like eyes on Ollie. 'Are you going to let him talk about me like that?'

'If it wasn't you, who was it?' Ollie demanded. He looked more fed up than angry, which clearly wasn't the effect that Tattie was looking for.

'He called me a *trollop*,' she reminded him, as if Ollie hadn't been standing there at the time. 'Are you going to let him get away with it?'

'Ollie hasn't the gonads to throw a punch,' drawled Quincy, picking an olive from a bowl on the bar and popping it in his mouth. 'He doesn't know what his little-girl fists are for.'

'Oh, I think he does,' said Tattie, goadingly. 'And he knows how to defend a lady.' It was as if the twenty-first century hadn't happened. 'Don't you, Ollie?' she pushed, when Ollie didn't move, and it was almost with a sense of resignation – as if he didn't have a choice – that Ollie drew back his arm and aimed his fist at Quincy's jaw.

As Quincy's head snapped back, several cast members swooped in, and, among the ensuing scuffle, Tattie looked straight down the camera, a smile playing around her glistening lips, before the screen went blank.

Mum had been right. And Sheelagh. Ollie *had* had a raw deal. Anyone with eyes could see Tattie had engineered things – though I wasn't sure I understood why.

After slipping my phone in my bag, I stepped out of the car, wondering – too late – whether I should have called the school first. Jill Edwards was bound to be busy with the end of term approaching, but it was lunchtime and she might have a few minutes to spare.

Childish shouts and laughter reached me, as I spotted the sign for Nightingale Primary School. As I approached the green-painted railings surrounding the playground, I saw a group of well-wrapped-up five-year-olds with a smiling teaching assistant, clustered around a dark-haired man. Drawing closer, I noticed he was holding a little brown dog and was showing the children that it only had three legs.

'It's making me very sad,' said a little girl with spirals of brown hair and a duffel coat slipping off her shoulders.

'You don't need to be sad,' the man said, crouching down so the girl could stroke the dog's silky ears. 'Hovis doesn't know that he should have four legs.'

'Does it hurt where his leg should go?' One of the boys shoved the girl aside and briskly patted the dog's nose.

'No, it doesn't hurt him at all.' The man smiled at me as I passed. He was wearing medical scrubs and I guessed he must be a vet. 'He was born this way.'

'My great-granddaddy's only got one leg,' the little boy was saying as I crossed the frosty playground to the low, red-brick building. Inside, I paused to breathe in the heady, familiar scent of plasticine, poster paints and fairy cakes, instantly transported back to Kingswood Primary and my class of five-year-olds, their expectant faces turned up like flowers to the sun.

Feeling oddly choked, I opened my eyes to see Jill Edwards striding towards me, her rather stern expression converting into a smile.

'Miss Ambrose,' she said, arm outstretched. 'Sheelagh said you might drop by.'

As we shook hands, I saw Sheelagh over her shoulder, ushering a small, crying girl along the corridor in my direction, probably to see the nurse. She didn't look at me as she hurried by, and I was surprised by how much it hurt.

I'm not responsible for what comes out of Ollie Matheson's mouth, I wanted to say. *And, by the way, your husband's having an affair.*

But Ollie *was* my guest and he'd insulted Barry in my home. And even if she suspected her husband was cheating on her, and she was secretly in love with Ollie, she was bound to side with Barry.

'Come through to the office,' said Jill Edwards, leading the way, her low-heeled shoes clicking against the parquet floor.

The corridor walls were decorated for Christmas, covered in paintings of big-bellied Santas and oddly-shaped reindeer, and draped with tinsel and handmade paper chains. I peered into one of the classrooms as we passed, and felt a pang when I saw a teacher sitting behind a tidy desk, biting into an apple as she marked some work. That could have been me, a year ago. Only I'd have been eating cake.

'That's Miss Anderson,' Jill said, breaking her stride. 'She's the one who's leaving us.'

Miss Anderson looked up with an apologetic smile. 'Sorry,' she said, hunching her shoulders around her ears, and I guessed it wasn't the first time she'd been moved to apologise. Good teachers were like gold dust and I knew she'd be missed. *Had I been missed?* None of my ex-colleagues had been in touch after I'd left, which had hurt almost more than my break-up with Max. 'I've told you, Jill, you have to blame Jason for landing a job in New Zealand and dragging me there with him.'

'Oh, I do,' said Jill Edwards. I had a feeling she wasn't joking. 'I'm so glad you changed your mind,' she said when we were seated in her office, which was decorated in soothing shades of sage and cream. 'About the interview,' she added, when I looked at her blankly.

'Oh, no… I haven't,' I said, unfastening my coat as I tried to get comfy in a chair designed for bottoms smaller than mine. 'That's not why I'm here.'

Opposite, Jill folded her hands on the desk, her face lapsing back into sternness. 'Why are you here then, Miss Ambrose?'

'Please, call me Lily.'

She continued to stare, like an interrogator waiting for her witness to crumble.

'I, er, it's… I came to ask a favour, actually.'

'A favour?' Her eyes shrank. 'I'm not in the habit of doing favours for strangers, Miss Ambrose.'

Oh heck. 'It's not for me,' I said hastily. 'And it's more of a suggestion, really.'

She looked resigned. 'Go on.'

'I know you must be busy with Christmas at the moment…'

'We certainly are.' She tilted her head. 'Do you know, we suggested that on the last afternoon of term the children bring in some board games and most of them had no idea what we were talking about?'

'Oh, I know!' I said. 'We tried that last year and one of the mums came in and complained that her daughter had asked her what "nomopoly" was, as if I'd been teaching them swear words.'

'I suppose we have to move with the times.' Jill was watching me closely.

'Or introduce them to some of the old games,' I said, leaning forward. 'I took in my old Monopoly set and some Cluedo, and some simple packs of playing cards, and taught them Snap and Go Fish, which is great for learning numbers. They loved it.'

'What a clever idea,' said Jill. 'Sounds like you were a real asset.'

I sat back. I knew what she was trying to do. 'Anyway,' I said, picking my bag off the floor and putting it down again. 'Would it be possible for Alfie Blake to give a talk to the children about his job? In the New Year, obviously.'

'Alfie Blake?' Jill straightened. 'He used to attend this school. Recently started working for his father.'

'He showed me round Seaview Cottage,' I said, and told her about him being picked on in Cooper's Café and how I thought it might instil some pride in him to talk about what he did for a living, as well as inspire the children. I got a bit carried away and started talking about how bullying could lead to low self-esteem and how we had to take care of our young people, as though Alfie was my younger brother, rather than an estate agent I'd met twice.

Jill held up a hand as I started talking about suicide rates being high among the young, male population.

'I'll give him a call,' she said.

I paused, mid-sentence. 'You will?'

'We often have parents and locals come in to talk about their jobs.' She nodded at the window and through the slatted blind I saw the children lining up to pat the three-legged dog. 'Tom Hudson comes in now and then and I have to say he's by far our most popular visitor. Half the children want to be vets at the moment.' To my relief she was smiling again. 'Carrie, his fiancée, has been in too, but accountancy's a harder sell.'

'The same could be said of being an estate agent,' I pointed out. 'But Alfie's enthusiastic. At least, he was the first time we met. I think part of him believes real life is waiting to happen somewhere else.'

'Like London?'

'Exactly.'

Jill searched my face. 'Why did you give up teaching?'

Too startled to think up a lie, I ended up telling her the truth. 'I felt like I'd let everyone down,' I said, hands twisting in my lap, when I'd finished. 'How could those children respect me, after what I'd done?'

'Sounds to me like you believed the husband was single and on the verge of a divorce, so you can't really blame yourself.'

'Yes, but parent–teacher relationships were discouraged at the school, so—'

'I understand that angle,' Jill interrupted. 'But I still believe he was the one in the wrong and not you.'

My head whipped up. 'But if it had happened here, with one of your teachers...'

'I'd have acted with discretion,' Jill said. 'The situation wouldn't have been ideal, but it would be unlikely to happen again.'

'It wasn't that simple,' I said miserably.

'Look, I can see why this man's wife turning up to confront you might have reflected badly on the school, but I still say you weren't at fault.' Jill's words came at me like a breath of air, blowing away my feeble attempts to protest. 'If you'd ridden it out, I'm sure things would have blown over.'

'You don't know the head teacher there.' I felt a bit wobbly and light-headed. This wasn't a conversation I'd intended having. Ever. 'She made it clear I wasn't welcome to stay.'

'Probably jealous.' Jill's blue eyes glinted. 'Good-looking single dad? I bet she fancied him herself.'

The thought of the head teacher fancying Max made me want to giggle – until I remembered how often she used to call him in to talk about his daughter. She'd always refresh her lipstick, and on one occasion had offered to go to Max's house to discuss Harriet's behaviour there.

'I couldn't cope with the gossip,' I admitted.

'School mums can be the worst.' Jill sat back. 'You just have to rise above it. As long as you're doing the best job you can—'

'But they'd lost respect for me, and who knows what they told their children about me at home?'

Jill inclined her head. 'OK, I can see your point,' she said. 'But that doesn't mean you should give up teaching altogether.'

'I fancied a change.' I tried to hold her gaze.

'Sounds to me like you're punishing yourself.'

Now she sounded like a counsellor. 'I've always wanted to be a writer,' I said, shifting in my chair. It wasn't true and I had a feeling she knew it. 'Story time was always my favourite part of the day.'

I waited for her to point out that reading stories and writing them were two very different things – like Mum had, when I was defending my decision to her – but instead she said, 'Year One has a free session after lunch.' She flicked her wrist and glanced at her watch. 'Why don't you come and read them a story?'

I unwedged myself from the chair in record time. 'I'd love to,' I said, taking my coat off and hooking it over my arm, anticipation flowing through me.

'Jolly good.'

It probably wasn't wise to remind myself what I was missing, but as I trotted after Jill I realised I was looking forward to it more than anything since coming to Shipley.

Chapter 26

After Jill had introduced me and explained why I was there, the children insisted they didn't want a story from any of the books on the shelf.

'You have to make one up, Mith Ambroth,' lisped a tiny girl with solemn eyes. 'Thath the ruleth.'

'Ah, yes,' said Jill, her gaze sweeping over the eager faces in front of us. 'We freestyle sometimes. Anything goes, it doesn't have to be Christmassy.'

'Right,' I said, sitting on the wooden chair that Jill had pulled from behind the desk, after sending Miss Anderson to the staffroom with an order to eat a slice of Christmas cake. 'In that case, I have a story I think you're going to like.'

It felt so natural to be in the slightly overheated classroom, surrounded by colourful wall charts and tables scattered with exercise books, pencils and crayons, hearing the sniffles and whispers of thirty-odd children, that I didn't even mind that Jill was obviously testing me.

'It's a story about a little black cat with magical powers,' I said, loving how their eyes grew saucer-like and they instantly stopped shuffling.

Dropping my voice to a hush, I launched into a tale about 'Sabrina' (a friendly, female version of Marmite), who moved from family to family, transforming their lives by bringing them good luck – as long as they deserved it – and when I'd finished, to a touching round of applause, I finally knew what my book was going to be about.

After rashly promising Jill that I'd let her know by the end of the following day whether I wanted to take the job, I drove back to the cottage as fast as the speed limit would allow and crashed through the door to fire up my laptop.

Without even taking my coat off, I sat on the sofa and wrote an outline for *Sabrina the Magic Cat* and a couple of scenarios I could flesh out later. It made total sense that I should write a children's book, and I couldn't understand why I hadn't thought of it before.

I wanted to tell Craig, but realised – when I paused to stretch my fingers – that I appeared to be alone. I got up and checked each room, in case he was playing hide-and-seek, but obviously he'd got better things to do than wait for me to come back and start rambling about a witchy cat.

The book wouldn't take long to write, even if I made it into a series. Maybe I should carry on with my adult novel as well. I sat back down listlessly and opened my previous document, then shut it again, my head too full of Sabrina. I'd need an illustrator to come up with some drawings. My artistic skills didn't stretch beyond basic sketching, and although I pulled out my notepad and attempted some more cat doodles, they weren't very realistic. More like whiskery rats.

Perhaps someone local could help. One of my neighbours might know somebody. I went outside, wondering whether Craig was in one of the other houses, talking to a housewife or husband, prising out their secrets...

I felt self-conscious standing outside the cottage, so turning up my collar I walked a little way down the hill, peering discreetly into windows as I passed. Most had Christmas trees blocking my view, but Mr Flannery was standing outside Number 2, scratching his head as he stared at his roof, where a rosy-cheeked Santa appeared to be wedged in the chimney.

I tried to back up, but Mr Flannery turned and spotted me. 'Still think Lambert will win?' he said, with what might have passed for a grin if his eyes had been smiling. Instead he looked slightly unhinged. 'I've definitely got the edge, wouldn't you say?'

'W-e-e-e-ll…' I checked out his display, which was as much of a mishmash as Barry's. Although the house was heavily decorated there wasn't a coherent theme – just endless, multi-coloured flashing lights attached to the roof and walls, while every available space in front of it was stuffed with festive inflatables, grinning and gurning and – in some cases – twisting their heads from side to side in a spooky, robotic fashion. The only impressive feature was a giant globe, the snowflakes inside twirling down on an alpine scene, but the effect was spoilt by a cable leading to an ugly generator humming like an angry hornet. 'It's… nice,' I said carefully. Clearly Mr Flannery had no eye for design, yet he looked as proud of his lights as if he'd hand-crafted every single one himself.

'Nice?'

'Obviously, I have to be impartial,' I said quickly. 'I can't show any favouritism.'

'So, you *do* prefer mine.' Triumph written on his face, he folded his arms across his bobbly jumper and leaned back for a panoramic view of his display. 'When I win, I'm hoping to entice a lady away for the weekend.'

He was obviously dying to tell me who. 'Any lady in particular?'

'Ruby Dashwood,' he said, a zealous light in his eyes. 'She runs the flower stall, in the square. I've had my eye on her for quite a while.'

Poor Ruby. 'Well, good luck,' I said, leaving him to his contemplation and walking back the way I'd come, in time to see Sheelagh with her finger pressed on my doorbell.

'Oh, there you are,' she said, turning, and I was relieved to see her expression was friendlier than it had been at the school. 'I've just finished,' she said, glancing over at her house and back at me. 'Could I have a quick word?'

'Of course,' I said. 'Would you like to come in for a cup of tea?'

'No, no, here will be fine.' As she moved away from the doorstep, my heart sank. I had a feeling that without Sheelagh's endorsement, none of the neighbours would like me and I didn't know how to get back into her good books. 'Listen, about what Ollie said…' I began, but she held up a hand.

'The man hasn't a clue what he's talking about when it comes to Christmas lights.' She seemed to inflate inside her mustard coat. 'But I'd still… you know.' She widened her eyes, meaningfully. 'He's still *hot*.'

I relaxed a little. 'He's very… hot,' I agreed. 'Are you sure you won't come in?' I was freezing now. Dusk was gathering and I wanted to get the fire going inside.

'I heard you telling a story to the children,' Sheelagh said, suddenly. 'You were good.'

'Thanks.' I felt a flush of pleasure. 'I really enjoyed it.'

'Jill liked you.' Well, that was something. And Sheelagh didn't sound too surprised, so maybe she didn't hate me after all. 'I told her you were very interested in the post.'

'Sheelagh!' I shook my head. 'Why would you say that?'

Her eyebrows rose a couple of centimetres. 'Because you are.'

'Look, I… have to get the dinner on,' I said, even though there was enough leftover food to feed myself for a week, and I had no idea where Craig was, or when (if) Ollie was coming back.

'Did you see anything while I was away?' As the words burst out, her face crumpled like a collapsed tent.

I stiffened. 'Such as?' *Please don't say a woman in nightwear.* 'I saw Marmite,' I said, before Sheelagh could reply. 'He actually gave me my idea for the story I told the children—'

'I know,' she cut in. 'It was pretty obvious it was based on him.'

'Oh.'

'It's just, I think Barry might have —'

The sound of a horn cut her off and we were caught in a beam of headlights as Barry's car swept into their drive, almost bashing Sheelagh's Honda.

'Listen, forget it.' She flapped her hand as she backed away. 'Make sure you let Ollie know that we worked *very* hard on our display and that he must keep an open mind,' she said, extra loudly, so Barry could hear as he clambered out of his car.

I sensed him glaring at me, but thankfully couldn't see him properly in the shadows. 'Let's get these lights switched on,' he called, and Sheelagh sprinted home.

Within seconds, their house and garden were comet-bright, and as the competing houses lit up, as if by some secret signal, I had the feeling I'd moved to a distant planet, where the rules were different and I'd never fit in.

Deflated, I entered the cottage. After shrugging my coat off, I flicked on the light and went into the kitchen, where the sight of Marmite on the windowsill squeezed a scream from my lungs.

'Are you trying to kill me?' The cat must have slipped in when I'd opened the front door, and was now observing me calmly. 'You have to stop doing this.'

He leapt down and, to my amazement, curled around my ankles, purring.

'Cupboard love,' I said, opening the fridge. 'You just want me to feed you.' But I was pleased all the same. I looked at the turbot I'd bought before Ollie and Craig arrived. It seemed wrong to cook it for the cat, but it didn't take long and he sat patiently while it cooled a little. 'See?' I said, placing it on a plate in front of him. 'You only had to ask nicely.'

His look said, *You bore me deeply*, but he ate the fish in delicate bites and I followed him into the living room, where he arched his back and started clawing the rug.

'Make yourself at home, why don't you?'

I switched on the tree lights and drew the curtains, and by the time I'd coaxed the fire into life, he'd curled up and gone to sleep.

I smiled, then wondered if it was weird to be happy that the cat appeared not to hate me any more. Maybe if I fed the neighbours some turbot, it would have the same effect.

I was in the kitchen making a risotto, using leftover fish and some peas, when Craig came in, his face pink with cold and snow melting in his hair.

'It's snowing again!'

'Just started,' he said, grinning when I punched the air. 'You like the snow, then?'

'Love it,' I said. 'If it settles, I'll be out there building a snowman.'

He put down his camera. 'It would be nice to see one that isn't inflatable,' he said. 'Something smells good.' He came over and peered into the pan, sniffing appreciatively. 'I'm starving.'

'It won't be long,' I said, wishing I hadn't started a risotto that needed constant stirring. 'You've time for a shower, if you want one.'

'What are you trying to tell me?' He sniffed his armpit, though all I could smell was fresh air and a hint of cinnamon.

'It was just a suggestion.'

'In that case, I'll take you up on it.' He smiled and a pleasant ripple went through me.

'Have you been bothering the neighbours?' I asked, as he hooked his jacket over the back of a chair.

'I tried the Lamberts, but no one answered.'

I felt a jolt, remembering what Sheelagh had been about to ask me. What would I have told her if Barry hadn't turned up? The truth? She wouldn't have asked if she hadn't wanted to know, but I didn't want to be the one to confirm her worst suspicions. Maybe I should have a quiet word with Barry; tell him Sheelagh suspected something was up.

'…lovely family at Number 9, but the parents have got their hands full with those twins,' Craig was saying, as I tuned back in, and I realised he was talking about the Harassed Couple. 'Bella would like to go back to work but can't bear to leave them, even though Mark is happy to stay at home.' He stopped. 'You OK?'

'I'm good.' I resumed my stirring, deciding it wasn't my place to tell anyone that Barry Lambert was cheating on his wife.

'How did it go at the school?'

'Great,' I said, increasing my stirring to ward off any awkward questions. 'They're a nice bunch.'

There was a short silence, as if he was waiting for more, then he went upstairs, whistling snatches of 'Mistletoe and Wine'.

We ate in front of the fire and I told him about my plans for Sabrina the cat and her magical adventures. He seemed genuinely interested and promised to put me in touch with a friend of his father's, whose daughter illustrated children's books.

'She's really good and especially likes drawing animals.'

Marmite, curled between us, opened his eyes and studied me coolly until I promised I would give him an acknowledgement, which earned a laugh from Craig.

We talked easily for a while, exchanging snippets from our childhoods and university stories, and discovered we had a mutual love of bluegrass music, hated horror films, and could eat a whole tub of cookie dough ice cream in one sitting. Eventually, we were yawning and it seemed natural to suggest turning in.

As I said good night – as comfortably as if we'd been doing it for years – and left him on the sofa, I realised two things: we hadn't talked about Ollie, and I liked Craig being there.

When I opened the front door to let Marmite out, he gave me a knowing look.

'Oh, shut up,' I said.

Chapter 27

A rumble of voices from below woke me from a deep sleep, and I lay in the darkness, smiling at the memory of Craig, dopey-eyed and patting his belly, simulating an 'ice-cream high'.

As Ollie's voice rose, I threw back the duvet and leapt out of bed, almost collapsing as the muscles in my legs seized up.

'Ow, ow, ow, ow,' I chanted, fumbling my dressing gown on and shuffling my feet into my slippers. I was never going running again. Not without warming up, at least.

I hobbled downstairs, panting through the discomfort, and paused on the threshold of the living room.

'What's going on?' I said, blinking in the brightness of the overhead light. Craig was upright on the sofa swaddled in his sleeping bag, looking at Ollie, who was cradling Marmite in front of the fireplace, dressed for a night at the theatre – in Victorian London. Was he wearing a *smoking* jacket?

'Life is what's going on,' Ollie said, a delighted smile spreading over his face when he saw me. He dropped Marmite, who landed on all fours and streaked past me. 'Little Lily, Lilliput, I've had the time of my life,' he sang in a tuneless baritone, crossing the room to where I was gripping the door frame. 'Don't put your daughter on the stage, Mrs Worthington.' He beamed, his eyes almost vanishing. 'Noel Coward,' he elaborated.

'Yes, I know the quote,' I said.

'Anyway, it's nonsense.' He looked from Craig to me, clearly seeking a stronger reaction than tired irritation. 'I want to put everyone's daughter *and* son on the stage, and I want to direct them like they've never been directed before.' His eyes blazed with a passion I suspected many women would like to see directed at them.

'Do you know what time it is?' I wondered how he still managed to look groomed in the middle of the night – apart from a sprinkling of stubble, which lent him a devilish air.

'The time, madam?' He tweaked his cuff and squinted at his watch. 'It's fifteen minutes past two in the morning.'

'I meant, do you realise how late it is?'

The pad of his thumb travelled across his lips as he attempted a thoughtful look. 'I expect it's *very* late,' he said in a ponderous tone. 'Although… it's also *very* early.'

'He's drunk,' Craig said, rubbing his face with both hands. 'I've told him to go to bed, but he wants to go out and look at the Christmas lights.'

'No,' I said, lifting a hand from the door frame. 'You caused enough of a disturbance last night.'

'Are woo cwoss wiv me?' He stuck out his bottom lip and gave me a sad-eyed look.

'Very cwoss. I mean, cross.' I travelled slowly to the armchair, aware Craig's eyes were following me.

'Something aching?' he said.

'Just a bit.' I lowered myself down like a pensioner with brittle bones. 'I probably shouldn't have run so far.'

'You can't be cross,' Ollie cut in. 'Not when I've had such a splendid day.' It struck me afresh how comprehensively he dominated a room and a conversation. Even at this ungodly hour. 'If I say so myself, I was an absolute whiz on the directing front and I loved it.' He gave a little shake of his head, as if he couldn't quite believe it. 'What a troupe! You wouldn't believe they were amateurs. There wasn't a single wobbly-curtain moment and they're all fine actors, especially your mother, Lily. She totally rocked as Letitia Blacklock.' I felt a sweep of pride. I knew Mum was good but it was nice hearing someone else say it. 'The show brought the house down, and I have to say I didn't mind not being in front of the audience.' He lifted his chin. 'In fact, I don't want to be an actor any more. Directing is where my heart is.' He slapped his chest. 'Ow! That hurt.'

Craig and I traded looks.

'I'm pleased for you, really,' Craig said, sounding genuine. 'But maybe we could talk about it in the morning.'

'How come you're so late back?'

'Lily, I'm delighted you asked.' Ollie sat on the arm of the chair, so I had to crane my neck to look at him. 'We went to this café after the matinee called The Greasy Piglet. It's a tradition, apparently.'

I nodded. I'd been there. They did amazing bacon butties.

'We had an absolute wheeze. They're *such* fascinating people.' He sounded awestruck, as though he'd encountered a rare, uncivilised tribe that spoke perfect English. 'Anyway, upshot is, I decided to stay for the evening performance, and then we went for drinkies in the pub next door to the theatre.' He wrinkled his nose. 'Annie, who works in that hilariously named shop with your mother was there and started getting frisky, so after I'd given everyone a bit of a show with the trumpet—'

'You took your trumpet?'

'I always take my trumpet.'

'He always takes his trumpet,' Craig said at the same time, and I noticed the case flung down next to the sofa.

'—I decided it was time to weave my way back to Sibley-by-the-sea, or whatever this place is called…'

'Shipley,' Craig and I murmured.

'…so I got a cab.'

'All the way from London?'

'For a price.' Ollie lurched into my lap, radiating alcohol fumes, and began fiddling with the belt of my dressing gown. 'I might have had a little tipple of whisky in the car,' he said. 'It's a *very* dull journey and the driver wasn't keen on me playing my trumpet. He said it was distracting.'

'I don't blame him.' The weight of him on my legs was unbearable, and I shoved him away. Unprepared, he toppled to the floor, turning the fall into a breakdance move, before reaching for Craig's camera on the sofa (*had he been cuddling it in his sleep?*).

'Hey, why don't you film me and Lily doing the lift from *Dirty Dancing*?' He was on his knees, panning the camera around.

'I can barely move,' I said, raising my legs a centimetre to prove it.

Craig untangled himself from his sleeping bag and yawned into his hands. 'Ollie, I'm shattered.'

'Look at you two.' Ollie swung the camera past our faces. 'It's like the aftermath of a gas explosion and someone's taken you in, but you know you've got to go back to your burnt-out homes in the morning.'

'Great,' I said.

Craig covered his eyes with his palms. 'What we look like is tired.'

'It's a big day tomorrow,' I reminded Ollie. He was fiddling with the buttons on the camera, not really listening. 'Switching on the tree lights?' I added. 'You should get some sleep so you're nice and fresh.'

''M always nice and fresh,' he muttered, staring at the viewfinder. 'Where am I?'

'Sorry?'

'Seaview Cottage, Maple Hill.' Craig spoke with exaggerated patience. 'Maybe we should write it on your hand.'

'No, I mean, where am I?' Ollie waggled the camera. 'On here.'

I looked at Craig, my heartbeat speeding up.

'Let me have it.' He held out his arms, as though waiting to be delivered a baby.

'Where've I gone?' Ollie was hitting the buttons again and squinting at the screen. 'Can't find me.'

'I think it's time for bed,' I said, bracingly. It was too late for a showdown and we needed Ollie in a good mood for the next twenty-four hours.

I attempted to stand up, but Ollie had thrust the camera at Craig and was scrambling onto the sofa beside him. 'C'mon, show me,' he said, putting a brotherly arm around Craig's shoulders. 'Why are you wearing this?' His fingers plucked the material of Craig's running top. 'You need some proper PJs, bro. I can lend you a pair of mine, if you like.' He gave a winsome smile. 'We had a matching pair when we were kids, remember, Craggers? Ma bought them for our birthdays.' He gave me a fuzzy look. 'We both have birthdays in June, would you believe?' He ruffled Craig's hair. 'This little chap could be my twin, if he wasn't a year older.'

It was hardly the best time to be reminiscing about his 'brother from another mother' – not when he was about to discover there was no footage of him and there wouldn't be a 'one-off' show.

Craig was looking a bit queasy, twisting the camera around in his hands, as if unsure what to say.

'I wiped it all by mistake,' I blurted out.

Craig's head whipped up and I widened my eyes, signalling him not to argue. 'But there'll be plenty of opportunities for mingling tomorrow, and lovely things will be happening, so we can… replace it,' I steamed on. 'With something better.'

'Wiped it?' Ollie was looking at me as though I'd spoken in Spanish – although if I had, he would no doubt have understood. '*Wiped* it?'

'I was… messing about and pressed the wrong button.' I looked past him to avoid his slightly bloodshot stare, fixing my gaze on the smooth surface of the wall. 'But it's OK, because it wasn't that good anyway. I mean, it was all… blurry.'

He switched his gaze from me to Craig. '*Wiped* it?' He looked back at me, trying to focus his eyes. 'Only the bits with me in?'

'I… don't know how that happened,' I said, voice wobbling a little. I'd never been good at lying and, even drunk, Ollie could probably tell it didn't make sense. 'I'm so sorry.'

'I've been wiped,' he said to Craig. He sounded bemused, rather than angry, but that might have been the cushioning effect of the alcohol. 'Eliminated,' he added. 'I no longer exist.'

'Ollie, mate…' I could tell from the set of Craig's shoulders he was about to tell him the truth.

'Look at my toes!' I said, kicking off my slippers in an effort to skirt the issue, but Ollie was on his feet looking galvanised.

'We have to get out there this minute and start shooting,' he said, and I had to admire his ability to bounce back from what must have been a catastrophic discovery – that all of his performing had gone unrecorded. 'This is actually good,' he said, combing his hands through his hair as he paced up and down in a whisky haze. 'It'll be more naturalistic,' he said, barely slurring his words. 'You film me walking down the street, like this,' he slipped his fingers in the pockets of his silky jacket and mooched from the door to the fireplace and back. 'I'll be looking at each of the houses in a considering way.' He paused, hand cupping his chin, eyes scanning imaginary Christmas lights in a thoughtful fashion. 'Then, maybe Lily could run after me—'

'I'm running nowhere,' I muttered.

'—and take my hand,' he demonstrated by lifting my palm and linking his fingers through mine, 'and say something like, "Isn't it magical?"' He put on a falsetto voice, mimicking a love-struck expression that almost prompted a giggle. 'And then we could stand for a moment, admiring the Santas, or whatever, before I kiss her.' As he tilted my chin with his finger, I jerked away.

'Why does it have to involve a kiss?' I said, glancing at Craig, who was studying the floor with apparent interest. 'And I thought you'd changed your mind about being an actor.'

Ollie looked as if I'd pinched him. 'I was actually directing just then. I won't be acting.'

'But if you're directing yourself, you're not being natural,' I pointed out. 'You have to let things *unfold*.'

He looked uncomprehending. 'Wouldn't that be awfully boring?'

Craig gave a noisy sigh. He was still wrapped in his sleeping bag like a chrysalis. 'It's all in the editing, mate.' He lifted his head. 'Or at least it would be if we were—'

I cut him off. 'We're not filming in the middle of the night,' I practically shouted.

Ollie jumped. 'Fine.' For a moment, I thought he was actually agreeing, but then he dived for the camera. 'I'll do it myself,' he said, and left with astonishing speed.

A gust of cold air hit my ankles as the front door opened, and by the time Craig had extricated himself from his sleeping bag, Ollie had gone.

'Shit,' Craig muttered through gritted teeth, stuffing his feet in his trainers, and as he hurtled after Ollie, laces flapping, I saw he was wearing black boxers and that his calves were surprisingly muscular – probably from all the running.

'For crying out loud.' Forcing my own legs into action, I tightened the belt of my dressing gown and staggered after them.

Chapter 28

Outside, I gasped.

A layer of snow had settled, cloaking Maple Hill in a soft white blanket and enhancing the twinkle of Christmas lights on the houses. A huge, round moon hung over the rooftops, casting a silvery light, and I wanted to lie in the garden and make a snow angel.

Instead, I followed the footprints through the gate, like Bridget Jones rushing after Mark Darcy – except I wasn't wearing animal-print knickers and a cardigan. I'd stopped to pull on my boots and parka, which was just as well as it was freezing and my face already felt numb.

'So, here we are in the festive season, hours before I switch on the Christmas tree lights in SHIPLEY.' Ollie was in the middle of the road, camera aloft, giving a running commentary. 'I'll also be judging these houses, where the lighting rivals the NASA space station. Forget Blackpool Illuminations and come to SHIPLEY, where no Christmas cliché has been ignored, from whisky-nosed Santa' – he focused on the Lamberts' front garden – 'to Creepy Elf' – he swung the camera to a house a few doors down – 'to Rudolph the wonky reindeer.' As he panned to the roof of Number 10, Craig made a grab for the camera, but Ollie swung it up and out of his reach.

'At least keep your voice down,' Craig said, and even though quietly spoken his words carried on the frigid air.

As lights came on in a couple of bedroom windows, I tried to speed up, boots crunching the powdery snow. Hopefully, I could get Ollie back inside before someone reported him for breaching the peace… again.

'Forget the new runway at Heathrow,' he continued, clearly enjoying himself. 'In future, aeroplanes will land on MARBLE HILL.'

'Maple,' I muttered. Why couldn't he get it right? 'Ollie, will you please stop shouting?' My words seemed amplified and I lowered my voice to a hiss. 'People are sleeping.'

'We can sleep when we're dead!' he shouted. A glowing Rudolph nose from a nearby garden briefly bathed his face red, so he looked like the devil. 'Lily, you're adorable.' He lowered the camera and gave me a playful grin. 'Now, keep walking towards me but try to look as if you're out for a late-night stroll.'

I kept moving forwards, while Craig closed in behind him.

'Maybe don't stare at the camera like that.' Ollie clearly fancied himself as the next Woody Allen. 'And perhaps soften your face a bit. You look like a serial killer.'

'I want to kill *you*, right now.'

He gave a burst of laughter. 'You're hysterical, Lils. I've never met anyone like you.'

'In that case, you need to get out more.'

He pulled the camera back. 'I like this feisty you,' he said, eyes dancing with mischief. 'It's very Scarlett Johansson.'

'Ollie, give the camera to me,' Craig said.

With a look of surprise, Ollie swung round and slipped, and as the camera fell from his grasp, Craig deftly caught it.

'Hey, well done, my man.' Recovering his balance, Ollie slapped Craig on the back. 'Knew those baseball games would come in handy one day.'

'It's not even switched on,' Craig said, checking for damage. His lips looked blue with cold – though it could have been a lighting effect – and his teeth were chattering. He hugged his camera like a much-loved puppy, and the sight of his shins, naked but for a soft coating of darkish hair, made me feel a bit tearful. Or it could have been the cold, stinging my eyes.

'Let's go in,' I said to Ollie, holding my hand out as though trying to coax a deer, but he ducked down and scrunched some snow between his palms.

'Ollie, no!' I backed away as a snowball whizzed through the air and caught me on the shoulder.

'Catch me if you can,' he taunted, crouching like a rugby player waiting to be tackled – if rugby players wore loafers and gold velvet jackets with silky linings.

I brushed snow off my coat. 'Not right now, thanks.' I'd loved a gentle snowball fight with the children at Kingswood Primary and, years earlier, I'd given Chris a black eye with a badly aimed snowball that took him years to live down. But it was almost three o'clock in the morning and more windows were lighting up.

'Coward,' teased Ollie. He tossed another snowball, which I managed to dodge.

'Ollie,' Craig warned, but Ollie's face was bright with daring and the urge to respond was irresistible.

I gathered a handful of snow, compacting it into a sizeable ball, and lobbed it at him before he had chance to react.

It hit him square in the face.

'OUCH!'

He reeled back, one hand cupping his nose, and, to my horror, I saw blood dripping through his fingers.

'Oh, Christ.' Camera swinging in one hand, Craig clutched at his hair with the other. 'He's got sensitive sinuses.'

'Well, how was I to know?' Guilt made me snippy. 'Here.' I fished a tissue out of my pocket, not bothering to check it was clean, and shoved it into Ollie's groping hand. 'He started it,' I said to Craig.

'I know, I wasn't blaming you, I—'

'I can't believe how much that hurt,' said Ollie, tipping his head back and pressing the tissue to his nostrils. 'More than the punch at the book-signing, actually.'

Brilliant. 'I'm really sorry,' I said, hands hovering uselessly. There were vivid red spots of blood in the snow and the sight of them made me feel sick.

I began to shiver as the cold penetrated my coat and nightclothes, and Craig looked on the verge of hypothermia. Only Ollie seemed untroubled by the sub-zero temperature, as if he had warmer blood than the rest of us. 'There are a lot of stars in Shipley,' he said, his head tipped right back as though on a hinge. 'You never really notice them in London. Light pollution, you see.'

'Why don't we go inside and have a hot drink?' I managed, through clattering teeth. I wasn't in the mood for stargazing.

'Now, that sounds like a marvellous idea.'

'It really does,' said Craig, hugging himself awkwardly as he swayed from foot to foot.

'What on earth's going on out here?'

I swung round to see Sheelagh approaching, in her emerald coat and a pair of fleecy ankle boots, looking suspiciously well-turned-out considering the hour – unless she always slept in full make-up.

'Sorry if we disturbed you,' I said, heart sinking when I saw the look of reproach on her face. 'Ollie was just—'

'Oh, my goodness, what's happened to him?' Her hands shot out as he staggered towards her, but it was only because his eyes were still skywards and he couldn't see where he was going.

'I think Lily broke my nose,' he said, the tissue muffling his voice so it sounded like he was crying.

Sheelagh threw me a horrified stare. 'Fighting in the street in the middle of the night is not what we expect from our neighbours,' she said, in the manner of someone who'd been let down by a favourite niece. 'We had such high hopes of you, Lily.'

Craig jumped in. 'Hang on, it was an accident.' He moved between us like a referee. 'It's not like she hit him or anything. Well, only with a snowball.' His lips looked bloodless, and as she clapped eyes on him, Sheelagh's mouth gaped.

'You're not dressed!' she cried. For a moment I thought she was expressing concern that he might get frostbite but, instead, she covered her eyes with her hand. 'Wandering about naked in the middle of the night is hardly socially acceptable behaviour,' she said, though I had a feeling that if Ollie had been in his pants, or even capering about nude, she wouldn't have minded one bit. 'It was a big mistake you inviting them to stay.' She removed her hand and, thanks to the snow, the Christmas lights, and the glaring moon, I couldn't avoid the disappointment in her eyes. 'It's caused nothing but trouble.'

'I agree,' said a voice behind me.

'Me too.'

I swivelled round, my mouth falling open. More neighbours had emerged, some in coats and bobble hats, others wrapped in blankets, and one in a duvet, as though attending some outdoor event.

'This was a quiet, respectable street, until *he* came here.'

'Until *she* came here.'

'Who's she going to invite to stay next? One of them idiots off *The Only Way is Essex*?'

'Maybe it'll be a murderer and we'll all be killed in our beds.' The woman who'd spoken poured steaming liquid from a Thermos into a mug, and I marvelled that she'd had the foresight to prepare refreshments. It was Annabel from the beach, glaring from under the peak of a knitted hat. 'You need to keep your London boyfriend under control,' she said.

London boyfriend? I wanted to say something, but my brain felt as frozen as my fingers.

'We don't want any trouble,' Craig said, smoothing the air in front of us. There was a lot of steam from our combined breaths, and the unusual lighting lent the scene an air of unreality. 'We were just going in, actually.'

'Ooh, I'm not talking about you, my lovely.' Annabel threw him a dimpled smile. 'I'm talking about lover-boy here.'

'Lover-boy?' Ollie's head resumed its normal position, his gaze sweeping over what was possibly his most unreceptive audience to date. '*Lover*-boy?' There were scraps of bloody tissue stuck to his nose and his hair had flopped into an unflattering middle parting. It wasn't his best look. 'I'll have you know, I haven't laid a finger on this lovely lady.' He pulled me to him, causing my heels to slip so I ended up clutching at him for support. 'I can assure you her honour's intact.'

I knew he was trying to defend me but wished he'd be quiet. They were imitating him now, in exaggerated vowels.

'Oh, I *saaaaaaaaaaay*, he hasn't laid a finger on her, milord.'

'Would one like a cucumber sandwich, my lady?'

Gales of laughter followed.

'Hey, come on, that's a bit harsh.' Ollie let go of me and spread his arms like a preacher. 'How would you loike it if oi talked loike you lot?' He lapsed into a hideous Dorset accent. 'Oo-arr, where's me combine 'arvester?' He hooked his thumbs through a pair of imaginary braces and did a horrible jig. 'I'll 'ave me a pint of zider, please, sir.'

'Ollie, don't,' I said, tugging his sleeve, while Craig laid a hand on his shoulder. 'Let's just go inside.'

'Better listen to your girlfriend,' said Annabel, eyes bulging. 'And don't think we'll be turning up to watch you switch on the lights tomorrow – or should I say, later *today* –because we won't.'

'Yeah, you've ruined that for us, so thanks.' It was a skinny youth in a beanie hat, who looked like he might be Annabel's son.

'But what about the competitors?' I glanced round, hoping to see a friendly face or two, but Celia Appleton lived at the top of the hill, and Jane and Dennis – and Doris – near the bottom, and they were probably fast asleep. And I doubted they'd be feeling friendly, once word got around that Ollie Matheson and his 'girlfriend' had fought in the street in the middle of the night and woken half the neighbours. 'They'll have to be there for the prize-giving,' I said.

'Oh, I'm sure we will be,' Sheelagh interjected, glancing towards her house. I was surprised that Barry hadn't emerged to lend his weight to the argument, but guessed his dream of beating Mr Flannery (also notable by his absence) temporarily outweighed his dislike of my visitor, and he was keeping a low profile.

'I'm surprised at you, Sheelagh.' Annabel gave her a filthy look, and I had a horrid vision of a street forever divided into those who'd supported Ollie's visit, because of the competition, and those who blamed him for disrupting their peaceful lives.

I'd probably have to leave, like Isabel Sinclair had, in order for peace to be restored.

'Listen, now you're here, why don't we sing a few Christmas carols?' Amazingly, Ollie was smiling again, seemingly unaware that his blood-stained chin and jacket gave him the look of a recently fed cannibal. 'There's nothing like a sing-song for creating a feeling of harmony.'

'At this time of night?' Disbelieving looks flew around.

'Is he right in the head?'

'He's definitely takin' the piss.'

''TIS THE SEASON TO BE JOLLY, TRA-LA-LA-LA-LAAAA,' Ollie sang, in the style of Pavarotti, and the pin-drop silence that followed was broken by a long, piercing wail, closely followed by another, higher-pitched wail.

'Now, look what you've done,' hissed Annabel. 'You've woken the Desmond twins.'

'Are they Shipley's answer to the Kray twins?' Ollie queried, feigning a worried expression.

'They're babies, you idiot.' Annabel looked like she might spit at him. 'It probably took Bella and Mark hours to get them to sleep.'

We listened to the ghostly sounds emerging from the house where Craig had interviewed the parents just hours earlier.

'Shall I sing a lullaby?' Ollie said.

'Sounds lovely,' Sheelagh whispered, resting a mittened hand on Ollie's arm. 'But now might not be the right time.'

'Ollie,' Craig said tightly. 'Let's go. Now.'

Annabel drained her mug. 'Take your friend's advice,' she said, a frothy moustache of milk on her upper lip. 'Because if you sing so much as a single note I'll set Brian on you, and he'll go straight for your crown jewels.'

'That sounds awfully like a threat.' Ollie seemed genuinely disturbed at the level of resentment radiating towards him. 'Fine,' he said huffily, throwing off Craig's hand. 'I'll let you get back to your beds and do whatever it is you do there.'

'Sleep?' The sarcastic voice came from a figure so thoroughly wrapped in a duvet that only a pair of baleful eyes and a thatch of dark hair were visible. 'Dream?'

Ollie gave Annabel the first properly snooty look I'd seen from him. 'Well, I doubt it'll be anything sexual in your case. I actually feel sorry for *Brian*.' Turning, he walked away, his exit somewhat spoilt by rapid, stumbling steps as his loafers slithered on the freezing snow.

Craig and I looked at each other, and I saw the same resignation on his bone-white face that he probably saw on mine. There was nothing we could do but follow Ollie and, as we did, I pretended not to hear Annabel's parting words, despite them being loud enough to wake the dead.

'Did you hear that? He just accused me of sleeping with my *dog*.'

Chapter 29

It was almost ten when I woke, and I didn't want to get up.

Once we'd returned to the cottage, Ollie – finally sober – had expressed deep remorse at disturbing the neighbours and had wanted to go and apologise, and offer to pay for a spa day for Annabel and Brian. By the time Craig and I talked him out of it (and explained that Brian was a dog, which elicited a shocked, 'So, I basically accused her of bestiality'), it had been nearly four o'clock. Ollie eventually agreed to 'sleep on it' and Craig had dived into his sleeping bag with a fervently muttered, 'Thank Christ.' By the time I'd staggered upstairs, Ollie had washed his bloodied face in the bathroom and was fast asleep, his clothes tossed at the end of the bed, and I'd lain awake shivering for nearly an hour, cursing the day he'd arrived.

Now, I bunched deeper under my duvet and squeezed my eyes shut, but all I could see were the angry, scornful faces of my neighbours.

How was I ever going to win them round? And did I even want to? They had every reason to be annoyed with Ollie, but he hadn't meant any harm. If anything, he'd given them a bit of excitement, and something to dine out on for years. It's not like he deserved an ASBO and, anyway, he'd be gone in a couple of days.

The thought brought a little pang. I could barely remember what I'd been doing before Ollie and Craig arrived. Obviously, it would be nice to get back to writing, especially now I knew what I was doing, but it was going to be quiet without them. Perhaps I should invite my mum or Erin to stay the following weekend.

Poking my hand out, I plucked my phone from the bedside table.

Erin had texted the day before, asking how Ollie was 'behaving' and I hadn't known how to reply, what with him zipping to London to direct Mum's play (she would probably have found him and fired him) and had sent another an hour later, saying, *'he's not there, is he?'* that I hadn't seen. I'd had my phone on silent since visiting the school and there were a few missed calls.

Her penultimate message read: *'If you don't respond, I'm going to assume you've run away with my client, or that you're hiding something'*, and her final one, sent a couple of hours ago, made me sit up. *'I'll see you this afternoon.'*

I tried her number, but it went to voicemail, so I texted: *'Sorry I didn't get back to you, everything's under control, I PROMISE!! X'* before slumping back on my pillow to stare at the ceiling.

I had no one to blame but myself for things going wrong. If I hadn't gone to that stupid meeting in the first place, and tried to ingratiate myself with my neighbours, I might have been watching the tree lights being switched on this afternoon, just like everyone else, and have seen either Barry or Mr Flannery receive the award for best display as a spectator. Perhaps I'd have joined in with the good-natured gossip about who should really have won, and whether Mr Flannery was related to the judge, and one of my neighbours might have invited me round for a mince pie. As it was, I'd be attending the event as Ollie's escort, praying our angry neighbours didn't turn up to pelt him with eggs, or start heckling, which the local reporter would have a field day with. The story would get picked up by the national news, and end up on social media, further ruining Ollie's reputation, meaning he'd never work again, and I would be forever associated with his downfall, which meant Erin would hate me too…

My tumbling thoughts were cut off by a knock on the door, and I pushed back the duvet to see Craig's head. 'Cup of tea?' he enquired.

'Oh.' I sat up, aware of my bed-hair and morning-breath, as he cautiously approached with a mug and set it down on the bedside table. 'Thanks.'

'No problem.' He was dressed in jeans and a sweater and smelt like he'd showered, though I hadn't heard a thing. He looked mysterious in the half-light, his hair flatter than usual, and it struck me that I'd had two strange men in my bedroom in less than a week and they couldn't have been more different.

Craig was already backing out, his gaze cast down as if to preserve my modesty. Perversely, I wanted to detain him.

'Is Ollie up?'

He paused in the doorway. 'I thought it best to let him sleep off last night,' he said, in a low voice. 'He does better when he's properly rested.'

It sounded as if we were discussing our hyperactive child.

'Did you sleep OK in the end?'

'Once I'd warmed up.' There was a smile in his voice. 'I couldn't feel my feet for about an hour.'

'Me neither.'

The exchange felt oddly intimate and, as if he felt it too, he said, 'I'll make some toast,' and left the room.

I sat for a moment, trying to remember whether Max had ever brought me a drink in bed. It had happened once; after we'd slept together for the first time and I'd developed a raging thirst. He brought me some lukewarm water in a coffee cup, because he couldn't find a glass in his tiny, cluttered house.

I sipped my tea, which was just how I liked it, with only a splash of milk, and tried to locate my earlier panic and annoyance, but it had faded. It was impossible to stay mad with Ollie, however infuriating he was.

He didn't emerge until after one, striding into the living room wearing his 'dressed down' outfit of jeans and hooded sweatshirt, and looking like he'd slept for twenty-four hours.

'Where's Craig?' he demanded, dropping into the armchair.

'Gone for a run and to do some filming,' I said. He'd half jokingly asked me to join him for a run after breakfast, but I'd reluctantly declined on account of my legs feeling like they belonged to someone else. He'd advised me to have a long soak in a hot bath and I had, letting my mind drift with the steam, thinking about nothing in particular.

Now, I was welded to the sofa, my slippered feet propped on the coffee table, panic-buying last-minute Christmas gifts on Amazon.

'I dreamt I was giving Barack Obama a lift to the airport,' Ollie said, swinging one leg over the arm of the chair. 'He was telling me that the best way to carve a turkey was to use a spoon and I wanted to tell him that was rubbish, but I couldn't because… well, because he was Barack Obama.'

I looked at him over my laptop. 'Right.'

'He was wearing a really nice tie,' Ollie went on, stroking his hair back. 'Sort of stripy with little lambs on.'

'Are you still talking about the ex-president of the United States?'

'Yah.' He smiled sheepishly. 'I think I owe you an apology for last night,' he said. 'I shouldn't have got drunk in the cab.'

'No,' I agreed. 'You shouldn't have done a lot of things.'

He grimaced. 'It wasn't that bad. Was it?'

'You caused quite the stir.'

'Well, you did give me a nosebleed.'

'I doubt I'll be the last,' I said.

He guffawed. 'They're a bit uptight around here, aren't they?'

'Probably not used to middle-of-the night disturbances,' I said. 'Some of them are quite elderly.'

He sat forward, eyebrows bunched. 'Sounds crazy, but I don't know many old people,' he said. 'My grandparents on both sides died when I was young, and… well, let's just say there weren't any octogenarians on *Players* or in any of the clubs I go to, and although Ma and Pa must be in their sixties, they're not what you'd call *old*.'

'What about when you're doing your appearances?'

'It's mostly younger women and gay men that turn up,' he said. 'Though I must say, some of the mums can be keen, too.'

'I get it,' I said. 'To you, old people are like a different species.'

'I'm a bit scared of them.' His slightly haunted expression made me want to giggle. 'They just say what they think and it's often not very nice, like that Doris Day woman.'

'There are a few oldies at Mum's theatre group,' I said. 'How was that?'

'The older ladies seemed to like me, but the blokes were harder to win over.'

'Ah, the curse of being a lovely, handsome charmer.'

'I'll take that as a compliment,' he said with a grin, before turning serious again. 'Actually, the charm helps a bit when I'm directing, but in a *good* way. I'm not just getting girls to like me, like on *Players*, I'm using it to bring people onside so we can work together. Well, mostly. You always get some swine – it's usually a bloke – who doesn't like being directed, and thinks his vision is better, but the secret is to engender loyalty in your cast and crew, and I really think I can do that.' He formed a pyramid shape with his fingers and nodded sincerely. 'I really do love it.'

I'd never heard him so engaged. 'Then I think you've found your new career path,' I said. 'Congratulations. You'll never have to work another day in your life.'

'What?'

'Oh, nothing,' I said, embarrassed. 'Just something Craig said.'

'Ah, yes.' His eyes lingered on mine a beat too long. 'The wise words his teacher imparted to him when he was seven. Craig, I mean, not the teacher. You couldn't have a seven-year-old teacher, that would be ridiculous.'

I was impressed that Ollie had retained this information. It was proof that he valued Craig's friendship – not that I needed proof. In fact, it was nothing to do with me. I'd never see either of them again, after tomorrow.

'Are you looking forward to the ceremony this afternoon?' I said, breaking the little silence that had fallen.

'I'm not sure, after last night.' He sank back in the armchair, mouth pursed. 'I don't think I'm going to be very well remembered in Shipley.'

'Most of the locals are friendly,' I reminded him. 'Just not the few you've woken up two nights running, but hopefully they won't be there.'

'I suppose it's just a job,' he said, pulling the hood of his sweatshirt over his hair and adopting a hard-man expression. 'I'll be my best professional self then leave them in peace.'

'So, have you decided who is going to win the competition?'

He tapped the side of his nose and winked. 'You'll have to wait and see, sweet Lily,' he said. 'But I promise I've been fair-minded and not let any of the shenanigans sway me.'

'In that case, what could possibly go wrong?' I said.

The square was buzzing when we arrived, which made it easier to go unnoticed. In the car, Craig had primed Ollie to keep his head down until it was time to switch on the lights, and to try not to attract too much attention.

'I thought the whole point of me being here was to attract attention but, yah, whatever.' He'd changed into a crisp lemon shirt and navy wool coat over dark blue jeans, and his boots were slightly more workmanlike than his usual footwear. When I'd queried how he could possibly have fitted all these clothes into his holdall, he confessed to having a couple of suitcases stashed in the back of Craig's car. 'I change outfits a *lot* at home,' he'd said. 'I like to keep things fresh.'

I'd stuck with my jeans and sweatshirt combo, under my parka and woolly scarf, hoping to blend in, while Craig was back in his running gear, which seemed to be his uniform of choice. He looked fresh-faced and alert, his camera at half-mast, and I wondered if he was relieved he'd soon be returning to his normal life – hopefully with a new TV series to look forward to.

Disappointingly, the snow had gone as if it had never happened, but the square exuded festive cheer in the dark, late afternoon. Apart from strings of illuminated stars and baubles spanning the shops on Main Street, a market had sprung up in the square, selling everything from roast chestnuts to wooden toys to mulled wine, each stall decorated with tiny fairy lights, like fireflies. People were milling about, wrapped in a colourful array of hats, gloves and scarves, their faces bright and smiling as they browsed the goods on offer.

Next to Ruby's Blooms was a twinkling Santa's grotto, where a tall girl dressed as an elf was entertaining a queue of children by telling Christmas jokes.

'What do you get if you cross Santa with a duck?'

'*Christmas Quackers*!'

'Who's Santa's favourite helper?'

'His wife?' offered a girl with plaits, to the obvious mortification of her blushing mother.

'I'm actually a feminist!' she trilled, but everyone was too busy laughing.

'It's *Elf-is* Presley!' sang the Christmas elf, which provoked a chorus of groans from the parents and baffled looks from the children.

'I thought that was rather funny,' said Ollie, giving the elf a round of applause. A few people cast him sidelong looks but no one seemed too interested in his presence. 'How about a glass of mulled wine to get the party started?'

'How about we go and find Barry,' I said, worried Ollie might get drunk, or start singing, or break out his trumpet to attract attention. He was already scanning the crowd for a receptive face. 'Not long to go now.'

'Spoilsport,' he grumbled good-naturedly, burrowing his hands in his coat pockets.

Craig, who'd been looking around with interest, slid me a glance and smiled.

Luckily, Barry was already in the Christmas tree area, where a small stage had been erected. 'Councillor Gerald Finch, this is Oliver Matheson,' he said, gruffly.

Mr Finch was short and broad, with squat legs like a bulldog. In a seasonal nod, a pair of flashing antlers had been clamped over his thinning, metal-grey hair. 'Good to meet you, Oliver. Never seen the show, but my wife loves it.'

'Actually, it's Ollie. Only my aunt ever calls me Oliver, and only when I've been terribly badly behaved.' Ollie was actually flirting with the councillor, as if he couldn't help himself. Craig shook his head in mock despair.

'It says Oliver on the board,' said Mr Finch, and sure enough someone had chalked: OLIVER MATTESON FROM TV SHOW PLAYERS WILL BE SWITCHING ON THE LIGHTS!!

They'd also spelt his surname wrong.

Ollie looked about to protest, but I gave him a warning look and he subsided, making a strangling gesture when Mr Finch turned to speak to Barry.

'When you get the signal, you need to pull this handle, OK?' Barry said to Ollie, a few strands of hair drifting from his ponytail as he vigorously mimed the gesture. 'It's a dummy switch, the power comes from a street lamp so the lights will be triggered remotely.'

'Sounds straightforward.' Ollie rubbed his hands together.

'Local paper's here, and News South-West will probably turn up too, so when you've done the lights and presented the competition prize to Barry here' – the councillor sniggered – 'just kidding. Obviously.' He cleared his throat and adjusted his antlers, which were listing to one side. 'When you've finished, give a shout out to the people of Shipley, thank everyone for the warm welcome' – he didn't appear to notice Ollie's snort – 'and then you can plug your show if you like.' Ollie made a *pah* sound that also went unnoticed. 'Oh, and the tradition is to meet for a drink in The Anchor afterwards, so we'll see you there.'

He patted Ollie's arm and stepped aside.

'You ready?' Ollie said to Craig, presumably meaning filming for the 'show', and Craig raised his camera as Ollie stepped on to the little stage and continued trying to charm Mr Finch, while Barry backed away, holding his phone as though about to take a call.

'Are you really filming?' I asked Craig.

'Not much point, if the local news is covering it,' he said, and I noticed a small camera crew, sporting Christmas jumpers with penguins on the front, chatting to bystanders, while Chris Weatherby from *The Shipley Examiner* – a piece of gold tinsel wrapped around his man-bun – snapped photographs of the stalls. 'He'll get his coverage.'

'Let's hope it's enough.'

'Listen, you didn't have to say that last night, about wiping the recording,' he said. 'But thanks.'

'He was surprisingly OK about it.'

'That's because it was you and he can't resist a pretty girl saying sorry.' Craig gave a wry smile, while I tried not to react to him calling me pretty. 'I'll tell him the truth when we leave, so you don't need to deal with the fallout.'

'If he's serious about moving into directing, he probably won't mind,' I said, stamping my feet, which were starting to numb with cold. 'And, anyway, it'll be too late by then.'

'Unless he suggests doing another one-off show. A shorter one, to wean himself off being in front of the camera.' Although Craig spoke lightly, his face had tensed and I guessed he was feeling guilty for deceiving his friend.

'You'll have to be firm and say no,' I said. 'Take your teacher's advice and start doing what *you* love, instead.'

He gave me a considering look. 'Maybe.'

Flustered, I looked at my watch. 'Nearly time for the big moment.'

Craig nodded, hoisting his camera over his shoulder by its strap. 'Nice atmosphere,' he said, glancing around so that the fairy lights reflected in his eyes, giving them an extra sparkle. 'I could see myself settling somewhere like this, one day.'

My heart bumped. 'Well, I can highly recommend Shipley,' I said, dismissing my earlier notion of having to leave. When I'd looked for somewhere to run to, Shipley had been the first place that had sprung to mind. Grumpy neighbours notwithstanding, I had happy memories of being here and I planned to stay around and make some more. 'Maybe you could come back and visit some time.' I felt my face go red as I said it, and hoped he hadn't noticed.

'If my show gets the go-ahead, I'll have a permanent link to the place.' He reached for my hand and pulled me aside as a family in matching reindeer hats jostled past, carrying cones of chestnuts, and the warmth of his touch ran through me like an infusion.

For a moment, it felt as if all the air had left my lungs, and when he looked at me his eyes were shocked, as if he'd felt something too.

'There you are!' said a familiar voice. 'I thought I'd never find you in this bloody crowd.'

I turned to meet a pair of wide blue eyes and a full-lipped smile. 'Erin!' I pulled her into a hug, thrilled to see her in spite of everything. 'I texted you this morning to say everything was fine.'

'I wanted to see for myself,' she said, drawing away and surveying my face, as if checking it was really me. 'You look great,' she said, with an air of surprise. 'Living in a tight-knit, small-minded community obviously suits you.'

I laughed. 'You look great too,' I said. She was wearing her cow-print coat with high, red boots, her blonde hair sweeping over her shoulders beneath a black beret that was, thankfully, more Marlene Dietrich than Frank Spencer – another of my grandfather's favourites.

'I don't know how,' she said with a grimace. 'Traffic on the way over was awful, I've been mainlining coffee, and I'm dying for a wee.'

'Well, you'll have to hold on,' I said. 'I'm glad you're here.' I thrust my arm through hers and gave it a squeeze. 'He's over there, by the way, where he's supposed to be.' I pointed to where Ollie was tapping a microphone that had been placed in front of him. 'Testing, testing,' he said through a screech of feedback, and sang a couple of lines from 'Silent Night'.

'Oh god,' groaned Erin, but there was a bright little smile on her face.

I thought about her kissing Ollie and wondered whether he even remembered, and turned to Craig, who'd been watching our exchange with a politely interested smile.

'Hi, Erin,' he said, raising a hand. 'Long time no see, though Ollie mentions you a lot.'

'He does?' Her eyes briefly widened in surprise, then her expression cooled. 'I've got a bone to pick with you, Craig Daniels.'

His face grew wary. 'Oh?'

'Tattie Granger came to see me.'

He went very still and gave her a prickly stare.

'Erin, what's going on?' I said, just as a loud countdown began behind us.

'*Ten... nine...*'

'Apparently, it wasn't someone on the show that Tattie slept with.' Erin had to shout above the din.

'*Eight... seven...*'

'It was Craig.'

Chapter 30

'*Six... five... four...*'

The countdown gathered in pace and volume, while I tried to process Erin's words, an uneasy feeling sliding through my stomach.

'*Three... two...*'

There was a dramatic pause, then Ollie pulled the switch and – as if by magic – the tree burst into glittering brightness to appreciative cries from the crowd.

'I declare this Shipley tree turned ON,' declared Ollie, twisting his head to admire the tree, the lights reflecting off his shiny hair. 'In fact, I'm turned on just looking at it.' He made seductive eyes at the crowd and a woman next to me tutted.

'Inappropriate. There are children here, for fuck's sake.'

Erin caught Ollie's gaze and made a throat-cutting gesture.

His face lit up as he spotted her and he gave her a happy wave, while I surreptitiously glanced at Craig, my heart behaving weirdly. He was staring ahead, teeth clamped to his lower lip, as if chewing over what Erin had said.

So, Craig was the 'other man'. I wondered whether Ollie had any idea. Clearly not, or there'd have been quite a lot of awkwardness between them.

I remembered the pad of scribbled plans I'd discovered on Craig's first day, and realised how much he was capable of hiding. Disappointment rose, thick and choking. *You barely know him*, I reminded myself. *Why are you so surprised?*

He caught my gaze and seemed about to speak, when another gasp went up.

The tree lights had gone out.

'Well, that didn't last long,' Ollie joked, to a stony silence. 'Looks like someone's pulled the plug.'

The councillor rushed forward and grabbed the microphone. 'Sorry about this,' he muttered, before pulling the switch himself, several times, his antlers falling over his eyes.

'First time that's ever happened.' The voice behind me was loaded with portent.

'It's bad luck if the lights go out,' said somebody else.

'It means someone's going to die!'

'Don't say that in front of the kids, you numpty.'

A doom-laden babble of voices joined in, until everyone was more or less predicting the end of the world.

'This isn't good,' murmured Erin, her eyes still glued to Ollie. 'He should say something.'

But, for once, Ollie seemed at a loss, glancing up at the tree and scratching his chin, as if the action would make the tree light up again.

The camera crew were filming, and the reporter was scribbling in his notepad, and I wondered whether they were going to somehow blame Ollie for this.

'Ollie Matheson's brought a curse to this town,' someone shouted. It sounded suspiciously like Annabel, but when I looked round, I couldn't see her.

'Bit harsh,' someone muttered.

Without warning, the lights flickered back to life and there was a palpable rush of relief from the crowd. As a tentative cheer went up, Ollie sprang back to life. 'And now for the results of the Maple Hill Christmas Lights competition!'

'He got the street name right.' I looked at Craig, the smile on my lips dying when I remembered Erin's revelation.

'Can we talk?' His eyes met mine at last. 'Away from here?'

'Not now,' I said, shoving my hands in my pockets. They hadn't felt cold, but now I couldn't stop shivering as I looked to the side of the stage where Barry stood, arms hugging his chest. He'd been joined by Sheelagh, who looked dressed for a night at the opera in a flowing black cloak, and Jane – who I'd spotted earlier, selling Christmas wreaths on the flower stall – had appeared alongside Dennis, the pair of them in matching bobble hats. The Harassed Couple, Bella and Mark, were each cradling a twin, and Mr Flannery had joined the line-up, eyes darting around as if seeking a sniper in the crowd. Only the Jensens hadn't made it; presumably because their high-powered jobs didn't allow them an afternoon off.

'And the winner IS…' Ollie paused, looking at each of the contestants in turn with an air of barely concealed excitement. He'd either got better at acting or was genuinely enjoying himself.

Jane and Dennis nudged each other like schoolchildren, while Sheelagh gazed up at Ollie with something approaching reverence, apparently unaffected by having a broken night's sleep. Barry stared at his feet, encased in biker-style boots, and Mr Flannery stared heavenwards, as if praying, fingers toying with a toggle on his duffle coat.

'Spit it out, my feet are freezing,' someone yelled.

'Why can't they leave him alone?' Erin whispered, even though I'd been wishing he'd get on with it too. 'He's doing a great job.'

I looked at her in surprise. Ollie was milking the moment for all it was worth and – as usual – not reading the mood.

'The winner IS… The GINGERbread House,' he boomed finally, in the style of the voiceover man on *The X Factor*, and the Harassed Couple broke into delighted smiles. They handed their babies to Jane and Dennis, before stepping up to accept their hamper and Hudson Country House Hotel voucher, and then opted for their fifty pounds to be donated to the local hospice, while the crowd politely applauded.

'Good decision.' Doris Day had somehow sandwiched herself between Erin and me, a bag of shopping in one of her mittened hands. 'They deserve it,' she approved. 'They need that hotel break. They've barely slept in a year.'

'I thought they might win,' I said, giving Ollie a thumbs-up, before realising his megawatt smile was directed at Erin.

I was amazed to see Barry and Mr Flannery applauding too, flashing each other oddly triumphant looks. 'I thought they'd be furious,' I said.

'They're each glad the other hasn't won.' Doris gave me a look that said, *Don't you get it*? 'The competition has always been between the pair of them,' she elaborated. 'They're fine with someone else winning.'

'Ah.' I clearly had a lot to learn about the politics of the Christmas lights competition. 'That's… good?' I said. Though, if I was honest, a teensy part of me felt a bit let down. I'd been curious to know what Mr Flannery would do if he didn't win. Especially as he'd been planning to take Ruby Dashwood away for a dirty weekend. Although, judging by the way she was laughing with Bob the Baker, who was selling mince pies from a nearby stall, she wouldn't have accepted anyway. A blonde-haired girl, who looked like a younger version of Ruby, was trying to attract her attention back to the flower stall, and I heard her shout, 'Gran, can you tell Dad these red plants have poisonous leaves, because he won't believe me?'

I turned back to Erin, who was saying to Doris, 'It sounds like he's been very fair with his decision,' as proudly as if Ollie was her firstborn. 'I can't wait to see this gingerbread house for myself.'

'He liked that one the best the night we arrived.' Craig had raised his camera and was filming the presentation, even though News South-West was covering it anyway. 'One for the archives,' he said to me, even though I'd been trying not to look at him. *He'd slept with Tattie Granger, for heaven's sake. How could he act normally around Ollie?*

'Traitor,' Erin hissed in my ear, as if catching my thoughts. 'As soon as this is over, we'll be having words.'

'In front of Ollie?'

'No.' Erin looked to where Ollie was emptying the food hamper, item by item, holding up a jar of goose fat and telling a story about his nanny's roast potatoes being the best he'd ever tasted, the secret being goose fat, which he'd loved ever since, and how he even took a jar with him to restaurants. The onlookers looked suitably bemused. 'I'll get Craig to tell him and if he won't, then I will.'

'And then what?'

Erin had a strange glint in her eye that I'd only seen once before: after The Actor had declared his intention to conquer America without her. 'I don't know,' she admitted, the glint fading.

'I've seen his fancy woman.'

I looked at Doris, noticing her discreet, Christmas tree earrings. 'Sorry?'

'Barry.' She flashed her eyes in his direction, while Erin moved in to eavesdrop.

'Where?'

'Well, as you haven't been keeping an eye out I thought I'd have a wander past the house myself, while Sheelagh was at school yesterday lunchtime, and I noticed a smudge on their front window—'

'You noticed a smudge from the pavement?' I said.

'Well, I didn't realise it was a smudge until I got closer, but I know what smudged glass looks like.' Erin and I glanced at each other, wide-eyed with the urge to laugh. 'Anyway, I saw her, brazen as anything, half-dressed on the sofa in front of that dreadful *Loose Women*, flipping through one of Sheelagh's books.' Her mouth pursed. 'I very nearly knocked on the glass to give her a fright,' she said. 'But I didn't want to add more smudges and raise suspicion.'

'Naturally.'

'Are you going to tell Sheelagh?' said Erin, grasping the situation right away.

Doris's face softened. 'I've written the evidence down, just in case, but I think I should wait for her to come and ask for help,' she said. 'She might already know but not want to know, if you get my drift.'

I was impressed by Doris's restraint. I didn't want to be the one to tell Sheelagh either, and was praying she wouldn't ask me again if I'd seen anything.

'You know, you should put your policing skills to good use,' I said. 'The Doris Day Detective Agency has quite a nice ring to it.'

'I'd call you,' said Erin. 'If I thought my husband was *cheating*.' She threw Craig a savage look, but the News South-West cameraman had wandered over and they were comparing equipment.

'Maybe I will,' Doris said, looking tickled by the idea. 'I used to help my Roger solve his cases, and *Midsomer Murders* is my favourite TV programme after *Without a Trace*.'

'There you go then,' I said.

Bella and Mark had stepped off the stage with their booty, looking far less harassed, and Ollie was speaking into the microphone again. 'In their own ways, all the residents were absolute winners,' he said, holding up a hand to still the crowd, who were starting to drift away. 'And as a thank you to everyone at Maple Hill, for putting up with me, I'll be making a substantial donation to The Christmas Lights Society, towards next year's festivities.'

'You shouldn't be encouraging people to compete against each other!'

Definitely Annabel. Luckily, apart from some tutting, no one seemed to agree and there was a rousing outbreak of applause.

Sheelagh looked overcome with emotion, her hands clasped as though she were praying to Ollie, clearly forgetting – or forgiving – his insults about Barry's lights.

'That's nice of him,' said Erin. 'I hope the cameras got that.'

Doris looked less impressed. 'I was rather hoping there wouldn't be a competition next year,' she said, adjusting the knot of her scarf. 'But I suppose it gives those two something to look forward to.' Mr Flannery and Barry were squaring up, like wrestlers, testosterone swirling like a cyclone. 'Pair of big kids.'

Before I could respond, Ollie shouted, 'Have a wonderful Christmas, SHIPLEY, and don't do anything I wouldn't, yah?' He'd barely finished before the councillor stepped forward, minus his antlers, to announce the Nightingale Primary choir was about to perform, and a clutch of rosy-cheeked children were herded on stage by a smiling Jill Edwards, wearing a holly-patterned sweater beneath her padded coat.

Ollie came over and stopped in front of Erin. 'Did I do OK?' he said, groomed eyebrows crinkling. He sounded oddly uncertain.

'You were fine,' she said coolly, pulling a compact-mirror from her black, silver- studded handbag to check her lipstick.

He visibly relaxed. 'If my agent's happy, then so am I.' He spoke with an air of solemnity, eyes sweeping her appearance and seeming to find it favourable. 'Love the hat,' he said, tugging it forward. She slapped his hand away and I realised she was being playful, which wasn't like Erin at all. Clearly the Ollie effect hadn't quite worn off.

'Isn't it traditional to repair to the pub?' he said to Craig, who'd stopped filming and was standing a little way off, looking as if he longed to be invisible.

'Well, I've got a pair of breasts to attend to.' Doris patted her bag. 'My Eric is coming for dinner and loves his chicken, and we're hoping to introduce Erica to a pureed Brussels sprout, so she can get a taste for them before Christmas Day.' She looked like she'd swallowed a bunch of fairy lights when she spoke about her granddaughter, and as she headed for the parade with a bright, 'Cheerio,' I half wished I was going with her. Anywhere but the pub, where things were bound to get awkward.

Plus, I loved Brussels sprouts.

Chapter 31

In the event, only Sheelagh came with us to The Anchor.

'We're really tired,' said Bella, with a pointed look at Ollie that he could hardly argue with, while Jane and Dennis apparently had a 'date night' scheduled (I didn't want to think about what that involved).

'My nephew can't be trusted on his own in there,' said Mr Flannery, before hotfooting it back the newsagent's, though I suspected he mostly wanted to keep a lovelorn eye on Ruby.

Barry melted into the night, without bothering to make an excuse, and Councillor Finch pleaded an appointment with his chiropodist for an ingrown toenail, which made Ollie look slightly nauseous.

'I can't believe there's only us,' Ollie said, as we launched into the pub after a short walk across to the harbour, during which he'd challenged Craig to build a sandcastle – tersely declined – and asked Erin again what she'd thought of his performance.

'Hardly Oscar-worthy,' she'd said, rolling her eyes at me.

On arrival at the pub, Sheelagh tripped on her cloak and Ollie offered her his arm, which she gripped with obvious delight.

'At least you've got me,' Sheelagh flirted.

'Ah, my lovely Loretta,' Ollie flirted back, while Erin pretended to gag.

The pub was modern but cosy, with a separate restaurant, and a bar area where a log-fire was blazing and a densely decorated Christmas tree sparkled in the corner.

It was early, and most people were still enjoying the festivities in the square, but the restaurant was busy with office parties, and the bar vibrated with piped Christmas music and the sound of people enjoying a drink.

'Barry's cooking a candlelit dinner tonight,' Sheelagh said, as we squeezed onto a leather banquette around a wooden-topped table, while Ollie went to the bar with Craig to order 'champers'. 'He always cooks on Fridays,' she added, eyes darting to me and away again. She was either making an excuse for him, hoping I'd forgotten she'd doorstepped me, or hadn't forgiven me for giving her beloved Ollie a nosebleed the night before. 'He can be very thoughtful,' she went on, as though daring me to argue. 'He would have come with us, but…' *He doesn't like Ollie.* The unspoken words hung in the air.

'It's fine,' I said. I was relieved he wasn't there.

Erin removed her coat to reveal a tight, high-waisted skirt, which accentuated her curves, and a baby-blue cropped sweater. I felt like the Beast to her Beauty in my jeans and sweatshirt, and decided to keep my parka on.

'Isn't Barry upset at not winning?' I said to Sheelagh.

Erin shot me a look of surprise as she sat down.

'Oh, he loves taking part, that's the main thing,' Sheelagh replied. 'And all the bantering with Clint.' I couldn't think who she meant for a moment, and suspected he'd always be Mr Flannery to me. 'They're like a pair of boxers squaring up,' she added, confirming Doris's theory. 'It'll all be forgotten, until next year.' She gave a honk of laughter and slipped her cloak off. 'Here come the drinkies!'

Ollie plonked down a tray of half-filled glasses with a flourish, and wedged himself next to Erin. 'I've ordered a bottle, it'll be over in a minute,' he said, raising his glass. 'In the meantime, here's to our last night in Shipley.'

'Oh.' Sheelagh gave a heartfelt sigh. She picked up a glass and drained it in one go. 'I'm going to miss you,' she said.

'You'll be the only one.' Ollie looked suddenly crushed. 'I think I've ballsed things up a bit, truth be told,' he said. 'Seem to have put everyone's backs up.'

'They're not used to people like you.' Sheelagh leaned across Erin to pat his hand.

'I'm not used to people like them,' he admitted. 'It's been a learning curve.'

'Really?' I said.

'Yah.' He pushed his hair back. 'I've learnt I'm never doing these kinds of public engagements again.'

'Hallelujah!' Craig said, lifting his glass. 'I'll drink to that.' He'd positioned himself beside me and I was aware of his thigh inches from mine, and as Erin's accusation spun through my mind I couldn't help wishing she hadn't said anything.

The waiter hurried over with a bottle of champagne in a silver bucket and placed it by the table. 'Could I have a selfie?' he said shyly to Ollie, who – for once – looked reluctant.

'Sure,' he said gamely, and we endured an excruciating few minutes as the waiter fiddled with his phone, trying to get the pose right and taking several shots 'for luck', his arm braced firmly around Ollie's shoulders.

'Gay,' Ollie whispered when he'd gone. 'A lot of my fans are.' He sloshed more champagne into our glasses, even though he and Sheelagh appeared to be the only ones drinking. 'Might as well get piddled,' he said, slumping against Erin and pulling a sad face. She shoved him away, clearly trying to maintain a professional agent/client relationship, even though Ollie kept trying to take hold of her hand.

'So, what's next for you, Ollie?' Sheelagh had gone a little cross-eyed after emptying another glass of champagne. 'I know!' She held up a finger. 'You should go back to *Players*.' She made it sound like a brilliant and original idea.

'I'm never going back there,' he said, as though he'd worked in an office on a charmless industrial estate. 'I'm on a new career path, lovely Loretta.'

'Well, I'm sure whatever you do, it'll work out for you.' She stood up, bosom straining at the material of her ruffled, leopard-print top. 'Now, if you'll excuse me, I need to powder my nose,' she said. 'I don't know why people say that.' She swayed a little. 'I'm actually going for a wee.' She clapped a hand to her mouth. 'I'm so sorry,' she said to Ollie. 'Have I shared too much?'

'Don't mind me,' he said. 'Have a number two, on me.'

'Ew,' said Erin, and punched his arm.

Sheelagh's face turned puce. 'I wouldn't dream of it,' she said.

Once she'd hurried off, Ollie angled a look at Erin. 'Why do you keep glaring at Craig like that?'

She gave a guilty start. 'Like what?'

'Like you want to hurt him.'

Craig shifted uneasily, a mix of dread and resignation washing over his face.

My heart started to race. This wasn't the place for a confrontation. 'Erin…' I began.

'Are you going to tell him, or shall I?' she said to Craig, colour suffusing her normally creamy cheeks.

'Tell me what?' Ollie was looking between them with deepening suspicion. 'You two…' he waved a hand between them, eyes widening. 'Oh god, please tell me you're not—'

'No, we're bloody not,' said Erin, slapping his hand down. 'For Christ's sake, Ollie, I barely know him and, anyway…' She took a breath. 'It's not me he's been messing about with.'

I had a feeling she hadn't really meant to say it and felt an unexpected surge of pity for Craig. Whatever had happened with Tattie was obviously over, and he must have been dreading Ollie finding out. Was that why he'd been so keen for them to get away? Had he been protecting himself, as much as Ollie?

'What's she talking about, Craggers?' Ollie looked from one of us to the other, his brow furrowed. 'What's going on, mate?'

Craig fiddled with the stem of his glass. It was the sort of flute I'd seen on the clip of *Players* and it looked too dainty in his hand. 'Can we do this somewhere else?' he said, quietly.

'Oh, come on, you can't leave me hanging.' Ollie looked at me.

Oh heck. 'I—'

'Tattie and Craig slept together,' Erin said baldly, and I experienced a moment's surprise that she was pushing this to its inevitably ugly conclusion. Was it to do with her own nasty break-up, and not wanting to see someone else get hurt? But that didn't make any sense. Why bring it up at all? 'She cheated on you, with your best friend.'

'Craig?' Ollie looked at Erin for confirmation.

'Of course, Craig, you idiot,' she snapped. She was being incredibly rude to him, under the circumstances. 'How many best friends have you got?'

There was a burst of raucous carol-singing from the restaurant, overlaying the chink of cutlery and loud chatter from another table, but it couldn't drown out the pounding in my ears as I waited for the penny to drop.

Ollie gave a shout of laughter. 'This has to be a joke, right?' He directed the words at Craig, who looked like he wanted to be sick. '*That's* what this is about?'

Erin and I glanced at each other.

'It's not true,' Craig said, stiffly. 'Tattie tried it on with me, but I would never—'

'Of *course* you wouldn't.' Ollie's face twisted with concern. 'You're my *friend*.'

Craig looked thrown, as if this wasn't the response he'd envisaged. 'I never even fancied her,' he said, warily. 'That was the problem, really. When I turned her down, she said if I told you she'd say I made a pass at her.'

Ollie gave a snort. 'As if I'd have believed that.'

'But… she said Craig had a freckle on his…' Erin lowered her voice. 'On his willy.'

Our eyes dropped to Craig's crotch, as if it might be visible through his jeans. 'How else would she have known if—'

'Because I told her, once,' cried Ollie, making us jump. 'I'd had too much to drink, and we were talking about birthmarks in weird places – don't ask me why – and I mentioned you had this freckle on your peen.'

'Don't say peen,' said Erin, at the same time as I said, 'How do *you* know he has a freckle?'

Craig squirmed in his seat. 'I might have told him once, for a laugh, when we were kids, Christ knows why, it's not even true,' he said. 'I can show you if you like.'

'Er, no, mate, thanks for offering,' said Ollie. 'I can't believe you lied about it.'

'I can't believe you told Tattie,' Craig countered.

'Well, it doesn't matter if it's not true and, anyway, it proves she was lying,' Ollie said. 'Not that I needed proof.'

Craig didn't sleep with Tattie. The words sent a spiral of warmth through me that had nothing to do with wearing too many layers in a pub with a roaring log-fire. 'But why tell Erin?' I said.

'And why aren't you mad as hell?' Erin turned to face Ollie. 'I thought you were crazy in love with the silly bitch.'

'Of course I'm not.' He looked genuinely horrified. 'Yes, I had a fling with her, but it was to make someone else jealous. Tattie fell for me in a big way – obviously – but when she realised I didn't feel the same she started this silly campaign to make me jealous, and when that didn't work she got me thrown off the show.'

'If you weren't jealous, why hit whatsisname?' I said.

Ollie shrugged, leaning against the banquette, one arm along the back, as if discussing his plans for Christmas. 'I never liked that idiot, Cuttlingtonson. He deserved to be punched, and I suppose it was a way of forcing things to change. I was pretty much done with *Players*. I'm too old for all that bull-crap.'

'So, why do you think Tattie went to Erin?' Craig said. I hadn't realised how pale he'd been until I noticed some colour had returned to his face.

Ollie shrugged again. 'She phoned me the other day, pleading with me to come back to her, saying she could get me my job back, and when I said no and told her why, she lost the plot and said she'd slept with you, and I guess she wanted to make trouble—'

'She said that?' Craig's glass slammed down on the table. 'And you didn't think to mention it?'

'What's to mention?' Ollie seemed puzzled. 'I knew she was lying, so I didn't bother you with it.'

'But didn't you think Craig might have been worried?' I said.

'I didn't know she'd made a move on you, bro.' He gave Craig a hard look. 'You should have told me in the first place.'

'How could I?' Concern creased Craig's brow. 'You were moping around like a lovesick puppy. I thought if I told you she'd tried to… *seduce* me, it might push you over the edge.'

'I'd have known it wasn't true,' Ollie said fondly. 'Mates before dates, right?'

'Right.' Craig gave a reluctant grin.

'Christ,' said Erin. 'It sounds like you two should be sleeping together.'

'That's gross,' said Ollie. 'Though to be fair, he probably does fancy the pants off me.'

'In your dreams,' said Craig, who looked like a weight had been hoisted off his shoulders. 'You're not my type.'

I still couldn't quite make sense of it all. 'But why did Tattie tell Erin?'

'Yes, why did she tell me?' said Erin. 'I feel like a total bitch now, accusing Craig like that.' She winced at him. 'Sorry, by the way.'

'No worries.' He lifted his glass in a toast. 'But, yeah, why did she tell you?'

'It's because of what I said when she called.' Ollie spoke as if we should know what he was on about. 'She knew Erin would come down and confront Craig, and probably hoped it would make trouble between us, and that I'd hate Erin for telling me the so-called "truth".'

'Sounds a bit far-fetched,' I said. 'What on earth did you tell her when she called that would make her go to those lengths?'

He took a deep breath and let it out slowly. 'That it's you I'm in love with.'

'WHAT?' I yelped.

'Sorry.' He flipped his eyes from me to Erin. 'I meant you.'

'*What*?' she hissed. 'Are you out of your tiny mind?'

'Erin, you know I'm crazy about you.'

Craig and I gave each other gobsmacked looks.

'Ollie, for god's sake, you don't mean it,' Erin said. 'Just because we slept together once—'

'Slept together?' I gaped at her. 'You said you'd kissed, not *slept* together.'

'Yeah, well. It wasn't something I wanted to admit to.' Erin picked up her glass, her hand shaking. 'I didn't want to be one of *those* girls. Plus, he's my client.'

'Bit late for that,' I said.

'You never said a word.' Craig sounded shell-shocked. 'So much for mates.'

'Look, I was embarrassed she'd knocked me back,' Ollie admitted, looking shame-faced and a bit sweaty around the hairline. 'It's never happened to me before.'

'You need to get over yourself,' muttered Erin.

'She won't believe I'm genuine,' he said, stroking her beret. She jerked away, giving him a furious glare. 'See? I've been trying to think of a way to win her over and thought agreeing to do this show might be a start.'

'You tried to kiss *Lily*, for Christ's sake,' she blasted. 'How was that trying to win me over, you… tosser?'

'It was for the one-off *show*,' said Ollie, earnestly. 'I mean, Lily's a wonderful girl, and absolutely gorgeous, but it didn't mean anything.'

'I wasn't interested anyway,' I said, trying and failing to locate some outrage at his nicely worded dismissal.

'You do know there won't *be* a one-off show?' said Craig, with the air of someone throwing all their cards on the table. 'You kept being Ollie Matheson from *Players* and I think you need to get away from that.'

'Fuck's sake, Craig.' Erin pressed her fingers into Ollie's forearm in an unconsciously protective gesture. 'Was that really your decision to make?'

For a second, I thought Ollie was finally going to erupt. He bowed his head and seemed in the grip of a strong emotion, then I realised he was overcome by the sight of Erin's hand on his arm. 'I'm glad,' he said finally, raising his eyes to Craig. 'You were looking out for me.'

Craig gave a slightly exhausted laugh. 'I was, but if you'd like to do another show, I'll—'

'No.' Ollie turned to Erin, and took both her hands in his. 'I'm going to be a director,' he said. 'And I'm firing you as my agent.'

Sheelagh chose that moment to reappear, her lipstick renewed and her curls loosened, as if she'd been running her fingers through them.

'What have I missed?' she said, and looked baffled when Craig replied, 'Where to start?'

'Well, I hope you weren't talking about me.' She sat back down and looked around expectantly.

'Oh look, it's our newest resident, having a lovely time with her boyfriend,' said a carping voice. It was Annabel, with her embarrassed looking husband and another couple wearing tinsel garlands round their necks. 'Planning to start a fight in the street tonight?' she said, to me. 'Is that what you're used to where you come from?' She flashed a dimpled smile at Craig. 'Hi, lovely.'

'Annabel,' he said, without any warmth this time.

'What a bitch,' Erin muttered.

'Why don't you wind your neck in, as Nanny used to say?' Ollie's imperious voice created a ripple among the group.

'Ooh, he had a nanny,' sniped Annabel. 'Why doesn't that surprise me?'

'Leave him alone.' My voice emerged, surprisingly strong and clear.

'I could say the same to you, my lovely.'

Suddenly, I'd had enough. It was like being in the classroom all over again, being insulted by Max's wife when I hadn't done anything wrong. 'Firstly, Ollie isn't my boyfriend,' I said, standing up on shaky legs. 'But even if he was, we're both single, so we wouldn't be doing anything wrong, or hurting anybody.' My cheeks felt scalded but I kept going. 'Secondly, why are you having a go at me? Women always attack other women, and I'm sick of it,' I said. 'And thirdly…' I faltered. What was the third thing? 'Thirdly, I come from the same place as you.' She screwed her face up, ready to protest. 'It's called The Planet,' I said. 'And you need to stop making out that I think I'm better than anyone here, because I don't.'

'You're better than her,' Craig said, as I dropped back down. 'You OK?' he murmured.

I nodded. 'Yes, actually, I am.'

Erin reached over and closed her hand over mine. 'Nice burn,' she said. 'I didn't know you had it in you.'

'Bravo!' Ollie started a slow handclap and a few people joined in before going back to their drinks.

Sheelagh looked at Annabel, her eyebrows lifted. 'I think some of you need to open your minds a bit,' she said, and I could see it had cost her to take my side against her long-standing neighbour, who was glaring as though Sheelagh had just betrayed her country. 'Now, go away because I want to make the most of this lovely young man before he leaves us tomorrow.'

Annabel looked like she swallowed a cupful of bleach. 'Sorry,' she murmured to Craig, but he wouldn't look at her.

'Miss Ambrose!' Alfie Blake pushed past Annabel, who had no choice but to scuttle away with her clearly embarrassed entourage, stumbling a little in her heels. 'I thought I recognised your voice,' he said, beaming. 'We was just 'aving our Christmas party, Dad's treat,' he said, sweeping an arm towards the restaurant. His cheeks were rosier than ever, his curls squashed beneath a floppy Santa hat, his baggy grey suit replaced with a Christmas jumper bearing a cross-eyed reindeer. 'Jill Edwards called me and said I could give a talk to Year Five in the New Year.'

'That's great,' I said, tears leaping to my eyes. It had been an emotionally draining evening and it was barely eight o'clock. 'You'll be great.'

'I'm going to do a Powerpoint display.' His big hands smoothed his sweater. 'Thanks. You know. For having a word.'

'My pleasure.'

As he headed off, Sheelagh beamed at me. 'Good girl,' she said, and, although it was silly to care, I was glad to be back in her good books. 'Now, I'm going to make a move or Barry's Beef Wellington will be overdone.'

'I'll give you a lift,' said Craig, scrambling to his feet as Ollie rose to help Sheelagh on with her cloak.

Disappointment flooded through me. 'But it's your last night,' I protested. It felt as if there was more to talk about, and now the air had been cleared I was in the mood for a drink. 'Are you coming back?'

'I'm pretty shattered,' he said, not quite meeting my eyes. 'Would you mind if I had a shower and something to eat at yours?'

Why wasn't he looking at me? 'Sure,' I said flatly, taking my keys out of my bag and handing them over.

'How are we going to get back?' said Ollie.

'I've got my car, you twat.' Erin swiped his shoulder. She couldn't seem to stop touching him, albeit in a slightly belligerent manner. 'Why do you think I'm not drinking?'

'You are staying tonight?' I said.

'She'd better be.' There was a glint in Ollie's eye. 'There's plenty of room in my bed.'

'Only if I can sleep with you,' Erin said to me.

'Of course you can.'

Sheelagh swooped to gather Ollie in a hug, her cloak enveloping him like a crow's wing as she planted a kiss on his cheek. 'Oops.' She swiped at the lipstick imprint with her thumb, but it wouldn't budge.

'Better do a matching one.' Ollie proffered his other cheek and Sheelagh didn't hold back. For a ridiculous moment, I could have sworn that Erin looked jealous.

Sheelagh finally joined Craig, who was standing by the table with his camera in one hand, keys jangling from the other, as if he couldn't wait to leave.

'Nice to meet you, love.' Sheelagh smiled at Erin. 'You'd make a lovely girlfriend for Ollie.'

'What did she say that for?' said Erin, as Craig opened the door to let Sheelagh through. I thought he might look back or give me a wave – something – but he disappeared without another glance. 'I'm nobody's girlfriend.'

'Not yet,' murmured Ollie.

'Must have been tough for him, wondering when Tattie was going to unleash her accusation,' Erin said, watching the pub door swing shut. 'What a good guy, though. I like him.'

If she was trying to prompt a response, she'd be disappointed. I couldn't muster more than a non-committal 'Mmm' as I splashed champagne into my glass. If Ollie hadn't been there I'd have turned the tables and asked her about sleeping with him, but he was gazing emotionally at the exit, as if the ghost of Craig was standing there. 'He's the absolute bloody best. I love that guy.'

'Oh god,' said Erin, but although she flicked her eyes up, I could tell she wasn't serious. They'd shuffled a bit closer together, but just as I felt loneliness descending she fixed her bright blue eyes on me and said, 'Now, tell us how you're getting on with your writing.'

'Ooh, yes, do tell,' said Ollie, properly interested. For once, he wasn't looking around to see if anyone had recognised him, or bursting into song, and although his trumpet was nestled in its case beneath the table, he didn't seem in any hurry to get it out.

Erin was good for him, I realised, and he brought out a protective side in her I'd never seen before. It was just a pity that she was too stubborn to see it.

Chapter 32

It was gone eleven by the time we crept upstairs at the cottage.

'Can I have a tiny good-night kiss?' Ollie asked Erin, when she came out of the bathroom after washing her make-up off.

'Get lost, and keep your voice down,' she stage-whispered, inclining her head to where Craig was asleep downstairs. The living room had been in darkness when we came in and there'd been no movement from the sofa, despite Ollie tiptoeing in and prodding Craig's sleeping bag. 'And don't be coming into Lily's room in the middle of the night, pretending you're looking for the bog.'

'That's a great idea.' Ollie mimed sleepwalking up and down the landing with his arms outstretched like tongs, which made me giggle.

'Idiot.' Erin looked more intoxicated than I was, even though she'd had nothing stronger to drink than lime and soda, while Ollie and I had worked our way through the champagne. Around nine, she'd declared she was starving, so Ollie had persuaded the doe-eyed waiter to talk the chef into rustling up a festive pizza with a turkey-and-cranberry topping, which we'd shared. I'd thought about leaving them to it, but Erin wouldn't hear of it, and neither would Ollie. He'd been at his most entertaining as he brought Erin up to date with all the ways he'd upset the neighbours, and although I knew he was hamming it up to impress her, it helped take my mind off Craig deserting us.

'Careful, or you'll give him another nosebleed,' Erin said now, as I closed the bedroom door in Ollie's face.

'I told you that was an accident.'

'He's got sensitive sinuses,' she said.

'I know that *now.*'

Erin contorted herself into a pair of my pyjamas. The heating was off and the bedroom felt chilly. 'I can't remember the last time I had a sleepover,' she said, tossing her clothes onto the chair.

'I can,' I said. 'It was with my mum last week.' This struck me as hilarious and I spluttered with laughter.

'That's tragic,' said Erin, which made me laugh even more.

Once we'd wriggled under the duvet, I calmed down and switched off the bedside light. 'So,' I said. 'You and Ollie?'

'There is no me and Ollie, and if you mention it again I'll smother you with your own pillow,' she said. 'How about you and Craig?'

'There is no me and Craig.' A tight feeling spread across my chest. I wondered if he was really asleep, or lying awake in his sleeping bag, desperate for morning, so he could escape.

'There you go, then.'

'That doesn't make sense.'

'You're not making sense.'

'It's quiet here, isn't it?' I said.

'It's nice, like having earplugs in but without hearing your own heartbeat.' Erin turned over, dragging a portion of the duvet with her. 'Shipley suits you,' she said. 'You should definitely stay.'

'Did you really like my idea for *Sabrina the Magic Cat*?'

'S'great,' she murmured, starting to sound sleepy. 'She could wear a diamond collar, or maybe a velvet bow. A purple one, because purple's supposed to be magic.'

'I like that,' I said, imagining it. 'I thought I could still write an adult novel as well,' I went on. 'What do you think of *My Neighbours and Me* as a title for a book about a woman's struggles to integrate into the local community?'

'Boring as fuck.'

'Don't hold back,' I said.

'How about *In the Dark*?'

'Ooh, that's good.' I wrenched a handful of duvet back. 'It would be a thriller, obviously.'

'Or, it would be a story about a woman who got a bit lost when her father died, had a disastrous relationship, and threw away the job she loved to write about a cat.'

'Erin, that's mean.' I tried to kick her, but she shifted just in time.

'Sorry,' she mumbled, yanking the duvet back. 'The cat idea's great, but you're a fantastic teacher. You should do that too.'

By the time I'd thought up a response, her breathing had deepened into sleep. I lay for a while, picturing myself at Nightingale Primary School, teaching a class of eager-faced children the alphabet, then felt myself drifting off.

What felt like minutes later, a shout from outside woke me up.

'Wha…?' Erin sat up. 'What was that?'

I snatched the duvet and parcelled it around me. 'A seagull,' I said, drowsily. 'Go back to sleep.'

'Seagulls don't shout.' She leaned over and switched the light on. 'It's nearly two o'clock.'

Another shout went up and I dived out of bed with a sinking sense of déjà vu. 'Ollie must be out there.'

'*Ollie*?' Erin's hair was a rumpled mass, but her eyes were bright and alert. 'Why would he be outside?'

'It's what he does,' I said, belting myself into my dressing gown. 'He wakes up the neighbours every night.'

A fist hammered on the door, and Ollie's head poked round. 'Next door's house is on fire,' he said, before vanishing.

'Fuck.' Erin leapt out of bed.

We were halfway downstairs, when Craig came out of the living room, wrapped in his sleeping bag. 'Not this again,' he said, blinking owlishly in the brightness of the hall light. 'Carol-singing, or snowball fight?'

'Fire!' I yelled, dragging my boots on and following a fully dressed Ollie through the front door, where I was greeted by the sight of orange flames dancing in the Lamberts' downstairs window, and smoke curling round the frame.

'Oh, good god,' said Erin, behind me. 'I'll phone the fire brigade.'

'They're on their way,' called Doris from the street. 'I called them as soon as I saw the blaze from my bedroom window.' She must have been having a late-night snoop with her binoculars – which was probably just as well.

In a horrible parody of the night before, I saw more neighbours emerging, blank-faced with shock as they took in the spectacle in front of them.

I followed Ollie as he raced round to the Lamberts'. 'Is anyone inside?' he said.

As he spoke, the front door flew open and Sheelagh ran out in an old-fashioned, full-length nightgown. Wild-eyed with terror, she clutched at Ollie's hands. 'Please help,' she cried, her cheeks streaked with mascara. 'Barry… Barry won't come out.'

'Won't or can't?' I said, but her eyes seemed stuck to Ollie.

'Please help him,' she whimpered.

Craig materialised. He'd pulled his jeans and a jumper on, and his hair was sticking up. 'How did it start?' he said to Sheelagh, eyes scanning the rows of Christmas lights on the house, which had mostly gone out.

'I told Barry the circuit was overloaded.' Her breath caught on a sob. 'Something must have blown in the hall, and we wouldn't even have known if Marmite hadn't come up and jumped on the bed.' She let out a wail. 'We have extinguishers everywhere so Barry put it out, but then it flared up again, and Barry's locked himself in the dining room to wait it out.'

'Wait it out?' I swapped an incredulous look with Craig. 'But that's dangerous. The fire could spread and the smoke will be toxic.'

'I know,' Sheelagh sobbed, chest heaving. 'And I don't know where Marmite is.'

'I'm going in,' said Ollie, and before anyone could stop him he'd charged through the front door, just as sirens sounded in the distance.

'Christ's sake,' Craig said. 'I'd better go and help.'

'No!' I grabbed his arm.

'It'll be fine,' he said, gently unpeeling my fingers. 'I'll be right back.'

'Where's Ollie?' Erin had reappeared, white-faced, in her cow-print coat. 'Don't tell me he's bloody gone in.'

'He's gone in,' I said.

For a second she seemed dumbstruck. 'I can't bloody believe this.'

'Craig's in there too.'

She shook her head. 'They're a pair of bloody idiots.'

No one else seemed inclined to speak. They were too busy watching the drama unfold, their solemn faces at odds with the sagging, but still grinning, Santa and a smiling Mrs Snowman.

As the flames in the window leapt higher, Sheelagh began making a keening noise, and Doris bustled over and wrapped an arm around her. Jane was there too, making soothing gestures, and Celia Appleton appeared with her Labrador, a voluminous nightdress under her patchwork coat, and placed a blanket around Sheelagh's shuddering shoulders.

As the fire engine roared up the road, its flashing lights slicing through the darkness, Craig emerged with a furry bundle in his arms.

'Oh, my baby,' Sheelagh sobbed, taking the cat and cradling him to her bosom. 'Look at my poor little pussy,' she cried. 'His fur's gone flat.'

Craig came over, rubbing his arm. 'Bloody thing attacked me,' he said, wincing. His jumper was on inside out, and the sight of the label sticking out made my chest feel tight. His sleeves were rolled up, and his forearms were criss-crossed with scratches.

'I've got some Savlon in my emergency drawer,' I said, through a lump the size of a ping-pong ball in my throat. 'I'll get it for you, if you like.'

'I'm OK.' He smiled briefly. 'Thanks, though.'

I looked at Erin, who had her hand crushed to her mouth, staring at the house as if willing Ollie to appear. 'What's he doing?' I said, wondering why Craig didn't seem particularly anxious.

He ran the heel of his hand over his brow. 'He's, er, trying to persuade Barry to come out.'

'What's his problem?' I said, tightening my coat around me. 'Surely if he's able to, he should. It can't be safe in there.'

'It's not that simple.' Craig looked distinctly awkward now.

'But Barry's OK?'

'He's fine.' He glanced towards the house, where one of the firemen was extending the hose, while another assessed the situation. There was a palpable sense of tension as the living-room window shattered, and flames started licking upwards.

'BARRY!' Sheelagh screamed.

Craig started to move back towards the house, just as one of the firemen aimed a jet of water at the blaze and Ollie appeared at the front door, struggling under the weight of a body slung over his shoulder.

'Thank god,' said Erin, so softly I was probably the only one who heard it.

'It's like Father Christmas, but in reverse,' someone said.

'Except that's not a parcel of presents, he's carrying.' I recognised Mr Flannery's voice.

'That's not even Barry,' said someone else. 'It's a woman.'

As Ollie staggered down the path, backlit by the blaze from the house, I stared. I recognised that red hair. It belonged to Barry's mistress. Her sizeable bottom was barely covered by the skimpy robe she was wearing, and a pair of fluffy mules dangled from her feet.

'My god, were they having a threesome in there?' said Erin. 'No wonder they didn't want to come out.'

'Not exactly.' Craig moved back to join us as Ollie lurched past a row of illuminated angels and deposited the woman in front of Sheelagh like a heavy parcel.

'Oh, my darling,' she cried, placing Marmite gently on the ground before throwing herself into the woman's arms. 'Thank god you're safe.'

'Anyone else in there?' called the fireman.

'No,' said Sheelagh. 'We're all here.'

'What's going on?' I looked back at the house. 'Where's Barry?'

'Yes, where is he?' said Doris, looking as mystified as everyone else.

'I'm here,' said the woman. Reaching up, she removed her long red hair, and suddenly it wasn't a woman at all. It was Barry, in crimson lipstick and dangly earrings, the silky camisole under his skimpy robe barely covering what looked like an ample bust.

'Fuck,' whispered Erin. 'And I thought it might be boring living in Shipley.'

The firemen were concentrating fiercely on the house, even though the fire had been put out.

'I know what you're all thinking.' Sheelagh turned to look at the stunned faces of her neighbours, brightly lit from the surrounding houses. She was holding on to Barry as if to stop him legging it back into the house – though I doubted he could in those mules. 'But he's not doing anything wrong. He likes wearing women's clothes sometimes, so what?' Through the bravado, her voice shook. 'I expect we'll be targets now you've found out, like at the last place we lived, which is why we left, but I'm not ashamed and Barry shouldn't be either. And just so you know, I love him very much.'

So that explained the self-help books I'd seen her carrying, and why she'd been worried that I might have spotted something the night she was at her sister's. *Poor Sheelagh.* I wondered whether it explained why their daughter rarely visited, and felt even sorrier for her.

'My dear, you don't have to be ashamed,' said Doris. 'My Roger always wore a pair of frilly knickers under his uniform.'

'Dennis is partial to a bit of make-up now and then,' said Jane. 'He was wearing eyeliner just this afternoon.'

'Well, I think Barry's got an excellent pair of legs.' Ollie rested a firm hand on Barry's drooping shoulder. 'I say, embrace your inner woman, but get some advice about the underwear, yah, you need to dress for your size, not the size you think you are.'

'That's what I keep telling him,' said Sheelagh, eyes shining. 'Ollie, you saved his life,' she added. 'I can't ever thank you enough.'

'He would have been fine, but I wasn't taking any chances so got him in a fireman's lift, which was astonishingly difficult. I need to get back to the gym.' With a final press of Barry's shoulder, Ollie came over, his face alight with satisfaction. 'I think that's rounded off my stay in Shipley rather nicely,' he said, a smile breaking over his face. 'And at least it wasn't me disturbing the peace this time.'

'Why were you dressed?' was all I could think to say. 'Normally you sleep like the dead.'

'Oh, I had things on my mind.' He glanced at Erin, eyes shining like marbles. 'Like how to win this beautiful lady over.'

'Oh, for fuck's sake,' she burst out. 'You just did.' And with that, she threw herself at him and pressed her lips to his.

Craig and I arched our brows at each other, and the warmth in his eyes when they fixed on me made me dizzy. Or maybe it was the drifting smoke from the house.

Ollie's arms were wound around Erin's waist, and hers were tight around his neck. They clearly weren't going anywhere, any time soon.

'Shall we?' Craig nodded at the cottage.

I couldn't stop grinning. 'I'll put the kettle on,' I said.

Chapter 33

'I'll actually miss this place,' said Ollie, accepting the plate of smoked salmon and scrambled eggs I'd rustled up for what he was calling The Last Supper – even though it was breakfast. 'It's been hashtag memorable.'

'Don't say hashtag,' Erin scolded.

He grinned, checking her out. She looked undeniably sexy in my stripy pyjamas, even with tangled hair and no make-up, and he was clearly having carnal thoughts. Erin had refused to sleep with him on the grounds that it would be disrespectful to me – as well as to humanity, considering he was a massive idiot.

I'd never seen him happier to be insulted.

'It feels like you've been here longer than a week,' I said, sliding a plate across the worktop to Craig. He looked tired, but then none of us had slept much, rehashing what had happened over mugs of hot chocolate and mince pies, once Erin and Ollie had joined us in the kitchen.

Ollie, hyped up on adrenaline and love, had been full of admiration for Barry and Sheelagh, and how 'marvellous' it was that she accepted her husband 'warts, knickers, and all'.

'That's all a man really wants,' he'd said, gazing longingly at Erin, who looked at him like something on the bottom of her shoe, as if they hadn't been kissing each other's faces off minutes earlier.

By contrast, Craig had reverted to his earlier self, despite my best efforts to engage him in the analysis of our neighbours' private lives.

'That must be why they didn't want you to interview them,' I'd said, which had led to Craig explaining to Ollie and Erin his plans for a 'talking heads' type show, which they'd both declared was 'genius'.

He was eating his breakfast standing up, as if to underline the fact that he wouldn't be hanging around for much longer.

'Did you have a nice run?' I said, forcing a broad smile, noticing his trainers on the mat by the door. I was going to miss seeing them. 'It looks like it might snow again.'

'I didn't go for a run,' he said, politely. 'I was loading the car, then I went to fill it up with petrol.'

'Sexy,' said Erin.

I would miss her too, I realised, as she turned away to pile her plate with food. I was about to ask if she'd like to stay for the weekend, when my mobile vibrated with an incoming call.

'Lily, are you OK?' Mum said, sounding panicked. 'I just saw it on the morning news.'

'It?' I said, putting the empty egg pan in the sink. 'What do you mean?'

'Ollie Matheson saved someone from a fire,' she said. 'There was a little bit of wobbly footage and I recognised your neighbour's house.'

'Footage?'

'Lily, why are you repeating everything?' She sounded exasperated. 'Doris knew what I meant right away and explained everything, but I wanted to check for myself that you hadn't inhaled smoke, or anything.'

'Doris?'

'Lily, for goodness sake! You weren't answering, so I called her.'

'I'm fine, I'm fine.' I looked at Craig. He was washing his plate at the sink, as if he'd been doing it for years. 'Hang on a sec,' I said to Mum, and Craig turned, as if alerted to something in my voice. 'Mum says Ollie was on the news.'

'What?' Ollie stopped trying to fork eggs into Erin's mouth. 'How so?'

Craig slowly dried his hands. 'Nothing to do with me,' he said. 'I didn't have my camera. One of the neighbours must have filmed it on their phone.' He aimed a small grin at Ollie. 'At least there's something real to show for your time in Shipley.'

Ollie looked overcome. 'I didn't even notice anyone recording me.'

'That's a first,' Craig said drily. 'At least you were being *you*. And now everyone else will see that, too.'

A thought struck. 'What about Barry?'

There was a rush as they dived for their phones. Erin got to hers first and found the news website. 'You can see it's Ollie and that he's carrying someone, but not in any detail… then it pans to a shot of the house and that smoking-hot fireman,' she said, as we craned over her shoulder for a look.

'He's not that hot,' grumbled Ollie. 'And his helmet's too big.'

'Well, whoever cropped the footage and sent it in meant well.' I felt a swell of emotion. 'It was a nice thing to do.'

'Awesome,' Erin agreed, looking a bit shiny-eyed. 'Maybe the neighbours won't hate you now you've rescued one of their own,' she said to Ollie. I noticed her bare foot was resting on his trousered knee, and that he didn't seem to mind one bit.

'You know what, I don't care.' He looked like he'd had a eureka moment. 'As long as the people I care about know the real me, who gives a fig about the rest of the world?'

'Oh god, he's gone all Disney,' groaned Erin. 'Pass the sick bucket.'

'I think that's amazing.' Crossing the kitchen, I kissed Ollie's bristly cheek. He'd announced he was growing a beard again, because shaving was a 'total bore'. 'And it only took you thirty-odd years to realise.'

'Lily!' screeched a tinny voice.

'Oops, sorry, Mum.' I lifted my mobile once more. 'Did you hear all that?'

'You sound very affectionate towards him, Lily, but remember what I said. Men like Ollie Matheson—'

'It's fine, Mum, you've no need to worry,' I said. 'I told you Ollie was in love with someone else.' Erin pretended to vomit. 'She's right here, actually.'

'I thought I recognised Erin's voice.' Mum sounded pleased, as if she'd known all along that Ollie was in love with my friend. 'Tell Ollie he's welcome to come and direct our next production,' she added. 'We're doing a spoof of *The Mousetrap*, set in the future.'

'I'll tell him,' I promised, though I had a feeling Ollie's plans wouldn't involve any amateur dramatic productions.

'Anyway, I've got to go.' She made it sound as if I was the one who'd called her. 'I'm meeting your brother for brunch.'

'At the hipster café?'

'It's not a hipster café.' She tutted. 'He wants me to try their new deconstructed English breakfast tasting plate,' she said. 'Apparently, it's very playful.'

'All good with the Ambroses?' Erin said, as I ended the call with a smile.

'All good.'

'Right then.' Ollie stopped massaging Erin's toes and stood up. 'I guess it's time to say ciao.'

'Only if you're Italian, you chump,' said Erin, buttering some more toast.

'Are you going to your parents'?' I asked him, aware of Craig's barely concealed impatience as he pushed his feet into his trainers.

'Yah, I'll probably catch up with the folks and then…' He looked a bit lost for a moment. 'Actually, I don't know what's next, except that it involves sorting out some training if I want to be a top-notch director, and then whisking this amazing woman somewhere exotic.' He brushed a crumb from the corner of Erin's mouth. 'What do you say?'

'I say, forget that,' she said. 'I'm spending Christmas with my family, and no doubt I'll be coming back here to visit Lily.'

'What about you, Craig?' I said, keeping my tone light.

'I'll pop home and see my dad,' said Craig, pulling his jacket on over his long-sleeved top. 'Check Linda hasn't been over-feeding him.'

'I'd love to see your home, some time.' The words flew out and landed in an awkward heap. No one spoke for a second, but I noticed Ollie and Erin swap a look. 'What I mean is, it would be nice to stay in touch.' I gave a silly laugh. 'Don't you think?'

'Of course we'll stay in touch.' It was Ollie who came over and drew me into a bear hug. 'We're practically family now,' he said, while I discreetly inhaled his delicious scent. 'You can't get rid of us that easily, you know.' He pulled away and planted his hands on my shoulders. 'Now, how much do I owe you for our stay?'

'Don't be silly,' I said, feeling almost tearful. 'You've just said, we're practically family. Family don't charge for staying.'

'Say ten grand,' said Erin. 'He can afford it.'

I ignored her. 'I really don't want your money.'

'Well, how about an open invitation to the chateau,' he said, eyes twinkling at full pelt. 'Call it a Christmas present, and bring Fiona. She'd love it.'

She would. It would increase her status no end at the shop, and with the Acting Out bunch. 'We might take you up on that,' I said.

'I'm counting on it.' Ollie's smile held genuine affection, and it struck me how different he seemed to the man who'd turned up a day early, supposedly to avoid detection, but really to attract attention. Although part of it was down to Erin, I liked to think there'd been a shift in his attitude, and felt glad that I'd played a small part.

It was just a shame that Craig seemed distant, rather than happy that his friendship with Ollie was intact, and Tattie was off the scene.

'Sure I can't take you back with me?' Ollie turned to Erin, who was on her third slice of toast.

'Nope,' she said, cheek bulging. 'I'm staying with Lily, if she'll have me. I need a proper tour of the cottage, and to see Shipley by daylight.'

'Of course,' I said, pleased. It wasn't that I couldn't face being on my own – although it would be strange – but I knew once they'd gone I'd either have a little cry, or spend too much time wondering whether I'd upset Craig. Probably both. 'There's a nice café on the seafront where we could have lunch.'

'You will come out for dinner with me next week, though?' Ollie said to Erin, sounding unusually anxious for a 'player'. 'Chiltern Firehouse?'

The name rang a bell. I remembered the receipt I'd come across among Ollie's things, and wondered if he'd kept it for sentimental reasons. The notion was heart-warming.

'Or we could try my local, The Dog and Duck.' Erin's tone was lofty.

'Ooh, it's nice there,' I said. 'They've got fancy tiles.'

'O-*kay*.' He chewed the corner of his bottom lip for a moment, then sighed. 'I suppose I'd better go and get my things,' he said, not taking his eyes off Erin as he left the kitchen, closely followed by Craig.

'I'm *never* going to be one of those girls,' Erin said fiercely, when Ollie was upstairs out of earshot. 'I won't roll over and be his little plaything.'

'You're not a plaything,' I said gently. 'And he knows it.'

Craig had gone outside, leaving the front door ajar. An icy breeze made me shiver, and the melancholy sound of a seagull seemed to reach inside me.

'Come and wave us off then,' said Ollie, reappearing with his holdall. He'd thrown his navy coat on and looked as handsome as ever – in spite of the trilby, which Erin immediately plucked from his head and tossed into the kitchen. 'You look like a buffoon.'

'Oi, you minx.' But he didn't bother to retrieve it.

'It's bloody freezing.' Erin pulled her coat on and I followed suit, reflecting that I'd been outside a lot this week with my coat on over my nightclothes. Perhaps I'd start a new trend and become known as the eccentric coat-lady.

To my surprise, a congregation had gathered in the garden, and when Ollie emerged they applauded and gave him a cheer. Even Doris had defrosted enough to join in, putting down her gingham-covered basket to clap, alongside a thirty-something couple I didn't recognise.

'The Jensens,' Doris mouthed, stabbing a finger in their direction when she saw me looking. They must have taken time out from their high-powered jobs to see what the fuss was about.

'I gave everyone a heads-up that we were leaving,' said Craig, joining us on the doorstep. He folded his arms, as if unsure what to do with them when he wasn't holding his camera. 'I thought they might want to make sure we were actually going.'

'Ha, ha,' I said, happy that he wasn't waiting in the car, and that he'd clearly wanted Ollie to have a good send-off.

'You're a hero,' Annabel shouted to Ollie, as if her memory had been wiped and she'd completely forgotten our encounter in The Anchor. 'Come back any time, you'll always be welcome.'

There was a chorus of 'hear, hears' and Ollie gave a modest bow, before pulling me forward and placing his arm around me. 'I've had an amazing time, thanks to this wonderful lady,' he said. 'Be nice to her, or I'll come back and annoy the hell out of you all.'

There was a quiver of laughter, and I noticed Mr Flannery navigating the festive inflatables in the garden next door. He was leaving the Lamberts' house, which was remarkably unscathed, apart from the boarded-up window where the curtains had caught fire, and some smoke damage around the frame.

'What's he up to?' I said, seeing his shifty expression.

'Saw what happened on the news, this morning,' he called, pushing through my gate to join the assembled neighbours in the frost-tipped garden. 'Just wanted to check they were OK.'

'Oh.'

He looked shifty, even when he was being nice. 'I told Barry, ages ago, to just come out and tell folk.'

'You knew?' I said.

'Saw him with a cross-dressing mate in John Lewis, buying underwear.' He jabbed his hands in his anorak pockets. 'Said I wouldn't say anything, if that's what he wanted.'

I could only gawp, while Doris gave him a huffy look, presumably because he'd found something out before she had.

'We don't need to discuss it any further,' she said, adding without irony, 'it's really none of our business.'

As if on cue, the Lamberts' front door opened and Barry and Sheelagh materialised arm-in-arm, like royalty putting on a brave front after a scandal had rocked the family. As they came into the garden, another cheer went up, and Sheelagh looked as if she might explode into tears.

Barry kept his head high as he came forward, and he shook Ollie's hand without looking as if he'd like to snap his arm off. 'Just wanted to thank you for last night,' he said gruffly. There was a trace of lipstick at the corner of his mouth, but in his trench coat and bandana he was very much the male version of himself. 'There wasn't any need to shoulder the door down and throw me about like that, but' – he glanced around, almost meeting people's eyes – 'I reckon you did me a favour.'

Sheelagh took hold of my hand and lowered her voice. 'I called our Bryony to tell her what had happened and she's flying home today,' she said.

'Oh, Sheelagh, that's wonderful.'

'Thank you for inviting Ollie to stay.' She looked at him, her eyes shimmering with tears. 'We'll never forget what you did for us.'

'The pleasure was all mine, Loretta,' said Ollie graciously, and there was another smattering of applause. The crowd parted to let him walk to the gate, where he paused to blow me a kiss before going to the car and slinging his bag in the boot.

'He'll have a Jesus complex after this,' said Erin. 'I'd better go and say a proper goodbye.'

She shot after him, and the neighbours jostled around as he bundled Erin inside the car, like a celebrity hiding his girlfriend from the paparazzi.

'He's forgotten his trumpet!' she called, as he dived into the back seat after her and slammed the door.

I followed Craig inside and through to the living room, where the case was standing by the Christmas tree. 'I can't believe he forgot it,' I said, feeling awkward.

'No,' said Craig, and I felt a powerful surge of emotion as I realised Ollie had left it on purpose to give us a moment alone.

Craig seemed to realise it too as he levelled his gaze to mine.

'Did I say something wrong?' I blurted out. I couldn't let him go without asking.

'Of course not.' His clear eyes widened. 'Why would you think that?'

'But…' *I thought you liked me* sounded childish. 'You've been off with me since last night.'

'I'm sorry,' he said, not denying it. 'It's just that, when you told Annabel off in the pub… it reminded me, you got badly hurt not so long ago.'

'I did,' I said quickly. 'But, to be honest, it was more what happened after the relationship ended than the break-up itself.' I had a feeling my face was brick-red but ploughed on, 'You probably overheard my mum telling Ollie about my encounter with Max's wife.'

He dropped his gaze and nodded. 'I also heard you tell her that you had no intention of having another relationship, that you just wanted casual flings—'

'I didn't kiss Ollie,' I burst out. 'I nearly did, but it didn't feel right.'

He lifted his head, a smile touching his eyes. 'I know,' he said. 'Though I wouldn't blame you if you had. I'd probably kiss him myself if I was a girl.'

I gave a shaky laugh. 'So…?'

He grew serious. 'I don't want to have a fling with you.'

'Oh.' My heart was thundering in my chest. 'Well, that's fine,' I said, hoping I wasn't about to cry, desperately reminding myself that I barely knew him. OK, so I thought we'd forged a bond, and had a connection, but it was obviously one-sided.

He took a step closer. 'What I mean is, I'd want more than a fling.'

'Oh?' My heart picked up speed again.

He reached out his hand and wrapped his fingers round mine, and their warmth flowed through me. 'I've had the best time, this week.'

'Me too.' Elation blossomed in my chest. 'Fire's featured a lot,' I said, hearing a crackle of burning logs in the grate. He must have got up early to get it going.

'It has.' A smile spread across his face. 'There's probably something meaningful in that, but I can't think what it is.'

Outside, a car horn blasted.

Craig tightened his grip on my hand. 'I suppose I'd better get going.'

I didn't want to let go, or for the moment to end. 'You'll call me?'

'Oh, yes.' He nodded firmly, keeping his eyes on mine. 'I've got your number.'

'You have?'

'I got Ollie to get it off Erin before we came here. I tried to ring to let you know we were coming, but Ollie grabbed my phone off me and threw it in the back of the car.'

I remembered the missed call I'd deleted, and laughed. 'That's such an Ollie thing to do.'

'It was,' he agreed. 'I'll put you in touch with that illustrator, too.'

'That would be good.' Oh god, we were being polite now. 'I'd better let you go.'

'For now.' Releasing my hand, he picked up Ollie's trumpet case, and after one last look he left, closing the front door behind him.

I stayed rooted to the spot, staring at nothing, until the doorbell chimed and I nearly shot out of my skin.

'I forgot something,' Craig said, breathing hard, something green and leafy crushed in one hand. Behind him, Ollie and Erin were grinning at me from the car, and I could see Doris handing out muffins to the neighbours who were waiting to wave goodbye.

'Your camera?' I said, confused.

'No, this.' Stepping forward, he placed his lips on mine, and I had no hesitation in winding my arms around him and pulling him close, our bodies slotting together with perfect precision. We came up for air to the sound of cheering and a shout of 'get a room', and Craig's arms tightened around my waist. 'Ollie gave me his mistletoe and said I should make good use of it,' he murmured.

'I don't really think we need it, do you?'

As he lowered his mouth to mine again, Erin hurried over to prise us apart.

'Children are watching,' she said. 'Take Ollie home before he gets his trumpet out, and that's not a euphemism.'

Craig gave me a long look and I knew he was reading in my eyes all the things I wanted to say. 'I'll be back,' he promised, cupping my chin with his hand.

'You'd better be,' was all I could manage.

He jogged to the car and I joined Erin and the others at the gate to wave them off, happiness racing through me.

As they pulled away it started to snow, and the neighbours began drifting off with friendly goodbyes. Sheelagh dabbed her eyes as Barry led her next door with a tender arm around her shoulders, and Doris said she had to get home because her friend, Ellen Partridge, was coming over for lunch.

'Well, that was intense,' said Erin, when we were back inside. 'What the hell's happened to us?'

'I don't know, but I like it.' I felt lighter than I had in a long time, and my face ached from smiling.

'And who's this little fellow?'

Marmite was on the arm of the sofa, calmly washing his paws.

'Ah, that's my inspiration for *Sabrina the Magic Cat*.' I thought of how Marmite had alerted the Lamberts to the fire next door, probably saving their lives, and leading to Barry's secret being revealed. 'I think he might *actually* be magic,' I said.

Erin pulled a face. 'Enough of that shite. Let's get dressed and go into town,' she said, patting Marmite's head. 'I want to buy a wreath for your door from that flower stall I saw yesterday, and some bon-bons from the sweet shop, and maybe we can feed the seagulls.'

'It's illegal to feed the seagulls.'

'You're such a killjoy,' she joked. 'Maybe you can show me that castle where your brother once got lost.'

I grinned. 'Sounds good,' I said, remembering there was still something I had to do. 'Just give me a few minutes.'

I found my phone in the kitchen and saw that I had a text.

'Look after my headphones until I get back ☺ C XX'

Smiling, I saw they were still on the worktop, where I'd left them the day before, and as I picked them up and hooked them round my neck, I noticed they'd been lying on a sheet of crumpled paper. Pulling it forward, I went clammy as I recognised my handwriting. *Jessica's cupcakes were the envy of all her friends. 'You should open your own café,' her friend ~~Craig~~ Carl kept saying. He was the biggest fan of her baking and never stopped trying to encourage her—* Oh god, he must have found my awful effort screwed up by the bin. *'If you find a job you love, you'll never work a day in your life,' he was fond of saying…* Craig had heavily underlined the quote in black ink, and surrounded it with arrows. Re-reading it, my eyes prickled with tears. *Message understood* ☺ *L XX* I replied, thinking how much Dad would have liked Craig. I could almost sense him with me, smiling his approval.

Wiping a hand over my eyes, I did what I'd intended to do since the night before, when the decision had slid into my head. I called a number I'd memorised without realising, my gaze moving to the window, where snowflakes were brushing against the glass.

Maybe we'd have a white Christmas this year, after all.

'Jill?' I said, when she picked up. 'I'd like to accept the job.'

A Letter from Karen

I want to say a huge thank you for choosing to read *The Beachside Christmas*. If you enjoyed it, and want to keep up-to-date with all my latest releases, just sign up at the following link. Your email address will never be shared and you can unsubscribe at any time.

www.bookouture.com/karen-clarke/?title=the-beachside-christmas-lights-society

It was a joy for me to return to Shipley for the final time, and to write a Christmas story, as Christmas is my favourite time of year. I have happy childhood memories of trying to stay awake on Christmas Eve, hoping to catch Santa delivering my presents (I never did).

In recent years there's been an explosion of Christmas light displays around where I live, with people seemingly competing to outdo each other, and it got me thinking about how easily it could get out of hand, and even lead to neighbours falling out.

A show in America called *The Great Christmas Light Fight* was a fun source of inspiration, and was particularly helpful when it came to setting a Christmassy mood, since I wrote most of the story during a heatwave!

We don't often get a white Christmas, but I wanted to leave the snow softly falling on Shipley as I said goodbye to my characters.

I hope you loved *The Beachside Christmas*. If you did, I would be very grateful if you could write a review. I'd love to know what you think, and reviews make such a difference to new readers who are discovering one of my books for the first time.

I love hearing from my readers – you can get in touch on my Facebook page, through Twitter, Goodreads, or my website.

Thanks,
Karen

karen.clarke.5682

@Karenclarke123

www.writewritingwritten.blogspot.com

Acknowledgements

A lot of people are involved in making a book, and I would like to thank the brilliant team at Bookouture for making it happen. Particular thanks to my wonderful editor, Abi, for her clever and insightful comments; to Anne for her seamless copy-editing; Emma for the gorgeous cover; and Kim Nash, for spreading the word.

Special thanks to Larissa Wainman for her very helpful snippets about primary-school teaching, and Fiona at Christmas Direct for explaining what happens when a town's Christmas tree lights are switched on.

As ever, I owe my lovely readers a massive thank you, as well as the blogging community, whose reviews are a labour of love, and Amanda Brittany, for her tireless feedback and friendship.

And last, but never least, thank you to my family and friends for their constant encouragement, my children, Amy, Martin and Liam, for their unwavering support, and my husband Tim for everything – I couldn't do it without you.

CPSIA information can be obtained
at www.ICGtesting.com
Printed in the USA
BVOW06s2300191117
500588BV00020B/390/P

9 781786 812728